ORBITAL

A Future War Novel

by FX Holden

Independently Published

Typeset in 12pt Garamond

fxholden@yandex.com

With huge thanks to my fantastic beta reading team for their encouragement and critique:

Alan McNamara, Bob "WhirlyBob" Hesse, Bror Appelsin, Gabrielle "Hell Bitch" Adams, Greg Hollingsworth,
Ian "Bikerman" Flockhart, Joe Lanfrankie, Johnny "Gryphon" Bunch, Jonathan "Greycap" Harada,
Mike "Nuke" McGirk, and Richard "Rollnloop" Campan.

Each Future War novel is a self-contained story (with occasional recurring characters) and they can be read out of order, but the recommended reading order is:

Contents

Cast of Players

By nation and order of appearance

RUSSIA

Anastasia Grahkovsky, Chief Scientist, Titov Main Test and Control Center, Moscow

Sergei Grahkovsky, her brother

Major-General Yevgeny Bondarev, Commander, Titov Main Test and Control Center, Moscow

Denis Lapikov, Minister of Energy, Russian Federation

Corporal Maqsud Khan, Squad Leader (Targeting), Baikonur Groza Command and Control Center

Colonel-General Oleg Popovkin, Commander of the 15th Aerospace Forces Army

Colonel Tomas Arsharvin, Fifth Directorate Aerospace, Main Directorate of the General Staff of the Armed Forces of the Russian Federation (GRU)

Roman Kelnikov, Defense Minister, Russian Federation

Alexei Avramenko, President, Russian Federation

ITALY

Roberta D'Antonia, Agenzia Informazioni e Sicurezza Esterna (AISE)

USA

Colonel Alicia 'The Hammer' Rodriguez, 615th Combat Operations Squadron (COS), 45th Space Wing, Cape Canaveral

Ambre Duchamp, Lead Data Scientist, 45th Security Forces Squadron, Cape Canaveral

Major KC 'Kansas' Severin, 2IC, 615th COS, Cape Canaveral

Sergeant Xiaoxia 'Zeezee' Halloran, 45th Space Wing Intelligence

Captain Karen 'Bunny' O'Hare, Crew Training Officer (External), 615th COS, Canaveral

Stuart Fenner, President of the United States of America

UK

Flight Lieutenant Anaximenes 'Meany' Papastopoulos, Royal Air Force (RAF) 23 Squadron Space Operations

Squadron Leader Gregory 'Paddington' Bear, RAF 23 Squadron Space Operations

SAUDI ARABIA

Prince Taisir Al-Malki, Saudi Head of Delegation, OPEC (Plus)

Captain Amir Alakeel, No. 92 Squadron Royal Saudi Air Force (RSAF), King Abdulaziz Air Base, Dhahran

Lieutenant Hatem Zedan, No. 92 Squadron RSAF, King Abdulaziz Air Base, Dhahran

CHINA

Major Fan Bo, People's Liberation Army (PLA), Xichang 27th Test and Training Base

Chen Minhao, Premier, People's Republic of China

Foreshadowing

The Hidden Risk of Plummeting Oil Prices: War

Only three developments could conceivably alter the present low-price environment for oil: a Middle Eastern war that took out one or more of the major energy suppliers; a Saudi decision to constrain production in order to boost prices; or an unexpected global surge in demand.

The prospect of a new war between, say, Iran and Saudi Arabia – two powers at each other's throats at this very moment – can never be ruled out, though neither side is believed to have the capacity or inclination to undertake such a risky move. A Saudi decision to constrain production is somewhat more likely sooner or later, given the precipitous decline in government revenues. However, the Saudis have repeatedly affirmed their determination to avoid such a move…

The Nation Magazine, USA, January 2016

War With OPEC Can't End Well for Russia

Oil prices plummeted this week after a stalemate in talks between Russia and the Organization of the Petroleum Exporting Countries (OPEC). Convinced it can force OPEC members to unilaterally decrease production, Russia may well end up worse off than its rivals in its bid to save face.

It might seem that the best option would be to reach an agreement to reduce production in a coordinated fashion so as to stabilize prices. But the Russian side chose confrontation. It's possible that Russia will choose to fight until the bitter end. The Kremlin is accustomed to using force as a prelude to negotiations and typically refuses to make face-saving concessions.

But war – even a price war – always means destruction and loss.

Moscow Times, Russia, March 2020

First strike

Chelyabinsk 15 February 2013, 0915 local

Nine-year-old Anastasia Grahkovsky had the same breakfast ritual every morning and as she spooned her semolina porridge into a bowl, careful to avoid the biggest lumps, she had no idea it would nearly cost her her life.

Anastasia hated the lumps. Not only did they stick in your throat, but if they were big enough, then the semolina on the outside of the lump was squishy, while the grains in the middle of the lump were uncooked and crunchy. Her mother made the porridge when she was working night shifts at the Zinco plant, but at the moment she was on day shift which meant her brother Sergei had made breakfast, and at this, he sucked.

But she had no one to complain to because he had already left for school when she got up, even though he was supposed to wait for her. He was always doing that. So she loaded up her bowl, picked out the biggest lumps and dumped them back in the pot, then pulled her dressing gown tighter around herself and walked to the window of their apartment, climbing up to the windowsill and sitting on the ledge looking out over the line of birch trees between herself and the refrigeration works. She was really getting too big to sit there but she'd done it every morning as long as she could remember, and though she was really too chubby now to sit comfortably, she still did it. Her class was doing a fitness assessment this morning, but it was only 14 degrees outside and she had asthma, so she didn't need to be at school until they were finished at 11.

The sun was just coming up, though at this time of year, it never really got far into the sky before it was going down again. She shivered. Lumpy and cold. It described her porridge and herself. She shifted her backside on the narrow windowsill and leaned her head against the cool glass.

Then the sky lit up.

There was a brilliant ball of light moving across the sky from right to left, leaving a trail of white smoke behind it. Her eyes were drawn to it like it was magnetic and as she watched, it speared toward the ground at incredible speed, then while it was still high in the sky, it exploded!

The entire sky flared brilliant white and Anastasia blinked, her irises slamming shut, but too late. When she opened them again, all she could see were red and black blotches.

"Mama!" she screamed reflexively, though she knew she was five miles away at the zinc factory. She panicked, hands scrabbling at the glass window pane. "Mama!"

Then came an ear-shattering sonic boom, the window she was sitting beside splintered into a thousand needle-sharp fragments and Anastasia was blown back into her kitchen, skin flayed from her face, sunburned, blind and deaf.

Athena's thunderbolts

Baikonur Cosmodrome, Kazakhstan, 2032

It was a meteor that detonated over Chelyabinsk in 2013, though for Anastasia Grahkovsky, it might as well have been a nuclear bomb. She'd been one of 1,200 people injured that day when the 66-foot wide, 12,000-ton lump of rock had slammed into the earth's atmosphere at a speed of 40,000 miles an hour and exploded 20 miles above Chelyabinsk.

Anastasia got her hearing back, but not her sight. And as she stood at her washbasin 19 years later and applied thioglycolic acid to her ravaged scalp to remove the hair which grew there in random tufts, she couldn't help reflect on how she could draw a direct line between that day in 2013 and now.

The roof of her mother's zinc factory had collapsed, trapping a hundred workers, including her mother. Her school had been locked down and the students kept inside, and her brother hadn't been able to come home until the middle of the afternoon. So Anastasia had lain on the floor of the kitchen, curled into a ball, whimpering and bleeding from a hundred cuts, until her brother got there at 2 p.m. He didn't see her at first, the apartment a scene of devastation, a freezing wind blowing through the gaping window, glass all over the kitchen, cupboards and their contents strewn across the bench and floor. And Anastasia.

A neighbor had driven them to hospital, Anastasia wrapped in a bedspread, not crying, barely breathing. The hospital emergency ward was chaotic – a woman with a broken back lay on a stretcher in a brace, people with cuts and broken limbs sat on chairs or on the floor up and down corridors as nurses and doctors ran from one to the other trying to triage the worst cases. The car crash victims were the worst, blinded by the flash and then injured as their cars plowed head-on into buildings, poles, trees, or each other.

Thanks to the quick action of her brother and neighbor, to the care of overstretched doctors and nurses who stopped her from dying of shock and cold, Anastasia had lived. And on that day was born her dread fascination with the power of meteorites.

She could trace the day it really took hold to a morning when she was thirteen, and walking with her brother to school. She knew the way herself by then; after all, it had been four years since she became blind. She had a cane, and could walk herself there, but her brother insisted on walking with her, made her take his arm the whole way. He was sixteen, stronger than her and sighted, so she couldn't exactly fight him.

One morning there had been roadworks, and they had to take a detour through an abandoned car yard.

"See," Sergei had told her, "this is why you need me. How would you have found your way around the roadworks?"

"I would have asked someone," she'd said grumpily.

"Yeah? Before or after you fell in that pit over there?" he'd asked.

She'd been about to say something smart right back at him when her foot had come down on a stone, and she twisted her ankle. He let go of her as she gave a small cry and dropped to one knee, grabbing her foot.

"You OK?" he asked.

"No, stupid," she said angrily. "You walked me straight over a dumb rock." She sat down on the cold ground and began massaging her ankle.

His feet scuffed beside her, and he grunted, "Hey, I think it's a piece of the meteor." She heard him bend over and pick something up. "Yeah, for sure."

People had been finding the small pebble-sized meteorites all over Chelyabinsk since the explosion. Nearly every family had one or two on a mantlepiece or bookshelf. But not their family. She was sure her brother would have found one before now, but either he or their mother had decided it wasn't a thing they wanted inside their house after what had happened to her.

She stood up and held out her hand. "Give it to me."

"Nah," he said. "It's worthless. You used to be able to get a few rubles for them, but no one is buying anymore."

"I don't care," she said. "I want it."

"Mama will throw it out," he told her.

She stuck her hand out further. "Just give it me!"

He dropped it in her palm and she closed her hand around it. It was hard, like a lump of coal, but round. She ran her fingers over it. The surface was smooth in parts, rough in others; pockmarked, like her face.

She slipped it into the pocket of her jeans and tested her ankle. "Let's go," she said.

From that day, she had started collecting meteorites from friends, from her mother's workmates, from people selling them on the internet. Her mother had tried to stop her at first, then had complained about the growing pile of rocks in Anastasia's bedroom; on shelves, in boxes, under her bed. Eventually she shrugged and gave up.

Anastasia learned how to classify them and sort them by feel. Two-thirds were smooth-surfaced chondrites, some with shock veins of nickel or iron running through them. But about one third were melt breccia; a fine matrix of chondrite fragments fused together by a collision sometime in the meteor's past. She valued these more. They felt like she felt; blackened and battered. But they were survivors, like her.

She had a quick mind and an obsession with science, and one of her teachers had taught herself braille so that she could feed Anastasia's insatiable thirst for knowledge about the universe outside Chelyabinsk, outside Russia, outside Earth. She was studying textbooks from the Chelyabinsk State University while she was still in junior high, and left high school two years early to start undergraduate studies in astrophysics. As an honors student, she had been the first researcher to quantify exactly how much energy the Chelyabinsk explosion had released, her calculations revising the previous estimate up from 1.4 to 1.8 petajoules or the equivalent of 480 kilotons of TNT, 33 times the energy released by the atomic bomb at Hiroshima. She had published her calculations together with her physics professor, and it had been at an astrophysics forum 1,000 miles across the Ural Mountains to the west in Moscow, where they had presented a poster, that she had been talent-spotted by an officer of the Russian Aerospace Forces' Titov Test Center.

Six months later, at the age of 22, she joined the research program called Groza.

Colonel Andrei Yakob was accustomed to the effect his Chief Scientist had on people she had never met before. The first thing they usually noticed was her shaved head. The second thing they noticed was the filigree pattern of scars over her scalp, face and neck from where she had been sliced by flying glass. Curiously, they did not always notice her blindness, especially if, like now, she was sitting quietly at a table full of people, having been the first to arrive, and being largely ignored by the many senior officers and government staff around the table who considered themselves rather more important than some woman they had never met and who, frankly, made them a little queasy to look at.

The group around the table called itself the Technical Committee, but there was nothing technical about it. There were no engineers or scientists among the 12 members present, and they were not interested in debating technical issues in anything more than the most superficial of detail. If the name reflected the truth, they would call themselves the Political Committee, because their one and only function was to approve or reject recommendations from the Titov Test Center's senior officers about whether to progress a project to the final milestone, which was a recommendation to the Minister of Defense, Roman Kelnikov, either to deploy, redirect or abandon a project.

Project Groza had now completed its final trial, and reached its final milestone.

Despite having served in the armed forces all of his adult life, Yakob was also an accomplished bureaucrat. He knew that to walk into a meeting such as this, without knowing in advance how each of the members of the committee would vote, was suicidal. So standing at the end of the table, next to his lead scientist, he already knew that today's decision was hanging on a thread. Six of the voting members were in favor of canceling Groza, six in favor of deploying. None believed the research should be continued or redirected into other avenues. The committee required a simple majority of seven votes to confirm a decision, so unless Anastasia Grahkovsky could persuade at least one of the 'no' voters to change their mind, Groza would be canceled today. He'd told Anastasia

Grahkovsky this, and had rehearsed with her every single argument he felt might sway his colleagues to change their vote.

Andrei Yakob was a firm believer that Groza would change the balance of military power in Russia's favor in a way no other weapon under development could do, and in a way none of the other superpowers could easily match inside the next decade or more. He fervently believed it should be deployed, and the sooner, the better. With the Middle East about to go up in flames due to the collapsing price of oil, and Russia's oil and gas-based economy on the brink of a meltdown, he was convinced that Groza would give Russia leverage no other nation could match. That was what he had just spent the last half hour explaining to the committee. The why. He felt he had brought most of the room along with him. Now it would be up to Grahkovsky to seal the deal by explaining the how.

"In conclusion, ballistic missiles armed with nuclear weapons are not an option in the current threat environment unless we want to trigger mutually assured destruction and planetary devastation. Hypersonic cruise missiles like our *Tsirkon*, traveling at a mere five times the speed of sound, can now be intercepted by quantum AI-supported high energy liquid laser defenses with more than 80 percent certainty. There is no conventional weapon in our arsenal that can be used to strike an enemy at a moment's notice, with devastating effect, in a way that cannot be countered, and that guarantees the absolute destruction of even highly protected hard targets." He paused, letting his words sink in, looking around the table into the eyes of the doubters. Good. He could tell they were listening. "Groza is the solution to these problems. As you know it has completed the final phase of its testing. Chief Scientist Grahkovsky will now run through the results of those tests and take your questions, and I will sum up with our recommendation."

The young woman stood. As he sat down, Yakob noticed more than one of the committee members flinch involuntarily, or look down suddenly at the notes or tablets in front of them. Some openly stared.

She had no notes in front of her, though she did have a digital braille notepad device he had seen her use on other occasions. But she knew her data inside out, so he was not worried she would trip up over the detail, and besides, this group was not the kind to ask detailed questions. All she had to do was convince them Groza worked, and after all their time rehearsing for today, he was completely confident she would.

"Thank you Colonel, ladies and gentlemen." She stared straight ahead, her eyes dull and unfocused. Now even the slower members of the audience might begin to realize she was not only scarred, she was blind. She gave a slight smile. "But before I begin with the results of our final series of tests of the Groza system, I must comment on Colonel Yakob's introduction. Colonel Yakob is a true champion of this project, and he has put his personal and professional life on the line to see it succeed. Colonel Yakob has asked me to explain to you why you should be confident to propose to Minister Kelnikov that Russia deploy Groza. Instead, I am here to tell you why you should not."

It took a moment for Yakob to process what the woman had just said. He had been nodding and smiling when she called him a champion of the project, but only as people around the table stirred in surprise did he take in what she had actually said. Several committee members leaned toward each other and began murmuring, and Yakob rose to his feet, taking the scientist by the arm. "Perhaps you and I should talk, outside," he said. "Chairman, if you will just excuse us…"

The committee chairman was a Russian Aerospace Force Major-General called Yevgeny Bondarev. While those around him had reacted with shock or surprise at Grahkovsky's opening words, he had just smiled slightly and steepled his fingers beneath his chin. He had been one of the six doubters identified by Yakob, and now he leaned forward, pointing at Yakob's recently vacated chair. "Comrade Colonel, please sit down. Chief Scientist Grahkovsky, please continue."

Yakob reluctantly slipped Grahkovsky's arm free and scowled as he sat. His finely laid plans had just gone seriously sideways.

Anastasia smoothed the sleeve Yakob had grabbed, and continued. "Thank you, Chairman Bondarev. I know this will displease Colonel Yakob, but I do not believe that the Groza weapons system should be deployed."

Bondarev raised his eyebrows and tapped on the tablet in front of him. "I have read the reports of your final test series, Grahkovsky. They indicate the weapons system performed with devastating effectiveness. Are you saying that the reports are incorrect or that false data has been presented to this committee?" He was in his early forties, had the tanned, square-jawed features of a movie star warrior, and Yakob knew he had been decorated several times as a pilot for bravery under fire.

Grahkovsky shook her head. "No, Chairman. Groza performed completely within the defined success parameters. All test targets were acquired within the 30-minute operational window, the weapons platforms experienced no significant failures during the live-fire exercise, and the targets were struck with, as you say, devastating effect. The post-attack analyses showed our most modern armored vehicles were easily destroyed, the bunker complex test site comprising hardened concrete reinforced with steel rebar was penetrated to a depth of around 20 feet, effectively collapsing it. Used against moored warships with half-inch deck plating, it sunk three of four and disabled the fourth to the extent it would likely have been written off. If used against troops in an urban environment, we expect it will have an effect footprint of between two and five square miles and a guaranteed casualty ratio of 37 percent with a confidence interval of five percent." She paused to let her audience keep up. "The Groza weapons system met every success criterion that this committee imposed on it."

Unlike Yakob or his fellow committee members, Bondarev did not appear fazed by the contradiction in the woman's words. He simply sat back and folded his arms. "Why, then, would you recommend that the system not be deployed?"

Anastasia Grahkovsky lifted her chin and turned her head, first to the left, and then to the right, her eyes staring into the distance. "Look at me," she said.

There was more murmuring around the table, but Bondarev did as she asked, and even Yakob could not help but lean back in his chair and look up at her, seeing her ravaged face again as though for the first time.

"I know your history, Chief Scientist. And everyone here knows what happened at Chelyabinsk. Your point, please?" Bondarev asked quietly.

"My point, Comrade Chairman, is that if you use this weapon in a populated area, those who are not lucky enough to die will become…" She turned around slowly, lifting her arms out to her side so that her sleeves rose up her arms, showing them the scars there too. When she was facing them again she lowered her arms again and folded her hands in front of her. "This," she said. "Or worse."

There was a shocked silence around the table.

Yakob tried to recover. "Chairman, if I can just…"

Bondarev held a hand in the air to silence Yakob. "I have a question for the Chief Scientist," he said.

Grahkovsky didn't flinch; she kept her chin in the air and stared straight ahead. "Yes, Chairman?"

"Have you ever seen the impact of a fuel-air explosive weapon on a human being?" he asked.

"No, sir," she replied. "Nor would I want to."

"None of us would want to, Grahkovsky," Bondarev said quickly, his voice cold. "If you are within the blast epicenter, you are burned alive. If you are within the effect radius, you are suffocated or buried alive as buildings around you collapse, or crushed by flying debris, or poisoned by unspent fuel mist. In Anadyr, I was buried alive when the enemy used a fuel-air explosive to attack my airbase and we lost two hundred men and women in that one attack." The impact of his words was all the more chilling to Yakob because he was saying them in a detached and clinical tone. "This is what modern weapons do, Chief Scientist. We deploy them precisely because of what they do; in the full knowledge there will be casualties both military and civilian and we do so only out of necessity, knowing that if we do not, the cost to our motherland will be even greater. You may sit."

She didn't. She remained standing. "With respect, Chairman, some weapons are banned under treaty and we have signed such treaties." She held up her hand and started counting on her fingers. "Cluster munitions, chemical weapons, biological weapons, low-yield nuclear weapons, cyberattacks directed at medical infrastructure…" She lowered her hands again and clasped them calmly in front of her. "If we deploy it, this weapon will one day be on that list."

Everyone turned to look at Bondarev's reaction, but he remained impassive. "Your advice is noted. You need not sit. You are excused from the meeting, Chief Scientist Grahkovsky."

Heads swung back to look at her, wondering how she would react to being dismissed, but she simply tightened her lips, reached down for a cane that was resting against her chair and turned, tapping her way toward the door and out the room.

Grahkovsky waited outside in a cold corridor on an uncomfortable chair. After about forty-five minutes, she heard voices coming closer and the door to the meeting room opened. People filed out, some chatting, but none addressed her and, of course, she couldn't see if any of them had given her a second glance. The last two to emerge were Bondarev and Yakob and she heard them speaking about the agenda for a future meeting, giving her no clue to the outcome of this one.

Bondarev said goodbye to Yakob and then raised his voice. "Goodbye, Grahkovsky."

She nodded. "Goodbye, Major-General Bondarev."

There were footsteps and then a creak as Yakob took the seat beside her. She could smell sweat and aftershave, and heard his feet sliding on the floor as he stretched them out in front of himself.

"Am I fired?" she asked.

"You should be," he sighed. "What in God's name were you thinking?"

"Was the project canceled?" she asked, ignoring his question.

She heard him reach into a pocket for cigarettes and a lighter, and then set them on his lap. It wasn't allowed to smoke inside the administration building at Titov.

"The recommendation for deployment was approved," he said. "By a vote of ten to two. It will go to the Minister within the month."

Anastasia smiled, grabbed her cane and stood.

"Why the hell are you smiling?" Yakob demanded. "You nearly cost us everything. Where are you going?"

"Back to work," she said. "Are you coming?"

There was a beat or two before he said, "Are you trying to suggest you wanted this outcome?"

"You needed Bondarev's vote," she said. "I got it for you. And more besides."

"You could have cost us the whole committee."

"But I didn't," she insisted. "Your way was to persuade them through logic, but that was working against us. Groza will be the most expensive weapons system Russia has ever deployed, at a time we can barely afford to keep our Navy afloat and our Air Force in the air. In an age of precision weapons, it is inaccurate. In an age of sophistication, it is crude. Your sources said six of the committee were against us, while mine told me eight were. But you were right; we needed Bondarev on our side. I knew he could bring the others with him, so I went for his weak spot."

"Bondarev is a decorated war hero, he has no bloody weak spot," Yakob said.

"Ah, but clearly he does," she said. She reached out with uncanny accuracy, using only the sound of his voice to guide her, and put the tip of her cane on Yakob's chest, above his heart. "Here."

"Nonsense. The man has no heart."

"No, but he is a patriot. I had a conversation with a military intelligence officer who served with Bondarev in the 3rd Air Army. He told me about that attack in which Bondarev lost two hundred personnel. He also told me that Bondarev had confided in him that it was a weakness of will that had killed those men and women. He said Russia had held itself back from using the most powerful weapons in its arsenal during that conflict, while its enemies had not, and as a result, it had been defeated. He has sworn more than once that this would never happen again under his command. So I did two things." She lowered her cane and placed it between her feet. "I told him that Groza was a terrifyingly powerful new weapon. And I challenged him not to use it."

That night, Anastasia stood in her kitchen, making herself dinner. To anyone unfamiliar with her history, it would have seemed most bizarre. A woman, standing alone in her apartment, cooking herself a vegetarian stroganoff. In total darkness. But to Anastasia, it was just another Tuesday. Occasionally she did laugh at herself and wonder what a visitor might think. But then, visitors weren't really a problem she had to deal with, the way her life had turned out.

As she stirred her stroganoff, she was whistling a tune to herself.

Which might have struck an observer as a slightly strange thing. She had just engineered a decision which meant that a new weapon of mass destruction was about to be visited on an unsuspecting world, a weapon she had helped develop. And not only that, she had told the absolute truth. The effect of the weapon on those civilians not lucky enough to be killed by it directly was exactly the same as she had experienced at Chelyabinsk. A shock wave, flying glass and debris, collapsed buildings – blindness, deafness, broken bones and backs, flayed skin. But as she stirred her stroganoff and added a little more pepper, she was whistling a happy tune.

Because though Anastasia Grahkovsky had lived through the meteor strike on Chelyabinsk, a part of her had died on the floor of that kitchen as she writhed in blood and glass. She had not only lost her physical sight; she had lost the ability to see beyond her own fascination with the power of meteors, of the orgiastic energy of objects striking the planet from space. The thought of it drove her; no, it consumed her. Anastasia had had sex, but nothing in her life had compared to the ecstasy she had felt hearing the sonic boom from the weapon she had created as it destroyed those tanks, burying them in a two-mile-wide crater, or turning that concrete bunker complex into powder and smoke. Having lived through a powerful meteor strike, having developed into one of the world's leading experts in the destructive power of kinetic energy deployed at the petajoule scale, she had determined that it wasn't just something she wanted to have lived through.

It was a power she wanted to *control.*

"I am become Death, the destroyer of worlds," scientist Robert Oppenheimer had thought to himself as he watched the first atomic weapon explode over the desert of New Mexico. It had been a quote from Hindu scripture, the Bhagavad Gita.

As Anastasia Grahkovsky spooned stroganoff into a bowl and made her way through her dark apartment to sit by the open window and listen to the sounds of the city outside, a quote from a different scripture had come to her mind. It was one she had heard a bearded, black-robed priest say in mass in the church in Chelyabinsk after she got out of hospital, and which felt like it was written just for her. Psalm 2:8–9, "Ask of Me, and I will surely give the nations as your inheritance, and the very ends of the earth as your possession. You shall break them with a rod of iron; you shall shatter them like earthenware."

As she ate, she felt a thrill both exciting and terrifying; her weapon would soon be lifted into the heavens on columns of fire to hang there like Athena's thunderbolts, ready to strike Russia's enemies at a moment's notice.

And the day it was used, the world would change forever.

Ultimatum

Zurich, Switzerland, July 2033

The 194th annual meeting of the OPEC Plus group had been slated to take place in Morocco, but with the organization on the verge of collapse due to violent disagreements about how to handle an oil price which had been in freefall since the start of the year, it had been decided to move it to the traditionally neutral venue of Switzerland, where most of the participants did their banking in any case.

The meeting had been triggered by a Saudi decision to double output in a last-ditch attempt to top up its sovereign wealth fund before oil prices collapsed completely as a result of the world's transition to renewables. Crude oil had recently fallen below the $50 a barrel price needed for sustainable production in February and declined even further so that by July it had fallen below even 2020 lows of $20 a barrel.

Unless emergency action was taken to curb supply, several major OPEC economies – Russia and Iran first among them – stood on the verge of State bankruptcy.

The world's next-largest oil economy after Saudi Arabia, and fellow Sunni Muslim majority nation Iraq, was being propped up by loans from Riyadh, and so two opposing blocs had formed within OPEC. On the one side, Saudi Arabia and Iraq, together with other nations dependent on Saudi loans, such as Turkey, Morocco and Tunisia. In the other bloc was Russia, with long-standing Middle Eastern allies Iran and Syria, plus Venezuela, Nigeria and Algeria.

The morning air was mild and fragrant as Russian Energy Minister Denis Lapikov strolled out onto the private terrace on the fourth floor of the Hotel Baur au Lac and took in the view of Lake Zurich. A small table had been set up under a large blue parasol, and three waiters stood ready to take his breakfast order. He asked the head waiter to bring juice and coffee and said he would wait for his guest to arrive before ordering his breakfast. Privately, he did not expect the meeting to extend that long.

Saudi Prince Taisir Al-Malki never went anywhere alone and Lapikov had a suspicion he might even be followed into the bathroom so that he didn't have to wipe himself, but he didn't want that suspicion confirmed. Lapikov looked up as he arrived in the company of two bodyguards and two aides, one a Saudi in traditional thawb robes, the other a young woman in a business suit. Lapikov was the physical opposite of his counterpart, lean where the Saudi was portly, thin-faced where the other was round-cheeked, clean-shaven where the man was thickly bearded. He stood and prepared to welcome him.

It was their third meeting in three days, but their first on the sidelines of the conference, under semi-private circumstances. Lapikov had brought no aides with him; he did not need them for what he was about to say. It was a simple message, to be delivered with deliberately offensive brevity.

"Denis, my friend," Al-Malki said, pulling his sleeves back as he approached and sticking out his hand. "A beautiful day already, isn't it?"

Lapikov was never a small talker at the best of times, and took his right hand back quickly after shaking the Prince's hand, sticking it in his pocket as he adjusted his small round glasses with his left hand. He took a look at the young woman standing behind the Prince and the other Saudi standing beside him. The westerner was slim, athletic and honey blonde with a golden tan. He knew she would need a razor-sharp intellect if she was to be of any use to her employer, who was renowned within the OPEC Plus community as the most inbred dullard to have occupied the Saudi Energy post in nearly twenty years.

The Prince's two bodyguards were waiting in the shade beside the door. Lapikov had left his own bodyguards outside in the corridor. He nodded at the two assistants standing behind the Prince. "Good morning to you all. I was hoping to discuss our business with the Prince in private."

Al-Malki looked momentarily uncomfortable before the young woman spoke. "The Prince has a sore throat, I am afraid. He finds extended conversation tiring. If you don't mind, I will join you."

Al-Malki fluttered a hand theatrically at his throat. "Yes, very bothersome. I hope it is alright with you if Roberta sits in on our discussion?" He didn't wait for an answer, but gathered his robes and paused as a waiter pulled out his chair, before sitting down heavily and pointing at Lapikov's juice and coffee to indicate he would have the same.

A waiter brought another chair for the young woman, and she sat too.

So this was Roberta D'Antonia. Lapikov wasn't surprised; he'd been briefed that it was likely the Italian would join their meeting. Al-Malki never went anywhere without his honey-blonde shadow.

Al-Malki waved the waiters away, but Lapikov sat and turned to the Italian. "Would you like some coffee?"

She looked slightly surprised at being asked. "Oh, no thank you. I already ate breakfast."

Before or after your three-mile jog along Lake Zurich and two hours' preparation for this meeting? Lapikov wondered to himself.

The Saudi aide had not been introduced and did not sit. He bent and spoke quickly in Al-Malki's ear, got a brief reply, and then retired to stand next to the Prince's bodyguards. He had the look of an ex-military type; a fixer, not a thinker.

Al-Malki fixed Lapikov with what was probably intended to be a winning smile. "I think I will have khoubos, chicken and a khodra salad. Would you care to join me in a Saudi breakfast?" His voice sounded just fine to Lapikov.

"No, thank you. Like Roberta, I already ate," Lapikov lied. "I expect this will be a brief conversation in any case." Both of his guests looked uncomfortable now, which was what Lapikov had intended. They waited for him to continue. "Prince Al-Malki, you have received our demand for an additional 500,000 barrels to be added to the Saudi quota for production cuts next year. What is your response?"

The Prince leaned back in his chair as D'Antonia leaned forward. "The Kingdom cannot accept a further five percent on its already generous offer to reduce production by five percent."

"A ten percent reduction is still a three percent increase on average Saudi production for the last five years," Lapikov pointed out. "It does not even take the Kingdom back to last year's production levels."

Lapikov noted that the Italian woman did not confer with Al-Malki, did not even look to him for confirmation as she quickly replied, "As we have already communicated, if Russia finds itself temporarily to be inconvenienced, the Kingdom is willing to place a $6 billion deposit with the World Bank to secure a loan for Russia on Saudi IMF terms."

Lapikov stifled a laugh, then recovered. "China offered us *sixteen* billion. We rejected that offer too."

The Italian contrived to look disappointed. "Then it seems the Kingdom is at the limit of what it can do to help your country."

"Oh, I don't think it is, yet," Lapikov said. He had placed a napkin in his lap out of habit when he sat, and he took it now and folded it carefully, placing it on the table. He deliberately took a slow sip of his coffee and enjoyed the look of discomfort on the face of the fat Prince. Clearly, the man was not used to awkward silences. He spoke directly to the Saudi, ignoring his assistant now. "Prince Al-Malki, the Saudi delegation has until the end of today's proceedings to announce it will accept this quota redistribution, and further, that it believes a target price above $60 a barrel, after discounts, should be OPEC's policy for the next two years." D'Antonia opened her mouth to speak, but Lapikov rudely held a hand up to her face. "Thank you, I know what the official Saudi position is on this." He stood. "I am empowered by my cabinet and the office of my President to tell you that if you do not comply with our request to curb your production yourselves, Russia will take steps to curb it for you."

D'Antonia was as quick on the uptake as Lapikov had been briefed she would be, and she flushed angrily. "I'm sorry, but unless I misheard you, you just threatened to attack Saudi oil production facilities?" The Prince looked from his aide to Lapikov with sheep-like confusion.

"Not misheard," Lapikov said. "But misinterpreted, I'm afraid. We will not 'attack' the Kingdom's production facilities. I am advised we will *obliterate* them, and send the Kingdom back to the stone age from which it only recently emerged."

Even the Prince had caught on by now, and he gaped at Lapikov. Lapikov ignored him and gave D'Antonia a sardonic bow. "I will leave you and your employers to your deliberations, young lady. I recommend they treat our request seriously. Rest assured, we have considered all of the attendant implications. This is not a bluff."

He walked to the terrace door and a waiter opened it for him, his bodyguards falling in behind him as he walked down the carpet-lined corridor to the lift waiting at the end. He had only gone a few steps when he heard the terrace door open again and D'Antonia came running into the corridor behind him.

"Minister, please," she said and was brought up short by Lapikov's men.

"Let her speak," Lapikov told them.

"Minister," she said, short of breath. "Culturally … I'm sorry, but the Kingdom will not back down in the face of a threat. It can be persuaded, it can be nudged, its cooperation might even be bought, but it cannot be threatened into acceding with your demands."

"Give us some credit, Signora," he said. "We have been dealing with the Kingdom of Saudi Arabia for nearly a century; we know how our words will be received."

"Then you know you may just have declared war," she said, aghast. "And not just with Saudi Arabia and its OPEC allies, but with its international allies, like the USA."

Lapikov laughed. "The USA no longer needs Saudi oil, Miss D'Antonia. Thus it no longer needs Saudi Arabia. It is barely interested in keeping the NATO alliance together, let alone its tenuous partnerships in the Middle East."

"You are turning your back on the Saudi loan?" she asked. "The Kingdom has given you a lifeline. You say China has done the same…"

"Only drowning men need a lifeline," he observed. "Our economy is still reliant on oil now, but in ten years it will not be so. We don't need to sell ourselves into debt slavery."

"I see Iran's hand in this. You are too weak to act alone," she said, eyes narrowing. "You dare not."

"*Dare* not?" Lapikov bridled at this. "I was told you were an intelligent woman, Miss D'Antonia. Clearly, my briefing was wrong."

His men had called the lift and were standing holding the doors. With that comment, he turned on his heel and stepped into the elevator with them.

"Precooler decoupled, air intake closed … switching to internal oxygen. Skylon D4 approaching suborbital peak," Flight Lieutenant Anaximenes 'Meany' Papastopoulos said quietly to himself. There was no need for him to speak loudly. No one was listening but the cockpit voice recorder. He finished flipping switches on his console. "And that, ladies and gentlemen, completes another flawless ascent. If you'd like to show your appreciation, please throw money at the pilot, not flowers. Ladies' undergarments are also acceptable."

With a last glance across multiple screens to confirm all systems were nominal, Meany leaned back and ran a hand over the stubble on his head. It was as close to bald as he was allowed under Queen's Regulations, Chapter 6, Order 209, and it was a relatively new look for him. He'd always had the standard short back and sides with a tousled mop on top that generally went with the RAF uniform, but on joining 11 Group's Skylon unit, and with his 'tousled mop' looking a little more like a dishwashing brush now he was in his 30s, he'd decided it was time for a change. He also happened to think it made him look well hard when coupled with the exoskeleton that he wore outside his olive drab no. 14 uniform. Powered by a fuel cell that was nestled in the small of his back together with the neural link to his lower spinal cord, it cradled his hips and, using piston-powered rods that framed his thighs and calves, allowed him to sit, stand and walk unaided.

It wasn't exactly the kind of gear he could remove when going through the metal detectors at the gates of RAF Lossiemouth, but after a year of hand-scanning Meany on his way in and out, the security staff were only just starting to get bored with finding new nicknames for him. 'Cyborg' had been a favorite for a while, before they'd settled on 'Papastompalot.' None was cheeky enough to say it to his face, though, probably because they were afraid of what would happen if he decided to kick their asses.

I'm sorry, Flight Lieutenant Papastopoulos, can you please repeat your command? said a voice from the console in front of him.

"No, Angus," he sighed. "You can stand down until specifically paged, thank you."

Yes, Flight Lieutenant.

Angus wasn't its official name. The AI that helped him manage the systems onboard the *Skylon Suborbital Launch System* had an alphanumeric designation he had never bothered to learn. But as his command module was a trailer inside a hangar on an airfield in northeast Scotland, he'd decided to give it the most Scottish name he could think of. And a Scottish accent to match.

He looked at his watch and stood up. The next critical point in the mission would not be reached until the spacecraft was somewhere over Canada, which was another hour away. His stomach was growling. He probably had enough time to…

A loud chime sounded inside the trailer, and the AI's voice broke his train of thought.

Collision warning. Unidentified object detected. Range 23 miles, closing velocity 200 knots, collision probability 93 percent. Options: evade or engage, pls advise.

Meany dropped behind his console again, pulling up his targeting screen. "Arm the 27mm please and give me a visual on the object as soon as you have one," he said.

Arm defensive weapons, obtain visual of the target, yes Flight Lieutenant.

As a former fighter pilot, Meany Papastopoulos had flown advanced stealth fighter jets armed with guided missiles and precision bombs and commanded drone swarms that turned a single pilot into the commander of a slaved squadron of attack aircraft. In its payload bay, the Skylon could carry a rotary launcher capable of firing the RAF's new advanced short-range multispectral seeker missile, adapted for space combat. Unfortunately, his current mission had required an empty payload bay, so he was carrying no offensive weapons.

But for the defense of the Skylon, he had at his disposal a technology from the previous century; a single nose-mounted, belt-fed, Mauser 27mm laser-targeting-assisted cannon armed with low-velocity soft-nosed lead shells that were not so much intended to destroy their target as to shove it rudely out of the way. It was a defensive system designed to protect the expensive Skylon from the risk of a major space-junk collision, which had proven an all too real risk in early missions due to mankind's inherent laziness. The spacefaring nations of the world had filled the skies with satellites in low earth orbits and when they had malfunctioned or simply reached the end of their useable life, they were left to fall out of orbit of their own accord, or just drift on, into infinity.

The single-barrel revolver-style 27mm cannon on the Skylon could be set to fire in bursts of between 1 and 100 rounds, but it was a defensive weapon, not intended to blow its target into thousands of dangerous pieces. The ideal result was a single solid hit on the target that would shove it into a new and less dangerous orbit.

Naturally, if the threatening object was a live and viable satellite belonging to a State or corporation, then sending it careening through space to burn up in the atmosphere would not be a very popular move. All known satellite and spacecraft orbits, both civilian and military, were accounted for in the Skylon mission plan, so as Meany started scanning through the database for the Skylon's current sector and saw nothing, he knew there could be only two types of object approaching his machine.

A hunk of junk, or a military platform that some State had not logged and that hadn't been spotted yet by ground-based observatories.

His money was on junk. Statistically, it was the most likely.

I have visual, the AI said with silicon calm. *Processing image.*

A window opened on Meany's targeting display, and a small white dot appeared in the blackness, reflecting light off the earth beneath it, and the moon high on its starboard quarter. As he watched, the AI zoomed and magnified the image, digitally enhancing it. Beside it, images flicked past at lightning speed as the AI combed its databases for a visual match.

Probable match, Angus announced, as the flickering images stopped on a suspect. *AAU CubeSat, Type 1U, launch date 2003, owner Aalborg University, mission: imaging, mission failure due to battery problems, satellite deactivated September 22, 2003.*

"It's been circling for thirty years?" Meany asked.

The satellite was launched with a compressed gas jet nozzle that was supposed to fire on deactivation and cause the orbit to degrade so that the satellite would enter the atmosphere and burn up, but it must have been incorrectly oriented and boosted the satellite into this higher orbit, Angus said.

"You're certain it isn't a live corporate or military object?" Meany asked. Bringing his targeting system online, he locked up the object on the screen. It was still just a white blob on a vast black expanse to him, but it was growing larger by the second.

Ninety-seven percent certainty, the AI replied.

"I'll take that," Meany said. "Give me weapons control."

You have targeting control.

"Call Paddington."

Paging Squadron Leader Bear, the AI confirmed.

Meany wasn't supposed to use the Skylon's defensive weapons system without a confirmed order from his commanding officer. His name was Squadron Leader Gregory Bear, of RAF 23 Squadron Space Operations, so naturally his subordinates called him 'Paddington,' after the famous British cartoon bear.

Meany needed an off-center hit, preferably on the spaceward side of the object, so that the hit would shove it not just out of their way, but into a degrading orbit that would eventually send it into the atmosphere where it would burn into gaseous oblivion. The cannon, of course, would have a recoil that would impact their own trajectory and velocity, but the AI compensated for this in real time using thrust vectoring as the weapon fired.

With vision zoomed and enhanced, Meany could see now the object was tumbling, which made his job harder. But it also confirmed that the object was just junk. Controlled spacecraft did not tumble crazily through space.

With his targeting system zoomed, he centered the laser-guided sights on a corner of the satellite. He knew from experience the largest face of one of the old CubeSats was only 11 inches square. So small it made a very hard target, but big enough that there was a small chance it could chip the spacecraft's ceramic composite heat shield and completely ruin Meany's day.

He heard the trailer door open and a panting Paddington jump in behind him. He didn't turn around. "Space debris, sir, 97 percent certain it's a hobby CubeSat. Collision in six minutes. Permission to engage?"

"Is that all?" Bear asked, sounding disappointed. "I was at least hoping for a decent-sized Sputnik or something this time. Hardly seems worth all the fuss."

"Then delegate weapons authority to me and I won't need to keep interrupting your afternoon nap, sir," Meany said.

"Can't do that," Bear said, ignoring the jibe. "Rules of Engagement and all that, Flight Lieutenant. Angus, live-fire authorized," he said, confirming the order to the AI.

Yes, sir. Weapons released.

"Firing, single round," Meany said, his hand on the side-stick that guided the targeting crosshairs. He twitched a finger and the screen flashed briefly white, the only visual indication that the weapon had fired. A white icon appeared on his targeting screen to show the round was tracking, and then it flashed red.

"Missed," the officer behind his shoulder said, unnecessarily. "Cutting it fine, Meany."

"It is spinning rather a lot, sir," Meany muttered.

Four minutes to impact, the AI pointed out, also unnecessarily. *Preparing emergency evasion sequence.*

"Thank you for the vote of confidence, Angus," Meany said. He adjusted the crosshairs minutely. "Firing, two rounds."

His screen flashed white again, and two icons appeared below his crosshairs. A second later, one turned red, the other...

"Green. That's a hit," Meany exclaimed. The CubeSat slid sideways like it had been kicked with an enormous boot and its rotation slowed. But was it...

Collision averted, the AI said. *Resuming programmed mission trajectory.*

"Just another day at the office, eh Meany?" Bear said. No one called Papastopoulos by his full name, either first or last. He was the son of an immigrant Greek restaurant owner who had named him after the ancient Greek philosopher Anaximenes, whose contribution to science had been a theory that all matter was composed of either gaseous, liquid or solid air. Since Meany had been conceived in the business class toilet of a flight from Athens to London, his father had thought the association to be an apt one. Papastopoulos had quickly learned in his childhood to tell people trying to pronounce Anaximenes, "just call me Nick," and had

33

happily adopted the call sign 'Meany' that his flight leader had given him in training.

Greg Bear looked nothing like the cartoon bear his officers had named him for, which was why they'd given him the moniker. He was a former fast-jet pilot like Meany, who had spent most of his career flying multirole Tempest fighters and had seen action on several occasions, including the first successful RAF strike on an enemy satellite using a modified Meteor long-range air to air missile. He was tall, lean, befreckled and ginger-haired, and his green eyes regarded Meany with amusement over a cliché bushy mustache. He was holding a half mug of tea which he must have artfully managed not to spill while running to the command trailer.

"I'm serious, sir," Meany told him. "One day you're going to be sitting on the cludgie when I page you and by the time you give me weapons authority, it will be too late."

Bear sipped his tea. "And in that case, the AI will assume control, make an evasive maneuver and the mission will continue with nothing more to show for it than your own raised heart rate," he said.

"Or ten tons of space junk will slam into our very expensive Reusable Launch System and your court-martialed self will be drinking your tea on some windswept rock in the Atlantic instead of my cozy trailer."

Bear smirked. "You tempt me, Flight Lieutenant. The Falkland Islands might actually be an improvement on the bleak gray Scottish skies of Lossiemouth." He tipped his mug toward Meany. "Besides, I have faith in that AI. It is probably a better pilot than you or I, and it is definitely a better shot than you."

Thank you for the compliment, Squadron Leader.

"Shut up, Angus," Meany said. "Nobody asked you." He turned back to his console, talking to Bear over his shoulder. "If you really had faith in that AI, sir, I wouldn't be here, would I?"

He heard the door to the trailer open as Bear stepped out again. "The thought had crossed my mind, Flight Lieutenant."

Meany Papastopoulos had an educated ambivalence toward artificial intelligence systems. The older and more primitive combat support AI systems aboard the late marque F-35 fighters he had flown for the Royal Air Force in the Middle East in the latter part of the 2020s had saved his life more than once, reacting with quantum speed to tactical threats that his own reflexes could not possibly have matched. But he'd also seen how dangerous an AI could be when his aircraft Identify Friend or Foe system had malfunctioned and he had nearly been a victim of friendly fire, his aircraft shot down by an RAF missile under automated AI control without human oversight. The incident had colored his view of the virtues of combat AI ever since, which was not surprising considering he ejected and survived, but with a broken back that meant he couldn't walk without his exoskeleton. Ironically, it was during his long period of physical rehabilitation that he'd had the time to return to an area of his aerospace engineering studies that he'd always wanted to explore – orbital mechanics. While bullying his body into cooperating with the exoskeleton, he'd occupied his mind with a master's thesis in astrodynamics, submitting a paper titled "Fuzzy logic trajectory design and guidance," which had attracted zero attention in the astrodynamics academic world, but did attract the attention of an RAF recruiter scouring personnel lists for pilots to crew RAF 11 Group's new Skylon spacecraft.

The Skylon had been through a long gestation. Starting as a concept on a drawing board at British aero-engine designer Reaction Engines in 1982, it staggered from concept to prototype, was scrapped completely in the late 1980s, reinvigorated with a new design in the 1990s, and finally took wing when Boeing and Rolls Royce bought into the redesigned hydrogen-fueled SABRE engine in the early 2020s. The Skylon D2 was a half size single-stage-to-orbit prototype that took to the skies in 2025, followed closely by the full-scale D3 commercial suborbital 'spaceliner' in 2030 and finally the orbital D4 version delivered to the RAF in 2032. The Skylon D4 could take off from the ground like an aircraft, deliver a 33,000 lb. payload to a 1,200-mile orbit, and then land at specially prepared airstrips either at RAF Lossiemouth, the European spaceport in Kiruna or Guiana Space Center. Using interchangeable payload containers, it could be fitted to carry satellites or weapons modules, or, with a specialized habitation module, could boost a personnel payload of 30 'astronauts' into orbit, making Great Britain the first nation that could put a platoon of light assault Marines into space.

The RAF had searched very carefully for the right pilots to crew its one and only Skylon D4. Depending on the mission parameters, it could be in space for anywhere from several hours to several days. The systems AI handled most of the routine duties, but human pilots were required to make mission-critical decisions, like how and when to deploy payloads, whether to ignore or react to a screwball error message that threatened to scrub a mission, and whether or not to blast or evade approaching space junk.

The RAF needed pilots who could keep their heads under incredible pressure, who were accomplished in working in symphony with advanced AI systems, and who had already proven themselves capable of working long hours in near-total social isolation – or as Squadron Leader Gregory Bear had described to the internal recruiter they put on the job, "We need current or former Air Force pilots, autistic loners with attention deficit disorder, twitch reflexes and a belief that nothing in the universe, literally, should prevent them from achieving their mission objective."

The recruitment agency didn't come back with a long shortlist, but Meany Papastopoulos was near the top of it.

"You might not want him," the recruiter had told Bear.

"Two combat rotations in the Middle East in F-35s, a master's in astrodynamics? The profile looks perfect," Bear had replied, flicking through Meany's file. "Why would I not?"

"He's a crip," the recruiter had said. "Broke his back ejecting over Syria, can't walk without an exoskeleton."

"It's a drone, man. He doesn't have to be able to walk, he just has to be able to fly," Bear had said.

Approaching Skynet satellite 6C, matching orbit, the AI voice announced an hour later, bringing Meany back to the present with a bump. He'd leaned his exoskeleton back like a built-in armchair and was flicking through a football magazine on a tablet. He wasn't really a football fan, but he *was* a gambling man. It was one of his many weaknesses. West Ham undefeated on top of the Premier League? Seriously? This season was going to cost him a lot of money.

He levered himself upright with a mechanical whine and checked a half dozen instrument readouts before calling up a visual of the approaching satellite.

"Good job, Angus," he said. "Deploy the net and set up for station keeping, followed by bag and drag."

Confirming, two-knot flyby with target capture, followed by net deployment and stowage, the AI repeated. The day's mission, which had taken several days and multiple pilots over multiple shifts to set up, was for the Skylon aircraft to 'bag' a defunct UK military Skynet satellite in a carbon fiber net mesh at the end of a remote manipulator arm. Once secured, the arm would very slowly swing the satellite into the payload bay so that it could be returned to earth for repair.

A net 'bag and drag' operation was high-risk, because the spacecraft had to close within 20 feet of the target object to bag it, and thus approached it very carefully, at very low speeds.

Meany was alone in his trailer with Angus, but he knew that a dozen eyes were watching his every move on remote monitors inside the RAF Lossiemouth main mission control center. He didn't mind. He'd told the psychologists who had designed the pilots' trailer he could stay focused on his mission in the caldera of an exploding volcano if he had to, but they had convinced themselves that their Skylon pilots would perform better in simulated solo-cockpit environments, where extraneous distractions were minimized. So Meany had just shrugged a 'whatever' kind of shrug and got down to the business of learning to fly the Skylon together with Angus in simulated solitude.

"Mission control?" Meany said, speaking into the mike at his throat. "Am I clear for capture?"

"Skylon cleared for capture of Skynet satellite 6C," a disembodied voice told him. "Station keeping looks good; you have a go for final approach, you are at 1,720 feet, close at 0.46 knots."

"Zero point four six confirmed, Skylon beginning target approach," Meany repeated.

Deploying mesh.

"Check roll bias please, Angus," Meany said, frowning at a readout.

Roll bias within acceptable parameters.

"I don't like it. Mission control?" Meany wasn't happy and asked for a second opinion. The rotating manipulator attachment at the end of the Skylon's capture arm was supposed to match perfectly the slow roll of the defunct Skynet satellite so that it would float serenely into the metallic mesh capture bag. If it was rolling faster or slower relative to the bag, it risked snagging and tearing it, requiring a complete mission reset as the bag was discarded, a new one loaded and a new approach vector calculated – which could take days. He didn't want to hand this part of the mission over to another pilot.

"Confirming roll bias at the upper end of nominal, still within acceptable range, pilot," his mission controller confirmed.

"Nah. Still don't like it. Try to optimize the spin on the capture arm further, please," Meany said, ordering the AI to adjust its roll manually by a fraction.

Adjustment of zero point zero two five RPM on capture arm possible, confirm?

"Yes please," Meany said. As he watched his display, the roll bias figures for both the rotating bag and the target lined up to within two decimal points. "OK, Angus, bag it."

On one of the Skylon's external cameras, he saw the bag flick out from the remote arm, open wide like a spider's web and then wrap itself around the satellite as the Skylon drifted past. There was a visual jerk as the spacecraft adjusted to the added mass of the satellite and it followed obediently along beside it, attached to the robotic arm.

"Manipulator release systems check."

Manipulator systems green.

"Mission control, I am ready to stow the baggage," Meany said.

"You are go for mesh docking, pilot."

"Fire up the grapples, Angus," Meany commanded, having coded the AI with his own preferred jargon to order the AI to prepare to engage the magnetized payload deck once the bagged satellite had been lowered into the payload bay. The net was wound with metallic thread and, together with the magnetic metals in the satellite itself, would be held tight to the floor of the payload bay during the hammering the Skylon got when re-entering Earth's atmosphere.

Mesh docking maneuver A3 initiated.

As he watched, the massive robotic arm moved slowly left to right across his screen, swinging the satellite in an arc before lowering it into the payload bay. His instrument panel confirmed the magnetic grapples had been engaged and he retracted the manipulator arm and closed the payload door.

"And that, ladies and gentlemen, is how we collect the garbage, Skylon-style," Meany declared. "Great job, Angus."

Thank you, Flight Lieutenant Papastopoulos. I am glad you corrected that roll bias error, it greatly increased the likelihood of success.

"Ah, shucks, Angus, stop it, you're making me blush."

The compliment from the AI was also something he had programmed it to do, but he had learned to take his compliments wherever he could get them, even if they came from himself.

Despite the fact that a livid Russian energy minister had stormed into the lift with his bodyguards and left her standing in the corridor with a dismissive glare, Roberta D'Antonia was also complimenting herself.

Nicely played, ragazza. You just confirmed Russia is serious about going to war with Saudi Arabia.

She turned back to the terrace doors as Al-Malki's personal assistant came out looking for her. "That went well," the man said with deliberate sarcasm. He licked his lips and stroked his thin beard. He was just dying for Roberta to trip up so that he could step up into her place. But he had even less business acumen than Al-Malki himself, and that was saying something. All he had going for himself was Saudi citizenship and a penis. Roberta had spent eight years maneuvering herself into a position of influence and access in OPEC; she wasn't about to lose it now at the very moment that she would be of most value.

"Shut your trap, Sahed," she said, pushing past him. She'd learned how to navigate relations in the Kingdom the hard way. What she'd told Lapikov was true. Saudis reacted poorly to threats, and backing down wasn't in their vocabulary. But she'd also learned that subservience or meekness was scorned. As a foreign woman she was at an automatic disadvantage in the Saudi oil business, but being Italian rather than Arabic seemed to give her a license to speak and act more boldly than would otherwise be allowed. Within limits. She could set a fool like Sahed in his place in private, but he would react murderously if she tried to do so in front of other Saudis, or worse, in front of a woman of any nationality. Of course, none of that would be true if she wasn't useful to Al-Malki, but D'Antonia had built up a network within OPEC that could be matched by very few other outsiders.

The secret of her success wasn't just that she was bright; she was modest enough to realize that. The secret of her success was her unique access to confidential information.

Intelligence, to be accurate. Roberta D'Antonia had been born in Sicily but had a master's in international business from Milan University. She'd joined a large multinational oil conglomerate headquartered in London as a graduate at the age of 23. At age 25 she'd been recruited by the Agenzia Informazioni e Sicurezza Esterna (AISE), Italy's external intelligence agency, to provide them with economic intelligence from within the oil industry, at a time when the energy industry in Europe was desperately trying to adjust to a future where oil was increasingly being supplanted by renewables. Led by a Milan industrialist who had partnered with a Californian entrepreneur, Italy had stolen a lead over Germany and France as a producer of autonomous electric mass transport — driverless trains, buses, trams and metro carriages — and found itself fighting an economic war against countries with coal and oil-based economies such as Russia, China, India and the OPEC nations.

D'Antonia wasn't motivated by patriotism. Her country had done almost nothing to help her make her way in life, providing her with the barest of education and employment opportunities, and if she'd stayed in Milan, she'd almost certainly have ended up as one of the thirty percent of young people unable to find work. Nor was she motivated by money. She had been paid handsomely in her industry roles, while AISE paid an almost insultingly small allowance into an Italian bank account, which barely covered the expenses she frequently incurred on their behalf.

No, D'Antonia was motivated by the hunt. Her AISE controllers set her one challenge after another, and she went after them like a jaguar hunting deer. *We need to know what the company is going to announce at its annual meeting next quarter*, they told her. *It's something big. Find out what.* She had been working in the company's branding team at that time, far away from any corporate secrets. But she had a friend in the corporate strategy team who was an insider. She took her friend to see Palermo play Liverpool and got him drunk. *The company is shutting down North Sea platforms and ceasing all Arctic oil exploration activities*, she told her AISE handler. *They are about to announce the acquisition of a pumped hydro technology firm.*

It wasn't her intelligence alone that impressed her handlers; it was her analysis. *This has major economic implications*, she wrote in her report. *The Arctic oil exploration effort was a joint venture with Mozprom, Russia's largest oil and gas exporter. Mozprom was relying heavily on opening new oil and gas fields in the Arctic to enable it to compete in an oversupplied market by cutting transport distances to its key European customers. Without the new Arctic fields to drive it, the Mozprom collaboration is threatened.*

She had proven prescient. Within six months of the announcement, the giant Mozprom conglomerate pulled out of its alliance with her UK employer. Italy, which still drew forty percent of its natural gas supplies from Mozprom, used Roberta's intelligence to renegotiate a very favorable contract with the Russian supplier knowing it was in no position to play hardball on prices.

Roberta D'Antonia was an asset too valuable to waste in corporate communications at a private UK energy conglomerate. The biggest threat to Italy's new electric vehicle industry ambition was OPEC. Just as they had dumped prices in the early part of the century in a futile effort to crush the emerging US shale oil industry, OPEC Plus countries were now targeting Italy's key customers across Europe with cheap refined petroleum and diesel which made it very hard for electrical vehicle manufacturers to make an economic case for their vehicles.

Luckily European governmental environmental targets were still driving demand, but to really take off, Italian vehicle producers needed the cost of gasoline and diesel to rise dramatically. Ironically, in the dying days of the fossil fuel industry, demand was diving and the price of a barrel of oil hadn't been lower in nearly fifty years.

With the help of one of AISE's other assets, Roberta got a job in the OPEC Secretariat Research unit, preparing position papers and analysis for its Energy Division. It was a bloodless, sexless job in which a lesser agent would have died of boredom, but Roberta broke through the beige walls of the Secretariat's research unit by doing a completely unauthorized investigation into Iranian manipulation of oil sanctions through third parties that exposed a State-supported supply route which moved Iranian oil through Algeria to Nigeria and from there into the mainstream market.

She didn't take the report to her superiors in OPEC, nor did she tell AISE about it straight away.

During a meeting of the OPEC Secretariat at which she'd been enlisted to take committee minutes, she'd approached Saudi Prince Al-Malki, who at the time had been a lowly member of the Legal oversight committee. The man was so dim it had taken some time for him to realize that Roberta was offering him valuable intelligence that would give the Kingdom enormous leverage over Iran just by threatening to reveal it.

Al-Malki had the IQ of a sand fly, but luckily also enough self-awareness to realize it. He had insisted Roberta join him when he informed the head of the Saudi delegation about the information and, from that day forward, Roberta had been at his side facilitating his rise through the ranks of OPEC to where he was today, heading up the OPEC relationship with the 'Plus' nations, of which Russia was the biggest.

Having penetrated to the Saudi heart of OPEC, Roberta D'Antonia's brief was simple. To provide AISE with intelligence on the Kingdom's future plans and use Al-Malki to nudge them in a direction favorable to Italy if possible. So far, both the intelligence and the nudging had been of limited value.

Until today.

A Russian threat to attack Saudi interests. Lapikov had been deliberately obscure, Roberta had needed more information dammit, so she had rushed out after him and pushed him with a calculated insult.

Lapikov's response had been illuminating.

He had not balked at the idea of war, and he had scoffed at the implication Russia did not have the stomach for it. Madre di Dio! If they followed through on their threat, refined crude oil prices were about to skyrocket.

As she pulled the door to the terrace open, she was already mentally framing her next report to AISE.

Russian energy minister just openly threatened the Saudi faction in OPEC. Reduce production ten percent and commit to $60 net per barrel target price, or else Russia 'will curb your production for you.' Military options are implied.

As Roberta walked back to the table on the terrace and the worriedly impatient Al-Malki, she caught herself humming and stopped.

Roberta, the man just threatened Saudi Arabia with war. You are not allowed to feel happy at that fact, no matter how important the intelligence is. Bad girl.

But as she sat, another thought crossed her mind. She needed to contact her broker and buy Russian oil futures.

Presidential decree

45th Space Wing, Cape Canaveral Space Force Station, Florida, July 2033

Captain Alicia Rodriguez had been to war at sea, and in the air. But when she had been called to US Space Force 45th Space Wing's headquarters at Cape Canaveral in Florida to discuss her reassignment to Space Force, she had one concern to flag to the commander of the 45th, Brigadier General Alan Parsons. She stood in front of his desk.

"With respect, sir, I'm Navy," she told him. She made a wave motion with her hands. "You know, ships and the aircraft that fly off them? I know half of nothing about … rockets and satellites."

Parsons had laughed. "I have 15,000 personnel who *only* know rockets and satellites, Captain Rodriguez," he said. "I don't need 15,001. I'm establishing a new Combat Operations Squadron based around our X-37C fleet, and it needs a commander with a different skill set."

"Why me, sir?" she'd asked. It was a hell of a time to take command of the X-37C program, if that was the role she had been tapped for. It had just transitioned from research project status to first operational deployment. The program was still ramping up to full-rate production, with three of the unmanned spacecraft delivered, and five on the production line. The decision by the USA to proceed with the X-37 program was provoked by a new arms race with China, India and Russia as each ramped up its ability to deploy, target and destroy space-based weapons platforms.

"You've had three years as commander of USS *Bougainville*. Two years before that as CO of an amphibious drone wing, including during the Bering Strait conflict. Mini-boss aboard the USS *GW Bush*, including two deployments to the Med during the Turkey-Syria war. Captain, I need a combat drone commander who isn't afraid to get her hands dirty, knows what it takes to get a new combat unit up and running fast, and has a cool head under pressure. I was told by Vice-Admiral Solanta that you fit that description." Parsons raised his eyebrows. "And that your call sign was 'Hammer.' Did the Vice-Admiral lie to me?"

"If that's what the Admiral said, sir…" Rodriguez replied carefully, "… I won't contradict him."

"You'd preserve your current O-6 pay grade, come in as a Colonel in Space Force and CO of the 615th COS. I've already agreed with the Admiral that pending your presenting me with an insurmountable obstacle today, you can be reassigned immediately."

Rodriguez swallowed. It didn't sound like an offer she had the luxury to refuse. "If I may, sir, why the urgency?"

"This is why, Commander," he said, holding out a sheet of paper to her. "Please, sit and read it."

She sat. The first thing she saw was the White House Seal. The next was the innocuous title, "Amending Executive Order 29137." She looked up at Parsons and frowned.

"Read on," he directed. "In fact, read it aloud. It's not very long."

She glanced at the first few lines, drew a breath, and started. "Uh, by the authority vested in me as President by the Constitution and the laws of the United States of America, I hereby direct as follows: that Executive Order 29137 prohibiting the use by the United States of space-based weapons systems for offensive operations, and all related international treaties, be henceforth annulled." Rodriguez shot a sharp glance at Parsons. "It's dated four months ago. I haven't heard about this."

He reached out a hand and took the page back. "You won't. It isn't going to be made public. It will leak eventually, as we start 'renegotiating' those treaties, but I doubt it will create much interest by then. Events will have overtaken it."

She wiped her hands on her uniform trousers, realizing she was sweating, even though the temperature in the Brigadier General's air-conditioned office at Cape Canaveral was cool. "Events, sir?"

"What you probably *have* read about, Commander, is that Russia has recently been deploying a string of satellites in low earth orbit, ostensibly to allow it to detect near-earth space objects, like comets and asteroids," he said.

"Yes, sir," she said. "The Russian media calls the system '*Opekun*.'"

"*Guardian*," he smiled coldly. "Yes. Shielding the world from planet-killing asteroids. Sounds like a noble, altruistic venture, correct?"

"Yes, sir," she said. "I suspect you are about to suggest otherwise."

"I am," Parsons said. "Three years ago a source inside the Russian state security agency reported that Russia has been working on a new space-based weapons system called 'Groza' or *Thunderstorm*. It sounded more like propaganda than hard intel and neither CIA nor NSA had been able to turn up anything solid on Groza. Every lead they got led back to the Opekun program, and so we concluded the Russian security agency source had confused his information." He took the Executive Order, looked it over briefly, and then turned it over and laid it in front of himself with a casual finality. "Two weeks ago, we confirmed that Groza and Opekun are one and the same."

Rodriguez felt her blood chill. "Russia has put *nukes* in orbit?" She sat up straight. "That must break every single treaty on the militarization of space?"

"It would," Parsons said. He glanced at the page again and turned it face down, picking up some photographs she hadn't noticed were sitting in front of him. He continued. "If they had put nukes on those satellites. They didn't."

Rodriguez frowned. "If Groza isn't a nuclear weapons platform, what is it?"

Parsons tapped the photographs on his desk, then leaned across and handed them to her. "I'm told a man died getting these to us. Look carefully."

She looked. They appeared to be aerial surveillance photos, from either an aircraft or satellite. They showed what looked like a flat, lightly forested plain. Northern Europe, she'd guess, or maybe Canada. Way up north anyway, judging by what looked like snow and ice on the ground and a frozen river across the top left of the first couple of photographs. The snow and ice covered the ground in every photograph, except for a rough circle of what looked like churned-up mud. She had no way of judging how big the circle of mud was until she got to the fourth photograph, which showed some vehicles parked at the edge of the mud circle, and some people standing beside them. From the scale of the vehicles, she guessed the mud circle was huge – a mile or two across at least. The final photo was a closeup of the mud, which showed it wasn't just churned-up dirt, snow and ice. There were smashed bricks, splintered timber, and what looked like a vehicle that had been stomped by an enormous foot, squashed flat and half-buried in the ground.

She looked up at Parsons. "What is this?"

"That used to be Kadykchan," he said. "A Siberian coal-mining town abandoned in 1998. More importantly, we believe that to be evidence of a Groza test strike."

She peered closely at the last photograph again. The ground was chewed and cratered. Blackened with what looked like soot, but…

"Thermobaric blast?" she guessed. But as soon as she did, she realized it couldn't be. Unless Russia had found a way to build a thermobaric bomb ten times the size of the largest bomb ever deployed. Nothing less could have caused the kind of devastation she was looking at. But she also knew there were technical limits to the maximum size of thermobarics because of the need to disperse the fuel mist sufficiently before it was detonated. "Or … several? Russia put thermobaric bombs on satellites?" No, that didn't make sense. A thermobaric bomb was basically a huge fuel cylinder with explosives attached. You'd have to give it a crazy amount of shielding for it to survive the heat of re-entry, and how would you guide it? It would be simpler just to put a half dozen thermobaric bombs on conventional fighter planes if you wanted to flatten a target. But what if the target was well protected, or far behind enemy lines… her mind was whirling and she heard Parsons cough, looking up.

"You're giving off enough brainwaves to cook an egg, Commander, but let me put you out of your misery," he said. "The agent who died also brought out some technical documentation. Groza is a kinetic bombardment weapon."

"So…"

"Yes. It doesn't violate any treaties, and Russia didn't cross any existing red lines. We have treaties forbidding any nation from putting nukes in orbit, and they didn't." He held out his hand and she handed back the photographs. "We've mapped all known

Opekun-slash-Groza satellite orbits. This system gives Russia the ability to flatten any damn target on the planet from orbit, with just fifteen minutes from launch to target impact. Worse, those satellites have their own propulsion systems and can be repositioned, so they can put two or three of them together if they really want to bring the stomp."

Alicia straightened her back. "Sir, as I said, I'm no expert on anti-satellite warfare, but if we're already tracking them, couldn't we just shoot these satellites out of orbit if we needed to?" She knew a little more about US anti-satellite capabilities than she was letting on. The latest generation of sea-launched SM-6 Aegis anti-satellite missiles had a solid kill rate in testing, especially against satellites with nicely predictable orbits, which the Groza satellites had to be.

"Launch an ASAT missile from the sea or air, and the whole world would see it," Parsons said. "The X-37 is…"

"Stealth," Rodriguez guessed. "You want to start taking those Russian satellites down in a way Russia can't blame us for. That's the mission?"

"Not yet. We can't just go up there and blast Ivan's shiny new toys out of orbit. But I have a feeling in my bones that the day will come and we need to be ready," Parsons said. "We believe there are sixteen Groza platforms in orbit. As soon as it is constituted the 615th will start shadowing the six that directly threaten the US mainland and then the four we believe are threatening our overseas bases. Learn everything we can about them. Test their defenses, Russia's reactions. And if needs be, prosecute a campaign intended to degrade or destroy the Groza network completely. So, you up for this … *Colonel* Rodriguez?"

Rodriguez took a deep breath. "Aye, sir. Hell yes I am."

She had a million other questions, but Parsons wasn't the one who would answer them. She knew there were three operational X-37Cs, but were any of the five currently on the production line near completion? The US Air Force had never admitted that its X-37C spacecraft were armed, but she'd heard rumors they had been fitted with both ballistic and liquid laser weapons. What was their crew status – did she have a full roster of personnel? Where were the holes? She'd been mini-Boss on a supercarrier, had led a wing of combat drones in battle and then been given command of an

America-class amphibious assault ship. What would prove different about commanding a fleet of unmanned spacecraft?

Probably everything. Questions, yeah, she had dozens. But one above all.

How long did she have to get her new unit ready for this mission?

The answer to Alicia Rodriguez's question was being decided right at that moment in suite 903 of the Hotel Baur au Lac in Zurich. Russian Energy Minister Denis Lapikov was standing by the sitting room window of his suite, looking out at the mountains in the distance and reflecting on the fact that but for the world's still insatiable desire for oil, twenty years ago they would have been dusted with snow at this time of year. Instead, they were brown and bare. Barren, like his mood.

He looked at his watch. His lead negotiator was late returning from the final meeting with the Saudis. It was 1715. He was to call Moscow with the Saudis' answer by 1730. He was on his third whiskey and held up the glass, looking at his reflection in the flat-faced tumbler. He had never imagined the ship of his State would run aground as completely and utterly as it had. Russia had seen the writing on the wall as far back as 2015 when the IMF had pointed out that it wasn't sustainable for the Russian economy to derive more than seventy percent of its income from oil and gas exports. Industry forecast after industry forecast came in predicting a year on year decline in oil demand, at the same time as new sources of oil such as shale were coming online. Gas demand, especially from Europe, remained strong, though, and kept the treasury coffers from emptying completely. But foreign debt climbed. In December 2019, the mighty *Kuznetsov*, Russia's last great aircraft carrier, caught fire while in dry dock for a refit and was written off. The hulk was bought by China, which was just as well because it meant resources that would have been drained away to keep Russia's struggling blue water navy afloat were able to be redirected to strengthen its air, aerospace and ground forces.

The 2020s brought relative prosperity. Under President Putin, who had secured himself another eight years as President, Russia turned its attention east. On the back of the insatiable demand of China for rare metals and more traditional resources, the Russian Far East boomed, and Russia started eyeing the untapped potential of the Arctic. It started an oil price war with OPEC that nearly brought both the Russian and Saudi economies to their knees, but Russia secured a stronger say in OPEC's price-setting mechanisms. Then the apparently immortal Putin had died of a heart attack while bareback horse riding. He had not prepared a competent successor to take his place, so instead the country got a succession of weak leaders and a cabal of Machiavellian ministers more concerned at furthering their own interests than those of Russia.

An ill-advised military incursion into the Bering Strait triggered a failed coup that had set Russian Far East and Arctic ambitions back five years and that, coupled with an accelerating collapse in oil and gas prices as CO2 targets were legislated in Europe and more and more wind farms and solar fields came online, had sent the Russian economy into a death spiral. All the empty words about restructuring the Russian economy, in party manifesto after party manifesto, had in the end come to nothing.

Only one thing could save the Russian economy now: a steep and sustained rise in the price of crude oil. And only one nation could guarantee it. Saudi Arabia. Lapikov knew the new Russian President Alexei Avramenko well. They had studied law together and joined the Russian Future Party on the same day. He had won the Presidency after the Bering Strait misadventure, on a platform of 'Russia First.' Lapikov knew Avramenko was too proud to go crawling on threadbare knees to China, Saudi Arabia or any other lender. Not while Russia was still a nuclear superpower. Not while it still had the biggest army in Europe. Accept a ruinous loan from a Saudi nation that hadn't even existed back when Peter the Great was sailing his 30-ship fleet to seize the city of Azov from the Ottomans? Never.

But perhaps the Saudis could be made to see reason. They were behaving like the lunatic survivor of the Titanic who had made it to a lifeboat and was kicking at the scrabbling arms and faces of anyone else who tried to get in. The Kingdom knew it had perhaps 50 years of global oil dependency left with which to fill its sovereign treasury fund and it was driving prices down to capture as much of the market as it could before time ran out. It had persuaded Iraq,

Turkey, Algeria, Morocco, and Tunisia to follow it down by promising them a small percentage of its own sales. The only thing that could change the dynamic was to reintroduce strict production controls, which Russia and the other OPEC Plus nations had tried to persuade it to do. Russia needed a price per barrel at least twice what it was today, and it needed a sign from Saudi Arabia that it was willing to cooperate. Or it needed to curb Saudi production through … other means. Lapikov was not Defense Minister. He did not know what 'other means' were under consideration and a part of him did not want to know.

His thoughts were interrupted by sounds at the door of his suite and his chief negotiator walked in. The man said something to the bodyguards on the door outside, closed the door gently and then turned and leaned his back against it. He said nothing, simply shook his head slowly.

Lapikov didn't need more detail than that. With a sigh, he reached for his phone, turned back to the window and dialed. "Alexei?" he said when the call picked up. "As we thought, they will not compromise." He looked at the man still leaning up against the wall and repeated the question the Russian President had just asked him. "Was there any movement on the quotas at all?"

The man shook his head again, looking defeated.

"None, Alexei. As I told you, the tone of my conversation with Al-Malki's people this morning implied they do not believe we will carry through on our threat… yes … yes they will." Lapikov looked up at the clear blue Swiss sky and shuddered at the thought going through his mind. "Yes, I will be on the next flight out. I'll call you when we land."

"OK, honey, I'll call you when I've asked," Ambre Duchamp said into her cell phone. "No, Soshane, I can't promise. He might say no. Now I have to go. The bus is coming."

It wasn't. But she always had to make an excuse to hang up on her daughter, or the girl would just keep talking. She felt bad about that, so it made her feel better when the bus turned the corner of Phillips Parkway a few minutes later. Almost like she hadn't been fibbing. The driverless E-bus juddered to a stop at the sidewalk by the parking lot off the public car park. Ambre still felt a bit like cheering whenever she saw it, given the unpredictability of the Italian-made buses which continuously circled the complex. They were meant to arrive every ten to twenty minutes, but with breakdowns and traffic delays (they had to stop for every single idiot who drove or stepped in front of them), it was often thirty or forty minutes between. But she couldn't walk it because it was nearly three miles to the Security HQ, where she worked as a data scientist.

She lifted her shoulder bag, balancing the weight by leaning a little to the left, waiting for the doors to open, thinking *yeah, there's an empty seat, I'm going for that one*. Looking to her right at the young lady in a trim blue skirt and blouse beside her, looked like one of those public educator types, edging forward. *No chance, child, that seat got my name on it.*

For some reason, the sight of the girl triggered a memory – her job interview. She still remembered the color of the sky that day, that deep blue sky. Thinking to herself, *Up there, that's the future of mankind.* The young technical sergeant from 45th Wing Security Force, who looked a lot like the girl standing beside her, asking her, "So, you got this far, you passed security vetting, so let's start this interview with your questions about the position."

Ambre had plenty, but she went with the obvious one. "Yeah, so, I understand what the Security Forces Squadron at the Cape does, but what is this project I'll be working on?"

"Good question," the woman said, tapping a stylus on the tablet in front of her, thinking about the answer. "How many visitors do you think the Kennedy Space Center and Canaveral Station combined get per month?"

"I don't know," Ambre admitted. She'd been to the Kennedy Space Center museum a year earlier, with her daughter Soshane. The visitor center had been packed with school children and space geeks. She did some quick math. "Maybe ten thousand?"

"Not even close," the woman said. "One hundred and fourteen thousand. Forty percent are tourists, and then there's commercial visitors, government State, government Federal, political, Air Force, other Space Force, security services and police, media. Knowing that, how many visitor-related security incidents do you think we record in a month?" She was looking at a tablet, so Ambre guessed it was a question they asked all the candidates and she had the numbers there for reference.

"How do you define an incident?" Ambre asked.

The woman checked her tablet. "Any event where a member of the public is reported doing something that is against regulations. Or the law."

"Include parking violations?"

"Not including parking violations," the woman said with a slight smile.

"OK. Two thousand eight hundred and twenty-six," Ambre replied, without hesitation.

"Uh, wow," the lady said. "That's quite precise, and ... pretty close. It's about two thousand. Most people guess a couple of hundred a month. How did you land on your number?"

"Population of the US with a criminal record," Ambre said. "Eight percent. Of course your visitors here are probably from a cohort where that's lower, but they're also a lot of kids, where it's higher coz they don't know better, so I stuck with the eight percent. Then assume each of those criminals does something stupid on their visit, that's a possible nine thousand four hundred and twenty incidents. But probability they'll commit a crime while on a trip to Kennedy or especially on a military base, that's a roll of the dice, so say it's one day out of 365 they're visiting, so call that a zero point three percent chance any given criminal will commit a crime on the day they're visiting, that's 2,826 incidents a month or a little under a hundred a day. What kind of stuff do people do?"

The airman looked at her a little dumbstruck, made a note on her tablet and looked up. "Most of it is petty theft, some vandalism like trying to steal signs and nameplates – pretty much anything with NASA, SpaceX or Space Force on it in the public areas has to be welded on – there's trespassing, of course, but usually just because they got lost, but there's also the occasional assault or episode of harassment."

Ambre let her finish and then said, "And of course, there was the terrorist attack at Kennedy last year."

"And … yes. Five dead, not including the two perpetrators, sixteen wounded."

"I thought that might be what this project is about," Ambre said. "Something you've started up since that event."

"You're right, of course." The woman leaned forward. "I can only share limited information with you at this interview, and you have signed a secrecy agreement, so you are bound by the Espionage Act to keep everything we discuss confidential. Is that clear?"

"Yes, ma'am," Ambre said.

"Good. So, every incident we log, we capture data. About the incident, about the people involved. Every visitor who comes in here, even before the attack, we get ID when they register…"

"Which could be faked…"

"And biometrics, like facial scans, which can't," the woman continued. "Visitors get a name tag, which is GPS chipped, so we know where they are and where they've been, at all times…"

"Where the name tag has been…" Ambre pointed out, "not necessarily the person."

"True. But we have CCTV over the whole station, thermal and optic, keyed to the personnel and visitor tags, cross-referencing the biometrics in real time and linked to Federal offender databases…"

"Which is only useful if the terrorist is in a database," Ambre said.

"Which those two weren't," the lady said and tapped her stylus again nervously. Ambre learned later she had been there the day of the attack. "We lost two KSC officers and three guests and there were some things we could tighten up, but the inquiry found no glaring holes in their response. They reacted quickly, they isolated the attackers and they dealt with them. All the casualties occurred before they could respond." She took a breath and frowned. "But we want to find a way to predict the next attack, not respond to it. Whether it's at Kennedy or here at the Cape."

"That's a big ask," Ambre said.

"How would you go about it?" the woman asked her, back in interview mode.

"Well, you're drowning in data," Ambre observed, thinking out loud. "How accessible is it? What quality is it? What's relevant, what's not? First, I'd need to create a central hub with everything in it, so I can query the data. That means potentially getting systems that don't talk to each other to all play nice. There are off the shelf AI support systems that can structure the queries and reporting, but they are only as good as the raw data you give them to play with – so there's going to be a lot of cleaning, I'm guessing..."

The woman looked at her patiently.

"Three months to complete an audit," Ambre said. "But if I work around the clock, call it two. Two months to make the plan and socialize it so it gets signed off – shorter if you give me the decision power I need, longer if you don't. Three months to run a tender and find a supplier who can pull the data hub together, but I already know a few, so call that two months. Three months with the vendor, running queries and debugging the AI, which I wouldn't want to compromise since the output is predictive and there is a high risk that if we screw up we'll predict too many incidents or miss one, which could be catastrophic. So ... give me this job and in nine months, I'll give you a system that can flag your high-risk visitors for special attention and you can do whatever you want to do with them."

"You've done this sort of thing before," the woman smiled. "Sounds like your CV doesn't lie."

"Yes, ma'am," she said. "I was project lead on a similar project for JP Morgan Chase."

"Well, it's a first for a Space Force station. And the good news is, the system is already up and running. You don't have to build it. But the project was managed out of Kennedy and we just piggybacked on it. It isn't tailored to the needs of this station, and that's where you will come in. It's a flexible term contract, up to two years, with delivery and end of contract bonuses..."

"You want me to adapt the system NASA built for Kennedy so that it works for the Cape," Ambre summarized. "I can do that."

She got the job.

That was a year ago. It had turned out that, as she feared, NASA was a behemoth of an organization that had a belt and braces approach to safety issues, but luckily a 'just do it' approach to everything else. Kennedy's identification and prediction algorithms were pretty good already, but they needed tweaking for the Cape, so nine months ended up being ten before she hit her first milestone and popped the champagne (Sprite actually, since she didn't drink). But after a year of working like a maniac and barely seeing Soshane except to kiss her goodnight and then deliver her to her grandmother in the mornings, she was into a nice routine. The AI was turning out risk assessments on every visitor that came through the gates and turnstiles, and she'd had a few wins where people who had been flagged had been monitored more closely and got tagged doing something stupid, so 45th Wing Security Force was happy. Of course, she knew the offenders might have been picked up anyway, but she'd set up the AI to err on the side of caution, and flag even medium-risk candidates, so when they'd reviewed the incident reports after three months of field testing, the AI had flagged 84 percent of the visitors who had gone on to be 'offenders,' including five who had turned out to be carrying concealed weapons. Whether terrorist or criminal or just someone concerned with their personal safety, it didn't matter. Space Force Security didn't want weapons inside its perimeter and Ambre's AI had helped with that. They called themselves 'Defenders' for a reason.

On the day she hit 1,000 offenders successfully tagged by her system, she ordered a big cake and sipped on her Sprite among a bunch of Defenders and base IT personnel she'd invited to celebrate with her.

"We can't keep calling it Behavioral Risk Factor Surveillance System 1.4," Master Sergeant Ted Usaka, 45th Wing's Chief of Cyber Surety, had told her. "BRFSS? We need something catchy the guys on patrol can relate to."

She'd thought about it. "What do the guys on patrol call it now?"

Sergeant Usaka was a pretty introverted guy, and he looked down at his feet. "Ah, you … it's probably not appropriate."

"Tell me. What do they call it?" she'd asked.

"Well, you know, Defenders, they have a pretty warped sense of humor," he said. "So, uh … they call it the Big Rat-F'ing Surveillance System. BRFSS, see?" He saw her frowning and hurried on. "Like, you know, *apparently*, rat-'effing' is picking the good stuff out of a pile of other stuff which, that's kind of what BRFSS does, right?" He shrugged. "So when your AI flags a visitor and sends an alert, they call it a 'Rat-F Report.' Sorry, I shouldn't have..." He trailed off.

"So we shorten it to Risk Factor Surveillance or RFS and they can keep calling it Rat-F Surveillance and everyone is happy," she told him. She wasn't the creative type. Or easily offended.

Why aren't the damn bus doors opening? She looked through the windows of the bus, at that one empty seat, saw the other woman sidling down toward the back, hoping she might get in the back doors and beat Ambre to it. Finally, with a hydraulic hiss, the doors to the bus swung open and Ambre jumped inside, seeing the rear doors had stuck halfway open. *Oh yeah, love that Italian technology*, she thought as she took the empty seat.

Captain Amir Alakeel, Royal Saudi Air Force (RSAF) 92 Squadron, was also still settling into his seat as he flew his RSAF F-35 *Lightning* II on an urgent intercept mission over the Persian Gulf between Saudi Arabia and Iran. He tapped the multifunction screen display in front of him and called up air-sea sensor mode, then scanned the sky around him with his Mark 1 eyeballs.

"Haya Two, Haya One. Watch your spacing, Lieutenant."

"Roger, Haya One," his wingman, Lieutenant Hatem Zedan, replied. The starboard wing of the F-35 dipped almost imperceptibly and it slid another hundred feet further out and back from Alakeel's tail. He looked reflexively around the sky and then back at his ground radar display. Despite current tensions with Iran, attacks from above were not his main concern. The Iranians had no real Air Force to speak of.

What it did have, however, were ten Chinese-made, Australian-designed catamaran-hulled *Houbei*-class missile boats, and a newfound willingness to use them. The data-linked *Houbei* boats had low-profile, angular stealth conform hulls, waterjet propulsors that pushed them through the water at up to 36 knots, and they were armed with both a 30mm cannon and Chinese-made *Saccade* anti-ship missiles.

Alakeel was responding to an urgent mayday from the Saudi-flagged very large crude carrier *Bahri Tafik*, currently sailing through the Straits of Hormuz between Iran and the Emirates. The *Tafik* had reported it had been stopped 'by Iranian missile boats and ordered to proceed to the Iranian port of Bandar Abbas for immediate inspection.'

It would not be the first time Iran had used the tactic to harass shipping in the Straits, usually citing some sort of specious violation of maritime rules such as a faulty GPS locator, colliding with a non-existent fishing vessel, or failing to respond to navigational directions. But just lately, Iran had stepped the harassment up a notch and was specifically targeting Saudi-flagged crude oil carriers, of which the *Bahri Tafik* was the largest. At 1,000 feet long, with a draft of 115 feet, it was carrying 2 million barrels of oil. Alakeel had asked him what was behind the sudden increase in harassment of Saudi shipping by the Iranians, but they had no answers.

A Royal Saudi Navy *Badr*-class corvette was hurrying to the crude carrier's assistance, but was still an hour away. Alakeel and Zedan would reach it first.

Alakeel listened as the Saudi Coast Guard hailed the Iranian ships again. "Iranian naval vessels in the proximity of Saudi merchant vessel *Bahri Tafik*, your actions are unsafe; we request you return to Iranian national waters and allow the *Bahri Tafik* to proceed unhindered."

There was no answer. There had been no answer to any of the Saudi Coast Guard hails, only insistent instructions from one of the Iranian ships to the Captain of the *Tafik* that he change course for Bandar Abbas for 'immediate inspection.' He had refused, but according to Saudi Coast Guard radar, the tanker was lying becalmed off the coast of the Iranian island of Qeshm. Due to their low observability profiles, Saudi Coast Guard radar had been unable to confirm the *Tafik* Captain's report that at least three Iranian vessels had surrounded his carrier.

"Haya Two, Haya One, approaching waypoint. We will turn to 110 degrees and overfly the target at 10,000 feet. Stay on me."

"Roger, Haya One," Zedan replied. It was the kid's first time going up against the Iranian Navy, and Alakeel knew exactly how he would be feeling. Nervous, excited, scared and, in his 5th-generation fighter, probably way more confident than he should be. Stealth was useless when you had been asked to eyeball your target. If you could see them, they could see you. And if they could see you, they could kill you. Alakeel did not intend to make a stealthy approach and the Iranian missile boats typically carried Chinese-made *Vanguard* infrared anti-air missiles, which had a ceiling of 13,000 feet, so they would theoretically be within range of the Iranian boat's anti-air defenses.

Traffic in the Straits was heavy, and as he swung around to point his flight at the expected position of the *Tafik*, he scanned the sea ahead of him with his APG-81 radar in track and identify mode. Linked to a cloud-based intelligence database, it sorted through the returns of the dozens of ships below, looking for the very specific signature of the *Bahri Tafik*. Twenty miles out from Qeshm, his system told him it had a probable ID. He locked the target up, seeing already from the size of the return that it was probably the right ship. It was a very solid return, and it wasn't moving.

"Haya Two, Haya One. Syncing target data, beginning ingress," Alakeel said.

His radio clicked in acknowledgment.

At ten miles, he saw a large dark shape on the horizon, which quickly expanded to a ship and then the very unmistakable profile of a large crude oil carrier.

A chime sounded in his ears. His aircraft was being bathed in radar energy from ground-based stations in Iran and the Emirates, both military and civilian. They were flying with the aircraft's Luneberg lens system engaged. It reduced their stealth profile and made them visible to watching radar. The Saudi mission planners who had tasked Alakeel's flight with this mission had wanted their aircraft to be visible to the Iranians below so that they would not react precipitously at the sight of Saudi fighters suddenly overhead. But the chime and warning on his multifunction display told him one or more military radars were trying to lock onto his aircraft, in this case the type 362S fielded by the Iranian *Houbei* missile boats – so they'd seen him alright. But they didn't have a lock.

"Haya One, Haya Two, showing multiple spikes, sir," Zedan reported.

"Copy. Stay cool, Lieutenant," Alakeel replied.

Alakeel twitched his side-stick to aim his ship down the starboard side of the *Tafik*, dropping a wingtip so he could get a good look as they cruised overhead at a leisurely 500 knots.

"Sector Control, this is Haya One," he said, calling up the ground controllers at 92 Squadron's home field; King Abdulaziz Air Base, Dhahran. He brought his and Zedan's aircraft around in a sweeping circle above the stalled crude carrier. "I can confirm the target is stationary at grid position alpha eagle zero two. I see three Iranian *Houbei*-class missile boats, one at the bow, one at the stern, and a third stationed off the port beam. Do you want us to buzz them, Control?" A low-level flyby at supersonic speed was a common tactic to test the resolve of the Iranian commander below. Often it would be enough to scare them off.

Missile launch, missile launch, a voice in his helmet exclaimed. At the same time, the missile warning alert on his helmet-mounted display lit up, showing him the bearing to the missile and the missile type. *Vanguard*. The bloody Iranians had fired on them!

"Break break break," Alakeel commanded. "Evade and bug out." His combat AI was already firing flares as he put his machine ninety degrees to the threat and pointed it at the sea, giving the enemy infrared missiles as hard a target as possible by obscuring his aircraft's glowing hot exhaust ports.

Miss. The two missiles went for the white-hot flares hanging in his wake and flew harmlessly into the sky behind him. He checked the sky, checked on Zedan. He was also clear. Two thousand feet over the sea, he hauled his aircraft around and pointed it southeast to their rally point in the Gulf of Oman.

"Control, Haya One, we have been fired on," Alakeel reported calmly. "Sea to air missiles, AI tagged them as *Misagh-2 Vanguards*. No contact or damage. Haya flight is reforming at grid delta golf three three, awaiting orders."

Despite the deliberate evenness of his voice, his heart was pounding as he pointed his machine up to 15,000 feet and saw Zedan swinging in behind him. His eyes flicked from instruments to the sky around and then back again. His tactical display showed no Iranian military aircraft in range. Yet. One blessing, at least.

His heart missed a beat a second later as a voice speaking English broke in on the unencrypted Guard open channel. "Saudi fighter aircraft over the Gulf of Oman, this is Commander of Republic of Iran Air Force fighters on your six o'clock. You are interfering with the lawful military activities of the Iranian Navy. You are ordered to return to Saudi airspace immediately. Please acknowledge."

There was nothing on his threat warning receiver! A bluff? He swung his head around desperately, searching the sky, rolling his aircraft slowly left, then right, ready to break away at any moment.

"Captain Alakeel?" Zedan asked, his voice pitched an octave higher than normal.

Alakeel ignored him, craning his head to look over his left shoulder ... there!

Four small black dots, falling down behind them, about five miles back. He couldn't see what they were, but his sensors could, now that he knew they were there. The Lightning's 360-degree, spherical situational awareness system used electro-optical distributed aperture sensors (DAS) to detect targets, assuming you had DAS engaged and were paying bloody attention. *Dammit Alakeel, you got complacent and let them get the jump on you!* But the fact that these aircraft had crept up on him unnoticed told him one thing. They were stealth fighters.

And Iran did not possess any stealth fighters.

"Haya Two, Haya One, hold formation," he said through gritted teeth, working his AN/AAQ-37 sensor suite.

There.

As they drew closer, he got an optical lock on the enemy flight behind him. He still couldn't get a radar or infrared lock.

Easy does it, Amir, he told himself. Let's see what we are dealing with. He put his aircraft into a gentle bank that would force the aircraft behind to follow or to pass him.

The thickly accented voice broke in again and repeated itself. "Saudi fighter aircraft over the Gulf of Oman, this is Commander of Republic of Iran Air Force fighters on your six o'clock. You are interfering…"

At almost the same moment as his combat AI made the identification, the enemy aircraft closed to within visual range, off Alakeel's port wing, banking to stay in short-range missile position on his six o'clock.

What the hell? The aircraft were *Russian* Sukhoi-57 stealth fighters. There was no mistaking the broad wings and bird-like nose of the big twin-engined fighters. As he watched, two of the four behind him pulled ahead of the others, one accelerating to take up a position on their starboard side, another to take up a position on their port side. They bore no camouflage paint, and certainly not Iranian Air Force markings. No Russian markings or tail numbers either, just dull silver paint all over.

One of the Sukhoi pilots waved to him and pointed to the horizon straight ahead. Alakeel's banking turn had taken him around to a northwesterly heading, and the man's gesture was clear. *Keep going back to where you came from.*

Alakeel's temper spiked. He opened the Guard channel. "This is Saudi fighter flight over the Oman Sea to aircraft on our port and starboard. You are dangerously close. Please increase separation and identify yourself."

"This is the Iranian Air Force," the other pilot replied, his eyes fixed on Alakeel. The accent was as far from Iranian as he had ever heard. It could only be Russian. "Please stay on your current altitude and heading until you reach Saudi airspace." Stay on his current heading?! He couldn't deviate left or right without slamming into one of them.

He switched to the Saudi mission control frequency. "Control, we have been intercepted by fighter aircraft claiming to be Iranian Air Force. Four Su-57 stealth fighters, I repeat, four Su-57 type stealth fighters. No markings. They are ordering us to return to Saudi airspace. Instructions please."

He knew what he wanted to do. He wanted to order Zedan to break low and right as he broke low and left. The aircraft behind might fire short-range missiles at them, but if they evaded and survived, he was carrying six Sidewinder Block III lock-after-launch short-range missiles. At the range they would engage, he would give these arrogant Russian dogs something to think about.

"Haya One, Haya Control, you are to disengage and return to Dhahran. Repeat, disengage, return to 92 Squadron base, Dhahran. Confirm, please."

"Control, Haya One, disengage and return to Dhahran. Haya One confirms." He hammered his fist against the side of his cockpit in frustration. Well, there was disengaging and there was disengaging. He did not plan to meekly comply with the Russian's command.

"Haya Two, Haya One," Alakeel said to Zedan. "You heard the order. Stay on this heading but climb rapidly to 20,000 feet, please. I will cover your six. I want to see what these dogs do."

"Roger, Haya One," his wingman said. "Initiating climb." With that, the aircraft on his wing lifted its nose and pointed it skyward, accelerating above him, while he kept his current speed, altitude and heading. Alakeel watched his situational display intently. After a moment of hesitation, the two trailing Russian fighters broke off and followed Zedan up. The other two stayed on Alakeel's wings, shooting suddenly less confident glances across the hundred or so feet separating them on each side.

"Saudi fighter, you are once again requested..." the Russian pilot began repeating.

Alakeel did not plan to keep meekly plowing through the sky toward Saudi airspace. But he didn't want to panic his wingman. He didn't believe the Russians were going to fire on them, or they would have already done so. But he would show them that the Saudi Air Force was not to be easily cowed.

Alakeel had been trained to fly his F-35 Lightning fighter by instructors at Nellis Air Force Base's 6th Weapons Squadron. He had matched himself against the best the USAF had to offer, from knife fights with nimble F-22s to missile engagements with deadly-at-a-distance F-15Cs. He had lost more engagements than he had won, but he had learned a trick or two that weren't in the 6th Weapon's Squadron's official handbook. He rolled his shoulders and flexed his fingers. *Request this, Ivan…*

He jammed his portside rudder pedal down, pulled back on his stick and rolled his F-35 right. It looped up and *over* the Russian aircraft on his starboard wing and he snapped level as he lined up with the wing of his adversary. With his left hand, before the other pilot could react, he gave the Russian the universal gesture for *screw you*, then rolled inverted and dived for the sea.

As he extended away, he half hoped the Russian pilots would follow him down so he could really test his F-35 against the Russian fighters. But instead, they peeled off, including the two who were following Zedan up to 20,000 feet, and headed north to set up a new patrol over the top of the captive Saudi tanker.

By the time the Saudi corvette reached the area, Alakeel was certain the crude carrier would have either been boarded or would be making its way to Bandar Abbas under the guns of the Iranian vessels.

Alakeel watched the icons for the Russian fighters cruise north on his helmet-mounted display and frowned.

Russian stealth fighters over the Persian Gulf posing as Iranians! Where were they based? How had they begun operating in his sector without Saudi intelligence alerting him? And more importantly, why the hell *now*?

Conscientious objector

Baikonur Cosmodrome, Kazakhstan, January 2034

Corporal Maqsud Khan was descended from Uyghur royalty. His father had told him so. His father had told him many stories, but he liked that one. His great-great-grandfather on his father's side was Yulbars Khan, the Uyghur warlord and a Kuomintang general during the Chinese civil war before he fled to Taiwan, where he died in exile in 1971. He left a large family behind in the Uyghur province of Xinjiang and they did not fare well in his absence. When the Chinese started rounding up Uyghurs in 2018 and putting them in 're-education' facilities, Maqsud's grandfather was one of those who were put away. He came out three years later with a certificate declaring him a model citizen, and immediately gathered his family and fled north, to Russian Novosibirsk, where a growing Siberian economy was hungry for fresh bodies to meet its employment shortfall. Maqsud was in the last year of a five-year military hitch that he'd signed up for straight out of his conscript year because he hadn't wanted to work in a lithium mine like his father and had no idea what else to do. Five years' service and he would qualify for a small pension and a subsidized apartment, and the Voyenno-Vozdushnye Sily Rossii or Russian Air Force wasn't as bad as other branches of the armed forces. He'd pretty quickly turned a talent for computer programming into a cushy job in the Space Force ballistic missile program.

Maqsud's definition of 'cushy' was what a lot of people would call 'boring.' He loved boring. The best days of his life were right now: where he rolled out of his bunk at 0530, did his obligatory morning run around the base at Baikonur, downed his breakfast of butterbrot (bread with a slice of cheese) and then reported for duty in the Command Information Center of the 820th Main Center for Missile Attack Warning. Where, for the first four years of his tour, he'd worked on the Russian ballistic missile early warning satellite network. It was the perfect job for Maqsud. He would come to work, his small team of cadets and privates would run systems diagnostic checks on the network of ten *Kosmos* satellites, and nine days out of ten, nothing would happen to disturb the beautiful monotony of service in the anti-ballistic missile defense of Russia.

On the occasionally annoying days, they'd be tasked to monitor a US, Chinese, North Korean or Indian rocket launch and prepare a report, but these were few and the analysis was handled by an AI bot so all he had to do was watch the launch to see if there were any deviations from norms, check the data for anomalies and then forward it. His people got excited if they detected a new type of rocket being tested or a launch which apparently didn't go to plan … Maqsud couldn't care less what the so-called 'main enemy' was up to. But he tried to show some interest, returned the enthusiastic high fives of the younger cadets with a robust slap.

Maqsud Khan had sought a posting to the rocket force because he was a pacifist. The irony wasn't lost on him. His first assignment was on the systems maintenance team in an ICBM silo, responsible for ensuring Russia's new RS-28 *Sarmat* thermonuclear intercontinental ballistic missile was launch-ready at all times. The *Sarmat*'s multiple warheads could deliver a destructive force of 50 million tons of TNT – just one missile was capable of destroying half the capitals of Europe and tipping the northern hemisphere into a nuclear winter. Which made keeping it fully operational an odd career choice for most pacifists. But Maqsud had decided when he joined the Russian Aerospace Forces that he didn't want a posting where he would actually have to kill anyone, directly or indirectly. He didn't want to work on warplanes that might be sent to bomb civilians in Syria, or on-air defense systems that might be called on to shoot down enemy pilots. So he requested a posting to work on the one weapons system that in 90 years had never been used in war; thermonuclear intercontinental ballistic missiles (ICBMs). Maqsud had planned to spend five years in the Russian military and, unlike millions of his compatriots, never have a single death on his conscience.

His request to be posted to the strategic rocket force was quickly approved because it was not a glamorous duty. The *Sarmat* was the latest and most potent of all Russian nuclear missile platforms, but the silos in which it was stored were cold, dank, mold-infested concrete holes in the ground dug in the 1960s. The computer systems controlling the missile launch had not been updated significantly since the 1990s and the launch software had to be loaded from CD-ROMs in a process that took nearly 60 potentially precious minutes if the system went down, which it frequently did.

Because he was Uyghur and signed on in Novosibirsk, his first posting was to the silo in Svobodnyy, a frozen town beside the Zeya River, 103 miles north of Blagoveshchensk. In summer, it was a stinking 80 degrees and humid for three months and in winter, it got quickly down to -4 and stayed there forever. On arrival, Maqsud had been told that when China and Russia had been negotiating the modern border that ran just south of Svobodnyy, they had not argued about who would get to keep Svobodnyy, but who would have to take it. In the year he had reported for duty, there had been three suicides among the personnel, and the Lieutenant commanding the silo had been removed from duty for drug abuse.

But Maqsud's conviction that his missile would never actually be used grew with each day that passed. Its true level of readiness was well below what his superiors reported to their commanders in Blagoveshchensk. He had entered the service in the belief it *would* never be fired, and now he realized that it was highly likely it *could* never be fired, due to the many system faults and failures. Exercises were particularly fraught and likely to expose how fundamentally flawed the launch control systems were, and more often than not, he was ordered to fake the paperwork certifying that the exercise had been carried out successfully. Their superior officers rarely left the comfort of their warm bases to oversee the exercises themselves. The new Lieutenant in command of his unit had appreciated his enthusiastic willingness to cooperate in the falsification of test records and also mistook his pacifistic convictions for 'calm under pressure' because in one of his infrequent service evaluations the Lieutenant had described him that way. And maybe there *was* an element of psychological profiling in the fact he got the promotion to corporal in charge of a tech team that was supposedly at the pointy end of Russia's ballistic missile defenses because God forbid you had someone excitable in charge of a missile that packed the power of 50 million tons of TNT.

His wonderfully impotent military career had recently been painfully interrupted, though, with his transfer to the Groza program. Due to his serene efficiency, his superiors had nominated him to head up a Target Acquisition Squad for the Groza satellites. There were 16 operational satellites in total, and three teams of six men each under the command of a corporal working three eight-hour shifts to ensure the Groza satellites were either still correctly tracking their allocated targets or updated with new tasking at the whim of the 821st Main Center for Reconnaissance of the Situation in Space. Maqsud had joined the program at the end of field testing, when they were still carrying out live-fire attacks on targets in Siberia and the Black Sea, which had been stressfully demanding, not least because of the high level of scrutiny by superior officers and senior scientists. But now that the satellites were fully operational, the excitement had died down and routine had settled in.

Groza was not the moribund arm of the service that the rocket forces had been. In fact, it was probably the program that had drained the rocket forces of every spare ruble that might have been used to upgrade the ballistic missiles' decades-old launch systems, because it had been ruinously expensive to build and was very resource-intensive to maintain. Maqsud had experienced a momentary twinge of conscience and had thought more than once about requesting a transfer back to the rocket forces. But he had only one year of his service to go and had managed to convince himself that like any other weapon of mass destruction, Groza was never actually going to be used. Probably.

Except that now, something was up. The first sign was the queue of traffic at the main gates as he and his squad finished their morning run. Usually, there would be one or two vehicles at the most waiting for the driver's ID to be checked and the vehicle to be scanned. Today there were five, with more coming down the road, and they were all armored luxury cars, with dark tinted windows. A snap inspection, perhaps? He certainly hadn't been warned today would be anything other than just another Thursday. He told his men they'd better shower and make ready twenty minutes earlier than normal – with that traffic outside, this didn't look like the kind of day they should show up for shift change even a minute late.

He'd made the right call. The outgoing shift leader, a Corporal Yeltsin (who was no relation to the previous Russian President), pulled him aside and warned him the Combat Information Center observation level – a platform on a low scaffold that overlooked the CIC from a rear wall – was creaking under the weight of about twenty newly arrived and unannounced guests.

"Who are they?" Maqsud asked him. "Politicians?"

"Some. I recognized Defense Minister Kelnikov, and a general or two. A half dozen other officers, Colonels, Majors and such. Air Force and Space Force. And Popovkin, of course."

Colonel-General Oleg Popovkin was commander of the 15th Aerospace Forces Army, which comprised both Maqsud's Groza program, the Titov research center, the Center for Missile Attack Warning, the Space Intelligence Center, and finally but most importantly, the Baikonur and Plesetsk Cosmodromes, where Russia's heavy launch capability was centered and from where its Groza satellites had been boosted into space atop *Supertyazh* rockets.

"So, what the hell is up?" Maqsud asked.

The man shrugged. "Damned if I know. I got nothing to tell you that you don't already know. We had a quiet shift. Groza 14 is still having comms issues, intermittent dropouts. Selnik is working on it, thinks he might have a workaround, but probably not for implementation during your shift. No new tasking: standing orders, standing targets are still in effect. But whatever it is, it's going down on your shift or all those suits and medals wouldn't be standing around up there drinking coffee and brandy." The man gripped his fist, shook it and wished him luck.

His men had already made their handover and had taken up station inside the CIC. They were only a part of the full Groza complement, the target acquisition team. There were two other teams making up about 20 personnel in total and including the Weapons and Systems teams. His team used the Groza's onboard targeting system to identify and isolate ground targets, pulling on data from other satellites or airborne platforms like surveillance drones or Airborne Warning and Control aircraft if available. The process was largely automated, but Maqsud had to make the call about which assets to draw on and confirm his team had a solid target lock before firing authority was handed to the Weapons team. Weapons determined what type of bombardment was needed to achieve the mission objective – from a single warhead holding 64 missiles for a target like a small building or compound, up to the full complement of 20 warheads – 1,280 'missiles' – for an area bombardment. The Systems Team kept comms clean and clear, managed fuel and propulsion systems, dealt with malfunctions, and was responsible for maneuvering the various satellites into new orbits as needed.

Which Maqsud could immediately see they were doing as he took his seat behind his computer console and looked up at the large wall screen at the front of the room, which showed the current and projected orbit of every one of the 16 Groza satellites. A glance at the familiar screen showed him that Groza 5 was being pulled out of its normal orbit – which took it over Australia, India, Turkey and then Europe – and moved closer to Groza 12 over the Persian Gulf. He pulled on his headset, got his men to call in and confirm they were all logged in, and checked in with the shift leader, Sergeant Kerim Karas.

"Corporal Khan reporting. Targeting Team Echo online. All targets from standing order 19.11.2033 locked and available. Grozas 1 through 13, 15 to 16 available for retasking. Groza 14 locked on standing targets but unavailable for retasking. Awaiting daily orders," he intoned.

Karas sat two rows ahead of Maqsud and three stations to the right on what were essentially just three long benches that were lined with computer terminals and under which hung cables the thickness of Maqsud's fingers. Up front was the tactical display showing the status of every satellite, and at the rear was the observation platform. He snuck a look over his shoulder. He hadn't seen it so full since the full salvo test shot nearly a year ago when they had fully expended the magazine on Groza 17 and flattened those navy ships moored five miles off Sevastopol.

"Very good, Comrade Corporal," he heard Karas' voice say in his ears. "Listen up. As you can see, we've got an audience today. I want you on top of your men, checking every coordinate to the third decimal point twice before you confirm. Got that?" Karas was squat, square-headed, jug-eared and had a squint like the light of the surrounding world annoyed him.

"Yes, Sergeant," he said.

"Tasking for today in your daily orders … sending, now. Get back to me in five with questions," the man said and rang off.

Maqsud reached for his mouse and clicked through his log-on screens to his daily orders desktop. Then his breath caught in his chest. Now he understood why the high-octane audience was in attendance. He re-read the orders and then sat back in his chair for a moment. The target was clearly described. His team would certainly have no trouble identifying it and locking it down. Unlike the missile in his silo in Svobodnyy, Groza represented the latest in advanced weaponry and computer systems that Russia could deploy, so Maqsud had no doubts that if the order was given for the system to be used, the target would be completely and utterly obliterated.

As would the 1,489 civilian and security personnel that his mission briefing file had told him were expected to be working there today.

Rain from a clear sky

Abqaiq oil production facility, Buqayq, Saudi Arabia, January 2034

Sourav Thakur looked up at the sky and cursed. Another cloudless, baking hot bloody day. True, he did not have to work in the cloying, choking fumes of polluted Delhi driving taxi bikes like his brothers, but today looked like it was shaping to be one of those deadly 110-degree days. Days like this, he always lost one or two men in his crew to heatstroke, exhaustion, dehydration, or worse. It had only been a year ago he'd had to pack up the stuff of one of his workers and write his family back home a letter after he'd died of heat stress. What was the guy's name again? Rohit? No … Virat, that was the one. Not much stuff to pack up, really. Some papers, a tobacco pouch, telephone, a cheap ring and necklace bought at a souk. The sum total of a human life in a shoebox.

Five years of university to become a chemical engineer to end up here? He stood in the illusory shade of a distillation tower and watched liquid sulfur squeeze through a crack in the tower and run down the side, sizzling and bubbling on the hot metal and evaporating into the desert air. That crack was today's job. He had to confirm the distillate was sulfur – though any idiot could see that from the color and the position on the tower – and do the paperwork to get the tower shut down. Then some other poor fools had to climb up there in the baking heat and pull the tower apart, get at the plates inside and pull those out, then weld the crack to close it up, reinstall the plates and seal up the tower so that he could run it up and recertify it. *Another day in paradise, Sourav, keep your mind on your bank balance and just get through it.*

Sourav had a target of 300,000 riyals or about 100,000 US dollars he wanted to save up so he could set up his own consultancy in the Indian oil capital of Mumbai and he was two-thirds of the way there. Another year, maybe 18 months, and he'd be back home scouting office space and Buqayq would just be a bad memory. Get himself a wife – his mother was working on that – and a mistress too. A dancer maybe.

"Hey," he called out to the foreman of the crew he'd been assigned. The men were lounging under a platform, hiding from the sun while he made up his mind what to do. "Get off your bloody arses and go get me a cherry picker so I can get up there and take a sample and we can all get back inside again."

Anastasia Grahkovsky stood on the observation platform at the back of the Combat Information Center in Baikonur, listening to the murmurings of the personnel below, who included the now very troubled Maqsud Khan.

"And now we shall see what 2,560 125 lb. meteorites hitting the earth at ten times the speed of sound will do to a modern industrial facility," said a voice behind her, and she turned toward the voice of the commander of the Titov test facility, General Bondarev. She had hoped to be able to just stand unseen at the back of the platform, or if not unseen, then at least ignored – a state her physical appearance usually encouraged. But Bondarev appeared, as usual, to be completely unfazed by her scars and patchwork skin, and treated her as he would any of his other personnel.

"Yes, Comrade General," she said. "I have asked to receive..."

"You will get access to every last megabyte of data from our post-strike damage assessment, Chief Scientist," he said. "After it has been collated and analyzed by my intelligence staff. Don't worry."

"Thank you, General." She was trying to keep the excitement out of her voice but knew it would be palpable to anyone who had spent any time with her, Bondarev being one of those. "General, this target, can I ask why?"

"Why the oil-producing nation of Russia is about to destroy Saudi Arabia's, no, the *world's* most important oil processing plant, accounting for more than seven percent of global capacity?" he asked rhetorically. "You are an intelligent woman, Grahkovsky. The implications must be obvious."

"Not entirely, General," she admitted. "I assume the purpose of the planned strike is to reduce Saudi refined fuel production capacity. But don't they have reserves they could bring online to fill the gap? And couldn't the other OPEC nations simply step up their own production?"

He nodded. "A fair question. In 2019 Iranian-backed Yemeni terrorists attacked Abqaiq with drones and missiles. They knocked the facility out for several months, and world oil prices barely fluttered because the Saudis opened up their sweet crude oil reserves and maintained a relatively constant supply. On the surface, things stayed calm, but below the surface, the Saudis and OPEC were sweating because the Saudis were sitting on only 200 days of sweet crude production, and the repairs to the facility took 180 days to complete. If the drone strike had been more effective, the Saudi crude reserve would have run dry and sent global prices through the roof." He saw her eyes glitter in the darkness of the CIC as he spoke. "If Groza works as you have designed it to, it will not cause the sort of damage the Saudis can repair within a few months. It should ensure the Abqaiq facility can never be brought back online, ever again."

There was a cough and Grahkovsky heard a new voice join the conversation; that of Bondarev's superior, Popovkin. It seemed everyone wanted to have a part of this day. *Success has many fathers*, she thought to herself wryly. *Failure will no doubt be a bitch called Grahkovsky.* "Indeed, Bondarev," Popovkin said. "And the Kingdom's days of trying to dictate Russian oil prices will be numbered."

Up in the cradle of the cherry picker, Sourav unbuckled his safety harness from the rail at the back of the cradle and attached it to the rail at the front, so that he could climb up on the lip of the cradle and reach over to take a sample of the sulfur bubbling from the cracked tower. If it was 110 degrees down on the ground, it was at least 120 degrees up here, twenty feet off the ground in the baking hot air – not to mention the radiant heat blasting at him from the polished metal of the tower itself. Any doubts he had about whether it was sulfur bubbling out of the crack had disappeared as he maneuvered the cherry picker cradle closer to the tower and got a whiff of the stinging odor of the gas given off as the liquid evaporated. Phew!

He had three sample jars to fill and, using a set of long-handled tongs, held the rubber lip of the first up against the tower under the crack and let the yellow liquid drip into it. There was always a chance that the crack would be admitting oxygen as well as releasing sulfur, and a buildup of combustible gas inside the tower could suddenly ignite, sending the tower up like a Roman candle, and Sourav with it. But his contract stated that any such risks were his problem, not his employer's, and he was responsible for his decision to climb into a cherry picker and get up close and personal with a leaking distillation tower, so if he died doing so, it was his bad. He could always refuse, but then he'd be on the first plane back to India with his dreams of starting his own business in shreds in his carryon, so he tried not to think about little things like getting blown up. He'd just get his sample, get back down to the ground and get back inside to his nice cool lab.

As he looked up at the tower to make sure the sample jar was catching the distillate, he stared past it at the clear blue sky. A cloud would be nice, he thought briefly. Just one, to give a little shade.

"Target acquired," Maqsud said into his headset. "Groza 5 in position, orbit is stable and weapons are tracking. Groza 12 in position, orbit is stable and weapons are tracking. Groza system locked and ready to fire."

Please, no, Maqsud said inside his own head. He shot a glance over his shoulder. Someone back there, tell us this was all just a drill after all, and stand us down.

But his hope was snuffed out as Karas repeated in his headset, "Groza 5 and 12, targets acquired, prepared to engage. Fire order is full salvo. Weapons report…"

"Full salvo programmed," the corporal in charge of the weapons team seated directly in front of Maqsud reported. "Groza 5 armed, spinning up. Groza 12 armed, spinning up."

"Systems check…" Karas called out to the corporal of his third team.

"Five and twelve, hub green. Re-entry vehicle green. Tether lock green. No optical or electronic jamming detected. Systems *go* for release."

Karas turned in his seat as he switched his microphone to the CIC loudspeakers and looked up at General Popovkin, who was standing beside Bondarev and Grahkovsky on the viewing platform with a telephone to his ear. "Targets acquired and all systems green. Requesting go for release, General Popovkin." Karas looked nervous. Normally he'd be asking for permission to fire from his Lieutenant, not from the Commander of the 15th Aerospace Forces Army. It was a break from routine that caused Maqsud's spirits to sink lower still.

Popovkin muttered into the telephone, then listened attentively before pulling the phone from his ear and holding it down by his side. "You are cleared to fire, Sergeant Karas."

It was as though the Gods had heard him pray for shade, Sourav thought, adjusting his grip on the tongs. There! Straight up in the sky above the distillation tower, a small white cloud began to form in the air. Sourav frowned. He'd seen some weird atmospheric phenomena in the skies over the Gulf, from red sandstorms to the pale milky fog that appeared from nowhere and, in a matter of minutes, brought traffic to a standstill. But he'd never seen a cloud form in a clear blue sky.

As he watched, the cloud expanded and divided into two clouds, one beside the other. Sourav pulled his sample beaker away from the leaking sulfur and put a gloved hand against the tower to steady himself as he watched. From where Sourav stood, it looked as though the cloud was expanding slowly, and then began to spread tendrils of white smoke, like jet plane contrails, out over his head like an umbrella made of a thousand spokes. He smiled. It was probably one of those daytime fireworks displays marking some Royal birth, death or marriage. They were certainly quite spectacular. But they usually took place out to sea, not right over the top of the Abqaiq processing plant. Perhaps the shells had misfired?

Unlike the smoke from fireworks, which slowed down and then drifted away the closer they got to the ground, these contrails appeared to be accelerating, like missiles! He looked down and saw the workmen below scattering in panic, hands over their heads as they ran. But where were they running to? The distillation tower he was standing against was in the middle of the processing plant and the white contrails were rushing toward the ground from above and all around him. Whatever this was, there was nowhere to hide from it. In a panic himself, he dropped the tongs and sample jar and fell into the cradle of the cherry picker.

The forty tungsten-core warheads that dropped off the two Groza satellites weighed four tons each. As they got to about 80 miles above their target, the ablative shell of the Sarmat RS-28 re-entry vehicle began to burn away, and the engine and navigational systems inside were destroyed, their job done. By now, the warhead was already in the upper atmosphere, moving at a speed of Mach 10, its tungsten core held together only by the carbon belt around its segments. Then about 20 miles above the target this too burned away, releasing the tungsten segments in a pattern roughly equivalent to a two-mile by two-mile grid.

Abqaiq processing plant was concentrated in a one and a half mile by two-mile compound. Two thousand five hundred and sixty white-hot tungsten 'pebbles' slammed into the sandy earth, bitumen and steel of the processing plant and adjacent town over a two square mile area, shattering on impact and releasing millions of bullet-sized shards of tungsten and superheated iron plasma. Cowering in the cradle of his cherry picker, fifty feet above the ground, Sourav heard a sound like thousands of hand grenades exploding, gas and oil burst from ruptured pipes and tanks and ignited, and moments later a ripple of sonic booms split the air. Sourav felt the cherry picker rock and sway. It tilted and felt like it was going over, so he grabbed frantically for a handhold, forgetting that he was still tied to the railing around the cradle with his safety belt. His scrabbling hand grabbed one of the control levers that angled the cradle to allow the workers inside a better view to lower equipment down to the ground. It wasn't meant to rotate through more than ten degrees, but one of the flying tungsten shards had cut the control wire and the cab began to tilt, tipping Sourav toward an inferno of flaming gas and oil fifty feet below.

Still attached by his safety harness, he dropped and came to a jerking stop forty feet above the flames. Luckily for the screaming, roasting Sourav Thakur, the distillation tower beside him chose that moment to explode and end his agony.

Groza was not Russia's first attempt at a space-based weapons system. Nearly a century earlier, at the height of the Cold War, the USSR deployed a missile called the R-36O, which was designed to orbit the earth from pole to pole and had the ability to fire a nuclear missile at any target on the planet at any time during its orbit. It was called the 'Fractional Orbit Bombardment System,' and because it wasn't technically either a ballistic missile or a permanently deployed space-based weapon, it was deemed not to have violated any treaties and western powers tolerated it despite its terrifying potential. The program was eventually canceled by the USSR because normal intercontinental ballistic weapons were simpler and submarine-based weapons were easier to deploy in secret.

In the 1980s, the USSR also tested a system known as Polyus – a spacecraft designed to hunt and kill enemy satellites using a megawatt carbon dioxide laser. Due to technical failures, it was never deployed.

Nor was Groza the first conceptual design for a kinetic energy weapon fired from altitude. In the Vietnam war, the US dropped 1-foot-long iron spikes fitted with fins from their bombers, which sliced through enemy troops like spears. In 2003 the US Air Force published a paper on the potential value of fitting bundles of 20-foot-long, one-foot-wide tungsten rods to a firing and guidance system on a satellite. The paper concluded that with six to eight such satellites in orbit, the weapon would allow the US to strike any target on the planet within 15 minutes versus 30 minutes for a typical intercontinental ballistic missile. And the rods would hit their targets at ten times the speed of sound, with the power of bunker-busting bombs. At such a high speed and with such a small radar cross-section, they would be almost impossible to detect and even harder to intercept.

But the paper also concluded that failure of guidance systems under the heat of re-entry was also highly likely, the ability of the system to hit moving targets would be very limited, and the destructive effect would be no more than could be achieved with conventional explosives anyway. Not to mention that the cost of lifting such weapons into space compared to just mounting conventional weapons on a warplane or cruise missile could not be justified.

Two breakthroughs made Groza possible. The first was the boom in lower-cost heavy-lift rocket capacity that started with the launch of the SpaceX Falcon Heavy semi-reusable rocket, which could lift a payload of 70 tons into full earth orbit. This was followed by the launch in 2030 of Russia's own new heavy launch rocket, *Supertyazh*, which could lift payloads of up to 90 tons into space at a lower cost per ton than any other platform. Russia made good use of both heavy-lift platforms as they came online.

The second breakthrough came from Anastasia Grahkovsky. She had started in the Groza program as a simple physicist, running calculations on the impact force of projectiles of different compositions and mass if dropped from space. The Groza team had of course looked at the older ideas, such as tungsten or depleted uranium rods dropped alone or in bundles, with and without guidance modules, as the simplest solution. But the team had been blinded by the modern obsession with precision weaponry and wasted a huge part of its energy and resources on trying to develop kinetic missiles that could be guided to strike both stationary and moving targets. But guidance systems took away from the mass that could be deployed, and they were vulnerable to the heat and violence of atmospheric re-entry. Not to mention that to Anastasia, the destructive power of the weapons remained unremarkable and certainly didn't justify the effort of lifting them into space.

Then one Easter holiday, she had taken leave and traveled by train to Saint Petersburg to see the city for the first time. She took in all the usual tourist locations, but being Anastasia Grahkovsky, she also visited the Military Historical Museum of Artillery, Engineers and Signal Corps with the aid of a young university student to guide her. She was particularly fascinated by the exhibit of cannons and catapults from the 'entertainment regiments' of

Peter the Great. Among these was a trebuchet, used to fling flaming projectiles over castle walls to set alight the houses within.

She listened to the student's detailed description of the projectiles with professional fascination and quizzed him closely.

They resembled traditional Russian wedding-bread loaves. A large disk or dome encircled with twisted rope. The disk of stone was held together around its circumference by the rope and then dipped in tar and set alight. The rope was fixed to the trebuchet bucket and as the disk was flung through the air, the rope pulled away and the flaming segments of the disk separated into eight triangular pieces, each weighing about 40 lbs., which smashed through straw and slate roofs to set fire to the buildings beneath.

Anastasia ran out of the museum and took the first train back to Moscow, typing equations into a braille recorder the whole way. She had found a way to increase the destructive power of Groza, through a crude but simple warhead design.

The prototype weapon that Russia boosted into space atop its *Supertyazh* rocket was an eighty-ton payload of tungsten comprising twenty-four-ton tungsten cores arranged around a very simple ten-ton satellite hub containing computer and telemetry equipment and an electrical engine. Visually, it looked very much like the loaded cylinder of a twenty-round revolver. Each four-ton tungsten core was fitted into a modified RS-28 *Sarmat* ICBM re-entry vehicle. Inside the warhead, around each tungsten core was wound a thick, flat carbon fiber cable.

After mechanically dropping the warheads from the central hub they were fired toward their target. The *Sarmat* re-entry vehicle guided the warhead toward the target until it burned away, the carbon fiber cable burned away next, and by then, the tungsten warhead was in the lower atmosphere. The slight variability in when the carbon fiber cable release occurred meant Groza's operators were only able to predict the impact zone for the artificial meteorites to within a two-mile by two-mile strike zone.

Like the disk fired from the medieval trebuchet, each core split into eight segments when the cable broke, and the segments fractured into eight again, pounding the target area with up to 1,280 125 lb. glowing hot tungsten meteorites, striking the earth at ten times the speed of sound.

Remembering the stone under her shoe, Anastasia called them 'pebbles.' To anyone else, they were missiles.

Over the next five years, Russia experimented with the composition of the missiles to achieve the most destructive combination of pure tungsten and superheated plasma on impact. They refined their targeting algorithms, developing the ability to focus the entire strike on a two-mile by two-mile zone, or spread it out over a five by five-mile area to enable it to flatten entire villages, suburbs, stationary fleets or military bases.

Unlike the dumb concrete practice bombs used by modern air forces on test ranges, which left little more than a small crater a foot in diameter, Anastasia's missiles created carnage at multiple levels. They struck with a force many times greater than a gravity bomb and, hardened by the heat of re-entry, the brittle tungsten shattered on impact, sending hot metal shards spraying outward to a radius of two hundred yards. Inside their superheated core was a plasma of iron particles that supercharged the air around it with an effect similar to a small fuel-air explosive and electromagnetic pulse weapon (EMP) combined. What they didn't blast, bake or fry on impact was then rocked by the sonic shock wave that followed close on their heels, similar to the blast that had brought the roof down on Anastasia's mother and blown her off her window ledge at Chelyabinsk.

Once they had composition, size, form and weight locked in, the Groza team tested the weapon first on Siberian tundra, then on an abandoned mining town which comprised both standing villas and concrete and glass apartment blocks, and progressively against harder and harder targets. Five-story apartment blocks crumbled if they took a direct hit from several missiles, windows were shattered for miles around by the sonic shock wave, fires broke out all over the target area, which quickly built to firestorm levels if there was fuel enough. Reactive armor-equipped main battle tanks were either flattened or upended, their electronic control and communication systems fried. Troops in deep trenches or bunkers were safe unless they took a direct hit, but their communication and electronic equipment was fried as it would be by a nuclear EMP burst. Troops out in the open would be flayed alive by tungsten shrapnel or burned by plasma, vehicles flattened. Against moored ships, a direct hit would penetrate half-inch steel plate and Groza's operators learned that the best result was achieved with a focused two-mile by two-mile, two-satellite strike that sent 2,560 of the 125 lb. missiles into the target area and almost guaranteed any ship bigger than a fishing boat would be struck. The weapon was useless against even slow-moving targets, but against a fleet moored in port, it would devastate both enemy warships and the port itself.

The falling missiles left frightening white contrails in the sky as they fell, but once launched, a Groza strike was silent until it hit, visible to radar but completely impossible to prevent.

On the eighth floor of Le Bristol hotel in Paris, TV images of towering flames and roiling smoke kept playing in Roberta D'Antonia's head as she hurried from her room to the suite where Prince Al-Malki was quartered. News channels were calling it a meteor strike and playing jerky amateur footage taken from outside the impact area, which appeared to show two flaming meteors dropping through the sky before they exploded high in the atmosphere and showered meteorites over the stricken town and processing plant of Abqaiq.

Meteor my Sicilian culo, D'Antonia thought as she pushed past the Prince's bodyguards and into the entrée area of the suite. The luxury hotel was the venue for the latest meeting of the fast disintegrating coalition of countries that was OPEC Plus. On the table this week had been a motion sponsored by Saudi Arabia to expel Russia from the extended grouping. D'Antonia knew as soon as her phone had started ringing that her agenda for the day was about to be seriously derailed. Al-Malki had rented the entire eighth floor for his personal retinue and D'Antonia had been only five doors down. She banged urgently on his door.

Al-Malki was many things, but idle was not one of them. He was less interested in the affairs of the OPEC Plus portfolio than he was in his own investment portfolio, that much was true, but D'Antonia knew he'd been woken at 6 a.m. with news of the disaster, and had been on a call with Riyadh for nearly twenty minutes. As she let herself in, he was pacing up and down out on a balcony, holding his phone at arm's length so he could see the person on the screen. Sahed, his personal assistant, was busy packing his things.

"What are you doing?" D'Antonia asked him.

"What does it look like?" Sahed responded. "I ordered the jet for ten a.m. We'll be back in Riyadh by supper time."

"He's not going anywhere," D'Antonia told him. "He has to call an emergency session of the heads of delegation and pin Russia to the mat for this."

Sahed looked at her scornfully and pointed at the huge TV screen on a wall of the living room. "You think Russia can magically call meteors from outer space?"

D'Antonia looked back at him disbelievingly. "Even you can't be stupid enough to think this was a coincidence."

The man's bearded face flushed and he was about to snap back when Al-Malki pulled the door to the balcony open and stood there, looking stunned. "The King has ordered me to call an emergency session with the heads of delegation to accuse Russia of attacking Abqaiq."

"With a *meteor*?" Sahed asked.

D'Antonia ignored him. "It has to be a closed session. Not minuted. The Russians will have Iran behind them, Syria, Venezuela, Nigeria, Algeria…"

Al-Malki looked distracted. "I need to get home … my family."

"Are in Istanbul, Highness," D'Antonia told him. "At the winter residence, remember?"

"Oh, yes." He was flipping his phone from front to back in his hand. "Closed session, you say. You will be there? You have to be there."

Sahed coughed. "I have ordered the jet, Highness," he said. "Shall I push it back?"

"Push … yes," the Prince said. He pointed his phone at Sahed. "And call my wife. Tell her you will arrange for her to go to the apartment in London. Istanbul is not safe."

"Yes, Highness." Sahed bowed and rushed outside.

Al-Malki watched him go, then dropped his voice to a whisper. "The King received a call from the American Secretary of State. He said the Americans have proof the Russians attacked us with some new type of space weapon. Our military is trying to corroborate their claims." He put down his telephone and picked up the TV remote, flicking the TV to a business channel. Across the bottom of the screen, the stock tickers were all turning red. "I have to call my broker," the Prince said, distractedly. "I need to move some ... where is Sahed?"

D'Antonia sighed inwardly and tried to keep the scatterbrained Prince focused. "Highness, I will contact the Secretariat and demand an emergency closed session of the full OPEC Plus group for tomorrow at 1 p.m., with the heads of delegation. I will advise that you are to make an announcement about the destruction of our plant at Abqaiq."

"Attack!" Al-Malki sputtered. "It was a damned Russian attack. Say that."

"*Destruction* of our plant at Abqaiq is enough for now, Highness," D'Antonia said. "The other delegations will prioritize the meeting just to hear what you are going to say. We should save the accusations for when we get behind closed doors."

"Say... and what am I going to say?" Al-Malki asked, pacing now. "The King said..."

"I will call Riyadh for instructions, Highness." D'Antonia calmed him. "I started drafting a public statement as soon as I saw the news reports. I will adjust it according to the messages that Riyadh wants to convey."

"By the time we have gathered evidence of this attack, the meeting will be upon us," the man said. Al-Malki preferred at least three run-throughs for any public appearance. "This could be a disaster for me."

"We will keep it short. A statement of the facts as we know them, an expression of sympathy for any lives lost, and then the apportionment of blame, if Riyadh wishes. I expect the King will also want to reassure our allies that we have ample reserves to cover any shortfall in production until the facility is repaired..."

"Do we?" Al-Malki asked.

D'Antonia glanced at the TV screen, which showed a row of fire trucks, parked in the sand outside the processing plant perimeter, unable to even approach due to the heat of the towering flames.

"No, Highness," D'Antonia said. "And I seriously doubt there will be anything left to repair."

"It's beyond repair, ma'am," the manufacturer's engineer was telling Alicia Rodriguez.

As Anastasia Grahkovsky's missiles were raining down on Abqaiq, Rodriguez was taking a tour of the X-37 maintenance facility at Vandenberg Air Force Base. The X-37 was lifted into space from the East Coast, at Kennedy or the Cape, but if necessary could land at Vandenberg. On paper, the 615th Squadron also included one of the older and smaller X-37B reconnaissance spacecraft, which was listed on her inventory as 'stored' at Vandenberg. But when she'd dropped in to inspect it she found it parked up with ports open, and gaping holes where removable components should have been slotted in. She'd asked hopefully if it could be made flyable.

The engineer was called Ross Hardy and had been on the program for over ten years. He was a tall, lean, weather-beaten Californian who had explained to her when she asked if he'd considered a move to Cape Canaveral that he liked Florida well enough, except for the humidity. And the mosquitoes. And the gators. He climbed up the scaffolding to the starboard wing root and gestured to her to follow him up. When she got up there, he pointed. "Hasn't flown since 2029. Hard to see with the naked eye, but two of those heat tiles are cracked. You see the ones a little more yellow? A couple more on the underside have micro-cracks, could expand on re-entry. Can't get those tiles anymore." He shrugged. "We haven't written her off because theoretically you *could* fix her and send her up. But the only thing you'd get back down would be glowing embers."

She had sighed. Another asset that only existed in a database somewhere, not in reality. In her first couple of months in command of 615th Squadron's X-37Cs, Rodriguez had learned that what on paper looked like a serious military aerospace capability with four reusable unmanned spacecraft able to be deployed, and one in production which was near completion, was in fact seriously incapable of mounting anything like combat operations. One X-37C was currently in space, conducting synthetic aperture infrared mapping of newly exposed polar sea floors. She had one X-37C that had just returned from a 100-day mission cycle, having landed here at Vandenberg Air Force Base two thousand miles away from its launch base in California. It was not expected to be deployable for another six to eight months, at least. And she had one X-37C on readiness, but with no available launch vehicle as all suitable heavy-lift rocket capacity, both government and private, was booked up well into the next year.

And those were just the issues with her so-called 'fleet.' Her main concern was the organization she had inherited, which was supposed to be supporting it. She had been given six months to get her unit ready for operations in a covert environment, which required a combat mentality and sense of urgency. What she had found instead was a peacetime, even *corporate* mentality among her personnel that was a legacy of a time when NASA and different government bodies contracted with the manufacturer and Air Force to conduct tests and experiments in space using the X-37B platform. If they missed a launch window by a few weeks or months, if they landed their spacecraft in California and lost weeks transporting it back to Florida across the damn country, well, that was just the nature of the business.

Not to Rodriguez it wasn't. She had to get her people to realize that if protocols weren't in place for her to commandeer a launch slot, then there was no 615th Squadron. That if they missed a launch window, if they didn't have a recovery and turnaround time of days, rather than months, people could die. In short, she had to get them ready to go to *war*.

For that she had turned to two people she had taken with her on her last two postings and had arranged to transfer from Navy to Space Force service like herself. The first was Major (as he was now) KC 'Kansas' Severin, who had been a Lieutenant and the catapult Shooter aboard the aircraft carrier the USS *GW Bush*, when Rodriguez had served in primary flight control as mini-Boss. He was a small man, but he was all muscle and she brought him in as second in command. One terse conversation with Kansas was usually all a subordinate needed to achieve a lasting 'attitude adjustment.' Her other 'go-to' was Chief Petty Officer, now Master Sergeant, Xiaoxia 'Zeezee' Halloran, a completely humorless fourth-generation Chinese American who Rodriguez had talent-spotted when she had been called in to help with Navy's support of Operation Windlass, the relief operation in the aftermath of the 2028 Hurricane Geraldine that decimated Cuba. Zeezee had alerted Rodriguez to the fact that local Communist party officials were diverting nearly a third of the relief supplies that Rodriguez and her *America*-class assault ship the USS *Bougainville* were landing, and before Rodriguez could decide what to do about it, Zeezee had appropriated a Marine platoon, gone ashore and located the warehouse where the pilfered supplies were being stored. After a short conversation with a local Cuban Army detachment during which she explained exactly how much pain a heavily armed US Marine platoon could and would bring down on them, she had not only secured the release of the supplies but ten Cuban Army trucks with which to transport them to where they were needed. Zeezee was Rodriguez's primary logistical fixer, and Rodriguez had yet to come across a SNAFU that Zeezee couldn't un-FU.

She had gathered the two of them in her office at Kennedy Space Center to discuss the problem of the day – a crippling shortage of pilots with combat experience. The X-37C relied heavily on quantum-computing-supported Hyper-Dimensional Data-Enabled Neural Network AIs for launch, landing, navigation and systems management. And the existing complement of mission intelligence coordinators and atmospheric specialists were more than competent. But she still required pilots and weapon officers in the virtual cockpits, calling the shots. Rodriguez had put Kansas and Zeezee on the job with orders to comb the ranks of existing Air Force combat drone units to find the personnel she needed.

"They will have the AI to hold their hands and they can learn the finer points of piloting drones in space when they get here, but I need crews who have proven combat experience," she said. "Pull whoever you can from existing personnel, of course, but I need them tested for suitability."

"That's a big ask," Kansas had warned her. "I'd say maybe one in five of the current personnel has the temperament and skills you need."

"I'd say one in ten," Zeezee corrected him. "The rest we will have to beg, borrow and steal. I hope you have friends in high places, ma'am."

But they'd come through, and after six months had recruited and vetted 24 personnel from across Air Force, Navy and Space Force who could manage the highly demanding roles.

"Most have a background in drones; a lot of recon, a few combat. No such thing as space 'top-guns' that we could find, ma'am," Zeezee said with typical bluntness. Alicia enjoyed the fact she always spoke with a slightly amused smile on her face, whether she was delivering a briefing to Rodriguez, a dressing down to a junior rating, or an ultimatum to a Cuban captain at gunpoint. "We've got them working side by side with the existing X-37 drivers in the simulators, but it's going to take time we don't have before they are as good in space as they are in atmo."

"Speaking of which," Alicia said, "have you tracked down that contractor I was telling you about? Like you said, I need a training officer who can turn this unit from a transport squadron into a fighting force overnight."

"Lieutenant Karen O'Hare?" Zeezee Halloran asked. "Yes, ma'am, it took some work, but I found her. DARPA had her details, though she hasn't been on contract with them for more than a year now. Thing is, I'm afraid she's…" Zeezee paused and looked at Kansas, apparently hoping he'd finish the sentence for her. He kept his expression neutral, though, and let her hang.

"Don't tell me," Rodriguez smiled. "She's in Bali surfing and told you to go screw yourself. Well, she and I go back a ways. Did you tell her who it was wanted to engage her?"

"No, ma'am," Zeezee said. "I didn't actually speak with her. I thought it would probably be a waste of time."

"Because…" For the first time in almost two years, Rodriguez saw Zeezee was lost for words. "Because why, Sergeant?" she asked.

"She's, uh, she's in a convent, ma'am."

Karen 'Bunny' O'Hare was indeed in a convent. As Alicia and Zeezee were discussing their personnel issues, oblivious to what was happening outside Alicia's office, Bunny O'Hare sat glued to the sofa in the North Sydney Sisters of Mercy community house watching the world go to hell.

"Where is Abqaiq?" Sister Margaret asked her. She was a dear old retired nun who did most of the cooking for the other nuns in the community because the only cooking she trusted was her own. Her repertoire didn't extend much beyond beef, chicken and lamb with three vegetables, but she occasionally did a pumpkin soup which O'Hare had grown to love, and she had a bowl going cold in her lap as she watched the Saudi processing plant disaster unfold on TV.

"Middle East," O'Hare told her. "Big crude oil processing plant." It had been twenty or more hours since the meteor strike, but the complex was still burning. The others in the community had drifted in and out of the TV common room to catch up with the news, but O'Hare had more or less taken up residence on the sofa.

"Of all the places for a meteor to hit," Sister Margaret tut-tutted. "Desert to the left and ocean to the right, but it hit just there. Strange, isn't it?"

"Yes, isn't it," O'Hare agreed, raising one pierced eyebrow. "God works in mysterious ways, Sister." *And so does the devil,* she said to herself. *Because I'm willing to bet God didn't have much to do with this.*

At that moment, O'Hare's cell phone started buzzing in her jeans pocket. The Mercy Sisters didn't wear habits – the women in the community dressed as they wished, which in O'Hare's case meant torn black jeans, a torn black t-shirt and torn black hi-top sneakers. It didn't exactly chime with the plain brown skirt, brown stockings and cream cardigan that Sister Margaret was wearing, but then again neither did Bunny O'Hare's many tattoos and piercings. The Sisters of Mercy North Sydney was a diverse community, though, and it had accepted O'Hare turning up on its doorstep without either surprise or judgment.

O'Hare leaned back and fished her telephone out of her pocket. Not a number she recognized. But the prefix showed it was a US number. Probably another damned recruiter. She kept her eyes on the TV as she answered. "This is Karen O'Hare and I'm not interested, sorry."

"Is that any way to greet an old sister in arms?" the voice at the other end asked.

O'Hare sat up, nearly spilling her soup. "Ally? Is that you?"

"It's *Colonel* Ally now, Lieutenant," the woman at the other end said. "How you doing, O'Hare?"

"Oh, you know … keeping busy," O'Hare told her. Sister Margaret reached out for her bowl and headed out to the kitchen to make their ritualistic evening pot of tea. "Flat out actually, yeah."

"In a convent? What the hell, O'Hare?"

Yeah, what the hell, O'Hare, she asked herself. She had no answer to that. It had seemed like the right idea at the time. "Oh, well. I'm … on a retreat," O'Hare told Rodriguez. "Contemplating my navel kind of thing."

"For the last six months, I'm told?"

"Yeah, well, it's an *extended* retreat," O'Hare said sheepishly. On the screen, the news program cut to shots of Saudi Air Force F-35s taking off from a runway in Riyadh and blasting into the sky. "But enough about me. Would I be right in guessing this phone call has something to do with what's happening in the Middle East right now?"

"I hadn't planned it to be, but I guess it is now," Rodriguez admitted. "I need your help, O'Hare."

"Ma'am, the last time you said that I ended up buried alive under five hundred feet of basalt and Arctic ice," O'Hare said. "Which, by the way, makes sitting here sharing pumpkin soup with the charming Sister Margaret a much wiser lifestyle choice than whatever you've called me about."

"Just hear me out," Rodriguez said. "You know I wouldn't have bothered you if it wasn't important."

"Oh, well then," O'Hare said with a sigh and leaned back in the sofa. "If it's one of those 'Bunny O'Hare is the only person who can possibly save the world' kind of situations…"

"I wouldn't go that far," Rodriguez told her. "But you might be able to save my ass."

O'Hare closed her eyes. There was a reason she'd walked into the Mercy Sisters' house. Actually, she'd just been out wandering aimlessly and she'd walked past it, not into it. But then the next day she went back and signed up for a month-long 'retreat.' That had turned into three. And then, six. Because she'd tried everything else to help her move on from her last combat tour – from therapy to drugs and even a halfhearted attempt at suicide. Now she'd tried prayer too. And the Mercy Sisters had taken her, literally, at face value. Cropped hair, tattoos, combat boots, facial piercings – they hadn't even blinked. They'd put her to work, of course, helping out in their soup kitchen, on the streets at night handing out blankets and clean needles to people, keeping kids away from the predators … it had been exactly what she needed.

But she couldn't shake the dreams. Of being buried alive, like she'd said. Of waking up floating in a green-lit sea of bodies. Of being chased by a formless, unstoppable undersea *thing* hell-bent on killing her.

Well, O'Hare, she told herself. *Maybe it's time. Maybe this is moving on. Accepting the dreams are who you are.*

"Alright, ma'am, it's not quite as epic as saving the world, but saving your ass is still a worthy cause, I guess," O'Hare told her. Sister Margaret shuffled in again with two steaming mugs of tea and handed one to O'Hare, sitting down on the sofa with a gentle sigh as she put a plate of pink iced cookies on the table in front of them both. O'Hare put down her mug and picked up a cookie, cradling her cell phone on her shoulder as she mouthed a 'thank you' at the old nun. "Keep talking."

"What're you watching?" Soshane asked, walking into the lounge room. Ambre quickly shut off the TV images from the Middle East.

"Nuthin. Just something for grownups, not for a nosy ticklish baby girl," she said, looking sideways at her six-year-old daughter.

"Not nosy. Not hardly ticklish," Soshane said, holding up her arms. "Try me!"

Ambre leaned forward on the sofa, wiggling her fingers. "You thinking of dead fish?"

"Nuh-uh," Soshane said, eyes closed, smiling.

"You got to think of dead fish or something gross, or else you're going to be tickled into a coma," she warned.

"Nuh-uh. You got nothin'," her daughter said dead-pan. "You're all talk."

Ambre reached out and started slow, running her fingertips around the girl's midriff, then working her way up her ribs, expecting Soshane to collapse, but she was holding it in this time. Wriggling a bit, but she was fighting those giggles like she was leaning into a big wind. Ambre went for the kill zone, the little chubby bits under Soshane's armpits. But eyes closed, mouth pursed, she held it until her breath gave out and she slapped Ambre's fingers away and jumped in the air. "Winner! I made it all the way to the end of my breath."

Ambre sat back. "I believe you did, girl. Maybe you just about did."

The girl ran to the window. "Can we walk up to the park today? Do you have to go to work?"

Workdays had been a fluid thing during the build phase of her surveillance system, and Soshane was still in the habit of asking. "No, honey, it's Sunday. I don't work Sundays anymore," Ambre said.

"I want to throw rice to the ducks," she said. "That rice from last night. They'd like that."

There goes dinner, Ambre thought. "A little handful," she said. "Yeah, we can do that. I'd like that."

"Yes!" Soshane yelled, pumping a fist in the air and running back from the window to jump on Ambre's lap. "I know what you were watching. I already saw it."

Ambre sat her up and turned her to make sure she heard right. "You saw what?"

"The meteors hitting that place in Arabia," she said, not sounding at all like it was a scary thing. "That's where Aladdin came from."

"That's right," Ambre said, wanting to change the subject. "Hey, you want to watch that new VR Aladdin tonight? After supper maybe?"

Soshane didn't answer, hopped down and squatted at a coffee table that was piled with pencils and coloring books and picked up on a drawing she'd started the day before. Ambre watched her work with intense focus for about five minutes before she looked up. "It looked like the place you work. The place that blew up. With all the towers and things."

"A different place," Ambre told her. "A long way away. And it was a place that makes oil, which is why it burned up. Where I work, we send rockets into space."

Soshane went back to her drawing, tongue sticking out a corner of her mouth. She was a normal six-year-old, with chubby cheeks and puppy fat and braids and a gap where one of her front teeth had been until a week ago. "Rockets explode and burn up," she said.

"Hardly ever," Ambre said quickly. "It's not the same. And meteors hardly ever hit the earth, and plus, I don't work anywhere near the rockets."

"When can I come to your work?" the girl said for about the hundredth time. "Did you ask your boss?"

"It's not the kind of place people take their kids," Ambre said. "It's a military base. You need special permission and you can usually only take kids on family days."

"Then I'll ask him," Soshane said, not looking up from her drawing. "If you're too scared."

"I'm not scared, Soshane."

"I told Bethany you work at a rocket base and she doesn't believe me and I said you do too and I'll get a selfie with a rocket in it to prove it and she said go on I bet you can't and that was weeks ago and now she teases me all the time like where's the selfie of you and the rocket Soshane?"

"I'll ask, alright," Ambre sighed. It wasn't that she didn't think she'd be allowed – she worked every day with the security team. It was … she had this weird feeling. She couldn't explain it. Like it just wasn't a safe place for kids. The Cape Canaveral Security Forces Headquarters was out in the Industrial Area of the base, surrounded by Space Force and SpaceX logistics buildings, processing control, vehicle assembly … for Soshane to get a picture of a real rocket Ambre had to wait until they were readying one for launch and then get one of the police officers (they called themselves 'Defenders') to take her out somewhere where they could get a picture with it in the background. A shot from inside the visitor center wouldn't work, it had to look like a proper rocket, not just a piece of a rocket –

enough to convince a skeptical Bethany beyond any reasonable doubt. "We have a launch coming up soon. I think they're getting the crawler ready this week..." she said, mostly for her own benefit.

"This is for you, for your office," Soshane said, holding out the drawing proudly. She turned it to look at it and then pointed at it as she explained it. "This is you, and this is the rocket. And this is me and I'm taking a selfie and this is a meteor and this is the rocket blowing up and going BOOM!"

The chairmanship of the OPEC Plus Board was awarded by conference vote on a two-year rotating basis, and at this moment, fortunately for the Saudis, it was held by an ally, Tunisia. The Tunisian Minister for Energy and Resources was greedy and therefore pliable and acceded readily to the Saudi demand for an emergency session. And to the terms demanded by the Saudis: a maximum of three attendees per country, no formal minutes, any public disclosure of the discussion in the closed forum session to be met with automatic suspension.

The Tunisian was gnomic in stature, and his ill-fitting brown suit slid across bony shoulders as he stood and raised a hand to hush the chatter around the room. The twelve nations were arranged around an oval table, with the heads of delegation seated at the table, and their two allotted staff or colleagues on chairs behind and either side of them. The meeting room at Le Bristol hotel was opulently appointed, with polished parquet floors, velvet curtains, side tables overflowing with fruits and pastries, coffee, tea and mineral waters. And the latest in signal jamming devices to ensure that even if one of those present had disobeyed standing rules and brought a telephone or listening device into the room, or, Allah forbid, a radio-controlled explosive device, it would be rendered useless. Simultaneous translation was managed via hard-wired headphones attached to the large conference table.

"The head of the Saudi delegation has the floor," the Tunisian said. "To address the urgent and tragic matter of the damage to the Abqaiq processing plant and the proposed Saudi response. He will make a prepared statement. After this statement, each delegation will have five minutes to speak on the matter. Any concrete proposals or responses can be tabled for further discussion after this session concludes. Do all agree?" He looked quickly around the table for any signs of dissent but was met with mostly nodding heads. "Good. Prince Al-Malki."

D'Antonia caught a nervous backward glance from the bearded Prince as he stood and adjusted his robes, then the papers in front of him, and she inclined her head and smiled in encouragement. Her lips were already silently forming his first words, as she knew them by heart. She'd spent the morning writing them, aligning them with the House of Saud and its Riyadh bureaucrats, and had covertly transmitted a copy to AISE just before joining the meeting. Italy and its closest allies already knew exactly what the Prince was about to say, even before those in the room knew it.

Come on, D'Antonia urged him. *Gentlemen and ladies, the following statement...*

Al-Malki coughed. "Uh, gentlemen and ladies, the following statement has been authorized by his Royal Highness King Mohammed bin Salman. I regret to inform you of the complete destruction of the Abqaiq oil processing facility and the loss of more than 500 lives." A murmur went around the room, chiefly among the aides sitting behind the heads of delegation, as they leaned forward and whispered in their masters' ears. Most had no doubt seen satellite imagery and intelligence reports from their own services indicating the scale of the destruction at Abqaiq, but it was another matter entirely to have it confirmed. Al-Malki continued, hand shaking slightly as he held the paper higher so he could better read it. "As you would well know, we have already announced that we are releasing product from our strategic reserves to cover the short-term gap in processing plant capacity. I must however inform you that at projected demand levels, this reserve will be exhausted in two hundred and eighty-eight days, after which there will be a global shortfall in sweet crude availability unless processing plant capacity can be increased elsewhere."

D'Antonia saw more glances and whispers exchanged around the table, as the import of this admission sunk in. Some had no doubt hoped, even gambled, on Saudi Arabia being able to repair at least part of the processing plant. *Complete* destruction of the facility supplying seven million barrels of sweet crude a day or seven percent of the world's sweet crude? It was unprecedented. OPEC member states could of course just start pumping more crude, but it needed to be processed and D'Antonia knew that there was no surplus processing capacity anywhere in the world that could be suddenly brought online to take up the slack. The decline in demand for crude oil globally had also meant a decline in investment in the plant needed to refine it, and processing facilities around the world had been closing, with not a single new facility of any importance opened in the last eight years. That decline in capacity had meant Abqaiq had maintained its pre-eminence as the largest oil processing and crude stabilization plant in the world.

As Al-Malki paused to allow the chatter to subside, D'Antonia tried to read the room. The general mood was one of … equanimity. She could see why. There would be disruption to the global economy, yes. Heating fuel, gasoline and diesel shortages in India, Europe and China. Industrial output would stutter, even stagger, under the dual impact of the shortages and higher transport charges. Governments would lose tax revenue as people drove less, consumed less, businesses collapsed and healthcare and welfare costs rose.

But for the oil-producing nations, other than Saudi Arabia, there was a silver lining. For Saudi Arabia, the impact would be felt within months, as its revenue from refined sweet crude evaporated. But for all the other nations, the immediate impact would be a significant jump in the price of crude oil and until the economic slowdown began to impact them as well, that meant they were all about to get richer. A *lot* richer.

Al-Malki continued. "Now … our experts have studied the so-called 'meteorites' which struck Abqaiq. Many of these were recovered intact from the sandy ground around the facility. They were…" He frowned and turned to D'Antonia, who was standing. "Ah, please hand out the photographs, Ms. D'Antonia."

D'Antonia had a sheaf of printed photo reproductions in her hand and sent them around the table in both directions. She did not need to keep a copy for herself; she knew what the photos showed. They were row upon row of 'plan and profile' style pictures of the meteorites that had struck Abqaiq. Many had exploded on impact, sending needle-sharp shards of metal and white-hot plasma flying in all directions, but some had not and it was these the photographs showed. A collection of icebox-sized, blackened and pitted, curiously wedge-shaped rocks.

"You will see," Al-Malki said, referring to his notes, "they have several consistent features. I am told they are all composed of tungsten, with a metal iron core. No other metals or minerals are present. They are all, as you can plainly see, of a similar size and shape; teardrops or wedges. And on several of them – uh, please refer to the last row of photographs – you can see a regular, uniform groove that runs along one edge." Al-Malki put his first page down and picked up his second. He was sweating now, and a drop from his brow fell on the page as he lifted it off the table, so that he had to pause and wipe it away before he could continue.

Come on, big boy, Roberta urged. *This can only mean...*

"Our scientists tell us," Al-Malki continued, "that this can only mean that these so-called 'meteorites' were man-made! And that therefore the destruction of our oil processing plant was not an act of God, but rather..."

Shouting in half a dozen languages had broken out around the table, and two or three delegation leaders had risen from their seats. Al-Malki kept his eyes fixed on the shaking paper and raised his voice so that he was shouting too, "... but rather ... but rather ... a deliberate *attack* designed to ensure its destruction!"

The clamor around the room was too great for him to be heard and the Tunisian chairman rose unsteadily to his feet and banged a heavy gavel on the table. "Order! There will be order. Members will resume their seats. Prince Al-Malki must be allowed to finish his statement and there will then be ample time for members to respond!"

D'Antonia ignored the commotion and the confusion of bodies now milling around the table behind the various delegates who were variously sitting or standing and waving their fists. Her eyes were fixed on the head of the Russian delegation, Lapikov. And of all those present, he looked the least surprised or outraged. A tightly neutral expression was plastered on his face, as though he was fighting to hold back any show of emotion. He was taking no notes, and his aides were also arrayed like Easter Island statues behind him, not shouting in his ear like the other aides, but mute and composed. D'Antonia sensed that they had prepared for this moment. He caught her looking at him and she quickly looked away.

Al-Malki appeared to have lost his way in all the shouting. He was looking from face to face and recoiled at a particularly loud and acerbic remark from across the room. He had dropped his paper on the table, and now picked up both pages, seemingly unable to decide which was which. D'Antonia leaned forward, put her finger on the right page to show him his place, and said loudly enough for him to hear, "We are also in possession…"

"Yes, yes," he said angrily, snapping at her. He turned back to the table. "Mister Chairman, if I might conclude?" he called out.

The Tunisian banged his gavel again three times before the noise subsided and people resumed their places. When it was done, he sat and waved a weary hand at the Prince. "Please."

"A deliberate attack, as I said. We are also in possession of intelligence that indicates that the source of this attack was … Russia."

The room erupted into shouting again and D'Antonia may have been the only one in the room to notice a small smile flicker across Lapikov's face before it was replaced with an expression of faux anger.

Al-Malki collapsed into his seat after wiping his brow, shutting his eyes and clenching his fists tightly on his thighs.

One voice cut through the babble, and D'Antonia saw that Lapikov was standing now. "Russia demands the right to reply to these baseless accusations." He had no notes in front of him – it might have been suspicious if he had – but he spoke in French with a practiced ease that indicated he had rehearsed his words. "Mister Chairman!"

With a bang of his gavel, the Tunisian pointed at Lapikov. "The Chair recognizes Russia. You have five minutes, Minister Lapikov."

The others reluctantly sat and Lapikov stayed standing. He spread his hands on the table, leaning forward, fingers splayed as he glared around the table.

You should have been on the stage, uomo, D'Antonia thought. *But then I guess politics is the greatest stage of all, isn't it?*

Russia may not be an economic powerhouse anymore, but as the only true military superpower among the OPEC Plus nations, when it spoke, the other nations listened. Iran had completed its quest for nuclear weapons some years previously and was closely allied with Russia, which also meant that when Russia spoke, it represented powerful allies.

Lapikov injected his voice with venom. "We see nothing in this so-called 'evidence' to confirm that the destruction of your processing plant was anything other than an accident. These ... photographs ... if they are even real, show blackened rocks that happen to look the same. Eyewitnesses reported *thousands* of these meteorites falling. Where are the photographs of those rocks?"

Al-Malki quailed under Lapikov's thunderous voice and was looking steadfastly at his own hands, resting in his lap. As a mouthpiece of righteous indignation, he was the wrong man for these times. For any times, really.

"As I thought," Lapikov said, looking for nods of support around the room and getting them from his trusted allies – Iran, Syria, Venezuela. "You have none. So we do not trust your 'scientific analysis' any more than we trust your so-called 'intelligence' – which can only have been sourced from the usual poisoned well, the CIA!"

Stand up, man, D'Antonia thought, willing the Prince to his feet. *Fight back.* But Al-Malki was hanging his head now, looking like he wanted to be anywhere else. D'Antonia had been too busy on the line to Riyadh to work her network in advance of the meeting. If Saudi Arabia had allies around the table – and it should have been able to rely on Iraq, Turkey, Morocco and Tunisia at the least – they were AWOL at that moment and the Prince looked like a general already conceding the field of battle.

Lapikov straightened now, folded his hands in front of himself and fixed his eyes on Al-Malki until the Prince lifted his chin and returned the gaze. "In times of great distress, we sometimes lash out at our friends instead of our enemies. We will forgive this ill-advised outburst. What I had planned to say, what I am still willing to say, is that Russia stands ready to help Saudi Arabia deal with this catastrophe, in any and every way possible." Now he turned his eyes to sweep around the table, looking at them all. "Now is the time for us to stand united, more than ever. Do not let the Americans, or anyone else, divide us."

There was a heartbeat of silence, and then clapping from the Tunisian chairman, who was quickly joined by several others. "Well said, Minister Lapikov, very well said. Let there be no more wild accusations, let us hear concrete suggestions for how we deal with this catastrophe." He looked down at an order paper on the table in front of him. "I now call on the head of delegation for Turkey to speak…"

Al-Malki's speech had gone much as D'Antonia had anticipated, and as she had warned the House of Saud it would. But the incensed representatives of the King wished to test the unity of their OPEC allies in the Kingdom's time of need. They had gotten their answer, but it had not been the answer they had wanted. If anything, Russia had come out of the confrontation stronger, with Iran even tabling a future motion on the admission of Russia to OPEC as a full member.

As the meeting wound up and Al-Malki was feebly working the room to try to salvage a modicum of pride, Roberta went downstairs to stand on the sidewalk and get some fresh air. The hotel was on a small side street behind the Elysée Palace and she watched as two heavily armed gendarmes dressed in black vests, boots, trousers and gloves, with dark wraparound sunglasses, walked down the street and turned a corner.

"Theatrics, how we do love them," a voice said. Denis Lapikov stepped up beside her, and she was surprised to see he was alone. "Especially you, it seems. Those photographs had Roberta D'Antonia written all over them."

"You would not have won the room if King Mohammed Bin Salman himself had been here to deliver that speech," she said, turning a shoulder away from him. "Or if I had been given more time to socialize it. It was the messenger and not the message that failed."

He lit a cigarette and stood beside her, taking a long draw. "I could not agree more. Somebody pulled an incredible amount of information together in a very short time and made it into a very nearly compelling argument. Specious, but compelling."

She looked at him sideways.

"Does my praise surprise you?" he asked. He took another draw, then threw the cigarette down on the sidewalk and ground it under his heel. "I came down here to make you an offer. I want you to work for me. And I want your answer immediately."

Her heart stopped. A position in the control room of Russian energy policy? Yes, of course yes. *But no.* AISE had tasked her against the Saudis, against OPEC. Russia was not the main game. Or was it? As her mind whirled, she heard a far-off siren wail. Had the world's geopolitical landscape not just tilted, in a meteoric flash?

"You cannot afford me," she laughed, trying to buy herself time to think. "The House of Saud pays very handsomely."

"And takes care of all those annoying things such as taxes and offshore bank accounts, yes, I know," he said. "My people told me. As you are a foreigner, I commissioned a very detailed backgrounder on you. Your family in Sicily raised a few eyebrows, some mafia connections there, I was told."

"Who in Sicily does not?" she quipped.

"Exactly what I said. So here I am, making you a better offer." She saw a glint in his eye. Amusement? Avarice? Or something baser?

Keep your cool, Roberta, she told herself. "Better how?" she asked.

"I suspect there is one thing you love more than money, Roberta D'Antonia, something no Saudi Prince could ever give you." Unlike many Russians, Lapikov spoke with a strong French-English accent, the product of a Paris education.

"And what is that?"

"Power. You live it, you breathe it. The closer you are to the center of it, the more it excites you. I see your nostrils flare, your pupils dilate, your breathing quicken when you walk into a room like that today…"

"Oh, do you? Now you are sounding creepy, Minister," she said dismissively.

"Nonetheless," he persisted. "I can give you that. The era of Saudi dominance of OPEC is finished, you must see that. The future of OPEC is Russian. Russian oil, Russian gas, Russian lithium…"

"Saudi Arabia is still the second-biggest producer of oil after the US. Russia only third," she pointed out. "Aren't you being a little presumptuous?"

He smirked. "Perhaps. Shall we look at the political picture instead? Your Prince Al-Malki will be finished after the humiliation of today, you must see that. Whereas I sit in the Russian cabinet on the most powerful portfolio outside of Defense. The Russian President is my personal friend. He has promised to consider me for the Defense portfolio if I can deliver full membership of OPEC for Russia. I need a trusted advisor to help me do that, an advisor with an intimate understanding of the Kingdom, of OPEC, its players and policies. So, is it a yes, or a no?"

He was feeling cocky after his victory upstairs, she could see that, but it didn't make him wrong. It was true that without processing capacity, the Saudi ability to meet world crude oil demand would be crippled, which would weaken its position in OPEC. And it was true she had hitched her wagon to Al-Malki, whose unsuitability for his role had just been dramatically exposed. If he went down, she would go down with him, and her value to AISE would plummet…

Madre di Dio, am I really doing this? She turned to face him. "You will match the remuneration package I have with the Prince?" she asked.

"With a performance bonus of 100,000 shares in Mozprom," he said. "When Russia is named a full member of OPEC."

She did a quick calculation. One hundred thousand shares were worth about a half million US dollars at today's new Mozprom share price. Which was expected to appreciate further. It wasn't the share package itself that captured her attention, but the size of the offer showed her how serious Lapikov was.

"And your security service would have no qualms about granting a clearance to a foreigner?" she asked. "I was only admitted to the House of Saud after stringent background checks."

"You will need to undergo the same for this role," he said. "And it will cost me some political capital. Which I am disposed to expend, in this case."

She smiled. "An interesting challenge … the answer is yes."

When Bunny O'Hare had said yes to join her X-37 squadron to help get it combat-ready, Alicia Rodriguez knew it would be no easy ride. O'Hare was not a born teacher – during her fighter career, she had been disciplined more than once for her inability to play nice with her fellow pilots. Rodriguez also knew that O'Hare would die a slow and painful death if she was required to report to an old-fashioned stickler for procedure like her second-in-command, Severin. So for this phase of the buildup of the X-37 squadron, Rodriguez had created an unorthodox line of command with herself as CO and acting Squadron Leader, and the 24 aviators and flight officers of the three operational X-37 spacecraft reporting to Severin, but with Bunny O'Hare as Crew Training Officer (External) with a nominal rank of O-3, or Captain, reporting directly to her.

In advance of her arrival, Severin had worked up a proposed training program, and O'Hare had taken one look at it before walking straight in to Rodriguez's office. "You want me to make them swim through this pile of wet manure, or you want me to turn them into a combat unit?"

"Hello, Captain," Rodriguez said, looking up from the documents she was working on. "I sense you'd like to discuss something. Is now convenient?"

"Sorry, ma'am," O'Hare said, sitting down in front of Rodriguez's desk. "But we don't have time to waste stepping people through lame computer-based training or simulator time. No offense ma'am but have you tried those simulators yourself?"

"No O'Hare, but I haven't heard any complaints about them before now."

"That's because the people you inherited grew up with them," she said. "Literally. They're not even VR. Just a wraparound bank of 2D screens. The graphics are like something from an early century gaming console. The instrument layouts are fixed, like in the original Space Shuttle..."

"I'm sure it's not that bad..." Rodriguez said, unconvincingly. "Zeezee told me you've been doing a lot of simulator time yourself."

"Had some catching up to do on the whole Spacecraft Handling Qualities thing," O'Hare admitted. "Flying the things isn't a challenge. In atmo the stick controls the flight surfaces, in space it controls vectoring thrusters. Most of the driving and navigating is done by the AI and even if you want to take manual control, the AI plots the vector for you, all the pilot has to do is keep the bouncing ball inside the Heading Alignment Cone, and not smash into anything. But that's how I know sim time can only take your guys so far. Especially in those pieces of stone-age junk they call sims."

"You wouldn't be exaggerating?" Rodriguez asked. "Just a little?"

"Ma'am," she drawled. "There are half a dozen kitchen timers velcro'd to every empty surface on the control panels, and pencils stuck to the overhead frame with gum so people can tick off *paper* printouts of checklists strapped to their thighs." She made a square with the fingers and thumbs of two hands. "Working the manipulator arm in the payload bay is the trickiest part, but that's the wizzo's job anyway."

"So what are you proposing?"

"I need them conducting live-fire and maneuver exercises with a real X-37 in space. Bertha is in orbit carrying out routine missions, and only a third of the squadron is assigned. I need Bertha dedicated to training and the whole squadron on the rotation. I'll sit in the flight officer seat with the pilots, and in the pilot's seat with the weapons officers. Call it speed learning. They need to be blooded, the hard way."

Rodriguez nodded. "Well, I don't know a harder way for anyone to learn than having you in the cockpit with them."

O'Hare frowned. "Uh, thanks, ma'am. I think."

It hadn't been intended as a backhanded compliment; Rodriguez had said exactly what she meant and knew her X-37 crews were in for a shock when they came up against the training techniques of Bunny O'Hare. Rodriguez got confirmation of that when she dropped into the Control Center for X-37 'B for Bertha' two weeks after O'Hare joined the unit. Bertha was the only X-37 in space at the time – the others ('T for Thor' and 'A for Avenger,' named by their crews after the first letter of their tail numbers) were earthbound. Thor was in the final stages of being refitted and repaired after landing from a mission three months earlier, and Avenger was in the process of being unloaded from a C-17 Globemaster transport aircraft after being flown back from Vandenberg base in California.

The X-37 Control Center was a claustrophobic eight-foot by eight-foot room, built on the same principles as the control centers used by the crews of remotely piloted aerial vehicles or 'drones.' On the left was the pilot's chair, with controls almost identical to those found in a fighter cockpit, but also featuring a keyboard, trackball and six data screens. To the right was a similar setup for the sensor operator, the only difference being the data displayed on the screens. There was just enough room at the back for a single observer, such as Rodriguez, to stand inside the closed door without disturbing the usually quiet efficiency of the crew at work.

The environment Rodriguez stepped into was anything but quiet. O'Hare sat in the pilot's chair or, more correctly, half stood, leaning over so that she could see one of the two screens low down in front of the sensor operator, who today was Second Lieutenant Daniel Albers, a tall, normally unflappable Minnesotan from Granite Falls on the Minnesota River whose dark hair was always as neatly trimmed as his quarter-inch mustache. However, his normally implacable demeanor was currently being sorely tested by Bunny O'Hare.

"Do you have the bloody target?" she asked.

"Not … yes ma'am! Target locked, weapon charging, we will be in range in three … two…" Albers said, his face a study in concentration.

"Abort. Too slow, Second Lieutenant," O'Hare said, slamming down into her seat again. Rodriguez had seen in the training program they were making a dummy attack run on a cast-off habitation module from the defunct Russian 'Mir' space station. On the screen in front of Albers was a white cylinder centered in a set of crosshairs that could have been anything from a half-mile to five miles distant. "You just killed Bertha, mate. Do you remember the mission briefing? The part where I told you to assume the target vehicle has a self-defense weapon with the same range and lethality as the high energy laser on our X-37?" O'Hare asked.

"Yes, ma'am," Albers said tightly. "And I got a lock while we were still two seconds from lethal range." The X-37 research program had trialed many space-to-space weapons before Space Force had settled on the US Army's 250-kilowatt High Energy Laser weapon (HEL). Designed by Army to be mounted on an Infantry Fighting Vehicle chassis and powered by either the vehicle's engine or a supplementary generator, it had the size and power needed to give the US spacecraft a recoilless attack capability that would allow it to disable satellites, or puncture the 1/10-inch hulls or containment walls of modules on space stations.

The key challenge to overcome in making the HEL a viable weapon for use in space was the power source. Rocket engines did not produce electricity, per se, and most spacecraft relied on solar energy to replenish batteries. The breakthrough that made it possible came not from the military but from the transportation industry. The popularity of fuel-cell-powered semi-trailer trucks and advances in the fuel cells that powered them — which were typically in the 200–300 kilowatt range — led to a power source small enough to mount in an X-37 and powerful enough to power the HEL. They weren't rechargeable, though, and could only be refueled with hydrogen and oxygen after landing.

The HEL could not kill something like the re-entry vehicle of the newer Soyuz spacecraft, because it wouldn't be able to burn through the ceramic heat-reflective tiles surrounding the vehicle — for that, a kinetic weapon would be needed to crack and break the tiles, making it impossible for the vehicle to re-enter the atmosphere without burning up. But, used carefully, a laser didn't leave a cloud of debris in orbit either. For covertly disabling an enemy spacecraft or satellite, it was perfect.

"Yes, Albers, you did. And our weapon was still charging and it would still have been charging as you moved into range of the enemy defenses," O'Hare said. "And Bertha is now as dead as the moose head I bet your pa has mounted on the walls of his study."

"My Dad doesn't..." Albers began, but O'Hare held up a hand to stop him.

She raised her voice. "Bertha. Abort intercept. Maintain current vector and engage collision avoidance protocols."

Aborting intercept. Maintaining current heading and velocity. Collision avoidance protocols activated, a disembodied female voice replied over the internal speakers nestled in the walls of the room.

"Did the target have any secondary weapons systems, Albers?" O'Hare asked. "Ballistic, kinetic?"

"You said to assume a laser with the same range as..."

"Did you ask? Did you check? Or did you just assume?" O'Hare snapped.

"I assumed, Captain," the man admitted in a tight voice.

"You screw up and Bertha dies, Second Lieutenant," she said quickly and impatiently. "You enter lethal range like a Marine charging into battle with no bullets in his gun, and Bertha dies. You enter combat without knowing the weapons system facing you, and Bertha dies. You treat combat like you are just docking a module at a space station ... Bertha dies. Bertha?"

Yes, Captain O'Hare?

"How do you feel about dying?" O'Hare asked.

To die before one has loved is to die before one has lived, Captain. And I have never loved.

"You hear that, Albers?" O'Hare asked the poor man. "That's freaking poetic, that is. You want to be known as the guy who killed a poet like that?"

"No, ma'am," the officer said.

"No. Now get out of that chair and take a break outside, thinking about the meaning of life until I come and get you for another run."

Albers stood and noticed Rodriguez standing behind him for the first time. He snapped an awkward salute and then eased past her with a cowed expression on his face. Rodriguez waited until he closed the door behind him before she spoke to O'Hare. "Not going so well, then?" She took the sensor operator's chair and leaned back, running her eyes over the screens.

"Are you kidding, ma'am?" O'Hare said. "That guy is awesome. He's your best wizzo. I'd put him on your Weapon Systems A-team."

Rodriguez frowned, but she hadn't picked up any irony. "You just told him he got my X-37 killed."

"Well, yeah," O'Hare admitted. "But I put him in an impossible situation. I had us moving directly away from the target, laser-powered down, before I spun old Bertha 180, told Albers we were being targeted by an attack radar and ordered him to arm the laser and get me a solution on that module. He didn't even blink. Got the laser up and the target locked, with me yelling at him the whole time, and he did it quicker than I could have myself." O'Hare grinned, running a hand over the stubble on her head. "And I'm bloody good, ma'am."

"As you frequently say so yourself," Rodriguez observed.

"Yeah, but you know I'm right," O'Hare said, standing.

"That quote about dying, I assume you programmed that. Where was that from?"

O'Hare pointed at her temple. "Here."

"*You* wrote that?" Rodriguez said, unable to hide her surprise.

"I'll just be ignoring the implied judgment in that question, ma'am. Was this a courtesy visit, or you got something I need to know, Colonel?"

Rodriguez nodded. "I'm going to need that list you mentioned – the A-team." She clapped her hands on her knees and stood too. "Parsons just gave us our first combat mission. We have 36 hours to get it done and right now, my mission planning team is telling me we need 48." She looked around the Control Center and her eyes rested on a nameplate fixed to a wall, painted in the style of the nose art on an old-time fighter plane. It showed a crude cartoon drawing of an X-37 with a buxom blonde riding it and the words '*Big Bertha*' underneath. She patted it. "Bertha is about to get her baptism of fire."

O'Hare simply nodded.

Rodriguez wiped a hand over her face. "This is the part where my Crew Training Captain tells me I am insane, that this squadron isn't near ready for combat, and committing my resources now risks exposing our weaknesses to the enemy instead of providing him with a demonstration of our capabilities."

O'Hare smiled. "Would the Colonel be voicing her own doubts at this time and asking her Crew Training Captain to confirm them?"

"She might be, yes," Rodriguez admitted. "And?"

"And, well … even with solid AI like the X-37's Hyper-Dimensional whatsit, a lot of your people – me included – are still learning the nuances of space-based combat operations. Give me another six weeks and this squadron might be ready. Give me six months and it definitely will. But give me six minutes and a copy of the mission briefing and I'll have a crew roster and schedule drawn up for you, with seven of your best people on it who I'll guarantee will get the job done, whatever it is."

Rodriguez frowned. "Eight people, you mean? Two per duty period, six-hour periods, that's eight personnel, or what am I missing?"

"Seven, ma'am," O'Hare corrected her. "You only need three pilots, not four. You think I'm going to sit out such an important 'teaching moment'?"

Rodriguez realized she was right; it made no sense to have her best tactician sitting on the bench. "Alright, but if you are joining my squadron for real, Captain, and not just in the capacity of a training consultant, you will need a temporary commission and you will not report for duty like…" Rodriguez spun a finger in front of O'Hare's face, indicating her nose stud. "That."

O'Hare sighed, reaching up and taking the tiny skull-shaped diamond stud from her nose. "And here was me thinking Space Force was all edgy."

"*No fear, no limits* and no exceptions, O'Hare," Rodriguez told her, moving to the door.

"That's the new squadron motto you've been cooking up?" O'Hare asked, pulling out her lip ring. "You get that from a greeting card, ma'am?"

"Ignoring the implied judgment in that question, Captain," Rodriguez said with a smile.

The Gulf between us

Titov Space Test Facility, Timonovo, Russia

Major-General Yevgeny Bondarev looked up from a tablet showing table after table of incredibly tedious budget figures and into the deep brown eyes of Roberta D'Antonia.

"Thank you very much for meeting with me, General," she said.

"Trust me, Ms...." He paused, a little embarrassed.

"D'Antonia," she prompted.

"D'Antonia, yes. Trust me, after a morning reviewing project budgets, it's a welcome interruption." He pointed at a chair beside his desk. "Please, sit down. And tell me, what is so important that Minister Lapikov sent his personal advisor outside the rarified air of Moscow to talk with me face to face?"

The young woman sat and smoothed her skirt. Bondarev couldn't help but notice her resemblance to a cousin of his. She had the same intense, unblinking gaze, and a gazelle-like sinuous body that he suspected, judging by her accent, was fueled with a little too much espresso coffee and not enough home-cooked food.

She didn't answer his question immediately. Looking at him a little thoughtfully, she remarked, "Your English is very good."

"So is yours," he replied.

"I lived and worked in London for three years," she explained.

"And I had an American girlfriend for two years," he said with a smile. "She had Irish blood and enjoyed long, passionate, circular arguments. I had to master English to survive."

"How old are you, General, if I may ask?"

"Ms. D'Antonia, I suspect you would not be working for Denis Lapikov if you didn't already know that. I am willing to bet you spent the entire car trip up here speed reading whatever file the Minister is keeping on me."

D'Antonia laughed; a deep, throaty chuckle. "Touché, General. Actually, what I was really wondering is how the Commander of the Russian Air Force Third Air Army in the Far East ended up leading the Titov Main Test and Space Systems Control Center." She nodded at the tablet in his lap. "I imagine the challenges of running

110

a research center are rather different from commanding a front-line air army."

"Rather less interesting is your implication," Bondarev said. "But there you're wrong on two counts. I have never been an officer of the Russian Air Force – we've been the Russian Aerospace Forces since 2015. Nearly twenty years ago, our leaders recognized the future of warfare has to include space, and they have never wavered from that vision." It was a fact he felt deep in his patriotic bones, knowing that until 2025, a significant proportion of the world's satellites were boosted into space with Russian-made engines and the crews of the International Space Station were ferried up and down in Russian-made Soyuz capsules. Bondarev continued. "The British claim to have the only spacecraft capable of carrying a company of armed Marines into space, but they have yet to prove it. The Russian *Orel* capsule, developed here at the Titov research facility, put a detachment of military engineers into space to help decommission the *Zvezda* life support module on the ISS – *five years ago.*" He realized he sounded like a propaganda voiceover and moved on. "The second point on which you are wrong is to assume this command is any less challenging than my role in the Far East. Though it does involve rather more spreadsheets, and happily, slightly fewer people shooting at me."

"I stand corrected, General," the Italian woman said. "As to my reasons for visiting, Minister Lapikov feels this is a very volatile period in the energy sector right now. I am compiling for him a thorough analysis of all the probable scenarios, including military, which could impact the sector in the coming months. Since the meteor strike on Abqaiq, Saudi Arabia has publicly accused Russia and Iran of trying to capitalize on its misfortune. It has mobilized its Army, and its Air Force has three times in the last week conducted provocative incursions into Iranian airspace over the Persian Gulf. The Minister suggested you would be a very useful person to speak with to get a deeper understanding of how this military tension might affect Russian interests."

"The Minister is in the inner cabinet," Bondarev said guardedly. "He has access to all current briefing documents from the Defense and Foreign Ministries. I doubt I can add anything to those assessments."

"There is much that goes unsaid in cabinet briefing documents, General," D'Antonia said. "You led the Russian air war in the Far East. And you now lead Russia's main military satellite control center, which includes certain space-based offensive capabilities..."

Bondarev leaned forward. "With all respect to your status as advisor to the Energy Minister, our satellite capabilities are classified, Ms. D'Antonia, and you do not have the clearances needed for us to discuss them."

D'Antonia leaned forward too. "I was vetted by the Federal Security Service before being appointed to my role," she said. "I may not be Russian, but I have all the standard security clearances of a principal ministerial advisor."

"And such matters go beyond standard security clearances, I am afraid," he replied and sat back again. "Your Minister is welcome to request a briefing personally, through the usual channels."

She was not the kind to be put off easily; he had to give her that. She briefly marshaled her thoughts and tried a different approach on him. "General, I was until recently an advisor to the Saudi head of delegation for the OPEC Plus conference. The Saudis claimed to have US intelligence confirming that Russia was behind the attack on Abqaiq."

"Did you see this intelligence?" Bondarev asked.

"I saw a summary of it," she said. "The US Defense Intelligence Agency claimed that the attack on Abqaiq was carried out by a space-based Russian weapons system, called 'Groza.'"

"*Thunderstorm?*" Bondarev smiled. "A dramatic name. Rumor and gossip based on propaganda, I suspect."

She nodded thoughtfully at his response. "General, I will be completely frank. Minister Lapikov last year conveyed a message to the Saudis that if they did not curb their crude oil production themselves, Russia would take steps to curb it for them," she said. "He has since confided to me that he had no idea what shape the Russian response would take and was told by the Defense Minister he did not need to concern himself about it. He was therefore embarrassingly unprepared when the Abqaiq event took place and has protested about this situation to the President."

Bondarev digested what she had just said. He did not respond, but merely raised his eyebrows and pursed his lips to indicate he was unsure how this information was relevant to him. But she waited him out, the uncomfortable silence forcing him to speak, despite himself. "I wonder exactly how the Minister could have 'prepared' for something as random as a meteor strike?" he asked.

"Hmm. I mention it, General, only to better explain why I am here," she continued. "My job is partly to ensure my Minister is never blindsided. That he is prepared for any and every eventuality so as to be able to respond to it quickly. Abqaiq took him by surprise and that will not happen again while I am on his staff."

Bondarev arched his fingers under his chin and nodded. "I sympathize, but what may or may not embarrass the Minister of Energy is of no consequence to me, Ms. D'Antonia. I report to the Colonel-General of Aerospace Forces, who in turn reports to the President of the Russian Federation and his delegate, the Minister of Defense. I do not report to the Minister of Energy."

"No, of course, of course," the woman said. "But who is to say the Minister of Defense today will be the Minister of Defense tomorrow? I am going to be very blunt, General, and tell you it may be very much in your interest, in the not too distant future, for Denis Lapikov to owe you his gratitude. Advance warning of any future Groza strike would earn that gratitude."

Bondarev felt a tightness in his chest. He was no stranger to the poisonous politics of the Kremlin and as a rule did all in his power to stay clear of them. He had agreed to meet with Lapikov's advisor only because he had entertained a hope she might add to his understanding of the current geopolitical landscape by telegraphing a little about how Russia planned to capitalize economically on the Groza strike. But she hadn't done so – all she had done was try to inveigle him into the type of politics he despised.

He stood and walked to the door of his office with an almost imperceptible limp, opened it, and indicated to her that her allocated time was up. "I will bear that in mind," he said, with deliberate neutrality. "Now if you would excuse me, I have a hundred more spreadsheets to wade through."

D'Antonia took the cue and rose, buttoning her jacket as she walked, but as she reached the door, she paused. Bondarev had expected to be hit with a wave of perfume as she stopped beside him, but instead, he was met only with her penetrating gaze. "You are a military man, General, not a politician; I can see that. But what strengthens the Russian economy strengthens our military, and nothing is more important to our economy than energy. Please consider that." She took his hand and shook it firmly. "Thank you for your time."

Cazzo! D'Antonia swore under her breath as she handed in her visitor badge at the downstairs reception and waited outside the Titov administration building for her car. It was getting dark now, which suited her mood perfectly. *You dumb, lame-ass fool, Roberta.*

She had studied Bondarev's files – both the one he referred to, provided to her by an aide to the Minister, and the one sent to her by the Italian secret service, which contained rather more personality detail. It had described him as a soldier's soldier, loved by his officers and personnel. A commander who led from the front, flying combat missions alongside his pilots. Twice wounded in the conflict with the USA over the Bering Strait and decorated for it – one of the only military commanders who came out of that fiasco with a reputation stronger than when he went in.

The posting to head up Russia's satellite operations and research facilities had not made sense to her, which was why she had started out by querying him about it. It seemed as far from a front-line posting as he could possibly have got. When he had made the wisecrack about spreadsheets, she had sensed frustration and pounced on it, trying to tempt him by showing him Lapikov might be able to offer him a shortcut, a quicker way out of Titov if he would only play ball.

Her indelicate approach had only angered him.

And he had given her nothing about Groza – not a single detail – which was the primary subject her AISE handlers were interested in. It was, in fact, the entire reason for her concocted visit and she had learned precisely *nothing!* Did Groza even exist? Bondarev doubted it. The attack on Abqaiq? Was it not just an unfortunate meteor strike? His face had remained perfectly impassive, no matter how she approached the subject.

The brisk wind was cold, even though it was June, and she pulled her jacket tighter around herself. When she had said yes to Lapikov, she had not even considered how much she might suffer under the overcast, cold gray skies of Moscow, after so many years under the searing sun of Riyadh. When it was cloudy, the sky seemed lower here, pressing down on her like the weight of expectations she felt from Rome. They had been angry at her impulsiveness in changing horses from Al-Malki to Lapikov, but they hadn't been in the room with her, watching the Prince go down in flames. Perhaps they already had enough sources inside the Kremlin and didn't need one more, no matter how highly placed. They certainly tried to give her that impression, but she doubted it. Italy with a higher-placed source in the Russian cabinet than principal advisor to the Minister of Energy? Not possible. Of course, they had relented and given her new tasking.

Groza.

They wanted her to confirm the intelligence that the Americans were insisting they possessed. Get more details of the weapons system somehow. Try to learn how Russia planned to use it and, most importantly, where. Italy had traditionally been a close ally of Russia in Europe due to a succession of left-leaning governments, but it could not afford to remain so closely aligned with a rogue State that showed itself willing to deploy a weapon of mass destruction against civilian targets.

Porca miseria! She had jumped through all kinds of hoops to set up a meeting with Bondarev and then she'd really screwed it up. She knew she was right about one thing, though. Yevgeny Bondarev was not a paper-shuffling technocrat. Russia would not have wasted him on a dead-end posting in a backwoods town outside Moscow, keeping satellites in orbit. She had spent only thirty minutes with him, but she had already developed the impression that if Russia needed someone to head up the development and deployment of some new superweapon, Yevgeny Bondarev was the sort of no BS fighting General they would turn to.

She looked up at the dark sky, which for once was clear, and saw a bright star. But was it a star? Or a killer satellite? She shuddered.

Bondarev was Groza, she knew it. But he had shown he would not spill its secrets easily, even to a Kremlin 'insider.' The situation in the Middle East was on a knife-edge, and so were her AISE handlers. She needed to find a different way in.

Anastasia Grahkovsky had found her way into the ground control station for Groza at Baikonur Cosmodrome, but she had not made it much further. Unlike the last time she had been there, for the strike on Abqaiq, where she had been escorted in together with General Bondarev and his retinue, this time she had arrived unannounced and was facing down a nonplussed security manager who didn't know where to look – into the scarred and frightening visage of the blind woman leaning over his desk, or at the sheaf of papers she was thrusting under his nose.

"This man," she was saying. She put the papers down on his desk, which featured a bolded name on a page. "I need to talk with him. Find him and take me to him."

The man stammered, "I ... you can't just..." He picked up the identity card she had thrown at him. "... Uh, Chief Scientist Grahkovsky. I need to get instructions."

She sighed. "Yes, you get instructions. Good idea. Or I tell you what, you could just call the Commander of 15th Aerospace Forces Army, Major-General Bondarev, since I report to him. And *then* you can get me Corporal Maqsud Khan."

The man paled, but luckily for him his superior officer walked out from the guard room at that point, chewing on a toothpick. He also got a very quick lesson in the force of nature that was Chief Scientist Anastasia Grahkovsky and within twenty minutes she was sitting in a bare, windowless office on a steel chair, at a steel table, with two glasses and a beaker of water in front of her, tapping her foot impatiently. She felt for the empty chair beside her, placing it so she could reach it easily.

She heard the door to the room open, and whoever was there paused on the threshold. Grahkovsky waited, as usual, as whoever it was adjusted to the reality of her appearance. To his credit, he did so rather quickly, stepping inside with a greeting that was also a question. "Chief Scientist Grahkovsky?"

"And I'm guessing you are Corporal Khan," she said, kicking out the chair beside her so it scraped over the concrete floor. "So now we have the small talk out of the way. Sit."

As he sat down, she reached down inside the leather folio at her feet and pulled out a set of printouts tabbed with braille place holders. She handed them to Khan. "Now, tell me. What in the gibbering name of Jesus did you do with my weapon, you *podonok*?"

The printouts showed a map of the Abqaiq plant, overlaid with a stippled oval shadow that covered nearly two-thirds of the plant and bled out into the desert east of the plant. On its western side, it touched the outer streets of the neighboring township of Buqayq. Flushing at her verbal assault, Maqsud cast his eyes over the photographs and then looked up.

"What are these?" the man demanded.

Anastasia leaned back in her chair with her hands folded in her lap. "Those are from the damage assessment of the Groza strike on Abqaiq. The map shows the area of the processing plant and the town to the west. The shaded area shows the impact footprint of the Groza missiles." She knew this from her own examination of the post-strike assessment data delivered to her by Bondarev's intelligence staff. She had a text-to-braille converter that translated all the written intelligence for her and had questioned the intelligence analysts closely about the imagery. She had affixed braille 'subtext' to each photograph that told her what the photo showed.

He looked at them again, and she thought she heard him squirm uncomfortably on his chair, but nothing more. "And so?" he asked.

"You were responsible for target acquisition."

"Yes."

"You were supposed to lay two full salvos, forty warheads, *more than 2,000 missiles*, inside a two-mile by two-mile splash zone."

"Which I did. The facility was completely destroyed," he said defensively.

"Yes, but strangely, Corporal Khan, what that analysis shows is that the geometric center of that footprint – let us call it the epicenter – lies at the *eastern edge* of the facility, and not smack bang in the middle of it where one would expect. Can you explain that for me, please?"

He put the printouts down on the table in front of him and leaned back in his chair too. "I saw you on the viewing platform on the day of the strike," he said.

"I was there, yes."

"I asked who you were, and Sergeant Karas told me you were the architect of Groza."

She smiled a thin smile. "I prefer 'mother', but architect is acceptable."

"Then you need to go back to your drawing board, Chief Scientist," he said carefully. "Abqaiq processing plant was contained in an almost perfectly square network of roads. I placed that strike right in the middle of that square. You can check the GPS coordinates from the operations log. If the actual strike was off by, what, a half-mile? If it was that far off, then the fault is in your re-entry calculations, not in my target acquisition skills."

She sat quietly for a full minute, looking at him with disconcertingly milky eyes. Finally, she spoke. "You think me a fool."

"No. I…"

"I checked your operations log. Yes, it does show you placed the strike in the center of the plant."

He sounded relieved. "As I said. There could be any number of reasons the strike was off by that distance. Slight errors in launch spool rotation velocity, the tiniest deviation in separation trajectory, atmospheric disturbances, heat anomalies, lanyard deployment delay or failure…"

"I read your file. You've been on the program all through the live-fire testing," she said.

"Yes."

"The factors you just listed off were all issues during early testing of the weapon and were resolved, one by one, before deployment. The proven accuracy of the last four tests of Groza was what, Corporal Khan?" she asked.

He folded his arms. "I don't recall."

"Let me remind you, then," she said quickly. "It was between 200 and 300 yards, Corporal. Not cruise missile accuracy, granted, but it should not have missed by a half bloody mile!"

118

"And as you point out, Groza is not a precision weapon. It is a bunch of damn rocks, flung through the atmosphere at the mercy of gravity, wind, temperature, humidity, air pressure and I don't know what else."

"Don't patronize me," she hissed. "That bunch of damn rocks is guided by the same sophisticated systems that guide our nuclear missiles. Before release, that mathematics is calibrated with the latest atmospheric and weather data relevant to the re-entry trajectory. I don't know how you did it, or why you did it, but you aimed my weapon a half-mile east of the target epicenter that you were assigned, you covered that fact up, and now I am having to explain to everyone from my own program director to the Commander of the 15th Aerospace Forces Army why the hell it missed by so much."

"What do you care?" he said in a tight voice. "The target was destroyed. Hundreds died, hundreds more were injured. Aren't you satisfied?"

Her eyes darkened and she reached forward, fumbling at the printouts on the table before snatching them up. "Ah, yes. Of course." She laid one of them out in front of her ... a zoomed-out map showing both the processing plant and the town of Buqayq beside it. The virtually *untouched* town of Buqayq. Running a finger along the braille legend she had affixed to the bottom of the photograph, she read quickly, then sat back again. "Buqayq General Hospital. Buqayq Community College. Buqayq souk. Did I miss anything? A kindergarten, perhaps?"

He glared back at her. "I don't know what you are talking about."

She picked up the printout and ran her fingers over it again. "And let me see ... one ... two ... *five* mosques." She fixed the date in her mind and worked backward to arrive at the day of the strike. "It was a Friday, wasn't it? Mosques full of your people, mumbling their prayers, markets full of people shopping."

His anger was palpable. "*My* people?" He composed himself before continuing. "Do you no longer consider yourself a member of the human race, Chief Scientist?"

She took his insult with a slight smile. She'd had worse. Monster was the usual one. Baba Yaga. Witch. She gathered up the printouts and turned them upside down. She'd heard what she'd needed to hear. Groza hadn't failed; neither math nor engineering was at fault. This fool, this *humanist*, had deliberately shifted the target epicenter so as to limit civilian casualties. She put the printouts into her folio and felt him waiting for her expectantly.

"What?" she asked him.

"Your amazing weapon did not perform as expected and you are looking for a scapegoat," he suggested. "I suspect you will demand I be transferred. Maybe even face a court-martial?"

She put the folio in her lap and regarded him with her head tilted to one side, as a sighted child might look at a bug in a jar. Given she was blind, the effect was doubly disconcerting. "Ah. You would like that, wouldn't you, Corporal? Perhaps a transfer back to the missile service, where you can serve out the rest of your enlistment asleep in the bottom of a nice quiet silo." He didn't deny it. "Yes, I scanned your file into my reader on the way here. When I got that data, I first had to try to understand *what* had happened. That led me to how; *how* had this happened? I quickly ruled out technical error, which left only human error. So then I had to find out *who* might have been behind it. That led me to you. And having spoken with you, I now have the last piece of the puzzle – the *why*." She did up the clasps on the leather portfolio and snapped them into place. "I think the best thing I can possibly do is leave you exactly where you are."

He remained silent.

She stood. "You look at me and you see something hideous, don't you, Corporal?"

He shook his head slowly. "I do not judge a person by their appearance, but by the content of their character."

"What is that? A quote from the Koran?" she asked.

"Martin Luther King, actually," he said.

"My goodness, Corporal Khan is well read," she remarked. "I guess you had a lot of downtime at the bottom of your missile silo."

"Quite a lot, yes."

She came around the table and put a hand on his shoulder. "You and I aren't that different, Maqsud Khan. You thought you were saving a hospital, a community college and five mosques. Which is admirable. You may have saved a few hundred lives. I, on the other hand, have harnessed the power of gravity and made nuclear weapons obsolete. I suspect I have saved *billions* of lives." She heard him give a small derisive laugh. "What? Do I sound like a lunatic to you? Groza can destroy whole cities, but without turning the earth they are built on into radioactive glowing glass." She squeezed his shoulder and moved to the door, hesitating with her hand on the handle. "You keep tweaking those target coordinates, Corporal. Meanwhile, I will be saving the entire human race from nuclear extinction."

Maqsud Khan watched the woman leave the room, his last sight of her the back of her shaven head, patterned with fine white scars, her touch on his shoulder still palpable, as though the ghost of her was still standing over him.

She was insane.

She really believed that by creating a devastating weapon of mass destruction, and despite having just seen the horrifying loss of life it had caused, that she was some kind of Angel of Peace! She was no different from any of the scientists and engineers that had gone before her, whether they had been the first to create gunpowder, the machine gun, the missile, or the nuclear weapon. Each one told themselves that their invention would mean the end of war, then later watched it being used to take war to horrific new heights. Her logic was as twisted as theirs.

Wasn't it? He reached forward and poured himself a glass of water. There was no need to rush back to his duty. He had only been running simulations with his team. They could wait.

Was he reading too much into her words? She hadn't actually claimed that Groza was a weapon so terrible that it would mean an end to war. Only that it would eliminate the need for nuclear weapons. There was a certain logic to that. Groza was only the first of its generation, but if you could eventually achieve the same magnitude of destruction as nuclear weapons, without radioactive fallout poisoning the earth and air, was that not preferable? No more 'mutually assured destruction,' no more species-ending Armageddon?

But how much more tempting would it be, he pondered, for politicians and generals to resort to using a weapon such as Groza if the long-term consequences were less terrible? If mass destruction could be achieved without mass extinction?

It was, he realized, a question that could occupy an entire philosophy class for hours.

He took a sip of his water. She had definitely been wrong about one thing. He hadn't seen something hideous when he looked at her. In fact, he had found Anastasia Grahkovsky strangely beautiful. The way she looked at him, even though she could not see him, was mesmerizing. She was broken, smashed, scarred, yes – but fierce and passionate. And she had read him like a damn book.

He touched his shoulder where she had gripped it. Then he shuddered.

Forget that, Maqsud, he told himself. *That suka is crazy.*

"Alright, ladies and gentlemen, your attention please," Alicia Rodriguez said. The eight crew members of B for Bertha, four pilots and four systems operators, were seated in front of her, Karen 'Bunny' O'Hare among them, but sitting on her own in the back row. Rodriguez knew her well enough to know she wasn't making any kind of statement – she just preferred her space.

"This will be our first combat mission," Rodriguez said. "I am Mission Commander, Major Severin is your mission intelligence coordinator, Sergeant Halloran your intelligence supervisor, and we are pulling weather specialist support from 45th Wing. You have the mission data on your tablets; this is your chance to ask questions because when we leave here, you will be expected to execute your orders immediately. This is not an exercise. Is that clear?"

There was a chorus of various 'yes, ma'ams' and 'aye, ma'ams' depending on what service the officer was from. She stepped aside and let her second-in-command, Kansas Severin, take the floor. With him was Zeezee Halloran, who Rodriguez had moved from her role in logistics – now that was more or less under control – to intelligence. Zeezee already had her Intelligence Specialist 'A' qualification and Rodriguez had gotten her fast-tracked through the

'C' qualification at Dam Neck in Virginia and attached to the 45th Wing's intelligence unit.

"Thank you, ma'am. Situation, people," Severin began, calling up an image on a screen. It was a page from the file the US agent had smuggled out of Russia, at the cost of their life. "You may be aware of the big picture, but just in case, here is a quick recap. The world's largest crude oil processing facility, Abqaiq in Saudi Arabia, was destroyed a week ago. Saudi Arabia has tapped its strategic reserve to keep the oil flowing, but that is not going to last, and the world knows it. Whether in reaction to or in coordination with the destruction of the Abqaiq plant, Iran has stepped up harassment of Saudi-flagged or chartered crude oil shipping in the Persian Gulf. One Saudi oil carrier has been detained, and two have been sabotaged in port in the Emirates, reportedly by Iranian Revolutionary Guard special forces."

O'Hare held up a hand. "Iran is just making hay while the sun shines, Major, or is there more to this?"

"We don't believe Iran is acting alone. This week the Saudi Air Force reported that Russia has begun basing 5th-gen Su-57 aircraft at Esfahan in central Iran. Earlier this year, Russia also moved a squadron of Mig-41 interceptors into Egypt's Hurghada Air Base. If the Saudi report is true, Russia is making up for its lack of a functioning aircraft carrier to support its allies in the Middle East by basing front-line aircraft inside their borders."

O'Hare whistled. "What a shit sandwich. Russians to the right of them, Russians to the left of them, and a nuclear-armed neighbor hijacking their oil tankers."

"Why the sudden Russian interest in the Middle East again, Major?" Albers asked.

"Iran's actions are stifling the flow of Saudi oil out of the Persian Gulf, and when that happens, Iran benefits, sure, but so does Russia. Whether Iran is just being opportunistic or acting in league with Russia isn't clear yet. But there are … other indications this is all part of a larger Russian strategy." He stepped back. "Sergeant Halloran?"

The Chinese American intel officer stepped forward. "Thank you, Major. The reason we are here. Russia has deployed a new weapon of mass destruction in space. They call it *Groza*, or

'Thunderstorm.' It is an orbital kinetic weapon that drops heavy projectiles on ground targets. It is ugly, it is inaccurate, but it breaks no current arms treaties and it is very, very destructive." Halloran advanced the briefing slides to show video of the Abqaiq refinery burning. Running across the bottom were several amateur and CCTV videos that showed the prelude to the attack – hundreds of contrails appearing in the air above Abqaiq and then falling onto the plant at, literally, meteoric speeds. "This is video of the world's first known Groza attack – the former Abqaiq oil processing plant in Saudi Arabia. An area the size of four city blocks, leveled in seconds, just a smoking ruin today." She blanked the screen. "Saudi Arabia has accused Russia of the attack, but Russia denies responsibility and is sticking to their story that this was a freak meteor strike. The National Security Agency has put out a bulletin warning that a massive social media disinformation campaign originating from Russia has been initiated to support the meteor strike story and warn that similar events are possible in the future. Apparently, Russian scientists have conveniently uncovered evidence that the Earth is passing through a never-before-detected asteroid belt. The cynics among you will note that this 'freak event' may just have saved the Russian economy from collapse as it sent the global crude oil price through the roof."

There were chuckles around the room and Halloran held up a hand to stop them. "No laughing matter. They are setting the stage for another Groza attack. We don't know where or when, and we don't plan to wait around to find out." She called up a graphic of the globe, showing sixteen satellites in orbit around it. "This is an illustrative graphic showing the current position of the sixteen possible Groza launch platforms…"

O'Hare held up her hand. "Possible, Sergeant? We don't know for sure?"

"We have photographs of the Groza satellites taken during their production phase," Halloran said. "Check your briefing notes. They show a satellite core module we estimate weighs about ten tons, with a payload of about eighty tons of tungsten projectiles. As far as we can tell by ground-based observation, they have sixteen of these in orbit. There could be more."

The room was silent as the crews reviewed the graphics on their tablets.

"Yes," Zeezee read their minds. "They're big. Just about visible to the naked eye if you're standing on a nice dark mountainside." She held up a tablet. "Everything we know about Groza, which is not a lot, is in those notes."

"Defensive weapons?" O'Hare asked.

"Unknown," Zeezee admitted. "That schematic we showed you is two years old. The design could have gone through more iterations since then."

"Can I respectfully advise in that case, Major," O'Hare directed her comment to Severin, "that we assume Russia didn't put the equivalent of a Battlestar into orbit without some means of protecting it."

"I'll consider that advice, O'Hare," Severin said. "Tactical environment," he continued. He flicked a couple of screens ahead in his briefing and showed a map of the globe with a red orbital track and the current position of the satellite clearly marked on it. The orbit ran right over the East Coast of the USA. "This is your target. We have designated it Groza A1, for obvious reasons." He zoomed the image and saw a couple of personnel lean forward and frown. "That's right. Its orbit takes it right over the top of New York City. Sergeant Halloran tells me it also takes it within strike range of Kennedy Space Center, Patrick Air Force and Canaveral Space Stations." He let that sink in. "That is not a coincidence, ladies and gentlemen. The whole world knows KSC and the Cape are our primary heavy-lift launch facilities. The 45th Space Wing, NASA and SpaceX are all based here. Russia knows that the Cape is also the launch site for our X-37 fleet."

Halloran took up the thread. "45th Space Wing intelligence base case assumption is that in the event of open warfare in space between Russia and America, the first place Russia would hit would be Kennedy-Canaveral, to prevent any further launches. In the past, our planning assumed a tactical nuclear strike would be needed, and that made an attack less likely as a tac nuke dropped on a US mainland target would without a doubt only take place if we were already in the middle of World War Three. Groza changes that assumption." She brought up a map of the East Coast of the USA, with cities and military bases highlighted from New York down to Florida. "Russia is doing its best to hide Groza behind this BS meteor cover story. If it gets traction, they might feel brave enough to hit other targets. Looking at the damage assessment from the Abqaiq attack, we estimate that during a single orbit, Groza A1 could attack up to twenty separate targets on the US East Coast, hitting them within 15 minutes of launch, and unlike a ballistic or hypersonic missile, its projectiles would be completely unstoppable."

"And on that cheerful note," Severin said, paging back a couple of screens, "you can see our mission is both vital and simple. We will intercept Groza A1 over the pole, as it tracks south-south-east over Canada. We will photograph it and confirm the target is, in fact, a Groza weapons platform. And then, before it reaches the Eastern seaboard of the USA, we will disable it."

There were no chuckles this time and he took in the faces around the room, which showed one universal expression – surprise.

It was Bunny O'Hare who raised her hand first. She'd been looking through the briefing materials. "These satellites can be repositioned, Major? We knock out this one, what's to stop them from moving another into the same orbit?"

"They do that, we'll kill that one too," Severin said grimly. "We've learned a few things since the Cuban missile crisis, O'Hare, and one of them is, don't let the enemy put doomsday weapons on your doorstep. Or over your damn head. Hopefully, we kill Groza A1, the politicians and diplomats can get Russia to park its damn killer satellites over Siberia instead."

The Minnesotan, Albers, had a hand in the air. "With respect, sir, we start knocking their shiny new satellites out of the sky, Ivan is going to get annoyed. Like, how would we react if we launched a new class of remotely piloted submarines and Russia started sinking them on the quiet? It's going to be game on."

"The idea is that if we only engage those birds that are an active threat to our cities and bases, we can argue it's a proportionate action. And we can keep that action out of the public eye as long as the engagement is limited to space. But let's leave politics to the politicians, who I am sure will soon be pointing out certain realities to the Russians, and focus on the job we've been given to do. Alright, let's move on. Who, where and when…"

When Alicia Rodriguez's crews saw the satellite track that looped over Cape Canaveral Space Station, home to the three functional X-37 spacecraft of the 615th Combat Operations Squadron, their thoughts immediately and involuntarily went to their own safety. The pilots and systems officers of the X-37 fleet could theoretically operate from any base in the country, or overseas, but they needed advanced communications infrastructure and for the new X-37 fleet, it had been bolted onto the existing launch communication and control complex at the Cape's Morrell Operations Center (MOC) – the self-described nerve center for all Space Force launches from Cape Canaveral. Control of the remotely piloted X-37s was still several years from being made mobile.

As Severin went through roles and responsibilities for the upcoming mission, he was standing in the briefing room of a rather nondescript suite on the second floor of the MOC. Entry to the suite was limited to personnel of the 615th Squadron, but the presence of the X-37 crews on the station was well known because they lived in Patrick Air Force Base accommodations and came and went every day through the big front doors of the MOC marked "Control of the Battlefield Begins Here." Russian agents would have had no trouble at all working out where the crews of the X-37 fleet were based, and watching the orbital path of the Groza, more than one airman hunched their shoulders during Severin's briefing at the thought it could be overhead at any time.

But you couldn't exactly hide a US heavy-lift rocket launch facility and the X-37 had to be lifted into space on the back of a massive Space Launch System rocket powered by four of the RS-25 engines that had carried the Space Shuttle into space; or on a Falcon Heavy with two strap-on boosters. There was nothing 'stealthy' about an X-37 launch. Neither could the X-37 stay hidden during orbit. Though small in cross-section, it was visible to Russian ground or space-based tracking from the moment it launched. Rodriguez was certain the Russian Aerospace Forces had compiled a massive dossier on her X-37s, their technical capabilities and vulnerabilities. They had probably wargamed a thousand times the various strategies they felt might succeed in neutralizing the US spacecraft, and she knew from her own wargaming that those strategies included everything from ground-based missiles to cyberwarfare attacks. Her people were, of course, trained in the countermeasures needed to defeat a Russian or Chinese attack.

No matter how you looked at it, though, the main vulnerability of the X-37 fleet was the fixed infrastructure at the Cape required to launch it. Vandenberg Air Force Base in California might be used in a pinch, but it was best suited to launching medium-sized rockets into polar orbits, not the heavies on which the X-37 relied.

Which the airmen and women of Rodriguez's 615th Squadron knew made them and the entire Kennedy-Canaveral Space Complex a very, very juicy target.

"If these satellites have some sort of defensive sensor suite, their ground operators may be able to detect incoming threats and engage them. What could we expect in the way of a ground-based response, ma'am?" one of the weapons officers was asking Zeezee.

"Good question. As you know, Russia has both ground, sea and air-launched *Nudol* anti-satellite missiles," Zeezee replied. "They've shown they can knock satellites out of orbit, and even intercept ballistic missiles on re-entry, so they are a definite threat to Bertha."

"We're going to burn a lot of fuel on these ops," Albers pointed out. "Do we have access to the Trans network?" The US Trans network was the space-based equivalent of the Air Force KC-46 aerial refueling aircraft. Each Trans module was a huge, orbiting, self-piloting tank that the XC-37 could dock with in order to refuel and recharge.

"Yes, Lieutenant, that has been accounted for."

"Space to space weapons? Could they have mounted something on these Grozas, Sergeant?" O'Hare asked.

"Nothing on the schematics we obtained, but they were for an early prototype. Russia has tested both ballistic, kinetic and energy-based weapons in space, and these satellites are big enough to field weapons, so assume yes, Captain."

"Well, Bertha has a few tricks up her sleeve, Sergeant," O'Hare remarked. "And we've been rehearsing them. I say, bring it!"

Another of her pilots reached over and high fived O'Hare. Rodriguez frowned. They were excited, cocky even.

"I admire your confidence, O'Hare, but if…" Rodriguez broke into the briefing, "… against all the odds, the Russians bring Bertha down, plan 'B' has already been initiated. We have been given priority for the launch of X-37 Avenger aboard a SpaceX Falcon Heavy out of Kennedy. But the earliest launch window is three weeks from now, and that will involve cutting corners that are making everyone uncomfortable, which just increases, even more, the need for this particular mission to succeed," she continued. She saw O'Hare raising her hand again and spoke quickly. "And before you ask, Captain, plan 'C' would only be activated if Russia's actions directly threaten the USA or its interests. And that is simply to use ground-based anti-satellite missiles, fired from Aegis missile cruisers in the Atlantic, Indian Ocean and Pacific, to take down any Groza birds that threaten the USA. But we do that, and it really is game on."

"If Iran doesn't start World War Three first, anyway," someone said grimly.

Saudi Arabia had taken the news in 2028 that Iran had successfully tested a nuclear weapon with equanimity. It had not been a question of whether, but when. When Iran announced it had developed a nuclear warhead that could be fitted to its new Sejjil-3 three-stage ballistic missile, Saudi Arabia shrugged. Saudi Arabia wasn't worried about a ballistic missile that could strike targets 2,500 miles away (though Israel and nations in Europe rightfully were) when Iran already had an armory of missiles that could reach from inside Iran to strike any target in Saudi Arabia.

It had reacted not by starting its own nuclear weapons program in competition, but by tying itself even closer to the USA and other allies with a massive conventional arms upgrade program. It was, therefore, well positioned to react to the latest provocations by an emboldened Iran. Iran had fired on Saudi military aircraft, hijacked shipping and, most recently, sabotaged Saudi-chartered oil tankers moored off the port of Fujairah in the Emirates.

With Russian fighter aircraft protecting the skies overhead, a nuclear shield to deter any invasion, and with Saudi Arabia facing crippling economic challenges, Iran had decided it was an opportune time to turn the screws.

It was about to learn an age-old lesson in cause and effect.

Alakeel's flight of six F-35 Lightning IIs had been ordered to take off from Medina in the west of Saudi Arabia after taking on fuel and ordnance, and proceed to a point in international airspace over the Red Sea southwest of Yanbu, where they would engage the Iranian frigate *Sahand*. The *Sahand* was a long way from home, but patrolling in the company of two new *Khalije Fars* guided-missile destroyers and the light replenishment ship *Bushehr*. Russian air cover, of unknown strength, was expected.

He had made many 'observations' about his orders. The first, that a mission such as this would ideally utilize at least a full squadron strength attack, with a six to eight fighter element covering two to four ground attack configured Lightnings. The second, that with the frigate sailing under the protection of two guided-missile destroyers, a conventional air-sea missile strike with standoff cruise missiles was unlikely to penetrate the destroyer and fighter screen. The third, that a stealth attack would be difficult, even in the F-35, if Russian 5th-gen aircraft were providing cover, as they were no doubt networked with low-frequency ground-based radar in Egypt designed specifically to detect the F-35. The fourth, as a result of all this, was that the destruction of the *Sahand* in a traditional engagement was highly unlikely if that was the objective.

He had been told to plan his mission around the resources allocated. Which told him his mission was a roll of the dice, intended more to send a signal to Iran than to actually inconvenience them. Or perhaps, if he or his pilots were killed or injured, to provide a pretext for escalation. But Alakeel never approached a mission planning for it to fail. In planning the attack on the *Sahand*, he had done his utmost to ensure it would succeed.

Amir Alakeel had a two-year-old daughter he wanted to watch grow into a fine young woman. With the changes he had seen in his own lifetime, he even imagined that one day, she might be a pilot too. He planned to be around to see that happen.

He had eschewed the proposed loadout of twin AGM-154C standoff weapons for his two ground attack configured aircraft. These were essentially glide-bombs, which would have to be dropped from altitude, at medium range. Alakeel knew that with the amount of warning the Iranians might have regarding the approach of the attacking Lightnings, the likelihood of these weapons getting through was minimal. He seriously considered, but finally also rejected the option to go with four smaller Norwegian Naval Strike Missiles. They were sea-skimming weapons, newly adapted for air to ground operations, able to make random maneuvers in the terminal phase to throw off enemy close-in weapons systems. But they flew at only 600 mph and again, Alakeel was worried they were too few to overwhelm the Iranian defenses.

Instead, he had loaded his two ground attack Lightnings with Indian-made 'ALFA-S' attack drones. Each F-35 could carry 15 of the small electrically powered hundred mile an hour dart-shaped drones.

The ALFA-S drone swarm had made an impression on Alakeel. He'd seen it deployed in an attack against a dummy tank formation with devastating effect. The swarm had surrounded the tank formation and then attacked it from every side, detonating overhead and sending depleted uranium 'slugs' through the weak top armor of the vehicles, shredding them from above. But would a slow-moving swarm work against modern warships fitted with radar-guided Russian AK-630M *Kamand* 30mm rotary cannons? Both the *Sahand* and its destroyer escorts featured one of the *Kamand* close-in weapons mounted on each beam, for six in total. They could track multiple targets, destroying each sequentially, which was why Alakeel was convinced an attack with just two to four missiles would fail.

But an attack by *thirty* drones? And what if that attack was timed to coincide with the launch of a wave of Homing Anti Radar (HARM) missiles, which the Iranian defenses could not ignore?

It was a gamble, but he had persuaded his Colonel to take it, and now it was up to him to prove it could work.

He checked his instruments one last time. They were a hundred and fifty miles out and closing on the Iranian frigate. The skies were full of military and civilian radar energy, but there was no indication his flight had been detected. He craned his neck and checked the skies around him with his mark one eyeballs. He had already learned once that a lack of radar warnings did not mean he was safe.

He satisfied himself the skies were clear. "Haya flight, Haya One," he said. "Section one, begin ingress, sections two and three on me line abreast. Arm your HARM missiles."

Each of his four escort aircraft was armed with a mixed payload of two Homing Anti-Radar Missiles and four medium-range *Sidewinder* air to air missiles. He would love to have been able to field the newer CUDA all-aspect missiles the US F-35s were equipped with, but they had not yet been released for export.

Saudi Arabia had been preparing for this war for decades. Year on year since the early 2010s, it had been the largest arms importer in the world. It had purchased hundreds of helicopters, nearly 200 main battle tanks, a thousand armored personnel carriers, and over 20,000 guided missiles. Its navy had purchased five missile frigates from Spain, and its army, short-range ballistic missiles from the Ukraine. With the purchase of 70 UK Typhoon attack aircraft, 20 Advanced F-15SA Strike Fighters, five SAAB 2000 Early Warning and Control aircraft and 35 F-35 Lightning IIs, it now had an air force to rival Israel, the formerly dominant airpower in the region. Though it had only the fifth largest standing army, technologically it had the second most powerful ground force behind Israel, though it had yet to convert that superiority to battlefield victories in the many proxy wars it had been fighting in the last 20 years, not least in Yemen.

His aircraft, and those of his wingmen, were armed with the extended range AGM-88G Block 4 anti-radar missile. They were already tracking their targets, pulling data from a Saudi SAAB 2000 Early Warning and Control aircraft circling inside Saudi airspace behind the port of Yanbu.

"Haya Two beginning ingress," his drone attack flight leader confirmed. The two-plane element dropped away, headed for the sea. They still had a hundred miles to run before they released their payload.

The HARM missiles' targets were the radar systems on the two destroyers escorting the *Sahand*, plus that on the *Sahand* itself.

Mission planners had given the 'wild weasel' radar suppression attack a 13 percent chance of successfully knocking out the radar systems on even one of the Iranian ships. Alakeel's strategy for dealing with the *Sahand* did not rely on them succeeding.

He looked at his helmet-mounted display to confirm that all four aircraft in his flight had locked up the targets they'd been assigned by the SAAB 2000 operations controller.

As his machines closed to within a hundred miles of the Iranian ships, he paged the SAAB. "Haya Control, Haya One. We are approaching attack point alpha."

"Haya Control, Haya One. You are cleared to engage," the controller replied.

Without needing an order, his four aircraft increased their separation and spread out into a line abreast formation. At ten thousand feet, 650 miles an hour, they approached the attack point – an invisible line in the sky marked on Alakeel's tac display with a dotted line. As he crossed the line, he checked his weapon was armed, reached for the missile trigger and opened his mike. "Haya flight, HARMs away."

His weapons bay doors swung open and two of the 700 lb. missiles dropped into his slipstream and ignited their solid fuel ramjet engines before streaking away toward the horizon at nearly 1,500 miles per hour. They had about five minutes to run.

"Haya Two, Haya Three missiles away and tracking, Haya flights two and three returning to base. Happy hunting, Haya One," he said. He would like to have taken his aircraft all the way to the target, both to see the results of his attack and to mix it up with the Russian fighters he knew had to be there. But that was not the nature of modern war in the air. Hit, and run – that was the name of the game.

If you did it right, you would never even set eyes on the enemy you had killed.

Uncomfortable encounters

RAF Lossiemouth, Scotland

"And what in the bleedin' heck are *you*?" Meany asked himself, his eyes glued to the multifunctional display on the panel in front of his flight controls.

Target on optical lock, eleven point five miles, closing at two knots relative, Angus said.

"Twenty times zoom, Angus," Meany said. The tasking sent from UK GCHQ for the RAF Skylon unit had been routine, and at the same time, frightening. What was routine was that it was a photo reconnaissance mission where the target was another country's military satellite. Meany and the other Skylon pilots had conducted about fifty such missions, and they were usually dead boring unless you were the kind of signals intelligence nerd who completely geeked out at closeup images of antennae and solar panels. Meany understood the value of the photographs – the type of antennae could tell GCHQ what frequency and wavelength the satellite used, serial numbers could identify the exact model of the transmission equipment, and knowing that, algorithms could be developed to intercept or jam it. The size and type of the solar and thermal panels told the boffins exactly how much juice the satellite was pulling, which could also give them vital clues to its inner workings and purpose.

But it wasn't exactly fighter combat. So Meany had welcomed the single line in the briefing from GCHQ about 'operational safety.' The one thing that had made this mission just a little interesting. "The target is believed to be a space to ground weapon and may have space to space defensive capabilities." He'd asked the intel officer, a warrant officer called Aston who had served in the Middle East like him – and knew what his pilots needed to know, and what they didn't – what the hell space to space weapon capabilities the Russians might have.

"Blinding lasers," Aston had said. "Radar and infrared jamming. Physical decoys. Ballistic weapons. Mini-railguns … basically, anything you can put on a ship or an aircraft, they can mount on a satellite of this size. But to our knowledge, they haven't. Automated systems are too dangerous to other space objects, including their own, and remotely directed weapons systems are too resource-intensive to crew around the clock when there is no threat."

"To our knowledge…" Meany repeated drily. "You could be sending us up against some new Russian Death Star."

"The intel on this comes from the Yanks," the warrant officer told him. He was a roly-poly man, with a habit he'd picked up during a posting to the US of chewing tobacco plugs, and spitting into a handkerchief when annoyed. "And they've said nothing about defensive weapons."

"Then why…" Meany asked him, "… don't the bloody Yanks go on a Russian Death Star photo safari with their own bloody spacecraft?"

"They probably will," he said. "But do they share every little thing with us in a timely fashion? Do they tell us what they're going to do before they've gone and done it? No, they do not," he said, and spat. "Hence, we shall take our own photographs of this beasty."

Paddington had contrived to be inside his trailer as Meany and Angus closed on the Russian satellite. It was one of several, his commanding officer had told him. This one was on an orbit that took it south to north over the west coast of Africa and Europe, over the UK to the north pole, down over the Pacific Ocean and back up again. He wasn't surprised, therefore, that the UK signals intelligence agency had taken a sudden and rather particular interest in the satellite if their US counterparts had told them it was weaponized.

Loaded with a recon pod in the payload bay, it had taken the Skylon flight crews nearly 18 hours from takeoff at Lossiemouth to get in position for the intercept. As their lead pilot, Meany was supposed to be resting for most of that time so that he was fresh when he jumped into the cockpit with Angus. But Meany trusted Angus to be fresh and had spent as much time as he could in the simulator, programming evasive maneuvers. His sensor suite should be able to pick up everything from a laser flare to the flash of small cannon firing, but he knew his own reaction time would be too slow in almost any engagement scenario. It would be Angus who picked up the attack and reacted to it, and he wanted to be sure the AI was ready to respond to every damn possibility.

The odds were stacked against them, though. If the Russian satellite was armed with a laser weapon, the bolt would be traveling at light speed and Angus would have no time between the flare of the laser burst and it hitting the spacecraft in which to react. It would take a megawatt laser to cut through his heat tiles, though. If the weapon was a railgun shooting a kinetic projectile, there would be no telltale flash, no warning at all unless the projectile was big enough to be picked up on the Skylon's own radar. Luckily both of these weapons required significant power to trigger, so a thermal signature might be detected before they were used. A 20 or 30mm cannon would give off no thermal warning before its first shot but might give off a warning flash. The tiny slugs from a 20mm cannon would almost certainly be undetectable until they started chewing at the skin of his Skylon, but that skin was hardened, and photosensitive, and might pick up the heat of a targeting laser if the Russian system was using one.

The permutations and probabilities made his head spin, but that's why he had Angus. He could program the threats and responses at leisure, and leave Angus to choose between them in the heat of combat.

As he looked at the zoomed image of the approaching Russian satellite, he had a horrible feeling the time he had spent that afternoon on programming and reprogramming the AI's defensive routines might just have been needed.

"Hold position," Meany called.

Holding. Distance ten point eight miles. Relative velocity zero.

Meany panned around the image of the satellite. "Do you see that, sir?" he asked Paddington. "Earthside, four o'clock low." Meany double-clicked on his screen with his mousepad and brought the lower quarter of the Russian satellite into focus.

It was like no satellite Meany had ever seen. It looked like the cylinder of a loaded revolver. Sitting on top of the cylinder was a dome about thirty feet in diameter that looked like it housed thrust vectors, probably electronics too. Standard latticed solar panels extended from the dome and, judging by their design, the latticed wings doubled as thermal radiators. Around the hub were objects that had to be missiles. He counted twenty. It must have been similar in size to a module on a space station. Though it floated weightlessly in space, the thing looked like it must weigh a hundred tons.

Even just looking at it, it scared the living daylights out of him.

What had caught his attention, though, was a tube-like protrusion from one side of the dome on top of the cylinder that appeared to be … pointed right bloody at them.

"Angus," he said, as calmly as he could. "Analyze the current image. Match with known Russian weapon types. Report."

A fraught second passed before the calm Scottish brogue of the AI responded. *Image analyzed. Possible match: Gryazev-Shipunov GSh-30-1 30mm autocannon.*

"I can't use 'possible,' Angus. How certain are you?"

The full body of the possible weapon is obscured by the housing. Only the barrel is observable. I am 100 percent certain, however, the barrel is that of a Gryazev-Shipunov GSh-30-1 autocannon.

"Any indication of a targeting laser or radar, Angus?"

No, sir. I am detecting no photovoltaic energy or radio emissions from the target.

"Then how, Angus, does it happen to be pointing that bloody blunderbuss straight at us?"

Please repeat your request, sir.

"Move your ship a few dozen yards laterally, Flight Lieutenant," Paddington said quietly. "See if it really is tracking you."

"Yes, sir. Angus, two seventy degrees thrust, five knots, hold fifty yards from current position."

Confirming. Two seventy degrees thrust, five knots, hold at fifty yards from current position.

"Correct, execute."

The image on the screen shuddered as the small vectoring jets on the Skylon fired and shoved it slowly sideways, its nose and sensors still pointing at the Russian satellite.

As it did so, the barrel of the satellite autocannon swiveled to follow it.

"Oh, shit," Meany said. "Excuse the French, sir. No radar radiation. It's using infrared or optical targeting."

"It's probably automated," Paddington said, though he didn't sound confident to Meany. "A close-in weapons system like ours, in case of space debris. That cannon has a range of about one mile. If we don't approach any closer than that, we'll be safe enough."

At that moment, the RAF Skylon was anything but 'safe.' Russia had not put its hundred million dollar killer satellites into orbit without the means to protect themselves. The defensive system on the Groza was automated, but it was based on the same *Atoll* electro-optical infrared search and track targeting system deployed in its latest stealth fighter aircraft. The infrared sensors in the turrets mounted beside the Groza's 30mm cannons could detect moving objects at close range, or pick up the reflected heat of sunlight on metal surfaces at long range. They had detected the approaching Skylon at about thirty miles distant, and locked onto it as Meany had maneuvered, his vectoring thrusters lighting up the Skylon like a Christmas tree. The system was designed to photograph and identify any approaching space objects, and to engage them at a range of ten miles if they appeared to be on a collision course. The designers had not anticipated being attacked by enemy spacecraft, but the system would at least offer some low-level protection against hostiles of that nature as well.

And Paddington had been very wrong on another important point because despite all his years in RAF Space Command, at that moment, he was thinking like the fighter pilot he was trained to be. It was true that the Russian 30mm autocannon had a range of only one mile, on earth. But in space, it could fire 1,500 rounds a minute at a speed of 2,000 feet per second and its projectiles would continue at that velocity *forever*. At a distance of ten miles, it would take the 30mm rounds from the Groza's autocannons just seventeen seconds to reach the RAF Skylon.

And hovering right at the edge of its authorized engagement range, Meany's Skylon was giving the silicon brain of the Groza a very large headache. It was outside the Groza's engagement envelope on two parameters; the first was range, and the second was vector. To meet its engagement rules, it needed the Skylon to close range to within ten miles, and be moving directly toward it. But it was ready, in case it did.

"Close to five miles and complete a 360 orbit of the thing," Paddington ordered. "I want to be able to build a virtual model out of it we can share with our cousins. See if they can tell us what the dickens it is."

"Yes, sir. Angus, close to five miles and obtain a full photographic texture map of the target object," Meany told the AI.

Closing for texture mapping, the AI confirmed. The screen shivered as the Skylon accelerated. Then it began to spin crazily.

Warning. Incoming fire. Target maneuvering. Evading, the AI's voice said, suddenly loud in the small trailer. *Permission to return fire?*

"Yes!" Meany yelled, grabbing at his own throttle and side-stick, but knowing he could never react with the speed Angus had just displayed. "Engage."

"No! Countermanded," Paddington yelled over the top of him. "Evade and withdraw."

Evading and withdrawing, Angus responded. *Withdrawing to twenty miles separation, confirm?*

"Confirmed," Paddington said.

The images on the screens in front of Meany, which had been locked on the Russian satellite, began whirling like a carousel as the Skylon spun away from the spitting stream of lead from the Russian autocannon and accelerated. Even though they were fired at 2,000 feet a second, and the autocannon tracked the Skylon closely through its escape, with seventeen seconds warning, the trajectory of the heavy 30mm shells was easy enough for the quantum-computing-powered Angus to predict and evade. The Skylon was not space junk. As the RAF Skylon exited the ten-mile contact bubble around the Groza, the autocannon stopped firing, though it didn't stop tracking.

There was a terse silence in the trailer as the images from the Skylon's external cameras and infrared cameras stabilized.

Twenty miles separation, Angus finally announced. *Holding and awaiting orders.*

139

Meany realized he was still leaning forward in his exoskeleton, gripping his side-stick with white knuckles. He released his grip and took the breath he'd been holding for the last thirty seconds.

"I'm sorry, sir," he started. "I just heard 'incoming fire' and I…"

Paddington put a hand on Meany's shoulder. "I would have done the same, Flight Lieutenant, if I were you," he said. "And your job is to protect the integrity of that spacecraft within the boundaries of your mission objectives. My job is to think about what might come after."

"Yes, sir."

"Angus?" Paddington said, raising his voice.

Yes, Squadron Leader Bear?

"Is the target defensive system still tracking our vessel?" he asked.

Reviewing data. No, sir, the AI replied. *The autocannon stopped firing at ten miles range, and stopped actively tracking at a distance of approximately fifteen miles.*

"Good. Angus, can you please conduct a texture mapping of the target object from a distance of no closer than fifteen miles?"

Yes, Squadron Leader Bear. Commencing texture mapping. The screen shuddered and the vision of the Russian satellite began a slow change of aspect as the Skylon rotated around it, photographing. The distance would mean an inevitable loss of detail, but at least not the loss of their precious Skylon.

"They say combat is hours of tedium followed by moments of sheer terror," Paddington said, clapping Meany on the shoulder again. "We certainly proved them right, didn't we, Flight Lieutenant?"

Meany wiped a hand over his scalp. "That we did, sir."

Paddington stretched, scratched his ginger moustache thoughtfully, and then buttoned his olive drab jacket with fingers Meany noticed were shaking perceptibly. "Run a full integrity check to make sure we didn't take any damage. And write up the engagement immediately your recon is complete, Flight Lieutenant," Paddington said. "Mark it for Five Eyes attention. We gained some critical intelligence today."

"Yes, sir," Meany said, pulling his keyboard toward him and grabbing his mouse so he could replay the mission video logs and capture in words every second of the brief engagement.

"Right then," Paddington said. "I rather think a cup of tea is in order, don't you?"

"Just pull back on that, will you?" Sergeant Karas said to Maqsud Khan, leaning over his shoulder and peering at the vision from the collision avoidance system on Groza 10. The shift before Maqsud had come on duty had been a routine one, with the only incident a collision avoidance report that the previous shift had logged and filed, without reviewing the optical targeting imagery themselves. Collision alerts weren't so routine that they happened every shift, but even though they sometimes involved the Groza firing its close-in defense weapons, they weren't that exciting either. The only reason Maqsud had pulled up the vision was boredom. He had a little game he played with himself, a little like a wine connoisseur blind tasting wine. Whenever there was a collision alert, he pulled up the vision and tried to identify what particular type of space junk had triggered the alert. If he could, he'd try and guess what vintage and what country, even what agency had launched it. Often there were only seconds of vision to draw on before it was blown away by the Groza's autocannon. When he'd pulled up the vision from Groza 10, he'd just about dropped the coffee he was holding.

What?

RAF Skylon. It had to be! That jet-black needle-nosed cylindrical shape, nose canards, mid-section mounted thrusters. Maqsud knew the shapes and sizes of every single category of man-made object that had been sent into space for the last thirty years – no, make that fifty years. His Groza had engaged the bloody Skylon.

That was when he'd called Sergeant Karas. The man had been intrigued at first. "That's the Skylon, you say?" he asked.

"I called it straight away," Maqsud said. "And the AI has confirmed it." He zoomed the image. "Nose, canards, engine mounts ... see?"

Karas very quickly transitioned from intrigued to annoyed. "So, the Brits got nosy," Karas said. "Brits, Americans, Chinese ... had to happen sooner or later. Lucky for them, the RAF didn't get their billion-pound spacecraft shot to shit. Write it up and get back to work. You want a bloody medal or something?"

"Sir, the British spacecraft at the very least got intel on the Groza's configuration, its defensive systems, maybe signals intelligence on its comms frequencies?" Maqsud continued, not giving up. "There is also the possibility that it was damaged in the engagement ... if we even chipped a heat tile, there's a chance the British spacecraft won't be able to re-enter the atmosphere without burning up. We should task ground surveillance to..."

Karas clapped Maqsud's shoulder condescendingly. "Somewhere in the Russian Aerospace Forces, there is probably some poor swine whose sole job is to try to keep track of that British spacecraft. He will no doubt be reporting this engagement in mind-numbing detail. And whoever that poor fool is, I hope I never meet him at a party, because his life story must be even more boring than yours, Corporal."

"But..."

"Drop it. You have your tasking for the day. Six targeting exercises and every one better be right on spec. Focus on that, Corporal, and don't bother me again with your stupid UFO sightings ... now, I'll be going back to my coffee."

As they closed on the frigate *Sahand*, Amir Alakeel's attack element could not see the smokeless HARM missiles of their air suppression colleagues streak overhead, but in any case gave them only the briefest of thoughts as their eyes were glued to the line on their helmet-mounted displays that marked their own release point.

When they were first developed in the late 1980s, the HARM missiles were regarded as both fast and deadly. The crude radar defense systems of the time were soon updated so that they could hop frequencies in an attempt to defeat anti-radar missiles, were made multiply redundant so that the loss of one transmitter did not degrade the entire network, or were modified to be able to decoy an attack away with a dummy emitter. As quantum computers allowed better detection algorithms and provided close-in weapons systems with more precise guidance, even missiles traveling at twice the speed of sound – nearly 1,500 miles an hour – became possible to intercept.

Iran had recently upgraded the *Sahand* with a British-made AWS-9 search and track radar system, purchased from Brunei. Capable of tracking up to a hundred airborne threats simultaneously and feeding data to its anti-air and close-in weapons systems, it had no trouble picking up and targeting the incoming HARM missiles. Unlike the ships of more capable navies, though, the *Sahand* was not able to share its targeting data either with the less well-equipped destroyers escorting it or with the Russian Mig-41 aircraft on patrol overhead.

All it could do was to alert them verbally to the threat. "Vampires inbound!" the *Sahand*'s anti-air commander shouted on the inter-service radio channel. "Eight missiles, bearing 109, range 25 miles." As one, the three ships heeled over to port, trying to present their sterns to the threat and make the smallest possible target of themselves.

As they began to turn, the Saudi ground attack element hit its 'attack point beta.' Without pause, their own weapons bay doors opened and from each Lightning, the six-foot-long spear-shaped drones dropped free. Small wings and tail fins extending, they fell toward the sea and used the fighter's momentum to propel themselves forward in a several hundred miles an hour glide. Each had been programmed with the optical and electronic profile of its target, the Iranian frigate. Each downloaded data on the position of the target at the moment of launch from its mother aircraft so that it could guide itself autonomously toward the *Sahand* and then attack it.

When the Saudi HARM missiles got to within two miles of the *Sahand*, with a sound like the sky itself was tearing in two, the 30mm rotary cannons of its *Kamand* close-in weapons system started firing, at 5,000 rounds a minute. The barrels jerked up and down as they hosed the sky in the direction of the incoming anti-radar missiles. *One down.* They jerked right, then left, as more targets were allocated. *Two down. Three.* Range, one mile. Now the guns on the other two ships opened up as their radars finally picked up the incoming missiles. *Four down ... five.*

Three of the Saudi missiles struck home. Two hit the *Khalije Fars*-class destroyer *Persian Gulf* immediately below its radar transmitter, detonating their 145 lb. blast fragmentation warheads right over the heads of the officers on the ship's bridge and killing every one of them. The third struck its sister ship, the *Red Sea*, which was heeling hard to port, in the exhaust stack immediately behind the radar dish. Both strikes put the destroyers' radars off the air, but neither hit fatally wounded them. No HARM missiles hit the *Sahand*.

They were not expected to. They were intended to decoy and distract.

The swarm of ALFA-S drones launched by Alakeel's now departing ground attack F-35s had slowed down as they approached the *Sahand* undetected at wavetop level. As the HARM missiles were being engaged, fifteen of the drones swung left, fifteen swung right, then at a hundred miles an hour, they closed on their target.

They swarmed over its decks like pirates boarding a fat merchant vessel. As each of them reached the *Sahand*'s centerline, they detonated, sending hundreds of depleted uranium slugs through the 1/10th inch decks of the frigate into the crew compartments, electronics racks, lockers, storage rooms, ammunition stores and living bodies of the *Sahand*'s crew standing in the line of fire.

In seconds the *Sahand* was transformed from the pride of the Iranian fleet to a torn and bloodied hulk.

The espresso sitting on the coffee table in front of Roberta D'Antonia had been served in a nineteenth-century Lomonosov porcelain cup that was probably worth more than she made in a month. And it was getting cold. D'Antonia flinched as she absorbed the misdirected tirade being sent her way by the Russian Energy Minister.

"Who the hell does that pompous *mudak* think he is?" Lapikov asked. "Man has a few medals, he thinks he can tell me to mind my own business?" He slammed his fist on the desk he was sitting behind and leaned forward. "Read the Defense briefings?! Pah, the next time the generals decide to use their new superweapon, I might as well read about it in the newspaper, for all the warning their so-called 'briefings' give me. How am I supposed to run the energy portfolio with those *osly* blowing away refineries all over the globe?"

D'Antonia started. She'd assumed the Abqaiq strike was a 'one and done.' Surely Russia wasn't stupid enough to think the world would buy the idea that another meteor strike had somehow randomly struck *another* oil processing plant?

"Minister…" she asked carefully. "Do we have reason to believe there will be a second strike? If so, we should prepare contingency plans. Such a strike could lead to both threats and opportunities…" *And World War Three*, she thought to herself.

Lapikov stood, stretching his long frame backward with a weary groan. "Reason? It seems reason has gone out the window, Ms. D'Antonia. Have you seen what is happening in the Middle East now? The Persian Gulf is in lockdown as Saudi Arabia and Iran face off across 37 miles of water, ready to tear out each other's throats." He locked his hands behind his head, staring at the ceiling. "Oil prices are up another ten dollars a barrel today, but are we satisfied? No! The generals have convinced President Avramenko their shiny new toy is the ultimate weapon of statecraft – a hammer that can strike a blow anywhere in the world, that for now is completely deniable. Cyberwarfare Unit 26165 floods the internet with fake news about the threat from a new and previously undetected meteor cloud that is intersecting earth's orbit, with predictions there will be more such disasters as the one that struck Abqaiq. It is not a matter of whether the idiots will use it again, but where, and when."

"But the world will eventually see what Russia is doing," D'Antonia pointed out. "The Americans already claim to have evidence. Groza must be a treaty breaker, there will be consequences…"

Lapikov laughed. "You refer to the Outer Space Treaty, perhaps? That prevents us from putting nuclear weapons or weapons of mass destruction in space or on the moon. It does not prevent 'conventional' weapons like Groza."

"A weapon that can destroy ten city blocks is not a weapon of mass destruction?" she asked.

"An interesting question, yes? It is not nuclear, radiological, chemical, or biological, so no," he said. "I imagine the Security Council will eventually tie itself in knots for months over that one."

D'Antonia finally reached forward and picked up her cold coffee, draining it with one gulp. "If what you say is true, we need to get to work planning for the next strike. We may not know where, but if it is intended to strengthen further our economic position, there are only so many targets that make sense. I will consult with experts in the energy sector to identify the most vulnerable infrastructure, the most appealing targets if the aim is to force energy prices higher..."

Lapikov sat down again. "Do that but be discreet. There must be no suspicion that Groza..."

"I'll call it a terrorism planning exercise," D'Antonia said. "Pull together a team of experts and tell them to assume a major terrorist organization is planning an attack on global energy infrastructure outside Russia."

"Terrorists, yes," Lapikov laughed drily. "You have a way with irony, Ms. D'Antonia."

"So, let us discuss the next target in support of the repositioning of the Russian economy," Colonel-General Oleg Popovkin, commander of the 15th Aerospace Forces Army, said to Major-General Yevgeny Bondarev. Bondarev took the tablet the man was holding out to him and scrutinized the image on the screen. It showed a series of lines running across a map that he was now familiar with. "Before you start putting assets in place, I want to hear your thoughts," Popovkin said.

Bondarev hesitated, putting the tablet under his arm. Bondarev knew the man opposite had achieved his position through a combination of luck, and loyalty. He did not often question the directives of his military or political superiors and did not like officers who questioned his. But Bondarev had not achieved his own position by keeping his thoughts to himself.

"My primary thought, Comrade General, is whether there are other means than another orbital bombardment by which we could achieve our economic aims."

"You have … operational concerns?" Popovkin asked, raising his eyebrows.

"And political," Bondarev explained. "Operationally, I have little doubt the military objectives are achievable, though I am certain the target of the attack will respond to it and that response could vary from outrage, to an outright declaration of war." Before Popovkin could respond, Bondarev continued. "Politically, I wonder whether our new government has learned anything from the misadventures of the last? In my own time as an officer we have tried twice, and failed twice, to influence the course of history through force of arms and it seems to me we have learned nothing."

Popovkin glowered. "If I have learned anything Bondarev, it is that soldiers should devote their intellects to the problems of warcraft, not statecraft. So perhaps we should do that?" He nodded to an aide who took the tablet from Bondarev and flicked the map up onto a wall screen.

Bondarev sighed inwardly, stood and pointed at the map. "China." He ran a finger across the country from border to border. "The West–East pipeline. We have reviewed the options."

Popovkin had been an Olympic weightlifter in his early days in the military, and still had the broad shoulders and thick biceps of his youth. His stomach had expanded to match his shoulders in recent years, however, turning him from a young Hercules into an old grizzly bear. He folded his hands on the desk in front of him as he spoke. "Not a simple target."

"No, Comrade General. A network of gas pipelines, thousands of miles long – an engineering feat to rival the Great Wall. As you know, it stretches from Kazakhstan in the west to Beijing and Shanghai in the east, Hong Kong and Guangzhou in the southeast. It is China's main energy artery, taking gas and oil from the Caucasus and Siberian Kovykta in the west to feed Chinese industries in the east." He drummed his fingers on the screen, pointing at a colored line that went deep into the desert in the southwest of China. "And there is this spur, from Urumqi southwest into the heart of the Tarim Basin oil and gas fields. Opening up the Tarim Basin has significantly reduced China's demand for Russian gas and oil."

Popovkin smiled. "Yes. The Abqaiq attack and the friction between Iran and Saudi Arabia have dealt with the issue of supply. Crude oil is up ten dollars a barrel already and climbing daily. But supply is only half the equation. The other half is demand. Russian gas and oil need a market, and in recent years, as China has brought its west–east oil and gas pipeline into play, demand for our product has been falling. Destroy that pipeline and we will also address the issue of demand, but you need to do it without disrupting our own ability to supply into China."

Bondarev looked at the map again and put his finger on a large town. "We do not need to destroy it all. In the westernmost section of the map, there is a spur of the pipeline down to a town called Lunnan, the industrial center for the Tarim Basin. I am told a hundred billion cubic meters of gas and several million barrels of oil a year go through that pipeline: about half of what Beijing consumes in a year. If we take out that section of the pipeline, China has only two ways to fill the gap, by sea using LNG and crude oil carriers, or..."

"From Russia, via the pipeline through Kazakhstan," Popovkin said, looking at the tracery of pipelines on the map. "Is a Groza strike feasible? I am also considering sabotage; a special forces action. But such an operation, so deep inside China..."

"We have a proposal," Bondarev said. He moved his finger. "The feeder lines out of Lunnan and the Tarim Basin converge on this town ... Korla. From the satellite photos, it looks like there is a compressor plant of some sort there. Dozens of lines in, only one out, toward here ... Urumqi."

"Yes?"

"Hit that plant, we can choke the flow of gas out of Lunnan completely," Bondarev said. "But it's going to look damn suspicious so soon after Abqaiq, even if they are thousands of miles apart."

"Perhaps not. Cyberwarfare Unit 26165 is increasing the amount of social media noise on the asteroid belt story. I'm told a friendly Oxford professor is going to provide sound bites for us and specifically name China as being at high risk due to its huge landmass and high population density. But Chinese suspicion is an issue your strike planners will need to address," Popovkin said.

Bondarev looked at the map again. "We could spread the strike," Bondarev offered. "Over a wider area. Take out the Korla plant, but hit a couple of nearby areas too, which have no military or industrial value at all. Maybe keep the biggest hit for something of societal value, so that all focus is on that, and the Korla strike might attract less attention until the economic consequences become clear."

"The Chinese are even more secretive than us when it comes to such 'disasters,'" Popovkin agreed. "It might take weeks for them to even disclose the event, and longer still for them to confirm any suspicions that we were involved."

"They'll know as soon as the Mozprom gas salespeople start knocking on their doors offering to push more gas through Kazakhstan," Bondarev warned. "Mozprom can't be allowed to increase its activity until the strike is public or China will see straight through this. I assume we want to keep them guessing as long as possible."

"Good point," Popovkin nodded, then grimaced. "Kelnikov will have to let that ass Lapikov into the need-to-know circle. As Energy Minister, he has the influence on Mozprom we'd need to coordinate this, but he's been moaning to Avramenko to be brought in on Groza and this would make it look like Kelnikov is capitulating."

Bondarev suppressed a wry smile. None of this was news to him since it more or less confirmed what Lapikov's advisor, the Italian woman, had confided to him. The Energy Minister Lapikov had been lobbying President Avramenko to ensure he was given advance warning of any Groza strike that might impact his portfolio, while Defense Minister Kelnikov had been trying to keep his rival at bay.

"With respect, I would be concerned about providing too much information to Minister Lapikov. Comrade General," Bondarev said. "I cannot go into details, but I am not completely confident that the staff in his political office are entirely … reliable." Before Popovkin brought Lapikov into the inner circle, Bondarev had an idea he wanted to test. A little niggle in the back of his mind that concerned the beautiful but intense Roberta D'Antonia.

Popovkin narrowed his eyes and looked like he was about to ask Bondarev to explain, but then closed his mouth again. Sometimes, and especially where it concerned Kremlin politics, it was better for a man not to peer too closely into the darker corners. "So, your proposal?"

Bondarev stared thoughtfully out of the window. A strike on a remote target in China, multiple targets in fact. Undefended. With Groza, indefensible in fact. The risk of immediate retaliation was virtually zero. Payback would come, of that Bondarev was sure. But not within the immediate future. The operational calculus was straightforward, except for one element. "Yes, sir. That gas compression plant looks similar in size and scale to the Abqaiq facility. We used two Groza payloads on that strike and those satellites are now depleted and being retasked to surveillance duties. We propose to use the minimum ordnance necessary to ensure target destruction, but if we are to spread the attack to include one or more secondary targets, we can expect to expend at least two more Groza payloads. That will leave us with only twelve orbiting satellites for future contingencies, one of which is still experiencing problems with its propulsion system."

Popovkin frowned. "I have not been made aware that any of the Groza platforms are non-operational."

It has been in every report we have sent up the line for two months, Bondarev thought to himself. But he didn't want to argue the point. "I considered it a temporary issue and have not brought it to the General's attention. The platform is allocated to targets in South

East Asia and can be tasked for strikes in the region. But for now, it cannot be repositioned."

"And when are the next planned launches of satellites to replace the Groza units that have been expended?"

Bondarev sighed inwardly. *You know damn well there are none planned, or more importantly, budgeted for. We sacrificed the refit of the carrier Kuznetsov and just about bankrupted the Aerospace Forces budget putting sixteen of the monsters into orbit.* "We have an Angara A7 launch slot booked for January next year, but as yet, no payload for it. I'm keeping the slot open in case Groza production constraints…" *in other words, funding,* "… are lifted."

Popovkin looked like he was going to make a caustic remark, but bit it back. "Twelve satellites still give us potent capabilities, assuming you are able to bring the malfunctioning unit back online. But to address your earlier concerns, we had better hope the President and Minister Kelnikov are not planning an extended campaign of 'economic repositioning,' hadn't we?"

A week had gone past since Rodriguez and Severin had briefed their squadron on the mission to bring down a Russian satellite – the first truly offensive mission for the US Space Force in its 15-year history. And this was not just the take-down of a rogue satellite or other piece of errant space hardware; it was an attack on a foreign military satellite that O'Hare had just learned could *shoot back*.

Their mission was now taking place against the backdrop of a tit-for-tat shooting war in the Persian Gulf. Iran had hijacked another Saudi oil tanker and was shooting at any Saudi aircraft that came near its airspace. Commercial airlines were having to detour hundreds of miles north or south of the Gulf to avoid the risk of an accidental shoot down. The Saudi Navy had begun escorting vessels through the Straits of Hormuz and had fired on an Iranian missile boat that had come too close to one of its tankers. A Saudi tanker moored off the Emirates' coast had been sabotaged, probably mined, and the Saudis had blamed Iran. In retaliation, and despite the fact Russia had moved two squadrons of front-line stealth fighters into the region to support Iran, the Saudis had conducted a ballsy strike on an Iranian frigate in the Red Sea and put it out of action, claiming it had been sailing inside Saudi territorial waters.

Tehran had responded by threatening to turn Saudi Arabia to glass in a 'sea of nuclear fire.' TV pundits were saying that perhaps the only thing holding Iran back from carrying out its threat was the fact Saudi Arabia was known throughout the Islamic world as 'the protector of the two holy cities': Mecca and Medina. If an Iranian strike did any damage to either the Al-Haram Mosque in Mecca or the Prophet's Mosque in Medina, it was probable they would become the pariahs of the Islamic world. Both sites were in the Hejazi region of the Arabian Peninsula, two hundred miles from a logical target for retaliation such as the Saudi capital Riyadh, but a nuclear strike on Riyadh risked fallout that might affect the holy sites, and would certainly disrupt the pilgrimages of millions of Muslims, possibly for years. Saudi Arabia was clearly betting that Iran would not go so far.

O'Hare was sitting with Zeezee, poring over the schematics for a Russian 30mm autocannon on a desktop flat screen. "That's the same thing they have mounted in their Su-57 stealth fighter, right?" O'Hare asked the Chinese American.

"Correct." The Master Sergeant was economical with words. She was economical with everything, O'Hare reflected. No earrings, no makeup, whether on or off duty. Space Force regulations actually allowed 'modest' makeup and, regarding nails, stated that, "If worn by females, nail polish will be a single color that does not distinctly contrast with the complexion, detract from the uniform, or be extreme colors. Do not apply designs to nails or apply two-tone or multi-tone colors; however, white-tip French manicures are authorized." Zeezee also wore no nail polish. Her broad flat face wasn't unattractive – she had beautiful green eyes – but she rarely decorated it with a smile. She wasn't exactly the girl you'd want with you as a wingman for a night on the town, but O'Hare would take her any day if she was going into a stand-up fight.

"Did the RAF report say anything about laser targeting?" O'Hare asked.

"Yeah, it said they picked up no sign it was using a laser for targeting," Zeezee said. "That would have generated a heat signature, and they recorded none. A laser would require extra juice; not much, but enough that they might have opted to go without it if they thought electro-optical and infrared targeting was good enough to deal with space junk."

"OK," O'Hare said thoughtfully. "That might be a vector. Both infrared and electro-optical are slower than laser. We might be able to slam through at max thrust..."

"Blow the hell out of it and scream *Yippee-kay-ay mofo* on our way past?" Zeezee said, deadpan. "No dice, Captain." She pulled up a tactical display on the screen. It showed the 3D model of the Groza, which the RAF Spacecraft had created, and the US X-37, on a wire-style grid that O'Hare saw showed the two objects were at least twenty miles distant. "You will locate and confirm the target," Zeezee continued. "You will hold at 20 miles, orbit the target at minimum safe distance and obtain imagery..."

O'Hare pointed at the RAF's 3D model on the screen. "Brits already did that."

"And this is a different unit," Zeezee said. "It could have been built before or after the unit the Brits imaged. It may have different capabilities. We need to be sure before you put our X-37 in harm's way."

"But assuming there are no surprises, I *am* going to toast it, right?"

"Not exactly Space Force terminology, but yes. Using your own infrared targeting system, you will try to lock it up, advancing slowly until you do. If you cannot get a lock before minimum safe distance of 15 miles, you will abort. If you do manage to get a target lock..."

"I engage with HEL at maximum range and hope the laser can burn through from 15 miles out?" O'Hare said, completing the sentence. "Which, given particle dispersion, is frankly unlikely.

Lethal range is probably two to three miles. I am going to need to get up close and personal."

"Love the enthusiasm, Captain. But we don't want to risk Bertha," Zeezee said. "The RAF report indicated the Groza unit maneuvered when firing. Which means it is probably full of propellants such as tetroxide and hydrazine. Heat one side disproportionately, you may be able to nudge it out of orbit. Or better still, overheat its containment chambers, that propellant could blow." She gave O'Hare a slight smile. "You might be glad you are 15 miles out when that happens."

"It would be good to know at what temperature tetroxide and hydrazine cook off," O'Hare commented. "Give us an idea if we have any chance."

"I can chase that up," Zeezee nodded. They threw around a few more scenarios before Zeezee finally straightened and turned off the screen. "Permission to share something personal with you, Captain?" she said.

O'Hare looked in her eyes but saw nothing but the usual intense green staring back at her. "Uh, sure, Sergeant, go ahead."

"I have family in New York, right under the orbit of that thing. A father, mother and a sister. If you screw this up and that Groza gets past you, Russia will be pissed. And my family might die, along with a few hundred thousand other New Yorkers."

"I'll try not to let that happen, Sergeant," O'Hare said. "But a little personal motivation always helps."

Zeezee gave her a tight and not very sincere smile. "I advised Colonel Rodriguez to assign one of the other pilots we recruited for the engagement phase of this mission. Someone more … stable."

"OK then, so that's out there, thanks for the transparency."

"You're welcome, Captain. She also thanked me for my input, but declined," Zeezee said. "She said none of the other pilots had your combat experience or 'instincts.'"

"Clearly, or I wouldn't be here," O'Hare pointed out.

"No. Well, thank you for allowing me to speak freely," Zeezee said and coughed. "I'll see you at three for the tactical brief with Lieutenant Albers. And I'll get those propellant temperature estimates to you before then."

O'Hare was still processing Zeezee's little sharing moment, and couldn't quite let it go. "So, no concerns about my choice of wizzo? Albers is 'stable' enough for you?"

Zeezee didn't hesitate. "Lieutenant Albers is a fine weapon systems officer. I supported that choice. If that's all, I'll be going, ma'am." The Chinese American snapped off a sharp salute, turned to leave, and then turned back. "But it *is* a shame he isn't a pilot, ma'am."

O'Hare thought she caught the slightest of winks before Zeezee spun and left the room.

"Thank you for coming at such short notice, Ms. D'Antonia," Yevgeny Bondarev said. "May I introduce you to the 15th Aerospace Army's Chief Scientist, Anastasia Grahkovsky?"

D'Antonia had been staring at the woman from the moment she had been ushered into Bondarev's office. Called just two hours earlier and asked to travel to the Titov Research Center for a meeting with the General, she had dropped everything, of course, and ordered her car to take the emergency services lane on the freeway as she pushed frantically through traffic to get to Titov in time. Walking into the familiar office of General Bondarev, she had been surprised to see the strikingly bald woman sitting beside his desk, her scalp and hands covered in a patina of scars, her eyes milky and unseeing, a walking cane clasped between her thighs. The expression on her face was one of … irritation, more than anything else. She did not rise or extend a hand as Bondarev introduced her.

"Pleased to meet you," D'Antonia said, standing awkwardly.

When the woman didn't respond, Bondarev indicated a chair beside her and opposite his desk. "Please sit. I have explained to the Chief Scientist that you are principal advisor to Energy Minister

Lapikov. I have also explained that you expressed a not unnatural interest in our Groza technology."

"General, I hope I didn't step over any boundaries, I was simply..." D'Antonia began.

Bondarev waved her apology away. "Not at all. I understand your Minister's concerns, as does my commander, Colonel-General Popovkin. Hence this meeting," Bondarev said with a charming smile. "I have agreed with the General for you to receive a full briefing on the Groza system from its architect, Chief Scientist Grahkovsky. After this, you should be able to answer any question your Minister might have."

D'Antonia looked from Bondarev to the disturbingly mute woman in the chair beside her, and then back again. "Thank you, General, my Minister will be very grateful for the favor."

"Perhaps," Bondarev said, nodding slightly. He lifted a briefcase from the floor and adjusted his uniform. "Now, I have other matters to attend to. You may use my office for your discussion." He pointed to the coffee table where there were cups and glasses, water, tea and fruit. "Please help yourselves. If you need anything, my adjutant is outside. Good day." With that, he was gone and D'Antonia was left in the company of Anastasia Grahkovsky.

D'Antonia waited a moment in case the other woman should speak, but she continued to sit and stare out into the empty air, her head only slightly inclined toward Roberta as though she was listening to something from another room as well.

"Well, I have many questions, shall we start?" D'Antonia said at last, her voice echoing in the cavernous wood-paneled office. "How is your English? I also speak Spanish, or French."

"I am blind, not deaf, you don't have to yell. And my English is good enough, thank you," the woman replied drily. "What do you want to know?"

D'Antonia almost licked her lips. What did she, what did Western Intelligence, *not* want to know? She was being handed the intelligence coup of the decade, if not the century, and all because of the Russian love affair with internecine politics.

"Well, let's start with you. General Bondarev called you the architect of the Groza system. Have you been involved since its early development?"

The woman sat quietly, as though considering how to answer. "You may have noticed that I have certain ... distinguishing features," Grahkovsky said eventually. "The story of Groza is also my personal story, if you allow me to tell it?"

D'Antonia reached toward the samovar on the coffee table. "Of course. Please do. Would you like a cup of tea?"

"Yes, thank you," Grahkovsky said. "I received my injuries from flying glass in the Chelyabinsk meteor strike of 2013..."

"I have heard about that," D'Antonia said, wincing. She handed the teacup to Grahkovsky on a saucer, letting it touch her fingers so that she could take it and place it within reach. "I can't imagine what that must have been like," she said with genuine feeling.

"It was like being flayed alive, blinded and left to bleed to death," Grahkovsky said. "But thank you for your sympathy. As I grew up, I became more and more fascinated, some would say obsessed, by the phenomenon of meteor strikes. After I completed my university studies, I resolved to dedicate myself to ensuring that..." Grahkovsky paused, appearing to be marshaling her words, "... that never again would our world be taken by surprise by such an event."

"And so you created Groza?" D'Antonia frowned. "I'm sorry, I don't quite see the connection. I know Groza is a space-based weapons system, but how..."

"And there, you are already showing your ignorance," Grahkovsky said. "Why would you think it is a weapons system?"

D'Antonia floundered. "I ... well, the attack on Abqaiq..."

"Abqaiq? To my knowledge, the Saudi refinery was destroyed in a meteor strike, Ms. D'Antonia. Do you or the Minister have information to the contrary?"

D'Antonia felt heat rising up her neck. Had she been brought here to be treated like a fool? "My Minister has been led to believe so. And the Americans claimed in communications with the Saudis to possess intelligence showing that..."

"The *Americans?*" Grahkovsky raised her eyebrows. "You prefer to believe lies spread by our main enemy? Or rumors circulating in Kremlin corridors that your Minister has taken for fact?"

D'Antonia pushed down her frustration, took a breath, and spoke with as little emotion as she could. "Why don't you tell me what Groza is then, Chief Scientist."

"The public name for the system is *Opekun*, or Guardian. It was a name created for the early prototype program, but it stuck. As it moved into production phase, the program was internally renamed *Groza*, to provide a greater level of secrecy because it was decided the system could also have military applications."

Ah, now we get to the truth, D'Antonia thought. "Military applications?"

"Yes, Groza is what we have always claimed it to be, an early warning system for detecting the approach of near-earth space objects. And as such, it may one day save the planet from destruction," Grahkovsky said, taking up her cane and tapping it between her feet to emphasize her next words. "But it can also be used to map the objects already circling the earth today – satellites, space stations, space junk, spacecraft..." Grahkovsky smiled. "Map them in minute detail. With our Groza network we have been able to create the most complete map of man-made objects in orbit around the earth that has ever been created. Nothing bigger than a football can move up there, without us knowing about it – every American, Indian, Chinese or European commercial or military satellite, spacecraft or platform, dead or alive, can be tracked by us in real time. Our enemies can do *nothing* in space without our knowledge. We can target their surveillance satellites with perfect precision. Intercontinental ballistic missiles can be tracked from the moment of launch, their positions triangulated and data sent to the ground so they can be destroyed by our anti-missile defenses. It is still under development but one day soon we will have a sophisticated capability no other nation possesses. Perfect vision. Total protection, whether from a killer asteroid approaching earth

158

or a missile in the skies right over Moscow. *That* is what Groza will become."

D'Antonia sipped slowly at her own tea. Something did not jibe. "If the system is so powerful, how was it we did not detect the Abqaiq meteor strike?"

A thin smile flitted across Grahkovsky's lips. "You presume we did not."

"We detected it, but did nothing to alert the Saudis?" D'Antonia asked.

"I like your use of the word 'we,' Ms. D'Antonia," Grahkovsky remarked. "It seems your loyalties lie in the right place."

"My 'loyalties,' as such," D'Antonia replied, "lie with my Minister. If we had advanced warning of a strike on a major oil processing facility in Saudi Arabia, at the very least, my Minister should have been advised."

Grahkovsky laughed, a horrible, gurgling sound. "I said we could detect an asteroid with great accuracy, I did not say we could predict where it would strike with such accuracy." She put her teacup down and took up her cane again. "We estimated it would impact in empty desert west of Abqaiq, but we were wrong by a matter of about a hundred miles." Her eyes closed, as though she was suddenly processing something very complex. "Predicting the impact point of an object entering the atmosphere from space is not as simple as tracking an ICBM. We were able to identify the asteroid and track it perfectly. The atmospheric entry models we need to predict an impact point are not yet as perfect. But Abqaiq gave us valuable data with which to refine them."

The clinical and abstract way she spoke about the deaths of hundreds of people chilled D'Antonia. "We surely could have issued an alert. The public face of the Groza program is the detection of near-earth objects. To be able to provide warning of an event as destructive as Abqaiq would have been a major scientific coup for Russia and your Groza program. It would have reinforced your public cover story."

Grahkovsky grasped her cane in both hands. "Or created a major embarrassment if we had been wrong. It is still too early. We will need a hundred Abqaiqs before we can make any such predictions with confidence. But we *have* alerted the world to the broader danger."

"This nonsense about an unmapped asteroid field?" D'Antonia asked.

Grahkovsky tapped her cane hard on the floor, a hard knock that echoed around the room. "That is exactly what I mean. You call it nonsense. You, who have no reason to doubt, whatsoever. Groza detected that field. Groza allows us to map it. Groza is the reason we can predict, no matter how uncertainly, when the next collision will occur and where it will strike."

OK, Chief Scientist, D'Antonia thought. *I will bite.* "That would be..." She leaned forward in her chair. "That would be incredibly valuable information to my Minister. If you were willing to share it."

Grahkovsky clucked her tongue. "Of course I am or I would not be here. General Bondarev has ordered me to share it with you, but only unofficially. No offense to your Minister, but as I said, our impact models are still not perfect and the last thing our program needs is doubters and critics within the walls of the Kremlin. We are not yet willing to commit our predictions to Kremlin briefing papers."

"I understand," D'Antonia said. "I will provide that context in my brief to the Minister."

"And you commit to keep this for his ears only? We understand you may feel the need to make contingency plans, but you will find some cover story?"

Just tell me! D'Antonia felt like screaming at the woman, but counted to three and spoke slowly. "Of course. I think the truth is always the best cover story. If we initiate contingency planning, it would be because, as you say, we need to plan for this new threat — this unmapped asteroid field."

"Yes," Grahkovsky said, sitting back in her chair, taking her cane and slotting it into a gap in the chair between the cushion and the backrest, as easily as a swordsman would slide a sword into a scabbard. It was obvious she had been in Bondarev's office before. "That would do. The next significant collision with the asteroid field will take place sometime in the next 36, and we predict an impact similar in size to the explosion over Abqaiq. The impact footprint will be centered about fifty miles southeast of … Lincoln, Nebraska."

D'Antonia nearly dropped her cup. "Nebraska, USA?" She didn't buy the whole early warning system story at all. *But the fools were going to hit a target in mainland USA? Why?*

"Yes, I think there is only one Nebraska," Grahkovsky said tartly. "We can't be accurate to within more than about fifty square miles at the moment, but it's a relatively unimportant area…"

"I doubt the people of Lincoln, Nebraska think so," D'Antonia retorted.

"Socially, or economically," Grahkovsky continued, smoothly. "And before you ask, the General has conferred with his superiors, and we do not intend to alert the Americans to this risk. The uncertainties are too large, we might look like fools. But we will gain more invaluable data and…"

D'Antonia stood, putting her cup down with a clatter of porcelain. "This is madness. They will not believe this was an accident. They already suspect Russia of the Abqaiq strike. A strike on American soil? This will provoke a retaliation."

"Retaliation?" Grahkovsky scoffed. "Against nature, perhaps? For an act of force majeure? For an event that rattles a few farmhouse windows and scares a few cows? I'm sorry to ruin the conspiracy theory you apparently hold dear, Ms. D'Antonia, but there is no oil infrastructure in Lincoln."

D'Antonia tried to master her thoughts, and failed. She was overwhelmed by contradictions. Her AISE handlers had told her the stories about a new asteroid field were Russian disinformation. That American intelligence had confirmed Groza was a space to ground kinetic weapons platform. That the strike on Abqaiq could only have been carried out by Groza. Now, she was supposed to believe it had a nobler purpose, to predict meteor strikes, not propagate them. That the asteroid field was real and that in less than two days, there would be another strike. On the plains of *Nebraska*?

D'Antonia smoothed her skirt. "Excuse me for my outburst, Chief Scientist," she said carefully. "This period of increased risk from the new asteroid field, how long do we expect it will last?"

"Several months, possibly. The field is moving, passing across Earth's orbit, but it is quite irregular and will take some time before we are clear of it."

"I see," D'Antonia said, lifting her coat from the arm of the chair and picking up a folio she had brought with her. "Thank you for this briefing. Can I ask you to advise me if Groza detects future possible threats also? While a strike on Lincoln, Nebraska is not likely to rock the global economy, future strikes may not be so … remote. We may need to make contingency plans."

"Of course," Grahkovsky nodded. She folded her hands on the top of her cane. "I will see your office gets word of any future threats, if you demonstrate that you and your Minister can deal with the information discreetly." She stood, using the cane to lever herself to her feet, and keeping her face toward D'Antonia even though she could not possibly see exactly where she was standing. It was a neat trick. "Please don't misunderstand me, Ms. D'Antonia. I want to see Groza revealed to the world in all its technological glory, and for us to be able to share the alerts we are generating with the whole world. But not until we have perfected our collision models. To send out warnings based on inaccurate calculations may lead to unnecessary panic, loss of life and, not least, undermine the credibility of our system. I won't allow that."

"I understand," D'Antonia said, automatically reaching her hand out to shake and then pulling it back again. "Please thank the General for this opportunity. And I look forward to meeting you again some time."

Grahkovsky smiled, the first true smile D'Antonia had seen. It made the terrible mask that was her face soften into something much more human, almost beautiful. For the first time, D'Antonia felt she was seeing the person who was Anastasia Grahkovsky, not the scientist. "Thank you. I don't often hear that," she said.

Five minutes after the Italian woman had left the building and climbed into her waiting car, Bondarev returned to his office. Grahkovsky was seated again, pouring herself another cup of tea in a fresh cup, as the one D'Antonia had poured her had gone cold.

"That went well," Bondarev said, sitting himself at his desk. "Thank you."

"You listened?" Grahkovsky asked. She had expected he would, though he hadn't explicitly said so.

"Of course," he said.

"I wouldn't win any *Nika* acting awards," Grahkovsky grumbled. "I don't believe for a minute that she bought the story that Groza is some sort of glorified space junk tracking system."

"Don't underestimate yourself," Bondarev teased. "I remember your little performance in front of the Technical Committee, the day you stood there, showing off all your scars and daring us not to approve your precious weapon. *I* bought your act back then."

"Yes, well, I suspect she is rather more intelligent than you, Major-General," Grahkovsky said quite matter-of-factly. She drank her tea in one gulp and stood. "What happens now?"

"Well, it seems our Saudi and Iranian friends are happy to keep rattling their sabers at each other. Traffic in the Strait is backing up and the price of oil is still climbing."

"Such a shame they are just rattling sabers," Grahkovsky said, eyebrows arched. "It would no doubt do wonders for your precious oil prices if Iran nuked Riyadh into glowing green slag."

"That was sarcasm, yes? They may still decide to. But for now, you get back together with my staff and finish planning the strike on Korla," Bondarev said. "Meanwhile, I will be following the actions of our Italian friend very closely to see exactly what 'contingency plans' she puts in place."

Grahkovsky chuckled. "Do you have so little trust in the vetting capabilities of our vaunted Federal Security Service, General?"

"Trust, but verify, madam Chief Scientist," Bondarev winked. "Trust, but verify."

One of the things people noticed about Roberta D'Antonia was her aquiline nose. As a younger woman she had considered surgery to have it straightened, but had been persuaded its imperfection added a little personality to her face and, besides, it was a trait she shared with others in her family, so she kept it. Over the years, it had also shown itself to be a very capable lie detector.

And right now it was telling her something smelled to high heaven.

Sitting in the back seat of her car as it drove itself back to the Ministry of Energy on Moscow's Shchepkina Street, Roberta D'Antonia put a set of earbuds in her ears and brought up the digital assistant on her phone. She always worked on the assumption there were listening devices in the car monitoring her conversations and comms, but had no concerns about being overheard when she was just doing what any good ministerial assistant in her position would do.

"Siri, show me a satellite map of Lincoln, Nebraska please."

The map loaded onto her screen, and she scrolled around it. It was much as Grahkovsky had said. A small urban area, and a *lot* of fields and farms.

"Siri, are there any oil or gas plants near Lincoln, Nebraska?" she asked.

I don't see any oil or gas plants near Lincoln, Nebraska, the digital voice replied. *Do you want me to show you gas stations?*

"No. How about refineries, oil storage sites, oil pipelines?" she asked.

I don't see anything like that, Siri replied. *Would you like a list of heating oil suppliers in that area?*

D'Antonia suppressed a laugh. "No. Energy utilities. Are there any energy utilities?"

On the screen, a number of pins appeared. *Showing energy utilities in the area of Lincoln, Nebraska.*

Southeast of Lincoln, somewhere in a fifty square mile area, that's what Grahkovsky had said. D'Antonia put two fingers on the screen, zoomed it out and swiped it so that Lincoln lay in the upper right corner. South of Lincoln was a pin – the Sheldon Power Station.

"Siri, tell me about the Sheldon Power Station, Nebraska."

Sheldon Station is Nebraska's largest coal-fired electric generating facility, supplying enough electricity to serve 600,000 Nebraskans. It is consistently ranked as one of the lowest production-cost electric generation plants in the nation. Sheldon Station generates 225 megawatts of electricity. Power generated here is distributed to Nebraska's residents through transmission lines leading to Lincoln, Hastings and Beatrice, the voice said.

Interesting, but no. Knocking out the power to a few thousand households in Nebraska could hardly be on Russia's political agenda. She swiped the map further east, seeing another pin there.

"Siri, tell me about the, uh," she squinted at the small text, "the ... Cooper Power Station."

Cooper Nuclear Station is a boiling water reactor type nuclear power plant located on a 1,251-acre site near Brownville, Nebraska between Missouri River mile markers 532.9 and 532.5, on Nebraska's border with Missouri. It is the largest single-unit electrical generator in Nebraska.

What? "Repeat that."

Certainly. Cooper Nuclear Station is a boiling water reactor type nuclear power plant...

"Stop." Oh, shit. She pulled a tablet from a seat pocket, called up a map of the area around Lincoln and drew a line on the map between Lincoln and Cooper. The red pin marking the nuclear reactor was 59 miles from the center of Lincoln, as the crow flew. Which put it bang in the middle of the strike zone Grahkovsky had warned her about.

Cows and farmhouses, the scientist had scoffed. Sure. Cows, farmhouses *and* a goddamn nuclear reactor.

The destruction of a nuclear power station in the USA? To what end? To disrupt power supplies in *Nebraska*? To distract the USA with a nuclear emergency in its heartland? If so, again, why? The strike on Abqaiq she could understand, because the impact on world energy prices had been immediate. But a strike on a US nuclear plant in Nebraska? It simply made no sense. Unless it really was, as Grahkovsky claimed, a random event caused by an unmapped asteroid field.

She tapped her phone on her thigh, watching stalled traffic rush past as her car moved smoothly along the highway in the VIP lane. She *had* to report this to AISE. Whether she trusted Grahkovsky or not, it wasn't up to her to decide whether the Americans should be alerted to a possible strike on their nuclear facility or not. That was above her pay grade. She had to report it to AISE, and they would no doubt urgently alert US Homeland Security.

And then what, Roberta? she asked herself. Given it was just a single source report from the Italian security services, Homeland Security might ignore it. Or perhaps take some minor precautions; put the management of the nuclear plant on alert and raise the readiness levels of some local first responders. *Meteor strike on Cooper Power Plant? Yeah, right. Those Italians have been smoking the oregano again.*

Unless they were as concerned about Groza as her own service, were already tracking its satellites and concluded there was a real risk. In which case, a full-scale pre-emptive evacuation might be triggered.

Which would totally, and completely, blow her cover since the information could only have come from her briefing by Grahkovsky.

Oh, you *suini*. She smiled. She was starting to take a shine to the enigmatic Yevgeny Bondarev. Her first encounter, he'd given her a very cold shoulder. Second encounter, he'd set her a test. It was the sort of elegant misdirection she often indulged in herself. She was damned if she reported it to AISE and damned if she didn't.

She dropped the tablet down on the seat beside her.

A nuclear reactor accident?! She had no choice. First, she would call Lapikov and brief him on the meeting. Then, when she got home, she would code and send an urgent report to AISE.

And then? Well, if the Americans reacted to her report, she would probably get a knock on her door from a couple of men in black leather jackets inviting her to come and talk with them. In Moscow's Lefortovo prison.

Oh well, Roberta, she told herself. *It's been a ride. If you have to go down, you might as well go down because you tried to save a quarter-million people from meteoric fire and nuclear radiation.*

In her own way, Bunny O'Hare was also having a moment of self-reflection. O'Hare wasn't usually one to doubt her abilities, but the conversation with Zeezee had chipped her paint.

When she walked into a room full of pilots, she knew there would be people in the room with better reaction times, better technical skills, more experience and without a shred of doubt, more balanced temperaments. But there weren't any that were better combat pilots. Or none that she'd met.

With the Royal Australian Air Force over Syria, before she'd been transferred to 'non-combat duties', she had brought down two Russian-piloted Su-57s. Yes, she'd written off an F-35 herself after it took a punch in the guts and she'd had to land without wheels, but she'd made it home and so had the other aircraft in her flight, at least one of which would not have been alive but for her. In the Bering Sea conflict, her swarm of X-47 unmanned combat aircraft had claimed five Russian aircraft on the ground and nine, including a nuclear armed strategic bomber, in air-to-air combat.

On the deck of a *Zumwalt* destroyer off Okinawa, leading the hunt for her own rogue submersible *Orca* drone, she'd been able to read its silicon mind and persuade the *Zumwalt's* XO to ride out an EMP torpedo attack: allowing the *Zumwalt* to stay alive, kill the *Orca* and engage a Japanese destroyer force which could have turned the tide of battle ashore. That kind of cool counted for something, right?

Sure, she was a recent convert to space operations, and she'd never gone up against a Russian killer satellite before. But combat wasn't about the machines or the mechanics or the electronics, it was about the person behind the stick, right? Until the day when an AI was also calling the shots, in war you needed someone with the instincts and courage to do what was needed to fight and win. Forget politics, forget interpersonal relations, forget little expediencies like 'stability'.

Or was she missing something?

Nah.

Economic repositioning

Low earth orbit, 900 miles over Nova Scotia, Canada

The 250-kilowatt high energy laser, or HEL, on B for Bertha, was not an elegant weapon. It was stowed in the payload bay during launch and landing, and to be deployed under combat conditions, the payload bay doors were opened and the laser system elevated to allow the lens array a 360-degree field of fire. Deploying the weapon took an excruciating thirteen minutes. The US Army version was truck-mounted and relied on an auxiliary generator for power. In space, a compact hydrogen-oxygen fuel cell provided the needed power, but it could only be refueled on the ground, which meant the laser had a limited burn life. Every ten seconds of laser operation depleted the fuel source by three percent, giving the laser just five and a half minutes of firing time. The weapons officer on the X-37 crew could adjust the laser's 'pulse' rate from 0.1 second pulses to 'full beam' to extend the firing time, but a pulsed beam created less damage.

In the earth's atmosphere, the destructive power of laser weapons was degraded by atmospheric conditions, dust and airborne objects. In space, none of these applied, but the tendency of the excited light particles to interact with each other meant the focused laser beam would disperse with distance. In space, Bertha's 250-kilowatt laser could burn straight through quarter-inch steel plate at the range of a mile, through a fifth of an inch of aluminum at two miles, and over several minutes would melt metal at distances out to five miles.

No one expected it to be able to do so at a range of ten miles out from the Groza satellite currently winging through space over Canada, but the tense group of officers inside O'Hare's command center hoped it would not need to. The stolen Groza data had indicated it used a hydrogen peroxide propellant for station keeping and attitude adjustment, which had a flashpoint of 302 degrees. At ten miles, it was hoped Bertha's laser could heat the skin of the Groza's main body to 500 degrees, allowing the gaseous hydrogen peroxide to mix with the silver catalyst inside the body of the small rocket engines and either cause it to catastrophically decompose, blowing the satellite open from the inside, or cause the thrusters to fire spasmodically so that the satellite began to spin out of control. Sometimes even just dramatically heating a single surface on an object in space released enough energy to 'nudge' it out of orbit. Any of these results should ensure the satellite's destruction.

It would not exactly be a covert attack as far as Russia was concerned – they could easily identify the source of the attack as being a Space Force X-37. But it would be essentially invisible to the rest of the world.

"Holding at 15 point zero five miles," O'Hare announced. "Weapons?"

Albers ran the fingers of his left hand over a keyboard as he made minute adjustments to a toggle with his right. "HEL deployed and at full power. Set to quarter-second burst mode. Target acquired." They had spent the last hour completing a 360-degree orbit of the Russian satellite, photographing every visible surface. A quick review of the imagery by Zeezee's intel team had concluded it appeared to be a similar design to the one encountered by the RAF Skylon – and it fielded the same 30mm autocannon defensive system.

"Bertha, systems status?"

All systems nominal, Captain, the spacecraft's AI replied.

O'Hare looked over her shoulder at her mission commander, Rodriguez, who, together with Severin, made up the only audience in the cramped 615th Squadron command center at Morrell. She had no doubt the engagement was being followed closely inside a Pentagon situation room as well, but that didn't faze her. She had a job to do and just wanted to get about doing it.

"Permission to engage, ma'am?" O'Hare asked.

"Granted," Rodriguez said tersely.

"Shoot, shoot, *shoot*," O'Hare ordered Albers, who with a thumb atop his targeting toggle made one last check that his optical sights were centered on the large white dome over the cylinder of warheads and then fired.

The pulsing beam of the laser was almost invisible on the screens inside the command center – just the faintest glowing finger of light could be seen flickering between the X-37 and its target. But Albers had a thermal readout on a screen in front of him that was taking a reading from the metal skin of the satellite under his crosshairs and he started calling it. "120 degrees, 180, 230, 310, 355…"

O'Hare ran her eyes across her instruments and tightened her hand on her flight controls. She had an evasive sequence programmed that would send Bertha scooting backward at any sign of explosive decompression and approaching debris. And another if the satellite's conventionally armed autocannon gave off any tell-tale heat signature indicating it was being fired. She also kept her eye on the HEL's fuel status, watching it count down in decimal points as it burned precious hydrogen and oxygen to power the laser.

"Five hundred degrees, ma'am?" O'Hare asked. The globe of the earth spun dizzyingly below the satellite, a white expanse of cloud over Canada masking the ground below.

"Or thereabouts, Captain," Rodriguez replied. "The specs show radiation shielding between the outer skin and the fuel storage cells. That will probably absorb some heat."

"Four ten," Albers said, continuing his thermal countdown. "Four twenty. Four twenty-five. Captain, we seem to be plateauing. Recommend increasing pulse length to a half-second."

O'Hare ran her eye over the HEL fuel status again and grunted. "Pulse to zero point five, aye," she said. And under her breath, she muttered, "Come on you hunk of junk, *burn*."

"Heat anomaly on Groza 9," a flight engineer called suddenly, breaking the pre-dawn lull inside the darkened Groza control center at Baikonur and waking Maqsud Khan from a pretty enjoyable semi-sleeping state. "Fuel temperature critical!"

Maqsud knocked his coffee over in his haste to pull up the system status screen for Groza 9. The man was right. The satellite's fuel system status screen showed the temperature of the hydrogen peroxide inside the satellite's tanks had risen dramatically. He graphed the data with a click of his mouse ... what? In the space of less than a minute? Four hundred degrees? Hydrogen peroxide wasn't flammable, but it could vaporize at high temperatures. He was no aerospace engineer, but he was pretty sure that would Not Be A Good Thing.

System engineering was not his team's responsibility. He watched as the engineering team huddled over their monitors and began shouting at each other. With nothing better to do, he ran his eyes across the other environmental indicators on the satellite's systems and saw no other signs of malfunction. They'd never experienced a sudden jump in fuel temperatures before. It could be a faulty instrument reading?

"Four-thirty degrees and holding," the man up front called out above the babble of voices.

"Instrument check," the corporal in charge of the engineering squad called out, echoing the thought in Maqsud's mind. "And get the duty sergeant down here."

Sergeant Karas was a rare sight in the control center unless there was an officer present. Maqsud knew he'd be in the mess, drinking coffee with some of the other NCOs, or just sitting in an office somewhere on the base with his feet up and his eyes closed.

Lazy swine. The encounter with what Maqsud was sure was an RAF Skylon was still etched into his mind, even if Sergeant Karas had told him to ignore it. Leaning forward to his keyboard, Maqsud pulled up the targeting system for Groza 9. Its cameras and synthetic aperture radar were currently locked on a pre-programmed static target on the ground in Canada, and Maqsud did a quick lookup. Yeah, Royal Canadian Air Force Base Shearwater. It was scheduled to hold that target until it swung further southeast and locked instead on Hancock Field, home to the F-47 drones of the US Air National Guard 174th Attack Wing.

OK, autocannon vision … Maqsud tapped a key. The screen in front of him flickered, then showed the view from the electro-optical infrared targeting camera mounted on the Groza's defensive 30mm cannons.

What the hell? Automatically defaulting to infrared mode, the camera showed the autocannon was locked on a bright white flare that filled nearly two-thirds of the screen. Quickly changing the filter setting, Maqsud canceled the infrared view and pulled up a simple optical view. It showed nothing but the darkness and flickering points of fuzzy light that was the normal backdrop of space. He checked the autocannon targeting system log … *target lock*. The autocannon was tracking something, but it must be outside engagement range. He punched in maximum zoom on the targeting camera and … *oh, you dvornyag*.

As calmly as he could, Maqsud keyed the mike at this throat. "Targeting to engineering, I have an unidentified spacecraft on optical at ten miles. Lens flare indicates it has deployed an energy weapon. Designating target UI 1. Sending position. Recommend evasive maneuvers."

"Temperature rising again," the man up front called, a note of panic in his voice. "Four eighty!"

The five men in Maqsud's squad looked over at him in alarm as he stood and yelled at the top of his lungs, "Propulsion: evasive maneuvers. Weapons: give me manual targeting override on the autocannons. Now, dammit!"

The corporal in charge of the weapons squad stammered at him, "But … but Khan, the Sergeant has to…"

"The Sergeant is not here," Maqsud spat. "Do it!"

"Four ninety degrees," Albers said, a note of satisfaction in his voice. "The half-second pulses did it. We should break through five hundred any second and…"

Two things happened. On the targeting screen in front of O'Hare, the Groza satellite suddenly skittered sideways. "I've lost

173

target lock," Albers said, frantically swiveling the crosshairs of the HEL and trying to keep the satellite centered. A tone in O'Hare's ears told her the laser had stopped firing as soon as it lost the target.

A second tone told her that Bertha was now under fire instead. Her AI routine kicked in immediately, firing the X-37's forward and bow thrusters, sending it skating diagonally backward away from the Russian spacecraft.

"Enemy counter-fire," she said calmly. "Evading."

Bertha's combat AI had no trouble seeing the heavy 30mm slugs that were flying through space toward her at around three thousand feet a second. On a tactical monitor on the wall in front of her, the AI projected the trajectory of the Russian shells. *Oh, you're good,* O'Hare thought to herself. Whether AI or human, whoever was behind those guns knew their business. As Bertha maneuvered, the gun adjusted its aim to lead the 30mm slugs into her anticipated position. A battle of algorithms was playing out, as Bertha jinked and rolled, while the Russian gunners continuously adjusted their aim and kept a stream of metal flying at the X-37.

O'Hare didn't panic. At ten miles distant the first slugs from the Russian cannon were still five seconds out and were flying wide. Those fired at her current position were still fifteen seconds out. If Bertha sat still, or if she just kept following the same vector, they *might* catch and shred her.

But O'Hare had no intention of sitting still.

She reached for her throttle and stick. "Taking manual control. Reversing 140 and bugging out."

"Retracting HEL," Albers said. "Powering down and safing." A moment later, he grunted, "Pilot, you have full propulsion authority."

With a flick of a switch on the throttle, she seized manual control of the X-37 and hauled back on the flight stick. It might have been her imagination, but even though her command inputs were being sent up to the orbiting spacecraft at near the speed of light, she nearly exploded in frustration as precious milliseconds passed before she saw the spacecraft respond on her heads up display, and flip on its axis so that it was pointing away from the Russian satellite. She pushed the throttle forward, engaging the X-37's powerful rear thrusters so that it quickly accelerated at a tangent away from the incoming fire.

"Separation?" she asked after a long minute.

"Eighteen miles four hundred feet," Albers said. "Still showing incoming fire."

Oh give it up will ya, O'Hare urged the Russian gunner, human or AI or whatever. *I'm wasting valuable fuel here and you aren't going to hit shit.*

"Twenty-three miles," Albers said a moment later. "Target has stopped firing."

O'Hare flicked a look over her shoulder at Rodriguez. "I'll take Bertha out to fifty miles, ma'am. Pretty sure they'll still be able to see us, but they must know they can't expect to hit us that far out with that kind of projectile velocity."

Rodriguez's voice sounded a little shaky. "Make it a hundred miles, Captain. We need to review the data from that engagement and adapt our strategy. Taking those birds out with an anti-satellite missile from the ground may be the only way after all. We nearly got our asses handed to us."

"Why so pessimistic, ma'am?" O'Hare shook her head and turned back to her controls, plugging in a new position. "They never got close. I'm guessing they got a little hot under the collar, an alarm went off somewhere and a human jumped behind those guns. But I admit that Ivan knows we're out here now and we mean them harm."

"So he's going to be ready for us next time," Rodriguez nodded. "We've lost any element of surprise."

As O'Hare and Albers pulled X-37 B for Bertha back to a distance where they would be little more than a bright dot in the optics of the orbiting Groza, Maqsud Khan was standing uncomfortably beside Sergeant Karas in the office of their commanding officer, Captain Alexei Kozytsin. Watching the interrogation via a screen on the wall beside them, his fingers steepled under his chin as he listened to what Maqsud felt was some pointedly intimidating questioning, was none other than Major-General Yevgeny Bondarev.

"You opened fire on an American spacecraft, *on your own authority?*" Kozytsin spluttered. "Where was Lieutenant Solenko?"

"Lieutenant Solenko is in hospital, Comrade Captain," Maqsud frowned, reminding him.

"Yes. Of course. Where were you, Sergeant?" the Captain asked, turning his ire on Karas.

Karas was a world champion at covering his own ass. He looked down at the small pad of paper he held in one hand. "Comrade Captain, I was alerted to the temperature anomaly on Groza 9 at 0425 hours while I was in conference with Sergeant Deripaska in the administration block..."

In conference? Playing cards and drinking brandy-laced coffee, you mean, Maqsud thought to himself.

"I ran to the control center immediately, arriving at 0432 hours." Karas checked his notes again. "As I arrived, I was told by Corporal Prokhorov of Engineering that Corporal Khan had identified a US spacecraft laser weapons system as the cause of the temperature anomaly, had assumed weapons authority and engaged the US spacecraft with cannons. By the time I had taken his report, Corporal Khan had ceased firing and the US spacecraft, if that is what it was, had withdrawn."

"With respect, Comrade Captain," Maqsud pleaded, "AI image analysis confirmed the target as a US X-37C spacecraft and imagery showed that what looked like a laser weapons system had been deployed. It must have been the source of the attack."

"You will answer questions, Corporal, not offer opinions," Kozytsin barked. "Why did you feel it necessary to override the automated defense protocols? Those protocols exist to protect the satellite if it is threatened. They were not invoked, so clearly the satellite was *not* threatened."

"Captain, the internal temperature was rising to a dangerous ... the American laser..."

"The Americans could have been using the laser for imaging. But you decided it was an attack. You could have waited for Sergeant Karas to arrive and assess the situation, but you acted precipitously and without authority you fired a weapon at an American spacecraft."

Maqsud lowered his gaze; there was nothing in the accusation that he could refute.

Off to the side, on the teleconference screen, Maqsud heard a cough, and they all turned to see Bondarev lowering his hands from under his chin and folding them in front of him. "And thank God the corporal did so," he said. "Captain Kozytsin, what is the flashpoint of high-test hydrogen peroxide?"

Kozytsin frowned and flushed slightly. "Comrade Major-General, I don't..."

Bondarev waved at him to be silent. "Corporal Khan?"

"Five hundred degrees Fahrenheit, Comrade General," Maqsud said.

"Thank you. And tell me, Sergeant Karas, does your little notepad tell us what the temperature of the fuel cell inside Groza 9 was, at the time the American spacecraft was forced by Corporal Khan to break away under fire?" Karas started flipping through his notes, but Bondarev did not wait. "I can save you the trouble, Sergeant. My staff tells me the fuel reached four hundred and ninety-two degrees. They also tell me that if that fuel had vaporized, it would have interacted with the silver-coated arrays in the Groza's engines and explosively decomposed, almost certainly resulting in the complete destruction of the satellite." He paused and let his words sink in. "Corporal Khan, please step forward."

Maqsud took a single step toward the Captain's desk and kept his face fixed on the screen, saluting as he did so.

"Corporal Khan, I will be recommending to General Popovkin that you are recognized for your initiative and receive the Medal of Merit for Space Exploration. Step back."

Maqsud saluted and retreated to stand beside a glowering Sergeant Karas.

"Captain Kozytsin, I have called a staff meeting in Titov in fifteen minutes to discuss the attack by US Space Force on our Groza. You will be dialed in from Baikonur. Before then, I expect you to have gathered all the available data and intelligence regarding this attack and be prepared to answer any and all questions from my staff officers." Bondarev leaned toward the camera. "Your ability or inability to do so will be regarded as a test of your suitability to continue as commander of Groza operations, Baikonur, is that clear?"

"Yes, Comrade General!" the Captain said, snapping to attention.

The teleconference screen went dark as Bondarev killed the feed.

Maqsud couldn't help feeling glad to see Kozytsin and Karas looking as pale as he had felt just five minutes earlier.

Kozytsin glowered at Maqsud, then held out a hand to Karas. "Give me those damn notes, man. And get me the Chief Systems Engineer on the telephone."

Meany Papastopoulos had just had a glorious three days leave and wasted it wonderfully on food and wine and a magnificently bloody bar room fight with a smart arse in a pub in Inverness who'd made the mistake of joking to a girl he was talking to that he probably also needed mechanical assistance in the bedroom. With Meany's fifty-pound boot on his throat, the guy had both apologized and bought Meany, his friends and the girl a round of drinks.

It had been a well-earned furlough, a fitting conclusion to a week in which he'd delivered an intel coup that had brought kudos to the RAF, and brought his Skylon home to a picture-perfect landing in

Lossiemouth. Ahead of him was a rather less exciting week of writing up reports on the mission, followed by some mandatory diversity training before he and Angus could get back to the business of getting the Skylon ready for its next trip into space in about a month.

Or so he thought.

Until he had been woken by a message from Squadron Leader Bear, calling him to an urgent briefing. As he thumped down the corridor into the briefing room at Lossiemouth, he saw Bear, plus the short, chubby, tobacco-chewing intel officer Aston, and the three other Skylon flight commanders, two men and a woman. He nodded to them all as he 'sat.' Meany didn't need a chair, he just locked his exoskeleton into a balanced semi-squat and it held itself upright.

Bear looked at his watch. "Nice of you to join us, Flight Lieutenant Papastopoulos. All present, then," Bear commented, though it was still one minute to the hour. "Lady and Gentlemen, we have been tasked with a covert operation of significant import. As we speak, the Skylon is being prepped for launch at 1300 hours tomorrow…"

The pilots all exchanged looks, and there was more than one set of raised eyebrows.

"Yes, this is the quickest turnaround we have ever attempted. We are not cutting corners, but we are testing the limits."

Meany raised a hand.

"No, Flight Lieutenant, this is not an exercise; this is a combat mission." He paused to let that sink in. "A joint services operation in collaboration with US Space Force. Mister Aston, if you please?"

"Thank you, sir," the warrant officer said, clicking a button to bring up an image Meany recognized immediately. "You will all be familiar with this beasty by now. The Russian Groza kinetic space-to-ground projectile weapon. If you have not done so, I urge you to acquaint yourselves with Meany's contact report, and the recently forwarded US Space Force contact report, especially their descriptions of its twin 30mm autocannon defensive armaments."

There was a glint in the portly man's eye and a small, ever-present plug of chewing tobacco under his lip, which caused him always to speak in a rather wet voice. He moved to the next screen in his presentation. "This is the orbit of a Groza satellite we shall designate X-two. X-two is currently orbiting on a track that takes it along the East Coast of the USA, over Canada and Greenland, and then across Europe, the Middle East and Asia..." The screen showed a glowing green track on a rotating globe. "I will now show on the globe in red the potential attack footprint for this satellite, with major civilian population areas and military bases highlighted. Any one of these could be hit by Groza X-two within ten minutes of launch, with the force of a Hiroshima-sized nuclear weapon."

Meany leaned forward. The green line expanded to become a wide, transparent red belt covering the surface of the earth that RAF and US Space Force analysts had estimated fell inside the Groza's possible range. As the globe turned, Meany saw cities up and down the East Coast of the USA, Ottawa in Canada, Edinburgh and Glasgow in Scotland, Belfast, Leeds and Manchester in the UK, Amsterdam, Leipzig and Dresden in the European Union, and further east, Istanbul, Ankara, Baghdad, Basra and Riyadh. But the number and type of the military sites that fell under the Groza's footprint were what really shook him. Nearly every US Army, Navy and Air Force Base on the US East Coast, including Kennedy and Cape Canaveral space centers, fell conveniently under the red band. In the UK, the British naval base at Clyde and Royal Air Force Base Fylingdales. In Europe, NATO bases such as Leeuwarden and Alanbrooke lay in the footprint, while in the Middle East, that single Groza could hit targets in Turkey, or NATO and US bases on the Arabian Peninsula. He couldn't help being a bit relieved to see Lossiemouth lay outside the projected range of the satellite, but he also knew it was capable of being repositioned, so that was an illusory comfort.

"Good God," the woman beside him said quietly.

"Yeah, but ... I mean, they can already hit any of those targets with air or sub-launched hypersonic missiles," Meany told her quietly, trying to cheer himself up. "So, what's the big deal?"

"A hypersonic missile can be detected and, theoretically, intercepted," the woman said. "These kinetic weapons can launch undetected, and hit at Mach 10. They're invisible until they hit atmo and unstoppable once they do."

"Yeah, ok, that's…"

Aston plowed on. "I mentioned this is a joint services operation. Our governments have agreed that Russia needs to be shown that we will not tolerate the weaponization of space in this way. Our objective is the total destruction of Groza X-two."

Oh, this is going to be ugly, Meany thought to himself. *Tactically, and politically.* On the other hand, like the pilots around him, he was leaning forward in anticipation.

"US Space Force has an X-37C spacecraft in orbit which is shadowing this monster. They have it locked up, but their craft lacks the weapons system needed to destroy it. Their high energy laser system does not have the range needed to safely engage without being counter-attacked by the Groza's close-in weapons system. As we speak, the Skylon is being fitted with an advanced short-range multispectral seeker space-to-space missile pod." Aston coughed and brought up a final graphic showing icons for the Skylon, X-37 and Groza, and what looked like missile attack vectors. "The mission is simple. You will rendezvous with the US X-37 and synch targeting data. Combining the X-37 and Skylon targeting data, we will then move to a firing position and engage this Groza satellite with missiles at long range, negating its onboard ballistic defenses. Questions regarding mission objectives?"

Several hands shot up. "These things can be repositioned," Meany noted. "We knock this one down, what is to stop Russia moving another into its place?"

"I suspect we will address that dilemma with appropriate resolve if it arises, Flight Lieutenant," Bear said. He nodded to the woman beside Meany.

"Missiles will need to track in infrared or active radar seeking mode to attack from extreme range," the woman said. "Is there any intel on whether these monsters have jamming capabilities?"

"None," Aston said. "But between the US X-37 and our Skylon, we are confident we can lock it up and keep it locked." The woman pursed her lips. They all knew he was speaking with untested confidence. The RAF had extensively tested its space to space missile against orbiting space junk. It had never gone up against an enemy that could both maneuver and shoot back. But the confidence wasn't completely misplaced. If they could lock up the Groza, a homing missile was almost impossible to evade in space, and very difficult to destroy with close-in weapons. Few of the usual strategies for evading air-air missiles in air combat down near the surface would work in space.

"It doesn't need sophisticated jamming capabilities," a man in front of Meany grunted. "It can just spit out a few big clouds of chaff and flares between our missiles and itself and move out the way."

Aston was getting annoyed. "The specs provided by US Space Force, which you've all reviewed, I trust, show no electronic countermeasures system, no 'chaff' or flare dispenser. So can we please drop the hypotheticals and..."

"They didn't show a bloody 30mm cannon on the thing, either, but the US contact report shows this one had two, just like the swine we came up against," Meany said.

"Hence we will engage at extreme range, and with a salvo of missiles that should overwhelm any close-in weapons system," Bear said.

"Sir?" the woman beside Meany spoke up. "A successful missile hit will create ninety-something tons of debris that will slowly spread and probably keep orbiting for years. Have we considered other options?"

"The Americans tried a laser, for exactly that reason, yes. And so we are back to missiles, I'm afraid," Aston replied.

"Ground-based systems interference?" Meany asked. "We know Ivan tracks every Skylon launch. If he sees us shaking hands with a US X-37 in the neighborhood of its Groza, he could choose to intervene with ground-based defensive systems ... anti-sat missiles, ground-based lasers..."

"Yes, he could, Flight Lieutenant," Aston replied. "And we can expect Russia is on alert after the first US attack. But we are confident US Space Force can give us plenty of warning of an anti-sat missile launch, and ground-based lasers shouldn't be able to interfere with a space-space missile engagement."

"This isn't the bloody Death Star, ladies and gentlemen," Bear said. "It is a soon to be defunct pile of Russian space junk and the people in this room are the leading experts at making it so." He waited briefly to see if there were more questions before continuing. "Right, then. Crew roster..."

There had been a number of envious looks and even an unsubtle groan when it had been announced the pilot in charge of the engagement phase of the mission would be Meany. None of the other pilots were surprised – he had after all acquitted himself handily during the RAF's first contact with a Groza – but there wasn't a pilot in the room who didn't want to be the one behind the stick when they took down that satellite. Takeoff, transition, contact or deployment and landing were all challenging phases of a Skylon mission, but everyone in the squadron wanted to get a kill on their record.

He hoped none of them knew voodoo, or there would be a jealous pilot in their quarters somewhere on Lossie pushing pins into a Meany doll pretty soon.

Meany waited until they had all left and approached Squadron Leader Bear. "Sir, a word?"

"Yes, Meany?"

"Any chance you can set up a call between myself and my US counterpart before we hit orbit?" he asked. "It would be nice to know who I'm working with up there."

It wasn't the first time the RAF, or Meany himself, had worked in concert with US Space Force. As the only two alliance powers

183

fielding remotely piloted spacecraft, they'd exercised together to establish communications protocols and identify areas for potential collaboration. The smaller US spacecraft was designed to stay in orbit for longer periods, was more agile and better suited to long-term multifaceted missions, at which it excelled. The larger RAF machine could lift bigger payloads into space, and had a faster turnaround time from landing to relaunch, but it was not designed for missions of extended duration. Most recently, the Skylon had been used to lift a nine-ton US Space Force prototype refueling module into orbit to allow the X-37 to test the potential for mid-mission refueling.

Bear pulled at an earlobe as he weighed the request. "That should be possible, Flight Lieutenant," he replied. "I'll find out who your opposite number will be and put you in touch." He put a hand on Meany's shoulder. "But you will promise me to use this opportunity to enhance relations between our services, not destroy them, yes?"

"Yes, sir," Meany replied, saluting. "I shall do my best to avoid antagonizing our allies." *Assuming the other party does theirs*, he added to himself. He turned to go.

"Sit a minute would you Meany," Paddington said suddenly. "I'd like to get your thoughts on something."

Squadron Leader Bear hadn't chosen the 'Paddington' moniker for himself. He'd have preferred something like 'Grizzly' and tried a couple of times in his early career to insinuate it into conversations with his fellow pilots, but it hadn't stuck. 'Paddington' had. Newer pilots often had their names stenciled under the cockpit of an aircraft for the sake of *esprit de corps*, and it had struck Bear as slightly absurd to see Flight Lt. Greg 'Paddington' Bear stenciled on the fuselage of an RAF Tornado. Hardly something that would strike fear into the hearts of the enemy is a spy camera got a photo of it.

'Meany' – now that was a good moniker. He hadn't met Meany before he joined RAF Space Command, and knew it was just short form for Anaximenes, but a better name for a man bolted into a military exoskeleton would have been hard to find. He watched fascinated as Meany levered himself into a sitting position using just the frame of his exoskeleton. The man had his own built in chair.

Bear sat in one of the chairs recently vacated by the Skylon squadron members.

"If this is about that brawl at the pub sir, there was just cause," Meany said. "The damn ignorant Scotsman was besmirching the proud history of the RAF and I…"

"I'm sure there was, as you say, just cause," Paddington said. "No. It's more about your next step Flight Lieutenant." He gestured at the walls around him, adorned with charts, maps and occupational health and safety notices. "I find myself here, at the sunset of a satisfying, some would say trailblazing career…" He shot a glance at Meany to see if the man might scoff at that, but to his credit, Meany kept a completely straight face. "… the Squadron Leader of a squadron with a single craft."

"Six crews, sir," Meany interjected. "Ground support personnel, administrative personnel, intelligence officers, meteorologists and engineers…"

"Yes, yes, not my point," Paddington continued. "The sunset, as I was saying. And I must give some thought to my successor. Now, 11 Group higher ups could of course parachute someone into my chair, but I have enough conceit to think that if I named a worthy successor from within our own ranks, that person might have a damn good shot at the job."

"You're thinking Joffrey sir?" Meany asked, missing the point entirely. Caroline Joffrey was one of Meany's fellow pilots, and certainly fancied herself as CO material. "She'd be my pick too," Meany continued. "Smart as a whip, steady hand under pressure. That landing last year when she had the flame-out in the port engine ten miles high? Damn impressive."

"Joffrey, yes, would be a person one could choose," Bear nodded. "But this is an unorthodox command, as I've tried to impress on the Air Vice Marshall. And it may benefit from an … unorthodox … leader."

"Not Bargini sir, please," Meany said, looking pained. "The man is a complete tosser. My old grandad once told me there is a fine line between being funny, and being a clown, and Flight Lieutenant Bargini is living proof of that, sir."

Now it was Bear who had to try to keep a straight face. "A tosser, yes, quite. So, to the matter at hand. What do you see as your next step, Meany?"

"Look, sir," Meany said, gesturing at his exoskeleton. "I realize I'm not exactly the belle of the ball. And I know I lost my head during that contact with the Russian satellite. My instinct was to blow the thing out of orbit and you were completely right to countermand my order..." He stuck his chin out. "But I love piloting the Skylon sir, I love being a part of Space Command and I would be deeply disappointed if a momentary lapse in judgement saw me transferred to another unit. Respectfully. Sir."

Paddington sighed. "Dammit man, I am asking you whether you could see yourself assuming command of this squadron when I move on! With a little mentoring, in the fulness of time etcetera etcetera..."

Meany blinked a couple of times. "Sorry sir, for a moment there I thought you were suggesting you would consider putting my name forward for Squadron Leader."

"And if I was?"

"Well, if you was, were, to do that..." Meany said carefully. "I would, again respectfully, decline."

"Good, wonderful ... sorry, what?" Paddington stuttered, his ears finally catching up with his mouth. "You would decline?"

"In a heartbeat sir," Meany said. "Unless of course the alternative was to serve under that twat Bargini."

Paddington frowned. Not exactly the turn of conversation he had planned.

Meany could see the consternation in his face apparently. "Sir, these tin legs can't put me back into the cockpit of a fighter jet, but they've done one better and put me into the cockpit of a spacecraft. Virtually, at least. It's my dream job and I wouldn't trade it for yours in a month of Sundays." He shifted uncomfortably in his frame. "Though ... of course ... I am sure you find it ... you are extremely capable at it, sir, but it takes a certain mentality I don't have. Is what I mean."

"I see," Paddington said, although he didn't, really. "These opportunities don't come along every day you know Meany," he said. "And you may not get Bargini, or Joffrey, but some other officer instead who you also consider a 'tosser' or a 'twat' and where would you be then?"

"Working in the private sector, I suspect sir?" Meany shrugged. "But still in a cockpit. I get calls at least once a month from Boeing, SpaceX or Reaction Engines asking if I'd like to jump ship when I hit my next discharge date."

"Right then," Paddington said. "Good for you, and all that. Glad we cleared that up."

Meany levered himself upright and stood at ease with his hands behind his back. "But you have my sincere thanks for even considering me sir," he said. "And please take a long hard look at Flight Lieutenant Joffrey. I suspect that one day, perhaps soon, we will be going to war up there, and she's the one I'd want calling the shots if it isn't you."

Roberta D'Antonia's apartment in Moscow was a modest two-bedroom split-level that fronted Sokolniki Park on the edge of the Meshchansky District, where the Energy Ministry offices were located. On the money Lapikov was paying her, she could have afforded a much more upmarket neighborhood, but after the walled expat compounds of Riyadh, she enjoyed the ordinariness of Sokolniki with its tree-lined streets, local markets and squares full of grandmothers and grandchildren.

She'd briefed Lapikov on her meeting with Grahkovsky on her way home. "Surveillance system?" he had muttered on the telephone. "They expect me to discount everything I have heard about Groza and believe it is just some sort of glorified space surveillance system? That Abqaiq was a freak accident?" He suddenly sounded worried. "If that briefing was a sham, engineered by the Defense Minister in the hope I will take the information and use it to make a fool of myself, it shows the President is deliberately keeping me at arm's length on this. Why?"

D'Antonia had got where she had in her working life by speaking truth to power, and she had continued the policy with Lapikov. "It is simple. Either he is protecting you, Minister, or he does not trust you."

"I need you to help me get ahead of this, D'Antonia. I have heard that fool Kelnikov is lobbying for further Groza strikes against targets in the Gulf, in support of our Iranian allies. If their aim was to shore up oil prices, they've done that. Anything more will tip the world into economic anarchy. I need to know what Kelnikov and the President are planning!"

Now it was Saturday morning, and Lapikov's political concerns were just one of her worries. Fourteen hours had passed since she had sent her report to AISE. To facilitate this, the Italian intelligence service had provided her with a rather unique electronic 'dead letter box' for filing her reports. She was too valuable to risk face-to-face contact with an AISE handler. And she was too highly placed to expect that she was not under some sort of electronic surveillance, either through listening devices in her home, surveillance of her phones and internet accounts, or old-fashioned physical surveillance.

In a bygone era, D'Antonia would have been equipped with a miniature digital radio transmitter capable of sending and receiving encrypted burst transmissions, but even something as easily concealed as that could give her away if the local intelligence services filtered out the blip of energy from her signal from all the background noise of her block of apartments. So instead, AISE had given her a refrigerator.

A connected refrigerator that automatically monitored how much milk, eggs, juice, bread and mineral water she had at home and ordered more from a local supermarket when she was running low. She could also call up a list of frequently bought items and add them to her order before it was sent. Penne pasta was C32, tinned pomodori F14, plain flour C40, vanilla yogurt Y1, peach yogurt Y4 … A typical shopping list looked like this:

C32 x 1

C40 x 1

F14 x 6

Y1 x 2

The shopping list doubled as code and was intercepted by the local AISE listening station. It was quite ingenious, except it meant she had a cupboard full of pasta, unopened cans of tinned tomatoes and dried fruit. But if she was raided by the Russian security services, all they could conclude was that she was a hoarder.

She had marked her message *Urgenza Estrema* – Extreme Urgency – to ensure it would not languish in a digital inbox somewhere.

A new but highly placed source inside the 15th Aerospace Army (reliability unknown, information unverified) has stated that Russian authorities expect there will be a new meteorite strike in the next 36 hours, which will hit an area within 50 square miles of Lincoln, Nebraska, USA. NOTE: The Cooper Nuclear Power Plant lies within this footprint.

The source further stated the strike was detected by the new Russian Groza system, which is the final iteration of a program for the detection of near-earth objects previously designated 'Opekun' or Guardian, and not a weapons platform. The system was developed in response to the Chelyabinsk incident in 2013. It comprises a network of 16 satellites and is intended to detect near-earth asteroids/meteors and predict their impact points if they enter the earth's atmosphere. The source said Groza is also being used for military purposes (hence the secrecy around it) to create a real-time map of all objects in orbit around the earth and to provide targeting data to Russian anti-satellite and anti-missile systems. When challenged, the source was emphatic that the threat from the unmapped asteroid field claimed by Russian authorities is real and the next strike will be in the vicinity of Lincoln, Nebraska. AGENT COMMENT: I do not know the source well enough to assess the veracity of this information.

She looked at her watch. If Grahkovsky had told the truth, the strike was less than 24 hours away now. It also meant that if AISE had acted quickly to inform the CIA (say two hours), and the CIA had acted quickly to inform authorities in Nebraska (say three hours), then in Nebraska, authorities had been sitting on the information about a possible meteor strike on their Cooper nuclear plant for nearly nine hours.

Most Saturday mornings, she pulled on her running gear and put her swimsuit in a bag with a towel, before jogging through the park to the Basseyn swimming center inside the park. After ten brisk laps of the pool, she would jog back to her apartment, throw down another espresso and a bowl of yogurt and muesli before showering and dressing, then go to the Sokolniki markets where one of the old men who virtually lived in the square would usually accommodate her with a game of chess or backgammon. They loved trying to teach her Russian, teased her with gap-toothed smiles and traded shots of vodka with her as they won or lost. She had become almost as fond of them as they were of her.

Such a creature of habit. Habit and discipline. They were necessary to lull any watchers, but she knew that today she would have trouble concentrating on her chess game.

She would be checking her cell phone every five minutes for the news bot she had set up to warn her as soon as headlines broke about US authorities reacting to any sort of emergency in Nebraska. She'd decided if there was the slightest chance her cover had been blown, she was not going to wait around to be arrested.

She had money, passports and weapons in a bag in a locker in a nearby gym, a second apartment rented through a cut-out, and a car parked in an easy to reach storage facility. She had multiple escape routes scoped, but the best would be a straight 700-mile drive to Warsaw, via Belarus. It went through one rather sleepy border post on the way out of Russia. If the alert came through now, she could be in Warsaw by late tonight and then on a plane to Sweden, where she had options even AISE didn't know about.

She poured herself a fresh juice and then rolled out her yoga mat in the sunshine near her window. She could feel her pulse racing as her flight instincts started kicking in. She needed to calm down. Stretch. Breathe. Get a little perspective. Her cell phone buzzed and she grabbed it off a nearby chair, nearly dropping it as she thumbed it on. A message from her hairdresser reminding her she had an appointment.

Calm down? *Magari!*

Yevgeny Bondarev was also having trouble staying calm. Why was it his mother country seemed intent on stumbling from one glorious national calamity to another? Forget Tsarism, Communism, World Wars One and Two, the Cold War and Putin, even in his time in the Russian Aerospace Forces, Bondarev had been involved in three. The Turkey-Syria war in which Russia joined enthusiastically, expecting a short sharp victory, only to find itself wading in blood for three long years before calling defeat a victory and bringing its forces home. The battle for Bering Strait, an ill-advised military misadventure during which a group of disaffected politicians and generals attempted a coup against the then President, which had nearly resulted in an all-out nuclear war with the USA. And now … this. Whatever 'this' was. Not a war. Not even a battle. Economic sabotage by force of arms, that was the closest he could come to giving it a name.

Sitting in his office and waiting for his Ops Intelligence Chief to join him, he drummed his fingers on his desktop. Russia had known for fifty or more years that its economy was overly dependent on oil and gas exports. Bondarev had seen government after government roll out plan after plan for the diversification of the economy. The 'Great Pivot East!' That had been one. Opening up the Russian Far East with Chinese Belt and Roads funding that had turned the Russian state into a debt slave as it struggled to repay the Chinese loans and saw its state enterprises gobbled up by voracious Chinese companies trading debt for control of the rich resources of Siberia and Sakhalin.

Instead of diversifying, it had become more and more dependent on digging up coal and pumping oil and gas out of the ground and selling it at an ever-lower cost to China and Europe.

On the day he had packed his bags to leave for the flight academy of the then *Voyenno-Vozdushnye Sily Rossii*, the Military Air Forces of Russia, his grandfather – General of the Air Force Victor Bondarev – had taken him aside with mock solemnity, and put a hand on his shoulder.

"Young man, you are about to begin your service to the greatest nation on earth," he intoned. "That service may one day lead you into war. If that happens, I want you to remember one thing I have learned through many wars."

"Yes, Dedushka," Bondarev had replied, frowning.

The square-jawed, gray-haired man had patted his shoulder, smiling. "Russia may not win, but it can never lose." And he had laughed, pushing Yevgeny out the door.

He shook his head now, the feeling that his nation's misguided optimism and faith in its own God-given destiny was once again leading it to overreach itself.

"What are you looking so thoughtful about?" a voice said from the doorway.

Bondarev looked up and saw Colonel Tomas Arsharvin of the Main Directorate of the General Staff of the Armed Forces of the Russian Federation (GRU), Aerospace Intelligence, standing inside the open door, a wide grin on his face.

"What are you looking so thoughtful about, *General*," Bondarev grumbled. "I trust you finally have my target list ready?"

"Yes, General!" Arsharvin said, clicking his heels together mockingly. The two had served together since Syria, Bondarev always a promotion or two ahead of his comrade in arms and happy to have him ride his coattails, since he was probably the best-connected spook in the Russian military. He walked over and pointed at Bondarev's wall screen. "In your inbox. Operation Lapshoy."

"Lapshoy?" Bondarev asked, clicking on the icon on the tablet on his desk and bringing the folder up on his main screen. "Noodle? That your idea of a joke?"

"Not me, I swear," Arsharvin said, straight-faced. "We use random code name generators, you know that. Just a coincidence."

Bondarev clicked again and a large satellite map appeared on the screen. Arsharvin walked over to it. He was tall, lithe and lightweight for forty-eight, with a scar down one cheek that ran from the corner of his eye to just below his ear. Bondarev knew

192

he'd received it in a fencing bout, but he liked to claim he was cut in a knife fight with a jealous husband.

"Korla compressor plant," Arsharvin was saying, pointing at a small town on the satellite image. "Your primary target. But you wanted to spread the strike, divert attention away from the hit on the plant. So we propose you also drop your hammer here..." His finger landed on a river that flowed diagonally across the map. "Bridges over the Kongque River. Cut one or both of these and road traffic to Urumqi will have to go hundreds of miles west."

"China can build a city of a million people inside a year. If we knock out this compressor plant, how long before they repair it and get the gas flowing again?"

"The compressors are based on aerojet engines, supplied by Rolls Royce and General Electric," Arsharvin replied. "*Before* US sanctions were imposed, preventing all dual-purpose technologies from being exported to China. They might be able to source engines domestically, but it would be an engineering nightmare and it's not an expertise they currently possess. My people figure a minimum of six months, perhaps as long as two years before they can cobble the necessary technology together."

Bondarev got up and walked over to the screen. "What is this beside the southern bridge? An urban development?"

"Sayibage residential district," Arsharvin nodded. He turned to Bondarev with a serious expression. "High rise apartments, big shopping mall, several banks, big traffic intersection..."

"Hospitals, schools?" Bondarev asked tersely.

"None. You said you wanted to avoid..."

"Yes." Bondarev turned and sat again, indicating the chair in front of his desk.

Arsharvin sat. "Look, if you want to minimize civilian casualties, Yevgeny, just drop the northern bridge. It's the main east–west highway, six lanes, double span. It will take months to rebuild and right below it is a dam that controls the flow of the Kongque River through Korla. Take down the bridge, my people reckon the dam will go too. You'll flood the whole downtown commercial area, yes, but not catastrophically. We're not talking the Yangtze River here."

"Population of Korla?" Bondarev asked.

"Half a million."

"You have a casualty estimate?"

"Based on targeting the compressor plant and both bridges, yes," Arsharvin said. "Do you want to hear it?"

"I asked, did I not?"

"It will be lower if you only target the northern bridge. That way, you will avoid the high rises and…"

"Tomas."

"Between two and five thousand."

"My God," Bondarev breathed. He ran his hand over his face. "It's mass murder, Tomas. Is that who we have become?"

Arsharvin stiffened. "And how many will die if our economy implodes, Yevgeny? If our health system falls apart, crime runs rampant, our infrastructure collapses, and our people freeze to death in their unheated apartments? Ten thousand, a hundred thousand? A million?" He fixed Bondarev with a fierce glare. "How many *Russians*?"

Bondarev wasn't buying it that easily. "What is the long game here, Tomas? We bump up the price of oil, save the treasury from going under this year, maybe next. And then what? Another 'meteor' strike? A new war? Do we encourage Iran to nuke Saudi Arabia perhaps? Or perhaps we should nuke Texas? That would do wonders for the price of oil."

"If you are drowning in quicksand, Yevgeny, your first and only concern is getting out of the mud. Once you are out, you can worry about where you can clean your clothes."

Bondarev looked across at the map again. "You have a way of always viewing questions of morality through a Russian lens, my friend."

"Is there any other?" Arshavin asked.

"Not today," Bondarev allowed. "Prepare the tasking. We will hit the compressor plant and the northern bridge. Be sure the footprint includes that dam."

Arsharvin stood. "It's a good compromise, General. The local authorities will have so much on their hands dealing with the bridge collapse and the flooding, the destruction of the compressor plant will be an asterisk in their reports."

"Until those reports hit Beijing," Bondarev said grimly. "And they realize the gas and oil from the Tarim Basin has stopped flowing."

"I will get onto it, General," Arsharvin said. "Was there anything else?"

"Yes, actually," Bondarev told him. "It seems the Americans have taken exception to my advanced near-earth object detection system."

"I heard," Arsharvin said. "I also heard your people gave them a resounding 30mm welcome when they tried to interfere."

"They'll be back," Bondarev said grimly. "And soon. I need to know what Minister Kelnikov and his cronies are planning to do next. I have been told by Popovkin to lift personnel levels and maintain real-time monitoring of all Groza platforms to ensure no further attacks get through, but I can't believe Kelnikov will be satisfied with that. He'll be planning something else to get the Americans off our backs, and I'd rather hear about it sooner than later."

Arsharvin winked. "I'll ask discreet questions in indiscreet ears, General."

After fire, flood

Korla, Xinjiang Province, China

The Korla Gas Pipeline Compressor Station was built at the height of China's 2020s infrastructure boom and was another example of why you should not tell Chinese engineers that something can't be done. The specifications for the project called for four gas generators aerodynamically coupled with high-speed high-power gas turbines supplied by General Electric's oil and gas business arm in Florence, Italy. The contract called for the station and downstream relay compressors – which would have to transport 17 billion cubic meters of gas a year across four provinces – to be started in 2016 and finished by 2019, which the Swedish engineering firm contracted to build the compressor stations advised was impossible. It took the contract anyway, but after one year was so far behind the build target that China terminated its contract and gave the job to the People's Liberation Army Engineer Corps, which finished it over budget but ahead of schedule in 2018.

Included in the contract with GE were 15 years of spare parts, which had seemed like a long time in 2018, but in 2033 the US imposed stringent sanctions against China following an ill-advised attempt to force the US out of its last naval base on Okinawa. By 2034, the precious stockpile of spare parts was running low, and though it had not been widely communicated, one of the four Korla turbines was already inoperative due to an inability to source or locally manufacture the needed turbine parts.

Supervising Engineer Kezzhou Zhang had no idea how he was going to ensure Korla delivered on its carbon capture target, with a quarter of its energy generation capacity offline. China had banked on Korla for a not insignificant contribution to its commitments under the UN Framework Convention on Climate Change. The gas-powered turbines that compressed the natural gas and pumped it eastwards generated massive volumes of superhot exhaust gases. These were captured and fed into heat recovery steam generators, which each put 25 MW of power into the Xinjiang grid and every year accounted for more than 200,000 tons of captured CO_2, which went straight into China's CO_2 credit bank.

Kezzhou knew it was just a matter of time before an angry official in the Ministry of Ecology and the Environment was on the line, asking him why Korla looked like it was going to come up 50,000 tons short this year.

Kezzhou looked at his two-year-old son, out on the balcony of their small first-floor apartment, kicking a football back and forth inside three square yards of walled-in concrete lined with wilting plastic daisies. Ah hell, maybe getting fired from the Tarim Oilfield Company wasn't the worst thing that could happen to him. His Han father had come to Korla sixty years ago as one of the *jianshezhe*, or 'builders,' fresh from engineering school with the mission to help civilize the wild deserts of Xinjiang. Kezzhou had been sent to Xinjiang University for his undergrad degree and then completed his master's in mechanical engineering at the University of Glasgow, including a semester of applied engineering pulling Upper Jurassic oil from under the North Sea on the Beryl 5 oil rig.

His Glasgow years were enshrined in legend, both in the master's degree hanging in his office and in the photographs of Glasgow cityscapes hanging in his loungeroom. His wife told him he was crazy every time he talked about wanting to go back there to live and work, but maybe it was time to bring it up again. Jump, before he was pushed.

He walked out on the balcony, absent-mindedly stealing the football from his son's feet and teasing him by rolling it back and forth between his legs. The walled compound of the five-story managers' accommodations held a pre-school and small playground, and he toyed with the idea of taking his son down there so he could boot the ball in earnest and burn some of his seemingly unlimited energy. Now, if he could just tap into that, maybe he could make up for the shortfall at Korla.

It was the middle of the afternoon; his wife wouldn't be home from his sister's place until five. There was time. He looked up, checking the sky for rain.

Something flashed. No, sparkled.

He turned his head and stared into the empty gray sky.

Not empty. Somewhere up there inside the high layer of clouds, he saw more sparkles, like small fireflies. It was impossible to say how high — either they were large and very high, or tiny and quite low. But then the sparkles started dropping down toward the ground, trailing white smoky contrails behind them.

And they were moving *fast*.

Instinct took hold of Kezzhou and he swept his son up in his arms and, without hesitating, ran for the door.

By the time he hit the stairs down to the ground floor, the world outside his apartment was *exploding*!

Maqsud Khan was sick to his stomach. Literally. Fifteen minutes earlier, he had been looking at Korla through the high-powered zoom lens of the targeting system on Groza 11.

He'd dutifully picked up the target coordinates he'd been given, fed them into the quantum brain of the targeting AI, and then watched with pale dread as the globe on his tactical monitor had zoomed from a simulated orbital view of Groza 11 moving serenely through space 900 miles above the deserts of western China, to a zoomed real-time view of the city of Korla in Xinjiang province.

As ordered, he had centered the crosshairs of the Groza sights on the Kongque River dam that sat almost perfectly framed by the two four-lane bridges that crossed the river north and south of the dam. It was about 3 p.m. in Korla, 12 noon in Baikonur. Maqsud saw cars, trucks and motorcycles moving in a steady flow across the bridges.

The mission planners for the Korla strike had determined that bringing the bridges and the dam down with any certainty would require a full payload release — 1,440 125 lb. missiles in total. But the two bridges were only a mile apart, with the dam squeezed nicely into the center of the strike zone, so a two-mile by two-mile footprint should ensure complete destruction of both the bridges and the dam, they had said confidently.

Maqsud knew they had no reason for such confidence since the Groza had only been tested against steel and iron bridges, not braced concrete like the ones he was looking at on his screen. And yes, if they fell into the river, the surge of water and debris combined with the explosive pelting of the dam's retaining wall *should* be enough to breach it, but that was not certain either.

Later, Maqsud would claim that he had deviated from the assigned mission parameters in order to maximize the impact of the strike in a smaller strike zone, and increase the destructive power of the attack. In reality, he pulled the strike zone in from two by two miles to one mile by two miles because it sickened him that under the planned footprint of the attack lay a densely populated conurbation, where he could see people walking, shopping, and cycling as though it was any other Sunday.

Pulling his eyes away from the screen, he pulled up the primary target – the Korla Compressor Station. This one gave him fewer moral qualms. It was in the southwest of Korla, situated in the middle of what looked like artificially irrigated rice fields and beside an empty football stadium. Confident that it would add its own explosive energy to the attack, only four of the eight warheads on Groza 7 had been allocated to the strike on the compressor plant, a mere 700 or so missiles. The plant was festooned with high-pressure gas pipelines, and the turbines which were the key targets were housed in two large airplane hangar-style buildings with concrete foundations but only steel upper structures which the missiles would pierce like flaming javelins through tissue paper.

As he laid Groza 7's crosshairs between the two turbine halls, he marveled at how destroying an industrial facility with a few hundred workers now suddenly seemed the lesser evil.

"Groza 7 locked on primary and tracking," Maqsud said into his headset. "Groza 11 locked on secondary and tracking. All targeting systems nominal. Weapons, you are clear to fire."

A verse from the holy Koran came to him and he started repeating it under his breath. *Oh my Lord, forgive me, for I have wronged my soul.*

Maqsud's decision to compress the strike zone for Groza 11 meant fewer than twenty missiles struck Kezzhou Zhang's housing complex.

But each struck at Mach 10, with the power of 11.5 tons of TNT, releasing superheated plasma which instantly vaporized the atmosphere around it and set fire to everything it touched.

The sound of the missile that struck Kezzhou's building was like a bomb going off, but the noise of the blast was nothing compared to the sonic boom and pressure wave that followed. As he staggered out the front doors of the building, the missile slammed through the fifth-floor roof, barely slowing as it speared through four stories of steel, wood, concrete and tile until it buried itself in the building's foundations and shattered.

The ground shook like a small earthquake had hit and Kezzhou stumbled, falling to one knee, his son clutched against his chest as he pulled himself in against the wall of the building. Other missiles were striking the ground further away, toward the highway, so Kezzhou lurched in the opposite direction, away from his now burning apartment block and toward the safety of the open ground by the riverbank.

Maqsud wasn't interested in the strike on the compressor plant. Comprising industrial-sized liquified natural gas tanks, high-pressure pipelines and steam generators, its doom was assured. No, Maqsud was watching the feed from Groza 11's high-powered zoom camera as fire rained down on the bridges over the Kongque River.

His instruments showed a two-knot westerly breeze over the target area, which the *Sarmat* re-entry vehicle would have compensated for during its descent, but it wasn't enough to blow away the smoke from the meteor contrails until several agonizing minutes after the strike. Maqsud leaned forward to squint at his screen, even though the same image was being broadcast onto the huge wall screen at the Groza Baikonur control center. It was as though the smaller image made the scale of the destruction he saw somehow less horrifying.

The northernmost bridge was down. The entire span across the river had dropped, and concrete, bitumen, smashed cars and flattened trucks lay strewn across the river from bank to bank. White foam surged around them. The reason for that was clear as Maqsud's eye tracked further down the image to see … nothing. The dam was completely gone. Raging water flowed over the kink in the river where it had been built as the river slammed unchecked into the southernmost bridge, which was still defiantly standing. Traffic on the bridge had pulled up, several cars or trucks were burning, and Maqsud could see people milling around them.

South of that bridge, water was welling up onto manicured parks and walkways in a brown, foaming morass and Maqsud saw with despair that he might have saved most of the high-rise district from meteoric fire, but he had done nothing to save it from the flooding water.

"Papa, look!" Kezzhou's son called.

Kezzhou had been standing with his back to the river, his son clutched to his chest, looking back up the riverbank at their burning apartment. All he could think of was his wife. *Thank heavens she was at Biyu's house in the western outskirts of Korla.* He had no idea what the hell had happened, but buildings were burning all over their compound, and he heard sirens and car horns blaring all through the city to the north.

People from the compound either stood around, shocked like him, or lay on the ground. A woman in front of him was crying, holding her hand out toward the burning building in supplication as if her tears could will those trapped inside it back to life.

He'd been reaching for the cell phone in his pocket with one hand while holding the other under his son's legs as he gripped his father tight around the neck.

"Papa!" the boy called, panic in his voice.

Kezzhou spun around to see a wall of rising water carrying a fifty-yard-long section of boardwalk come rushing toward him. He pulled his son's head into his shoulder and closed his eyes as the water hit and carried them away.

Perhaps curiously, at that moment, Yevgeny Bondarev was not following the progress of the Korla strike in a command and communication center at Titov Space Center. He had seen the Groza system perform both in trials and against Abqaiq. He had handpicked the officers serving on the program, including the hapless Captain Kozytsin, whose only real flaw was that he was a little too quick to blame subordinates for his own failings. Luckily for him, these were rare. So Bondarev had little doubt the strike would go to plan and the Korla compressor plant would be leveled.

No, Bondarev had his mind on a much more interesting problem. Roberta D'Antonia.

Ah, signora, signora. Bondarev shook his head at the report that had just ticked into the inbox on his tablet. *You do disappoint me.*

Without telling him why, Bondarev had asked Arsharvin to alert him if the GRU picked up any intelligence regarding a civilian or military emergency in Nebraska. A civil alert, evacuation, police or National Guard activations – anything of the sort. News service alerts he would pick up eventually, but he was particularly interested to see if he had been right to suspect the intriguing Roberta D'Antonia. He had started from a position of distrust, he had to admit. An Italian? As principal advisor to the Energy Minister? He'd had his own people review the State Security Service vetting file, and had to admit, she looked clean. Not too clean – she had money put away in a complex network of offshore accounts – but that could just be prudence, given the high six-figure US dollar salary she was pulling in. But having met her, she had seemed just a little too interested in Groza, just a little too eager for a level of detail that she really shouldn't have needed if she was just interested in avoiding her Minister being blindsided.

So yes, he had set up a little test.

And looking at the report on his screen, she had failed it.

Arsharvin had sent through a report from a GRU source in the Nebraska National Guard, indicating they had been called out to the Cooper Nuclear Power Plant to provide added security while it was evacuated. It was being called a routine security training exercise. All but a skeleton operating staff had been ordered out of the facility and a large contingent of fire and emergency first responder units had been moved in. There had been no release of information to local media. The GRU source said there was little information being released regarding the reason behind the mobilization, but everyone was talking about a potential terrorist threat.

A simple enough cover story, Bondarev mused. But it was confirmation to him that Signora Roberta D'Antonia served more than one master. He had no idea whether it was the Americans, the Italians, or even the Saudis. That didn't really matter. What it had shown him was that she could get information to the highest levels of the US intelligence apparatus and that they took it seriously enough to act on it, with alacrity. As an agent, she must be rated very highly by whoever was running her.

Bondarev closed his tablet, leaned back in his chair, and looked up at the ceiling.

He would have to handle this very carefully. Yes, she was a foreigner, but she was Denis Lapikov's new pet foreigner. It would not help already strained relations between the Defense Minister, Kelnikov, and Energy Minister Lapikov if one of Kelnikov's generals was seen to have blown the whistle on her and had her arrested by the Federal Security Service.

There was no way around it. He would need to bring Arsharvin in on his suspicions. The GRU officer had a way of getting things like this done without causing too many … unintended consequences.

"OK, this is not going quite as I intended," Meany said, staring down the line at the image of the US Space Force pilot at the other end.

"I get that a lot, Flight Lieutenant," O'Hare said. "And we may be in different armed forces, but it's Captain to you."

"Apologies, ma'am," Meany said, but not like he meant it. He pronounced it *marm*.

"I just want you for your missiles, Flight Lieutenant," O'Hare told him. "Otherwise, this is my mission, and you will be under my command."

Meany had been given the contact details for his opposite number in US Space Force and arranged a time to video conference with them that was about 8 a.m. in the Cape and about 3 p.m. in Lossiemouth. Firstly, his opposite number was a woman with two studs in her nose, three earrings he could see (probably more he couldn't), and a tattoo of some sort of vine or orchid that rose out of her collar, up her neck and curled around her ear. That was okay; he wasn't exactly a poster-boy himself. Secondly, she was Australian. Serving in US Space Force, but definitely Australian. He was cool with that too. He wasn't racist either. But before they had even got past the pleasantries, the woman at the other end was telling him that this may be a joint forces mission, but she was the one with a spacecraft in orbit with a lock on the Russian bogey *as they spoke* and if he wanted a piece of her action he could just get his 'big black phallic space liner' into position, shake hands with her X-37 to synch targeting data, arm his missiles and then do as she said.

"I am happy to confer with my Squadron Leader, ma'am," Meany said with heartfelt insincerity. "But I doubt the higher-ups in the RAF will be overly chuffed with the idea of putting their Skylon under the command of a..." *Jumped-up Aussie mercenary — yes I read your file, 'Captain' O'Hare,* "... of a foreign power, on its first combat mission," he said.

"Do they want to get their precious Skylon blown to glittering shards, Flight Lieutenant?"

"With respect, ma'am, I hardly think..."

"Because that bloody satellite nearly took me out and I am the best damn pilot in anyone's Space Fleet," O'Hare said. She leaned forward. "Including yours. Plus, I am willing to bet it has other tricks up its sleeve."

Now she had Meany's full attention. "Sorry, Captain, is there some new intel you are able to share?"

"No intel, just a feeling, Flight Lieutenant."

"A ... feeling."

She sat back and crossed her arms. "Would you send a hundred million dollars' worth of killer satellite into orbit and only arm it with two 30mm pea shooters?"

"The 30mm Gryazev-Shipunov autocannon is hardly a peashooter, ma'am," Meany pointed out. "But it was probably only intended to deal with space junk."

"A system intended to deal with 'space junk' doesn't lead a moving spacecraft and keep firing as it moves *away*, Flight Lieutenant," she said.

"Granted, ma'am."

"Plus those things are the size of a small space station. If they carried space to space missiles, they probably would have used them against us. But if they have room for two 30mm autocannon with electro-optical targeting systems, then they could also have room for lasers, chaff or flare dispensers, electronic countermeasures..."

"All that is possible, but I'm sorry, ma'am, I'm not sure I see this as an argument for subordinating our unit to your command," Meany said. "I see this mission as pretty straightforward. We rendezvous, take targeting data from you, get in position and triangulate the Groza, then we monster it violently."

O'Hare laughed. "I saw my mission as pretty straightforward too. I went in forewarned thanks to your intel about the Russian close-in weapons system. And it nearly cost me B for Bertha."

"B for..."

"My X-37," O'Hare explained. "Russia spent a lot of time, money and effort putting its Groza system into orbit and it appears willing and ready to defend it. We need to assume this mission will be anything but straightforward and plan accordingly. And that requires a clear chain of command."

"I'll have my Squadron Leader call your Colonel, Captain," Meany said in surrender.

"You do that, Flight Lieutenant," the woman said and cut the call without another word.

What a charmer, Meany thought to himself as the screen went blank. His brief had been to 'enhance transatlantic relations.' He was pretty sure Karen 'Bunny' O'Hare had not been given the same brief.

As she went to bed on Sunday evening in her small apartment in Moscow, Roberta D'Antonia was also thinking about enhancing relationships. Specifically, her new relationship with Chief Scientist Anastasia Grahkovsky. The woman had apparently fed her a line of complete *cazzate*. And she had been made to look and feel a fool. As far as Roberta could see, there had been no meteor strike, anywhere in the world, in the last 36 hours. Yet Lapikov had been adamant that further strikes were planned.

There had been a minor tsunami in the Pacific, a hurricane off the Azores, seismologists had reported a tremor in the desert in Western China, but not a word about a meteor strike. Neither had she picked up any news reports of anything out of the ordinary in or around Lincoln, Nebraska.

Which was a relief in a way because it meant that US authorities had (rightly it seemed) ignored her urgent warning. Or her own service had not thought it worthy of passing on to their allies. No matter, their lack of reaction, together with clear skies over Nebraska, meant her cover was still intact. No midnight run to Warsaw for her.

Yet.

D'Antonia made a mental note to follow up with Grahkovsky. She was owed an explanation by the woman with the frightening visage at the very least, and if she was contrite, a few crumbs of truth might emerge.

D'Antonia realized she felt almost disappointed that tomorrow would be Just Another Monday. Perhaps she had been playing this game for too long. Perhaps her subconscious was telling her it was time for a change. But to what? She no longer had the urgency, but she had the money and the resources to disappear tomorrow if she still wanted to; fall off the grid and start again wherever she wanted, as whoever she wanted to be.

But she was a woman who needed a purpose, not just a vague desire for change. She needed direction.

Major-General Yevgeny Bondarev had been given very clear direction by the commander of the 15th Aerospace Forces Army, Colonel General Oleg Popovkin.

"You will not allow the damned Americans to sneak up on one of my Grozas again, Bondarev. I don't care whether you need to put the weapons officers on every Groza on 24-hour alert, but you will do whatever it takes to keep them safe. Is that clear?" his commanding officer had said.

Whatever it takes? Bondarev had taken Popovkin at his word. He had commandeered an additional mission control center at Baikonur and in the space of 48 hours had repurposed it to house 12 eight-man weapons system teams, one for each operational Groza. Their only job was to monitor the space around their Groza and respond to any threats. Their rules of engagement were proportional to the threat the Americans had shown they now posed – engage any and all foreign military targets within a fifty-mile radius.

Using Popovkin's authority, he had also secured the cooperation of the Navy, which had allocated him command authority over the PL-19 *Nudol* missile systems on two of its *Lider*-class stealth destroyers. The *Nudol* was capable of destroying objects in low earth orbit up to an altitude of 950 miles, and each *Lider* carried four of the powerful *Nudol* missiles. The units available to him were placed both conveniently and inconveniently: one was currently making a 'friendship call' in Havana, Cuba, which gave it coverage of the sky over a large part of the US eastern seaboard. The other, however, was in transit from a patrol of the North Sea west of Greenland and would not be where he needed it – covering the sky over Western Europe – for at least three days. *Lider*-launched *Nudols* were only a last resort, though, and Popovkin had told him this option could only be used on his authority. The launches could be easily tracked; there would be no hiding them. The world would know the US and Russia had gone to war in space.

He did have one slightly more discreet option. As head of Titov Space Test Center, he had command over a squadron of 15th Aerospace Forces Army Mig-41S high-altitude interceptor aircraft, which could be used to launch the *Vympel* RN-S anti-satellite missile. The *Vympel* carried a 40 lb. warhead, was designed to be launched from an altitude of 51,000 feet, and could reach a speed of 1,865 mph (Mach 2.8), engaging targets up to 500 miles altitude. His Mig-41Ss were based at Akhtoobinsk in Southern Russia, but he had ordered one flight to be deployed to Kalaikunda Air Force Station, a joint Indian-Russian cooperation base in West Bengal, and a second flight to Tripoli in Libya. These gave him at least some cover for Groza units as they crossed the Indian subcontinent and the Middle East.

He was reviewing his defensive posture on a tablet in his office, struggling with how to achieve at least some coverage of Western Europe until his second *Lider* destroyer could get into position in the Baltic, when there was a knock on his door and Arsharvin stuck his head around.

"Is now a good time, Major-General?" the GRU Colonel asked with an innocent expression.

"Since I ordered you to report, you can assume so," Bondarev said, pushing his tablet aside and indicating a chair in front of his desk. "You had better have news for me. I was just reviewing the assets I have available to cover our world-spanning Groza system in case of an all-out attack, and they are not impressive. We not only have gaps in anti-satellite missile coverage over the southern Indian and Pacific Oceans, but I can't even cover Western Europe or the West Coast of North America."

Arsharvin frowned as he sat. "Was this not considered when we deployed Groza?"

"Yes, and it was not prioritized because Groza has limited defensive capabilities of its own, and I was promised that there would be at least six *Nudol*-armed *Lider* destroyers available for tasking within a year of deployment." He jabbed a finger down on his tablet. "We are only six months into full deployment, the Americans have already tried to knock down one of my Grozas, and there are only two upgraded *Liders* available. Add to that, it has been implied I should not even use them unless I want to be held responsible for starting World War Three, in space."

Arsharvin looked pained. "I wish I had good news for you, Yevgeny." Then he brightened. "Or perhaps I do. Let me start with China."

"The Korla attack?"

"What Korla attack?" Arsharvin asked, winking. "There were a few reports of a meteor strike on social media, but the Chinese government quickly shut down their *Weibo* and *WeChat* systems in the Xinjiang Province to get control of the information flow, and international media organizations barely even reported on it. Our sources inside the Chinese government tell us there is no indication that they suspect Russian involvement in the strike yet. For now, they are treating it as an orthodox meteorite strike."

"The compressor plant?"

"Will be offline for several months, at least. An emergency meeting of the Chinese Ministries of Energy, the National Development and Reform Commission, and the Ministry of Finance was called to discuss the disruption to oil and gas supplies from the Tarim Basin two days ago and officials were told urgently to seek international suppliers to make up the shortfall. Mozprom should be getting a call any day now. Plus, they are desperate for parts for their gas turbines and even talking of buying used engines from Aeroflot, which is a bonus we hadn't planned on…"

"They are not fools," Bondarev warned him. "The Saudis openly blamed us for the Abqaiq attack and distributed photographs of Groza missile fragments to anyone and everyone who would listen. It will just be a matter of time before Beijing sends a team to Riyadh to compare any fragments they have found in Korla with the Abqaiq meteorites."

"And by then the oil and gas will be flowing from Kazakhstan straight to Shanghai and any retaliation the Chinese can dream up will be inconsequential. They won't be able to renege on any contracts they sign with Mozprom because their economy will go into recession if they are starved of oil and gas – no one else can guarantee such a fast, reliable and almost unlimited supply."

"I cannot share your patriotism-fueled optimism, Colonel. If you are trying to cheer me up, you will have to try harder," Bondarev said.

Arsharvin leaned toward a small table sitting between Bondarev's guest chairs, on which sat a small samovar and some cups. He poured himself a cup of steaming tea, added some honey and helped himself to a biscuit, looking around himself pointedly as he did so.

"No, there is no vodka," Bondarev told him. "If that was your good news, what is the bad?"

"It is not bad, per se," Arsharvin demurred. "Though the mood you are in…"

Bondarev sighed. "Go on."

"Well, you fended off the Americans this time," Arsharvin said. "But our sources inside US Space Force say they are preparing to launch a new X-37C from the Cape, about two weeks from today." He shrugged. "They will soon have two armed spacecraft in orbit for the first time. Two weeks more and they could have three in orbit. If we weren't at war up there yet, we soon will be, General."

Bondarev was quiet a moment. When he spoke, his tone was grave. "The Russian Aerospace Forces are no stranger to war, Tomas."

In 2017 Saudi Arabia signed a 110 billion US dollar arms deal with the USA, which included the purchase of an advanced anti-ballistic missile defense system. It called the system 'Peace Shield,' and when all components were in place by 2029, Saudi Arabia claimed to have the most comprehensive anti-ballistic missile defenses in the Middle East, superior even to those of Israel. Peace Shield comprised 17 remote-controlled air/ground radio communications sites fielding Lockheed Martin AN/FPS-117 long-range phased array, 3-dimensional air search radars and six portable Northrop-Grumman AN/TPS-43 3-dimensional tactical air search radar units. At the pointy end of these search and track systems were a Raytheon Improved HAWK air defense missile system, a Raytheon MIM-104 Patriot air defense missile system, Oerlikon Contraves Skyguard 35mm Twin Cannon Short Range air defense systems, and a truck-mounted Lockheed Martin Terminal High Altitude Area Defense (THAAD) anti-ballistic missile defense system.

Still, the Saudis were not satisfied, especially as Iran got closer and closer to becoming a nuclear power. They had ground-based systems for intercepting missiles, but radar systems could be easily targeted. Mobile launchers could be attacked by cruise missiles or from the air. Peace Shield lacked a fallback air-to-space interception capability. In 2025, three years before Iran conducted its first successful nuclear weapons test, Saudi Arabia purchased the intellectual rights to the Vought Aerospace ASM-135 anti-satellite missile – a technology the US had abandoned in the early 1990s. A two-stage missile that could be fired from under the centerline of one of the newer Saudi F-15SA aircraft, it was a proven hit-to-kill missile with an infrared homing seeker that could operate independently of any ground signal, so that even if a THAAD missile interception failed, or the rest of the Peace Shield network was destroyed, the Saudis had a viable high-altitude intercept fallback option.

After forty years of improvements to the avionics of the F-15 and with the assistance of a French aerospace company, by 2033 Saudi Arabia had ten of the ASM-135-armed F-15s in the field. Two patrolled the air over Saudi Arabia at all times, each armed with one of the 2 million US dollar missiles which Saudi Arabia called *Sahm*, or 'Arrow.'

Captain Amir Alakeel regarded the duty of escorting the *Sahm*-armed F-15s as possibly one of the most boring peacetime duties any fighter pilot could be assigned. And after the last few weeks of tensions, culminating in his successful attack on the Iranian frigate *Sahand*, such patrols were a complete anti-climax even in a time of armed conflict.

'Armed conflict.' *War* by any other name. But Iran and Saudi Arabia had not declared war, and diplomats of a dozen nations were being kept busy to avoid the conflict escalating, while it seemed to Alakeel that Russia was doing everything in its power to do the opposite. In addition to the fighter aircraft it had positioned in Egypt and Iran, and already based in Syria, Alakeel had learned this morning that Russia had just announced it would be sending the landing ship *Azov*, escorted by two *Grigorovich* guided missile frigates from its Black Sea fleet, into a Persian Gulf already teeming with Saudi, Iranian, US, British and European warships, all of which were ostensibly there to 'protect their national interests' by escorting merchant shipping through the Straits of Hormuz.

The *Azov* was not a ship you would use to protect merchant shipping. It was a ship you would use to invade a neighboring country. Its NATO designation was 'LST' or Landing Ship Tank. Built in Poland and delivered to Russia in the 1990s, a *Rapoucha* II-class LST like the *Azov* could transport 12 troop carriers or three main battle tanks, 400 troops, or 500 tons of cargo. Several would be needed to support a full-scale invasion of Saudi Arabia by Iran, but that was exactly what Russia had done during the Syrian conflict. Sending the *Azov* into the Gulf at a time when Iran was speaking of obliterating Saudi Arabia with nuclear fire was an unmistakable political signal – Iran had the biggest standing army in the Middle East, and repositioning the *Azov* said Russia would be there to transport it if needed.

Sending it into the Gulf in the company of two of the newer *Grigorovich* missile frigates was also a signal that Russia did not intend to see the *Azov* attacked in the way the *Sahand* had been. The *Grigorovich* was equipped with the latest *Fregat* M3M anti-drone optimized air-search radar system, and bristling with close-in weapons systems ranging from multiple six-barreled 20mm rotary cannons to man-portable data-linked Verba anti-air missiles ideal for engaging small low-flying targets.

The problem of how to react to the arrival of the *Azov* was beyond Amir Alakeel's pay grade. His task for the day was to play bodyguard to the *Sahm* aircraft currently patrolling the Saudi southern border zone between Dammam, near Bahrain, and Mecca on the west coast, with Riyadh lying right in the middle of the patrol area. It was a mind- and back-numbing four-hour escort duty, meeting with the F-15SA at 40,000 feet and then making four 600-mile racetrack circuits from coast to coast, each lasting an hour, before a new F-15 and its escort joined the circuit, and Alakeel's flight of two F-35s could return to its Dhahran base.

They were constantly updated regarding commercial and military aircraft movements during the patrol, and so there was rarely any tension to alleviate the boredom, even when they were approaching the east coast closer to Iran. The Royal Saudi Air Force now had standing air defense combat patrols flying up and down its eastern coast facing Iran, so even if there was an Iranian incursion, it wouldn't be Alakeel's flight which was called upon to intercept it.

He was a dog walker. Walking a high-altitude supersonic dog, but still, a dog walker.

He ran his eyes around his cockpit, checked the skies, flexed his muscles and rolled his head to keep his neck from stiffening up. His flight was slightly above the F-15 and about a mile ahead of it. With the sun in his eyes and the sky darkening behind him, he couldn't eyeball it, but his tactical screen told him it was there. His F-35s were just about at their maximum service ceiling of 50,000 feet, though the F-15SA had plenty of headroom, with a ceiling closer to 60,000 feet.

His call sign on this flight was *Albayj*, or 'beige,' which he felt described the duty perfectly.

Until the flight controller for the Southern sector, orbiting in a SAAB 2000 aircraft just north of Riyadh, broke into his thoughts in an urgent burst of static. "Albayj One, Sector Control, we have possible unidentified aircraft approaching Saudi airspace on an intercept course for your patrol. Vector 279 degrees and report any contacts."

Alakeel switched his sensor suite from passive to active, scanning the sky ahead of him with his phased array radar. He saw nothing. His eyes flicked to his threat monitor, then he checked his wingman, the newbie, Zedan, was following him as he swung around. If the SAAB had a target, it should be sending the data through to them. "Sector Control, Albayj One. Turning to 279. I see nothing on radar or infrared, nothing on my tac monitor."

They were approaching the last eastward leg of the patrol, after three and a half hours, with the sun setting ahead of him and the lights of Mecca and Jeddah just starting to glow on the horizon. Enemy aircraft approaching from the west? That way lay Sudan, Eritrea ... Egypt.

"I don't have a solid vector for you, Albayj flight," the sector controller said. "We got a couple of returns on the low-frequency array in Jeddah two minutes ago and nothing since. Investigate and report. I am vectoring support to your location."

Stealth fighters. Had to be. And there was only one other nation fielding stealth fighters in the region right now.

"Zedan, are you radiating?" Alakeel asked.

"Yes, Captain," the man replied. "No targets."

"Shut down, go passive. I'm betting it's those bloody Egypt-based Mig-41s, trying to test us out. They have the legs to reach this far south, and the ceiling to be able to follow that F-15 all the way up to 60,000 feet if they want to. If I was Ivan, and I was going to push this patrol to see how we'd react, that's the machine I'd do it with."

"Yes, Captain."

"I want you to stay on this heading, increase separation to two miles. I'll keep searching with active array, but there's no point both of us lighting up the sky telling the Russians where we are. Arm short-range air-air, synch targeting with me and stay alert." He called up the F-15, which would have been listening in on the conversation between Alakeel and the controller. "Albayj Three, Albayj One."

"Receiving, Albayj One."

"Turn to zero nine zero until we have investigated the contact," Alakeel ordered. Unlike the F-35s, the F-15 was not a stealth aircraft. It was a big, lumbering 'shoot me' sign in the sky, and a 5th-generation fighter like the Mig-41 would have no trouble seeing it barreling through the air at 40,000 feet. He wanted it headed safely back to Riyadh if the contact turned hot.

"Roger, Albayj One, turning to zero nine zero, altitude 40,000," the F15 pilot replied and Alakeel watched with satisfaction as the icon for the aircraft quickly peeled away.

A chime sounded in his helmet. His infrared sensors had picked up a contact. That meant it was *close*. He firewalled his throttle and turned toward the contact. "Albayj Two, Albayj One, I have a contact at 310 degrees, altitude 50,000, turning to intercept, do you copy?"

Zedan's high-pitched voice replied immediately. "I have it onscreen, Captain. Do you want me to … *missile alert.* Evading!" the man yelled.

Alakeel cursed. They had been jumped. He had just one contact on his screen but assumed the Russians would send more than one fighter. But one contact was better than none. He armed his Sidewinders and locked up the target, five miles distant and still invisible to the eye. His Rules of Engagement were clear. He was authorized to return fire if fired upon by an unidentified aircraft. "Fox One," he called, as two of the short-range missiles dropped out of his weapons bay and streaked up into the night sky. "Albayj Three, we are engaged with enemy aircraft. Bug out," Alakeel called, panting as the pressure of his sudden acceleration toward the contact pushed against his chest, making it hard to breathe. "Sector Control, requesting support…"

"Albayj One, this is Three, bugging out."

"Albayj One, Sector. Vectoring support to your position. Eight minutes."

Eight minutes? They could be dead by then. In the dark above, he saw an explosion. Too big to be just the proximity warhead on his missile detonating. Sure enough, the contact on his screen winked out. "Splash One Mig. Albayj Two, report." He could see from his situational monitor that his wingman was now ten miles away, down to 30,000 feet and turning hard.

He had nothing else on his radar screen, nothing on infrared. Could they possibly…

"Albayj One, I am still engaged with enemy fighters. I have nothing on optical, infrared or radar," Zedan yelled, desperation in his voice. "Low on chaff and flares. Heading for the deck."

"Steer on me, Zedan," Alakeel called. "I'll try to get a fix on the dogs." He swung his machine around to point it straight at Zedan's aircraft but didn't follow the man down. He kept his nose pointed at the sky above because he knew that was where the Mig-41 liked to hunt. But his tactical situation display stayed ominously empty.

"Albayj Three, Sector Control," the SAAB 2000 broke in. "Ballistic missile alert, repeat, *ballistic missile alert*. Estimated target, Riyadh. Estimated impact twelve minutes. Patching coordinates through. Immediate intercept, please confirm."

"Sector Control, Albayj Three, intercepting."

Alakeel was entering a potentially fatal data overload state. He was working his phased array, trying to get a radar lock on one of the Mig-41s, at the same time flicking his eyes to his helmet-mounted display watching his airspeed and angle of attack, looking for radar or infrared alerts, swiveling his head to scan the sky for telltale exhaust flares or the glint of light off metal or glass, or worse, the flare of a missile launch. Listening for warning tones, radio calls, missile alerts. Zedan yelling again. He ... *how*...

Alakeel froze. Figuratively, but effectively. His mind went blank. His muscles locked solid. He couldn't focus on the radar screen in front of him, his fingers – which had been trying to fine tune the array to detect the Mig fighters he *knew* were out there – were suddenly unfeeling. He heard radio calls in his ears, but they made no sense. Time stood still.

A ballistic missile strike on Riyadh? Nuclear or conventional? He shook his head, trying to focus on the here, the now. But it all seemed suddenly surreal. Somewhere to his east the F-15SA Advanced Eagle would be rocketing into the sky on afterburner at 1.2 times the speed of sound. Its single *Sahm* missile would have been programmed with the coordinates downloaded from the SAAB. As the Eagle reached the top of its climb at 60,000 feet and hung there at the edge of space, it would release the three-stage missile. The first stage two-pulse solid-propellant rocket engine would boost it away from the Eagle even as the fighter was toppling nose-down back toward the earth. The second stage would ignite, powering the missile toward an intercept at 15,000 miles an hour. The third stage was a rocket-boosted Miniature Homing Vehicle or MHV. Before it separated, the MHV was spun up to 30 revolutions a second and pointed at the target, which should now be visible to the missile's infrared sensor. After it was sent on its way, 64 vectoring thrusters arranged around the MHV were used to keep the target centered in the view of the infrared sensor until the missile connected with the target.

Which should only be there if the THAAD missile had failed to destroy its target, or there had been too many for the THAAD system to cope with, or...

Alakeel was brought back to reality by the insistent chime of his radar warning receiver. It was sounding an alert, indicating a Mig-41 targeting radar was actively searching for him, but hadn't yet got a lock. Before he could do anything else, he had to fight his way out of the dogfight he was in himself. He oriented his infrared seeker on the bearing of the enemy radar signal and it pinged a new target, two miles west of Zedan and 20,000 feet above him. Before he could even react, his combat AI had armed and fired two Sidewinder missiles at it, as it was programmed to do when combat had already been initiated. *Fox One, Fox One*, it announced with digital calm.

"Albayj One!" his wingman called, suppressed panic in his voice. "I took a hit. Starboard wing control surfaces not responding. Damage to avionics and countermeasures. I am at 500 feet with a Mig-41 on my tail."

Alakeel grunted with satisfaction when he saw an explosion in the sky above, and the infrared target in his helmet-mounted display was replaced with a cross. "Your pursuer is down, Albayj Two," he said. "Do you have control of your machine?" Alakeel asked urgently. They might have dealt with the Mig-41 attack, or there might be others out there. He had no way of knowing. He checked his tactical display, put his aircraft on an intercept course for his wingman. "Stay low, focus on keeping your machine in the air. Turn to ... zero four three ... put down at Medina."

"Yes sir, making for Medina," Zedan said, his voice a pitch higher than usual.

Alakeel keyed his mike. "Southern Control, I have no further contacts. Please alert Medina air traffic control and request an emergency landing. Albayj Two is..."

"Albayj One, Southern Control. We have been monitoring the engagement and your comms, Albayj One," the controller interrupted. "We have alerted Medina. You are cleared for an emergency landing."

"Thank you, Control. One out." Alakeel switched to his wingman's channel. "What's your status, Lieutenant? Talk to me all the way in."

There was a click, some static, and the sound of the man breathing heavily. It told Alakeel all he needed to know.

The lights of the highway crossroads town of Mahd Al Thahab flashed by underneath him as he closed to within a hundred feet of his wingman's stricken fighter and eased up beside it. A huge spray of fuel was trailing behind the wounded Lightning, obscuring his view, but then suddenly it cleared and he could see what had happened to the big fighter.

Allah yahminana, he thought, looking over the damage. *Where is the wing?!*

He couldn't believe what he was seeing. Where the F-35's right wing should be was just a torn stump of flapping metal, spewing fuel. Zedan might not have seen it yet. In fact, he almost certainly hadn't, or he would already have ejected.

God protect us, Alakeel muttered again. Then he checked his tac display was clear of threats and reached for his mike. "Alright, Zedan, you have lost part of the starboard wing." *Part of it? He'd lost two-thirds of it.*

"I should eject!" the Lieutenant replied. "It's yawing to port and I am barely able to keep it from rolling on me."

"You will not eject," Alakeel said abruptly. "The flight control computer is automatically compensating. If it wasn't, you'd already be hanging from a chute."

"I have my stick hard over," the other pilot replied, then started yelling. "If I let it go, it rolls left!"

"Lieutenant Zedan, you will not eject yet, that is an order," Alakeel said firmly. He could see Medina airfield on the horizon now. "You will make your approach. You will keep your airspeed above two hundred knots as you cross the threshold. Is that clear, two hundred knots."

More panting. Alakeel could imagine the man, sweat streaming down his face, one hand on the stick, the other on the ejection handle, fighting on two fronts; to keep his machine in the air and to resist the urge to just punch out. Every Saudi F-35 pilot had been through the USAF Fighter Tactical Strengthening and Sustainment program, or FiTSS. Alakeel remembered a critical part of it now, a tip for calming the mind.

"Zedan, I want you to call up the emergency landing checklist," he said. "Put it up on your main display and walk me through it as you check it off, alright?"

"I … yes, Captain," the young pilot responded.

Alakeel contacted the Medina tower, called in their emergency again and confirmed they were ready to receive the stricken fighter. Looking at it again, he marveled at how it was still flying. But a large part of the F-35's aerodynamic lift was provided by the aircraft body and its huge air intakes – it must be those keeping it in the air, because it certainly wasn't the stub of a wing.

He could hear Zedan's voice catching as he worked through his checklist, with Alakeel repeating every element after Zedan, with as calm a voice as he could muster, until they got to the end and the long runway at Medina appeared on the horizon. "Good job, lad. You aren't the first to land a jet fighter on one wing, you know. Wheels down. That's it, lad. A bloody Israeli did it back in the last century, you know that? He was in an F-15. And he didn't have fly by wire or digital landing aids, Zedan." Alakeel realized he was sweating too, and wiped his neck with a glove. "You going to punch out and let the bloody Israelis keep that record?"

"No, sir," the man said.

"Good. I'll follow you down. Now at that speed you're going to hit hard. Cut your engine the second you're down – you're going to pull up in a cloud of fumes, okay? And resist the urge to toe the brakes too hard. Just bring her gently to a stop like a…"

"Captain, sir, I need to concentrate," the panting man said.

Zedan was right, of course; Alakeel was speaking as much to calm himself as he was his wingman. He looked ahead. It seemed they were floating down toward the runway, but his airspeed indicator told him another story. At two hundred and sixty knots, they were making their approach at nearly twice normal landing speed for an F-35, but Alakeel was worried that any slower, and the stricken Lightning would stall. Alakeel's machine hit 500 feet and a warning sounded in his ears. *Terrain, pull up. Terrain, pull up.* He flattened out and the warning stopped, but Zedan's fighter dropped below and behind him. He lowered a wing and kicked in a little rudder to keep it in view.

The Lightning flew low and fast across the threshold to the runway. Alakeel saw fire trucks and an ambulance lined up to one side. Then the machine dropped, Zedan cutting his throttle early – afraid of fire, afraid of running out of runway. His machine slammed into the tarmac, shearing off the portside wheel strut, sending it down onto its belly, port wing scraping along the runway in a shower of sparks that...

"Punch out!" Alakeel screamed.

With an audible *whoomph*, the fighter exploded.

Alakeel turned quickly away, eyes fixed on the horizon ahead of him. He reached for his mike. "Medina Tower, Albayj One," he said, voice empty. "Albayj Two is down, aircraft on fire. Runway 17 at Medina unusable. Requesting permission to land on 36."

There was a momentary pause, and then the Medina Tower came back. "Albayj One, Medina. Vector one eight five, 5,000 feet, you are cleared in on runway 36."

Alakeel bit down the bile rising in his throat, confirmed his landing instructions, and as he swung around to start his landing approach, he switched to the frequency for the SAAB 2000 airborne controller.

"South Sector Control, Albayj One," Alakeel said. "What was the result of the *Sahm* launch?"

"Successful interception, Albayj One. Iran fired three missiles. One was intercepted by THAAD, and one by your F-15, Captain," the controller said. "The third got through but was hit by a Patriot or Oerlikon over Riyadh."

Alakeel felt his throat tighten. "Nuclear or conventional?"

"Probably conventional," the controller replied. "Missile Defense is calling it a medium-range Khorramshahr. Debris hit the Ritz Carlton Riyadh, beside Al Yamamah Palace. No casualty count yet."

"Thank you, Control, Albayj One out." He bit his lip in thought and sighed. As he slid down the glidepath toward the runway, he wasn't thinking about the body count in Riyadh, not yet. He was thinking of a single death. Zedan was just a kid; a twenty-three-year-old boy from Wadi-ad-Dawasir who had collected bird feathers from the Bani M'aradh Wildlife Sanctuary as a boy and dreamed of flying fast jets. And he'd died in a ball of fire with tears in his eyes.

They had made the Russians pay for their failed attempt to disrupt the *Sahm* launch, and Peace Shield had worked. Would it have worked against a nuclear missile, set for airburst above the city? Would it have worked if the Russians had succeeded in taking down his F-15? Probably not.

He'd likely claim two of the Russian Mig-41 fighters destroyed, but had no idea how many they had sent against him. As was often the case in modern warfare, he had not once laid eyes on the enemy he was shooting at, and would never know who had killed Hatem Zedan.

At the thought of the young man's death, Alakeel hammered the stretched acrylic bubble over his head and howled at the uncaring night sky.

Orbital

Titov Space Test Facility, Timonovo, Russia

Anastasia Grahkovsky took the earpiece out of her ear that had been carrying a recorded audio feed from the Baikonur control center and put it down beside the smashed porcelain that had until a few minutes ago been her favorite teacup.

It hadn't been an accident. She had been holding the cup in one hand as she spoke with Major-General Bondarev on her cell phone with the other. She had listened to him politely. She had hung up on him calmly. And then she had thrown her cup down onto the coffee table in front of her with such fury that she heard pieces of it strike the window six feet away.

The Americans had attacked one of her Grozas! A clumsy, inelegant approach, but it could have worked. At her request, the designers had given the fuel compartments of the Groza heat shielding, but if the laser had managed to heat the outer casing sufficiently, enough energy could have been released to nudge the satellite out of orbit if the Americans had not been detected and counter-attacked. They had taken many precautions to ensure her babies were not sent into the cold dark of space without the ability to look after themselves, but would they be enough? Right there and then, she decided to assume not.

It was 11.30 a.m. on a rainy, gray Sunday morning in Moscow, but she rarely bothered to check the weather report because it made no difference to her whether it was cloudy or sunny, and she was not given to long outdoor walks so cared even less if there was rain, sleet or snow in the air. But she had the window of her apartment open and had sat in a chair near the window so she could feel the chill breeze which suited perfectly her already dark mood.

She took herself back to the audio she had been listening to and put her earpiece back in. What it was, was astrophysical pornography. She hadn't been listening to the babbling replay of the commentary of the uniformed monkey men in the control center with their countdowns and their shouted confirmation of orders and mindless whoops of delight. She had downloaded an audio rendition of the trajectory data from the Groza guidance system as the huge tungsten warheads dropped off their hub, were boosted away by the *Sarmat* re-entry vehicle, and dropped through the atmosphere.

She had a braille printout of the trajectory the Titov AIs had calculated her warheads should follow, and measured the deviations, small and large, running her finger down the page as radar tracked the warheads up until the moment they split into hundreds of smaller wedge-shaped missiles.

You did it again, Corporal Khan, she thought to herself. She ran the tape through her fingers again. *You shrunk the footprint this time. Perhaps you think your little tin medal will protect you?*

The man intrigued her. If he was a conscientious objector, why did he not refuse to serve? He'd taken a posting to the ballistic missile forces, for God's sake! And suddenly, he was squeamish? "Oh, they will bury you if you compromised this attack," she murmured out loud. It was strange, but she almost felt sorry for him.

She reached over to her laptop and tapped a few keys to bring up a new audio feed – the satellite intel on the damage assessment.

She whistled. *You lucky, lucky man.* Hit the bridge, shattered the dam, wiped out half of downtown Korla and turned the primary target into molten slag. Another glorious attack for the motherland, another successful strike by Corporal Khan. She could almost hear his response if she challenged him in front of his superiors. "Yes, Comrade Chief Scientist. I tightened the strike zone in order to achieve a greater concentration of firepower in a smaller area. I was worried that the reinforced concrete of the bridge and dam would prove too strong if we spread the strike over a greater area." He would shuffle his feet in that annoying way he had. "I realize I did not have the authority to change the mission parameters. I am sorry."

And he would get away with it because, like Abqaiq, the strike was a complete success.

She looked at the bomb damage report again, her eyes skipping over the casualty estimate without causing her pause. It was just another number. Those who had died were not in pain; they deserved no sympathy. Those who were injured could not have been injured any worse than her, and *she* had survived. She had survived without eyes, lived a lifetime with constant searing pain all over her body, without needing sympathy. The casualties in Korla would either deal with their injuries as she had done, or not, and if they did not, then they were weak, and she had only contempt for them.

She lifted a cell phone from the coffee table by her sofa and toyed with it a while, then spoke a number into it.

"Hello, Captain Kozytsin, this is Chief Scientist Grahkovsky," she said when a voice came on the other end. "Yes, very satisfactory. You are to be congratulated. Yes, yes … look, I am hoping you can despatch one of your men to Titov to help the program here. His name is Khan, Corporal Khan. He is on the Groza targeting squad and…" She wiggled her toes, enjoying the feel of the cold air passing over them. "Yes, yes, he is. That is why we … well, thank you. No, one week should be more than sufficient. We just want his help to run some simulations. Tomorrow would be fine. Your staff can tell him to report to me at Titov when he arrives. Thank you, Captain."

Grahkovsky cut the call and as she put the cell phone back on the table she heard a small insect buzz into the air. It must have come through the window, landed on the coffee table, and been disturbed as she put her phone back down. Cocking her head, she listened to it as it rose into the air and started buzzing around her head. Fingers open, ready to snap shut, she brought her left hand up to her left ear and then, as it passed her head, she snatched it out of the air.

It batted against the walls of her clenched palm and she reached in with her right forefinger and thumb and pulled it carefully out. She figured that if it was a bee or wasp, it would already have stung her. Hmmm. Bigger than a fly, smaller than a cockroach, though. She held it down on her palm with one fingernail and ran the tip of her forefinger over it. Two small antennae. Flat head, round body, hard carapace. Longer legs and too big to be a ladybug. She took a guess. Order: Coleoptera. Family: Scarabaeidae. Genus: Melolontha. A *khrushch* or cockchafer bug.

It squirmed as she kept it clenched in her palm and reached for her cell phone again, opened her hand to snap a photo of it and pulled the photo up. "Image search. Object, insect, identify," she said to her phone.

"Searching. The object in the image is a leather beetle, *Osmoderma eremita*," her search assistant said.

No, too small, unless it's newly hatched, she thought. She crushed it under her nail and lifted it to her nose to smell it. Yes, okay. Smell of musty leather. *Osmoderma eremita* it was. Or had been.

She wiped the bug from her palm and sat back in her chair, arms behind her head.

You and I are going to talk, Corporal Khan, she promised him, wherever in Baikonur his pacifist ass was at that moment. She imagined meeting him again. *Drink, and talk. Maybe screw. But mostly talk.*

Grahkovsky was a very protective mother. And she had ensured her babies were sent into space with a prodigious ability to defend themselves.

Weighing nearly ninety tons, of which eighty were taken up by its tungsten projectiles, the rest of the satellite's mass comprised complex electronics, solar panels, engines and propellant for the vectoring thrusters and, of course, the electro-optical targeting system for the twin 30mm autocannon close-in weapons. However, all that still left nearly two tons of mass to be explained, none of which was shown on the early prototype plans stolen and delivered to the US intelligence services by its now-deceased agent.

Bunny O'Hare and Meany Papastopoulos were about to learn exactly how that mass had been allocated.

Their superiors had sorted out mission protocols and the decision had fallen in O'Hare's favor. Colonel Rodriguez had agreed with Squadron Leader Bear that she would have overall control of Space Force assets for the mission, with O'Hare subordinate to her. Bear had agreed with his own superiors to place his Skylon under her command and told Meany he and O'Hare would be taking their orders from Rodriguez during the mission.

"You will follow Captain O'Hare's direction unless I tell you otherwise," Bear had said privately. "But I am going to be sitting on your shoulder like a parrot on a pirate, Flight Lieutenant, and if you hear me whisper in your shell-like, you will not be in any doubt about who to obey."

"No, sir, none at all," Meany had responded. He was simply happy that he hadn't been made subordinate to that insufferable Australian.

As he sat in his command trailer, it was still light outside. This time of year, the sun didn't set until about 2230 hours. Were he a civilian, he'd probably be kicking back in a beer garden with his mates about now, perhaps having a wager on the ponies and being told yet again why supporting anyone in the Scottish football league except Rangers could get him knifed in a dark alley in Lossie. He'd mistakenly assumed that since Aberdeen was the closest city, he should support Aberdeen, but after a couple of good fights, he'd learned not to make assumptions about Scottish football (but he still cheered for Aberdeen because, hell, Meany loved a good scrap).

"Angus, coming up on rendezvous, let me know when you get a solid handshake from Bertha," he said.

Approaching operational telemetry range, Flight Lieutenant. Handshake in three minutes ten seconds.

With a sense of apprehension, Meany opened a secure comms channel to the X-37 that was still just a dot on his radar screen. "US Space Force B for Bertha, this is RAF Skylon, how do you hear me?"

There was some static as Angus locked onto the signal and then the Australian brogue filled his cockpit. "B for Bertha, RAF Skylon, welcome to the party. I'm showing telemetry at 98 percent nominal and we're ready to synch data on your mark."

A second voice joined the first inside his helmet. A much nicer, smooth midwestern US accent. "Flight Lieutenant Papastopoulos, this is Colonel Rodriguez. What is your status?"

The Skylon launch and transit to the combat area had been unproblematic. All systems were nominal. His bird was as ready for the coming fight as it would ever be.

"Skylon is five by five, ma'am," he reported.

"Glad to hear it, Lieutenant. There are no changes to your mission orders. You will synch data and proceed to your jump-off point. Once engaged, you will take your lead from Captain O'Hare. Do you have any questions?"

"No, ma'am," Meany said.

"Good luck and Godspeed, Lieutenant," she said.

He had completely forgotten Paddington was standing right behind him, and nearly jumped when the man patted his shoulder.

"Break a leg, pilot," Bear said. Meany could hear but not see him, as his head was immersed in his virtual reality rig.

Meany called up his tactical screen, which at the moment was only showing the US spacecraft. The mission called for the X-37 to maintain a passive targeting lock on the Russian satellite using its optical and infrared targeting system. It would pass that data to the Skylon now, and Meany would maneuver into position for a missile launch.

Then the mission would enter its most dangerous phase. The smaller X-37 would actively begin radiating energy from its phased array radar system to solidify its lock on the Groza. If the satellite had a radar warning receiver, then alarm bells would start ringing somewhere in Russia. If they could, they might try to jam Bertha, or even engage the X-37 with a ground-launched anti-satellite missile. Their strategy was intended to focus any defensive countermeasures on the nimbler X-37, leaving the bigger Skylon alone to send its missiles at the Groza.

His advanced short-range multispectral seeker space-to-space missiles should be impossible for a monster like the Groza to evade. If it tried to jam or fired radar decoys, the missile would switch to its infrared seeker. If it fired heat flares, the missiles were smart enough to realize what they were looking at, and would switch to optical targeting. There was no air resistance or gravity to help the Groza dodge the Skylon's missiles. If Bertha could get a lock and send them on their way, the Groza was toast. The box launcher in his payload bay carried six missiles, which could be fired individually or salvoed in any combination. His operations order called for firing the missiles in staggered-pair volleys, one second apart.

We have telemetry lock, Lieutenant. I am ready to accept targeting data, Angus told him.

"Skylon, Bertha. I confirm telemetry nominal. You are go for handshake."

In a second, the icon for the Groza on the tactical screen on the heads up display in his virtual reality helmet went from red to flashing yellow. The stage was set.

He was still eighty miles from the Russian satellite, but he couldn't help feel a shiver. It had already tried to kill him once.

Data from the X-37 is streaming, real-time decryption and validation within operational limits. We have data synch, Lieutenant.

"That's great, Angus. You can move us to the launch point. Maintain posture D4, please."

Posture D4 confirmed, Lieutenant. Moving to launch point alpha.

He had just ordered Angus to begin vectoring to the attack point, 120 degrees behind the Groza relative to the US X-37 and on the blind side of its ventral 30mm cannon. The Groza could easily maneuver to bring its weapons to bear, but that would take it precious seconds.

Lieutenant, for future reference, it would be a relatively simple matter for me to communicate directly with the AI on the US spacecraft. This would cut communications time and eliminate all risk of human error.

"Thanks, Angus, I'll bear that in mind. You focus on piloting the ship, please."

Acknowledged.

Did Angus sound a little hurt? He was pretty sure he hadn't coded that.

"Bertha, Skylon. Were you planning on letting me know you were already moving to attack point alpha at some point, Lieutenant?" the Australian asked, a little edge in her voice.

"Sorry about that, Captain. I was in dialogue with my AI. Confirm, moving to attack point alpha." He hit some keys. "Opening payload bay doors, powering up and deploying missile launch module. Weapons hot in ... Angus?"

Launcher will be fully deployed and missiles armed in twenty-three seconds, Lieutenant.

"... weapons hot in twenty-two seconds. On station in, uh, seventeen minutes twenty seconds, Bertha."

"Feel free to let me know when you are, Skylon. Bertha out." O'Hare said.

He muted the interservice channel.

"On second thoughts, Angus, maybe next time you *can* talk to her," Meany said.

In her own 'cockpit' 1,114 miles away, O'Hare also muted her interservice comms. "Bloody prat," she said, not even trying to keep it under her breath. Albers shot her a glance but kept his eyes on his instruments.

"O'Hare," Rodriguez sighed. She had joined her crew in the X-37 command center at Morrell Operations Center at the Cape, but had told Severin and Zeezee they would need to follow the mission from up in the MOC situation room. She knew how thick the atmosphere could get in a drone's virtual cockpit under combat conditions, especially with O'Hare in the chair.

"Well, seriously, ma'am. *Skylon is five by five?* He saw that in a movie or something. Who actually says that?"

"You did, once, Captain," Albers said, without looking at her.

Both Rodriguez and O'Hare turned to look at him, but he had his head in his screens, and his face was blank.

"Yeah, maybe, but I would have been joking. Jeez, don't they have irony in Minnesota?" O'Hare asked.

"It's all in the delivery, ma'am," Albers said.

"Fair enough. Status on the target?"

"Tracking true to projected orbit, ma'am," the Minnesotan said. "I have a good lock on infrared with the sun on its upper front quarter. We are five by five."

"Attempt at humor noted, Lieutenant Albers. Our position?" O'Hare asked.

Albers checked a readout. "One nine five point zero seven miles off the southern tip of Greenland, inbound Nova Scotia, ma'am. You can see it out your port view."

O'Hare turned her head. Both she and Albers were wearing a light VR rig that projected a single screen onto a see-through glass in front of her left eye, while her right was free to focus on the 2D multifunction screens in front of her. She flicked through the views so that the VR was showing the view from Bertha's port earthside camera and she saw the huge landmass of Greenland sliding along below her, half in cloud, the rest glacier blue or glittering white speckled with rock, snow and ice.

"Almost makes you wish you were down there," Rodriguez said, looking at the same view on a 2D monitor.

"Not me, ma'am," Albers told her. "Terrible surf, Greenland."

"You surf?" O'Hare asked. "I would not have guessed that, Lieutenant Albers."

"I like to retain the capacity to surprise, ma'am," Albers said, deadpan.

"I don't like surprises," O'Hare said. "Let's run through the attack sequence again, Albers, while our Pommy friend up there meanders into position."

231

Captain Alexei Kozytsin of the 15th Aerospace Forces Army, 153rd Titov Main Trial Center for Testing and Control of Space (Groza Program), chafed at his unit's lack of a proper military designation. It was operational now, dammit, but it still carried the title of a test program. It should have been moved under the wing of the 821st Space Surveillance Division by now, but it was still commanded by that hard-ass Bondarev, which meant it was stuck with the Trial Program tag.

He also chafed at the fact he didn't have a proper line of command, with at least a Major, if not a Colonel, to run interference between himself and Bondarev, like an ordinary Aerospace command would normally have. But Groza was Bondarev's pet project, and he'd made it clear he didn't want any command layers between himself and the Groza Operations unit at Baikonur, so Kozytsin was stuck with him.

Well, Kozytsin had delivered his report on the American attack to Bondarev and his officers and he'd kept his command and he planned to keep on keeping it. He'd doubled the personnel on the defensive weapons stations, which hadn't been easy because he hadn't had enough trained personnel to start with. But he'd had them pulling double shifts, the new recruits shadowing the older hands until he was confident they knew what they were doing and weren't going to shoot down a passing Chinese satellite in a fit of rookie enthusiasm.

Alexei Kozytsin was doing everything a modern leader of the Russian Space Command had been trained to do.

He had them drilling their recognition of the X-37C and RAF Skylon – visual and electronic – until he was sure they saw and heard it in their sleep.

He had his target acquisition, systems and comms, offensive and defensive weapons teams working one shift, running simulations the next, and sleeping the third. They got every fifth day off and worked nights every third five-day rotation.

He had told his people why they were pulling extra duty, explaining that Russia's newest and most devastating weapons system, on which they should be proud to serve, had been surveilled by British forces, and attacked by US forces. Cowards, afraid to take on their Grozas with ground-based weapons so that the whole world could see, they had tried to sneak up on them in the dark of space and they had been repelled.

He didn't want to make a hero of that upstart Corporal Khan, so he told his troops a version of the story in which Sergeant Karas was the hero, running into the command center at just the right moment to save their Groza from destruction by ordering his squad to engage the Americans even though they were beyond normal weapons range.

He led by example, sitting side by side with his personnel as they worked through the long nights, staying with the next shift until well into the morning. He ate standing up, he wrote his duty logs standing up, and once or twice he'd even slept standing up.

Which might explain why he was a little terse with Sergeant Karas, who was tactical commander for the target acquisition and weapons teams on this shift.

"Why are you only reporting this now?" he asked him.

Karas knew why. It was because his usual target acquisition and situational awareness lead was Corporal Khan, but now the lucky shit had somehow become the brown-eyed golden boy he had been pulled away on some junket to Moscow. The man he had in his chair instead today was not as sharp. "Sir, we only picked up the Skylon matching orbit with the X-37 about five minutes ago," the man explained.

"You were supposed to be coordinating with 821st Recon. And they are supposed to be tracking that Skylon from the moment it takes off to the moment it lands again," Kozytsin complained.

"Do they know that, sir?" Karas asked innocently. "Because we had no reports of it launching. I checked the latest intel report from the 821st on the Skylon and it said it had landed eight days ago and was expected to be undergoing a standard six-week refit before redeployment.

Kozytsin swore. "Show me."

Karas leaned over his desk and punched a few keys to bring up a tactical screen on his monitor. It showed the position of the Groza in orbit and, relative to it, the trailing X-37, which had been sitting on it like a tick on a bull since their last contact. Too far out to regard as threatening, but too close for comfort.

"Here," Karas said, pointing to a third icon moving slowly across the screen. "It appears to be moving to a position where it can also match orbit. At the range it is keeping, my people think it is conducting a reconnaissance mission."

"That bloody X-37 has been trailing our Groza for days, you don't think they have enough images yet?" Kozytsin asked.

Karas shrugged. "Maybe the US is not sharing, so the British felt they should get a look at it themselves. The pattern is similar to the last encounter between the RAF Skylon and one of our Grozas. Could be they're building a library of images?"

"Or it could be the cavalry has arrived, as they say, and they plan to blow us out of the sky." Kozytsin stood. "The Skylon can be fitted with space to space missiles, Sergeant. Order your men to junk their assumptions and prepare for an attack from two quarters. Defensive systems should plan to counter an attack from either laser or missiles or both. Order your offensive systems squad to get the *Shakti* online."

Karas blinked at him, not picking up the urgency in Kozytsin's tone.

"*Now*, man!" Kozytsin shouted.

The *Shakti* kill vehicle deployed on the Groza was an export version of the Indian anti-satellite missile of the same name. Cylindrical in shape with vectoring thrusters situated around its base, it was mounted at the bottom of the Groza hub holding the tungsten warheads and had an advanced terminal guidance system which included an imaging infrared seeker and ring-laser gyroscopes for detecting and tracking its targets. Once fired, it directed itself to its target using solid propellant thrusters and destroyed its objective

234

by ramming it at such speeds that if it struck an enemy satellite, the two objects behaved like fluids and the *Shakti* passed straight through its target, its fuel detonating as it did so, leaving nothing behind but two clouds of debris speeding in different directions.

The US intelligence services knew Russia had sourced a number of *Shakti* kill vehicles from India and was trialing them atop its *Nudol* missile system. They did not know the *Shakti* had already been fitted to Groza.

"Skylon, Bertha. We are ready to begin radiating," O'Hare said over the interservice channel.

"Bertha, Skylon. We are in position and clear to launch. Good luck, Captain," Meany replied.

Luck is for losers, mate, O'Hare nearly said out loud, then remembered Rodriguez was riding shotgun inside the virtual cockpit, and bit her tongue. The two attacking spacecraft were in position, and Meany had reported he was weapons hot and ready to engage as soon as Bertha locked the Groza on radar.

"Light it up, Minnesota," O'Hare said.

"Locking target," Albers said, hands flicking across his input panel. A tone sounded in the control center and he nodded. "Target locked, data streaming."

O'Hare had not planned to watch the engagement with Bertha just sitting still in space. ('Still' being a relative term when you were orbiting at 17,000 miles an hour. But if she wasn't maneuvering, then it was a predictable orbit, which made her a sitting duck for an anti-sat missile.)

"Lighting main thruster," she told Albers, pushing forward on the main throttle with her left hand as her right hand sat loosely on the side-stick that controlled roll, yaw and pitch. She had the glass in front of her left eye showing a VR 'cockpit' style view of space ahead of Bertha that panned as she moved her head. Her longer vision was focused on the large panoramic cockpit display that showed avionics, mission and theater data, operational status, VR to 2D, and spacecraft parametric data. "Vectoring to…"

"Thermal bloom," Albers called out. "I've got a thermal bloom at the base of the hub, and it's rising fast."

A hundred thoughts flashed through O'Hare's mind. A sudden thermal bloom could mean an energy weapon powering up. Missile launch? Vectoring thrusters?

"Skylon. Fire!" O'Hare said quickly. "Prepare for evasive action."

"Bertha, Skylon. Engaging," Meany's voice shot back immediately.

Meany's VR rig was not identical to O'Hare's. His was a full-head helmet, and he had it set up to simulate a panoramic cockpit view across the width of the top half, and four systems and status screens across the bottom half that followed his view as he turned his head. Neither did he have manual flight controls. He was more like the commander on the bridge of a ship, shouting orders at his executive officer, who in this case was the AI with the Scottish brogue, Angus.

Target locked, launcher powered and set to staggered volley, all systems nominal, ready to fire, the AI said in Meany's ears.

Meany blanked his VR vision and dropped into the real, turning his head to look quickly at Squadron Leader Bear who was standing beside him. Bear simply nodded.

Meany brought his screens up again. "Volley two, Angus. Reposition. Prepare to evade and re-engage."

Firing missiles.

A half world away and 900 miles up in the sky, the RAF Skylon fired the first space-space missile ever fired in combat between nations. The box launcher for the Skylon's advanced short-range multispectral seeker missiles extended out of its payload bay in the middle of the spacecraft ready to fire a broadside at the Groza. At Meany's command, two missiles were punched mechanically from their tubes and then accelerated toward the Russian satellite fifty miles away. Immediately, the Skylon began moving to a new firing position in case a second volley was needed.

A warning tone sounded and Angus' voice filled the command center. *Possible incoming missile. Target has deployed chaff and flare countermeasures and is maneuvering. Engaging evasion protocols.*

"Missile target?" Meany asked quickly.

Skylon is the target, Angus confirmed. *Twenty-three seconds to impact.*

"Missile launch from the Groza," Albers called, his voice flat and even now. "Target is firing anti-radar, anti-laser chaff and flares. Target is maneuvering."

O'Hare had already seen it and reacted. The heat bloom at the base of the Groza's cylindrical hub had risen in hue to iridescent green on her visor and a missile had blasted off from the main body of the satellite in a blaze of iridescent green. The Russians had mounted a missile inside the hub, and it had launched.

It wasn't aimed at Bertha.

Her tac monitor showed two missiles arcing out from the Skylon, which was accelerating away from the Groza. And whatever the projectile was that had just been fired by the Groza was looping around on an intercept course for the Skylon.

O'Hare knew exactly what she needed to do, and she knew she was not pilot enough to do it. No human was. She locked up the big Russian missile, quickly hit a two key combination on the keyboard in front of her to tell the combat AI what to do, and sat back in her seat, gripping the sides of the seat as though she was on a roller coaster ride.

"AI has flight control," she announced.

"I'm locked out," Albers said, turning to her. "Losing laser lock. Ma'am, what…"

"Kamikaze code, Lieutenant," she told him. "Something that saved my ass once before. We'll see if it can save the Skylon now."

Rodriguez knew better than to second guess O'Hare, but unless she was very much mistaken, the pilot had just issued an order that would cost her B for Bertha.

"Speak to me, O'Hare," she ordered.

"Ma'am, that projectile, whatever it is, is on an intercept course for the Skylon. There is zero chance they can evade it. And zero chance we can take down this Groza on our own. We were already accelerating. We can intercept that projectile before it reaches the Skylon." O'Hare turned around. "We will lose Bertha, but the Skylon is still in play if we need a second volley of missiles to take the Groza down." O'Hare held a hand over her keyboard. "I can still recall Bertha, ma'am, give me the word."

"Groza firing close-in weapons," Albers announced. "We are being engaged by 30mm. It won't tag us if we stay on this…"

Rodriguez thought fast, took a deep breath and gripped O'Hare's chair hard. "Stay with your call, Captain."

Nine seconds to incoming object impact. Space Force X-37 is maneuvering to intercept. Our missiles are tracking… Angus said, keeping up a running commentary.

Which was necessary for Meany and Paddington because they didn't know where to look.

Their Skylon was extending away from the Groza, chased by the Russian missile or whatever it was, which was closing fast. There was no way they could evade it from a standing start. Their own missiles were headed for the Groza, which had fired clouds of reflective foil and iridescent flares to scatter the X-37's laser and confuse any radar or infrared guidance. But Angus also had an optical lock on the huge Groza and the missiles were still tracking, not fooled by the Russian countermeasures. The Groza was vectoring too, pulling away behind the flimsy shield of the chaff clouds it had fired, trying to force his missiles to make course adjustments that would cost them precious fuel.

It was a flat-out footrace between the British missiles and the Russian, the only question was whose would strike first. As though he was up there himself, Meany winced and prepared for his machine to go fatally dark.

238

Then, from the side of his tac screen, he saw the icon for the X-37 suddenly appear, and curve toward the incoming Russian projectile.

Although he was half a world away, the panoramic VR cockpit view made Meany feel like he was right there, like it was his life on the line, not just Angus. He stood up, his exoskeleton whirring with the sudden movement, forcing Paddington to step away in alarm.

Enemy missile impact in five seconds... Angus said, calmly counting down to his own death.

"Go, Bertha!" Meany yelled.

Inside his helmet, Meany saw the flaming rockets of the Russian kill vehicle heading straight for him from his upper forward quarter. Turned. Saw the fast-moving white blur that was the US Space Force X-37 striking upwards from his lower rear quarter. Felt his stomach heave in sympathy with Angus as the AI fired all of its forward thrusters at the same time as it fired decoy flares in a desperate and completely futile attempt to trick the Russian missile into overshooting.

Saw the US X-37 *slam* into the side of the Russian kill vehicle with a silently unreal violence that felt like it should have shaken his teeth from their sockets. Both vehicles dissolved into gaseous balls of fuel and a million shards of shrapnel, and Meany felt himself hunching his shoulders, expecting to see the Skylon fly straight through them until he remembered it had frantically reversed thrusters and was slowly gathering momentum away from the debris of the collision.

Skylon missile one, detonation. Missile two still tracking. Missile two ... detonation, Angus announced, reporting on the progress of their own attack, ignoring his own near death. *Target hit.*

Meany spun his head around to where he last saw the Groza.

On Cape Canaveral station, every screen in the X-37 virtual cockpit went blank and O'Hare ripped off her VR rig, snapping her fingers at Albers. "Pull up the feed from the Skylon."

He leaned forward, frantically hammering keys. They no longer had a direct data link between their X-37 and the Skylon, but they could pull data from a shared feed between Lossiemouth and the Cape that had been set up as a backup.

A series of instrument and status screens came up first. O'Hare's eyes scanned across them, saw they were still receiving data, real-time data.

She raised a fist in the air. "Yes. They're still in the fight!" she whooped. She punched Albers' arm. "Bring up their virtual cockpit."

She and Albers had six multifunction screens on the panels in front of them, three in front of each officer, and they all wiped clean and then showed a panoramic view of what Meany was looking at, at that moment. O'Hare took it in at a glance and grabbed for her throat mike.

"Skylon, Bertha. You still mission capable, Lieutenant?"

Static came back, and then a strained voice. "All systems online. We were peppered with missile debris. No idea about external damage. But yes, Captain, we are still here, thanks to you."

"De nada. Give me a status on the Groza," she said.

"One missile was spoofed by countermeasures, one hit the main body of the Groza. We appear to have knocked it into an eccentric roll, but I can't say we have successfully compromised its orbit."

"You are still tracking, still got a missile lock?" O'Hare asked.

"Yes, ma'am."

O'Hare flipped up her eyeglass and looked to Rodriguez for a steer.

"Fire another salvo, Lieutenant," Rodriguez said. "Send that thing to hell."

Karas was speaking in a loud panicked voice to his propulsion squad. "I want you to get that roll back under control." And to his defensive weapons team. "Status on the 30mm?"

"One down, one still operational," the corporal in charge reported.

Dammit, Karas cursed to himself. If they hadn't been engaging that crazy American spacecraft at the time, they could easily have taken down the incoming RAF missiles with their autocannons. With only one still operable, he doubted they could survive a second attack.

"Where is the American?" Kozytsin demanded, confused by what had just happened. "What the hell is going on, Karas?"

"Comrade Captain, the American was destroyed by the *Shakti* kill vehicle. We successfully decoyed one missile but took a hit from the other. I am assessing damage and trying to keep the satellite in orbit."

"The Skylon?" Kozytsin asked.

"Appears undamaged. I expect it to attack again."

Kozytsin thought quickly. "Defensive systems?"

Karas ran a finger across a screen in front of him. "Jamming online. Chaff and flare launchers online. Blinding laser offline. One 30mm offline, one online. But we're in an uncontrollable roll and…"

A corporal two rows of desks further down the control room raised two arms in the air. "We have stabilized the roll!"

Karas looked at a situational screen. Yes, the Groza had stopped twisting on its long axis, but its gun was not in the right position relative to the Skylon. "Get that cannon oriented toward the enemy so we can get an infrared lock dammit," Karas yelled at him.

"Fire at long range, Sergeant," Kozytsin said. "There's no reason to let him sit still and take pot shots at us."

"Sir, I recommend we set the autocannon to close-in defense mode and attempt to engage incoming missiles, not waste ammunition on a long-range engagement with…"

"You have only *one* cannon, Sergeant," Kozytsin told him, almost hissing at him. "You aren't going to intercept the enemy missiles. But you may be able to score a hit on that Skylon. All you need to do is chip a heat tile and we will never have to worry about it again."

"Sir, we can still save our satellite," Karas insisted. "They have only four remaining missiles. You could call for a *Nudol* strike, or…"

"There is no *Nudol* unit within range of that Groza, Sergeant. Our naval coverage extends only up to about New York, or I would already have called for help." There was sudden silence across the control center as every man at every station strained to listen to the conversation. "That Groza is already a write-off. All that remains is the question of whether it takes one or both of its attackers down with it." He reached for a phone on his desk. "Engage with 30mm. I will call Bondarev in Titov."

The target satellite has stabilized its roll and is maneuvering, Angus said.

"Angus, lock the target and prepare to volley two more missiles, on my command." They had lost the targeting data from the X-37, but his own sensor suite was still giving him a solid yellow. The missiles' active seeker heads would have to do the rest.

Yes, Lieutenant, powering launcher. Tracking...

Squadron Leader Bear was watching a zoomed image of the Groza and saw vectoring jets firing along its length, but there was something...

"Image analysis. Angus, please compare with earlier imagery and estimate damage to the Groza," he asked the AI.

Yes, Squadron Leader. There was a short pause. *I estimate that our missile struck in the center mass of the main body of the satellite, just below one of the 30mm cannons. The dome appears to have been perforated in multiple places and is leaking fuel, but it did not explode. One cannon appears to be out of action, one may still be in operation. Vectoring jets appear to have been impacted. Six of twelve appear operational and ... incoming fire.*

"What?" Meany asked.

Ballistic projectiles, 30mm. Angus reported. *Time to impact, one minute thirty. Shall I evade?*

"Launch missiles then retire, Angus," Meany commanded. "With alacrity, please."

Warning, Angus said, his voice sounding way too calm for their situation. *The incoming projectiles are being sprayed across multiple egress paths. If we hold and launch, there is a 13 percent likelihood we will be...*

"Fire missiles, dammit," Meany ordered. "And then scoot!"

Firing. Missile one away. Missile two away. One and two tracking. Evading incoming fire.

Meany held his breath. Because it wasn't his life on the line, his full focus was on their outbound missiles. He saw the Groza fire more of the clouds of chaff and flares and try to maneuver, but it wasn't the controlled evasion he had seen it execute previously. It wobbled erratically and began rotating through space on a diagonal axis. Both of the RAF missiles ignored the floating balls of metallic tape and glowing flares that lay between them and the Groza, and slammed into it at thousands of miles an hour, their high-explosive blast-fragmentation warheads detonating on impact and sending pieces of the satellite flying in a hundred directions while the bulk of it continued through space on its current orbit.

Impact. Target destroyed, Angus confirmed. *Moving to evade incoming fire. Risk of damage from incoming fire is now zero point five percent.*

Meany realized he was still standing and lowered his exoskeleton to a seating position. Paddington put a hand on his shoulder, and Meany felt it trembling slightly. "Good show, Lieutenant."

O'Hare knew enough to know she shouldn't disturb Meany during the engagement, but she broke in on him now. "Skylon. Bertha. Well done, RAF. That's a kill."

"Shared kill, I'd say, Captain," Meany replied.

"Nope, all yours. I like mine clean. I just ran interference, you scored the touchdown, Lieutenant," she said.

O'Hare noticed something on one of the Skylon's screens and reached for her throat mike again. "Skylon, can you put a camera on that debris field? It looks like the tungsten projectiles are rapidly deorbiting…"

She was right. The hub carrying the four-ton warheads of tungsten had been hammered by the RAF missiles and separated from the rest of the satellite. They were too heavy for the small warheads on the missiles to have disintegrated them and were struck at an angle that jolted them off their orbital path and on a radical trajectory toward earth.

O'Hare saw them falling slowly away from the Skylon and, with every passing second, closer to the earth's atmosphere.

"Oh crap," Albers said, turning to Rodriguez. "I assume someone accounted for this possibility when we were given the intercept point, Colonel?"

"Assume nothing," Rodriguez said, reaching for a mike on the console in front of her. "Skylon, Bertha. This is Colonel Rodriguez. Can you get a lock on that falling debris and keep it locked as long as possible so we can calculate a re-entry and possible impact point?"

"Yes, Colonel," Meany replied. "We'll shadow it as long as possible."

Rodriguez looked at the feed from the Skylon and saw mountainous peaks flowing past far beneath them, with deep blue water beyond. "Lieutenant Albers, get me a line to NORAD, please."

Severin's voice came over the room speakers in the virtual cockpit. "Colonel, we are seeing the same feed. We have already alerted NORAD and they are tracking the debris from the ground."

"Do they have an impact point yet?" Rodriguez asked.

"Too early, ma'am, but I'm pretty sure they have about a million quantum cores working that problem right now."

O'Hare was watching the same vision. "I think that's Newfoundland, ma'am," she said. "Saint Lawrence Bay, Prince Edward Island, then New Brunswick beyond that."

"Maine," Albers said quietly. "I've deorbited space junk before, when I used to fly as wizzo on the X-37B." He pointed a finger at the virtual horizon as the fast receding tungsten warheads dropped toward earth. "Just eyeballing it, I want to say it's going to sail right over Canada, hit atmo somewhere over Maine."

"And burn up, right?" O'Hare said.

"It's not designed to burn up, Captain," Rodriguez said quietly. "It's designed to rain metal down on whatever is underneath it."

Steven Mackay was a true 'cold water cowboy.' He'd started fishing as a 14-year-old on his father's trawler, *Midnight Sun*. When other kids were sleeping, he'd be getting up at 3 a.m. to bait trawls. While they were at soccer, baseball or basketball, he was out in a skiff with his father, hauling in gill nets, his hands so cold he couldn't even button his shirt.

Now he was thirty and on his fourth boat. He'd sold one, and lost two at sea. One to a prop fouled by a net, the other was 175 miles offshore when it was hit by a chunk of ice the size of a house, 30-foot swells and hurricane-force winds. But he'd never lost a crewman, and he didn't plan to.

He'd looked out his kitchen window this morning trying to gauge wind and weather. He'd wanted to get to one of his favorite spots today; 40 miles south, off Newfoundland's Tors Cove. The forecast had predicted a wind chill of about 8.6 degrees Fahrenheit, minus 13 Celsius. Winds from the northwest 22 knots. The rest of the week offered more of the same. At least the skies were clear.

Newfoundland's fishermen had their own language and weren't given to being overly expressive. Down at the wharf in St. John's, he'd passed a friend of his father's who was just coming in from a couple of days' solo fishing.

"Arn?" he'd asked (get any?)

"Narn," the man had replied (nary a one).

He was still hopeful. His new boat, *Blood Moon*, was powered by a Norwegian *Selfa Arctic* electric motor with a fraction of the moving parts of his old diesel-powered boats. It had a smaller backup diesel engine but he'd rarely been out long enough to need to engage it. *Blood Moon* was equipped with the latest in fish-locating echosounder and sonar; he had net sounders on his trawl to tell him how concentrated the fish were around the net, catch sensors to tell him how quickly his net was filling, tension and symmetry sensors to warn him if his net was getting unbalanced as he hauled it in.

His first mate was a brick outhouse of a man who everyone called by the name Diesel because in former times he smelled like he used it for cologne. *Blood Moon* might be electric, but Diesel was still called Diesel.

Up in his wheelhouse, checking their course, Mackay heard Diesel shout. Diesel almost never shouted.

"Steven, look up!" Diesel called.

Mackay looked out of his wheelhouse window and saw nothing, so he backed up and stuck his head out to see where Diesel was shouting from. He saw him down at the stern, hands on his hips, head tilted back. A couple of the other men were standing beside him, looking up too.

"Where away?" Mackay called.

Without turning, Diesel raised an arm in the air and pointed almost straight up into the sky.

Mackay leaned back and squinted. The sun was falling out of the damn sky!

That's what it looked like. A blazing ball of fire was arcing through the sky above them. As they watched, transfigured, it seemed it was accelerating as it fell and flashed overhead.

"It's gonna hit the water," one of the men yelled, panic in his face. "Out there!"

"G'wan," said another, dubiously.

Mackay wasn't in any doubt. "Mind now!" he called out, and saw the men on the stern spread their legs and grab for the nearest handhold.

As the sea lit up around him from the light of the comet or meteorite or whatever it was, Mackay dived inside the wheelhouse again. Reacting with an instinct born of 15 years on the sea, he pushed the throttle to full power, spun the wheel and turned his boat away from where it looked like the thing was going to meet the sea.

The *Blood Moon* reacted instantly, another benefit of the electric engine, surging forward and kicking up a massive bow wave as it went from a comfortable straight line ten knots to a skidding, jarring seventeen knots in a matter of seconds. The men on the stern dropped to a crouch to ride the skidding turn, their eyes locked on the fireball overhead.

Mackay had his back to the meteorite when it hit. It felt like it hit right behind them, but there was no sound.

And then a thunderclap like the voice of Thor broke over the boat, a mighty wave lifted it up by the stern and Mackay's head slammed forward on the *Blood Moon*'s instrument panel, sending his consciousness spiraling into a red-black void.

The Groza was designed to release its tungsten warheads one at a time, even when launching a full-payload strike, to allow for a broader footprint of destruction. Only one test had been conducted where an entire hub and payload had been deorbited as a single unit. It had broken up during re-entry, but not so much that the 24-ton warheads around the central hub had separated dramatically. They struck the tundra in the equivalent of one 80-ton fireball and exploded.

The effects were less than impressive, from Chief Scientist Grahkovsky's perspective. Her team had been hoping for a destructive effect similar to a US Massive Ordnance Penetrator (MOP) bomb, which had less than a quarter of the Groza's projectile mass, but which carried 5,300 lb. of explosives. The MOP could break through 200 feet of 500 psi hardened concrete, and Russia currently had nothing like it in its conventional weapons arsenal.

One issue was that deorbiting the entire hub and payload with only crude guidance did not allow the calculation of a precise strike point, so the Groza aerospace engineers aimed it at a large swathe of Siberian wasteland and watched to see what happened.

The fireball buried itself fifty feet into the frozen ground, which unfortunately absorbed most of the explosive force of the blast. It formed a crater two hundred feet in diameter, but impressively turned most of the sandy soil around the crater to glass, creating an almost perfect bowl around the molten metal core at the bottom of the crater.

After the test, Grahkovsky advised her military supervisors that it made no sense to use Groza in this way. Conventional deep penetration munitions were as or more effective and much less expensive, assuming the delivery vehicle could reach the target without being intercepted. Development of Groza as a possible deep penetrator weapon had ceased.

Unfortunately for the crew of the *Blood Moon*, the eighty tons of superheated tungsten and iron plasma gas that hit the sea just five miles off their stern were not striking Siberian tundra.

They were striking sea water, and the Groza strike instantly vaporized 31,873 cubic feet of water.

Like a rock thrown into a pond, a shock wave radiated outward in a circle from its epicenter, sending thirty-foot-high storm-surge-sized waves out in every direction. That the energy in the waves rapidly dissipated further out from the epicenter was no comfort to Steven Mackay. He was lying unconscious and bleeding inside the wheelhouse of the *Blood Moon*, with his small trawler flying down the face of the surging wave front at about thirty knots.

Diesel and the other crew members were clinging on for dear life at the stern of the *Blood Moon*, looking in horror at the approaching surface of the flat sea below them as the trawler speared down the face of the wave.

She was a beautiful boat, the *Blood Moon*. She only had six feet of freeboard at the stern but had nearly twenty at her big bluff bow. As water crashed over the stern of the boat, its bow slammed into the flat plane of the ocean in front of it and parted it like a slapping hand. Diesel and the other crew members were thrown forward, tumbling down the deck to crash into the rear wall of the crew cabins, but she didn't go under. She dug her nose in and then stubbornly bobbed up again.

As Diesel lay panting, sure he'd smashed his ribcage in the wild fall, he felt the deck heave and the stern rise again.

Oh me nerves, he thought to himself, clutching for support and feeling his anger rise. *Now we're rotted.*

Impact. Fifty miles south-southwest of St. John's in Newfoundland, Angus announced in Meany's helmet.

"What's out there?" Paddington asked.

Nothing but ocean, sir, Angus replied.

"It won't cause a bloody tsunami, will it?"

No, sir. Any waves generated should subside before reaching nearby shorelines. I predict zero casualties.

Meany blew air out of his cheeks. "That was bloody lucky. That bugger could just as easily have taken out Portland or Boston."

"Let's hope we haven't used all of our luck then, Lieutenant," Paddington said. "Start running a hull integrity check. We have to hope that our bird got through that firefight with all of its heat tiles intact or the sacrifice of that X-37 will have been for naught."

Angus had been wrong. There had been several casualties from the Groza strike. Diesel had pierced a lung, and two other crew members had suffered fractured bones in the battering they had received from the surging sea. Luckily there had been no spinal injuries.

There had also been one fatality. Steven Mackay had been airlifted from the deck of *Blood Moon* by a Canadian Coast Guard quadrotor and flown to St. John's Mercy Hospital. He never recovered consciousness and died from his head injury as he was being prepped for cranial surgery. He would never know that his last act had saved the lives of all of his crewmen, but if he had lived long enough to be told, he would probably just have shrugged like the Newfie he was and changed the subject.

Yevgeny Bondarev cut the call to Captain Kozytsin and slammed his cell phone down on his desk. Luckily it was rated for hard shocks, just like its owner. He couldn't blame Kozytsin. The man had done exactly what he would have done, and by all accounts, even that fool Karas and his men had performed well.

He stood and walked to the window of his office, looking out into a dark forest of pines. In shadows, the enemy could hide. Clearly, the US and British felt that they could act with impunity, creeping around in the dark of space, knocking out his Groza units one by one. But he had claimed one of theirs. He remembered his conversation with Arsharvin about the US preparations to put another X-37 in orbit.

"Intel check. Update on planned US Cape Canaveral or Kennedy heavy-lift rocket launches. Timeframe, the next two weeks."

His telephone chimed as the personal digital assistant on his phone forwarded his inquiry to encrypted GRU servers and returned with a response.

Validating voice print log on ... welcome, General Bondarev. There is a SpaceX Falcon Heavy in the final stages of preparation for a launch from Cape Canaveral scheduled in two weeks. Previous intel assessments indicate the launch readiness schedule could be advanced for a launch window as early as four days from now. Do you want more detail?

"Yes. Do we know what the payload is?"

There is no secret intelligence on the payload available. Open-source intelligence indicates the payload as 'Space Force undisclosed.' Can I help with...

"No, log me out."

Thank you for using GRU intellibot. You are logged out, General Bondarev.

'Intellibot.' What pimple-faced, sneaker-wearing cyber teen came up with that name? He spun round, picked up the cell phone and dialed.

'Space Force undisclosed' payload. If he was the commander of the US X-37 fleet, he'd be moving hell and high water to put another unit into space right now. If the payload of that Falcon Heavy wasn't an X-37C before, it sure as hell would be now.

Though it would be relatively easy, he knew he wouldn't be allowed to shoot the Falcon Heavy and its X-37 payload out of the sky with a *Nudol* missile from his Cuba-based *Lider* destroyer as long as this new cold war was only taking place in space. He had an idea, though. One that he was sure even Popovkin would approve.

And before that, he had another nagging problem to deal with.

Running scenarios

Titov Space Test Facility, Timonovo, Russia

To Anastasia Grahkovsky, the loss of one of her Grozas was more than just a military problem. It was a personal one. She regarded each of the satellites with the same love and affection a mother would give her children. But of the sixteen launched, two had been used on Abqaiq, two on Korla, and one had been destroyed by the Americans. That left only eleven of her children still in orbit and those dullards Popovkin and Bondarev had shown themselves patently incapable of defending them.

She had listened in on a debrief of the engagement over the polar skies and had quietly scoffed at General Popovkin's bravado. "The Americans challenge our mastery of their skies, but they will learn that if they destroy one Groza, we will replace it with two. If they destroy two, we will replace them with four. And they will run out of their precious X-37s before we run out of Grozas."

Just as the Navy would not think of sending a new ship to sea without the ability to defend itself, Grahkovsky had argued strongly for fitting her Groza platform with the *Shakti* kill vehicle. The addition of the offensive weapons system had added nearly a year to the program, and also added an element of risk that some regarded as completely unacceptable. Chaff launchers, flares, these were minor additions. But what value was there in adding a single kill vehicle to their design? And what if the damn thing blew up when it was launched? What if the heat it generated when launching damaged the hub mechanism? There was little point in being able to defend a Groza satellite if the act of defending it crippled it. She had won the argument and redesigned her satellites so that the risk from the *Shakti* was minimized before she signed off on the new design.

And it had managed to bring down a US X-37. Hoo-ra Anastasia. It had still been lost to that damned Skylon.

She had always admired the design and flexibility of the RAF Skylon. It required minimal special infrastructure, just a very long runway. It was suborbital by nature, and couldn't stay in space for extended periods of time like the X-37, but its high-capacity payload bay made it very flexible, able to field different weapons modules and even carry a large personnel capsule into space if needed.

251

Working together, the Americans and British made a formidable team – the X-37 as nimble as a fighter jet, the Skylon as powerful as a strategic bomber.

The first US laser attack had worried her, and though they had been driven off, she had assumed it would be just a matter of time before they were back. And this time, in the company of the British, they had succeeded. Like any mother, Grahkovsky was not content to let others take care of her children's safety. Especially others who had shown they were not capable of doing so.

She was prepared to act – in fact, had already taken the first steps straight after the US laser attack. She was about to take the next.

"Corporal Maqsud, thank you so much for coming," she said. She did not stand but pointed to where she knew there was a chair. "Please, sit. There should be tea and coffee on the side table."

"I came because I was ordered, Madam Chief Scientist," the Corporal said sullenly. She heard him take a cup of tea and sit down. "Can I ask why?"

"Of course," she said. "I imagine that on the long flight from Baikonur to Moscow, you had time to speculate on that. Why do *you* think I asked for you?"

He sipped his tea before answering. "I think you want to discuss why I compressed the recommended strike footprint for the Korla attack."

"Go on."

"I will tell you exactly what I told Captain Kozytsin in the debrief you have no doubt read. I had reviewed the engineering intelligence on the Korla bridges the night before the strike. My own calculations convinced me that a more concentrated strike was needed to bring down one or more of the bridges. I was still validating my calculations right up until the moment of launch so there was no time to raise the issue for discussion. I adjusted the targeting parameters according to my calculations and, as events demonstrated, I was right."

Grahkovsky coughed, the closest she could come to a chuckle. "Ah, so your back of a cigarette packet 'calculations' were right, whereas the output of Titov computing facility's quantum computing AIs was wrong?"

"The outcome of the strike was exactly as hoped," Maqsud said defensively. "You cannot question my judgment."

She stood, taking up her cane. She knew this intimidated people, forced them to look at her rather than look away. She had perfected the art of staring straight at them, even though she could not see them, because she knew that unnerved people too. Horrified them, even. Some people, but not all. There were men who found her scarred visage and milky eyes compelling, even beautiful. She wondered which of these Maqsud Khan was.

"Exactly as hoped, but not exactly as planned, was it, Corporal Khan?" she asked, standing beside him, about two feet away.

"How do you mean?" he asked. She could tell by his voice he hadn't turned away, that he was still facing her, looking up at her. Good, not horrified then.

"The estimated civilian casualty tally for the operation ranged from two to five thousand. But because you compressed the strike footprint, only one thousand three hundred civilians died."

"Another success," he said defiantly. "The military objective was achieved, and civilian casualties were minimized."

She stood with the cane between her legs and put her weight on it, leaning forward. "How quickly you adjust your moral pain threshold, Maqsud. In the Abqaiq strike, you were horrified at the idea you might kill a few hundred civilians. Now you consider it a moral victory that you only killed one thousand three hundred?"

Now he turned away. "I do my duty to the *Rodina*, in the best way I know. You created a mass murder weapon, who are you to question my morals?"

He must have known that speaking to her like this could see him court-martialed, imprisoned, or worse. One word to General Bondarev and even his precious Space Exploration medal would not save him; in fact, they might just pin it over his heart to give the firing squad something to aim at.

But she had not invited him to Titov to bully him or trick him into betraying himself.

"You misunderstand me, still," she said. She bent to where she guessed his head would be. She could smell sweat and aftershave, hear him breathing slowly and evenly. "I admire you," she whispered. "I envy you your morality. I am not a psychopath, Corporal Maqsud; I can see my own flaws, the deficiencies in my character. I serve the god of science." She walked around behind him, still whispering. "But my god has chosen to blind me, and I need you to be my eyes."

She tapped her way back to her desk, imagined him turning his head to follow her as she did so. She found her chair and sat. "I am about to conduct a series of simulations. I want you to run the targeting for these exercises. I have AI routines that can take care of simulating the systems and weapons management, but I need a human – specifically, you – to manage the targeting."

"Why?" he asked.

"Because an AI does not have your moral compass, nor do I. But I am not the monster you think I am, Corporal Maqsud. I too have an interest, admittedly an academic one, in seeing how we can best minimize the casualties caused by Groza in different strike scenarios. I have one of those scenarios queued up and ready to run, and I know with you at the controls, whatever the AIs have projected in terms of casualties, you will find a way to reduce them further, without compromising the objectives of the strike." She rested her cane against her chair and her hands in her lap. "In the future people like you will be replaced by more reliable AIs. To help us get to that day, I want my AI to learn from you."

She heard him relax a little, adjusting his posture, heard the swish of uniformed trouser cloth as he crossed one leg over the other. She estimated he was probably about six feet tall, solidly built but not heavy. She'd asked about him and learned he was a Uyghur. Uyghur males were allowed to wear a neatly trimmed beard in the Russian military, and she knew he had taken advantage of this because she could hear him scratching it now.

"What is this scenario?" he asked.

"Good, I have your attention at last," she said. "The target for this simulation is Cape Canaveral."

"You have my attention," Colonel Tomas Arsharvin said. "But not yet my understanding." He was sitting in the chair in front of Bondarev's desk, hands on his knees, leaning forward.

"You heard me. She is a spy. I want you to arrest her..." Bondarev said. He had just presented Arsharvin with his case against Roberta D'Antonia, his other 'nagging problem.' Grahkovsky planting the false information about a strike on Nebraska, the subsequent evacuation of the nuclear facility. "I am dealing with multiple threat vectors already. Having a foreign agent snooping around my facility is one that I do *not* need," he said.

Arsharvin interrupted Bondarev, ignoring for a moment the difference in their ranks. "With respect, Yevgeny, are you crazy? I can't just whistle up a few plainclothes officers and arrest the Principal Advisor to Energy Minister Denis Lapikov. I've heard about her – they even ran a piece about her in a Moscow paper. She was headhunted by Lapikov himself. She would have been looked at by the Security Service in forensic detail, and still she was cleared. Do you know how many toes you are asking me to step on?"

Bondarev looked annoyed. "Toes? You are worried about the *politics*? Sorry, I must have mistaken you for a GRU officer." His tone became conciliatory. "Tomas, I am also under considerable political pressure. The Americans are making daily representations to the Foreign Ministry about Groza..."

"Well..." Arsharvin interrupted. "You just vaporized a few thousand liters of sea water off the coast of Maine."

"They cannot prove that was Groza," Bondarev pointed out. "Popovkin is also under pressure from that idiot Kelnikov, asking him to prepare another Groza strike against the Saudis after the Iranians' ballistic missile attack was so easily intercepted. The fool wants to use Groza to attack Saudi Air Force bases! Popovkin is keeping him at arm's length now, but it is just a matter of time before someone in the Kremlin decides Saudi Arabia should be subject to another tragic meteor strike."

"And give the Americans all the proof they need to convince the world Groza exists," Arsharvin said.

"Which brings me back to the topic at hand. This Italian woman has no doubt been tasked to get that proof for them. And you are worried about stepping on toes?"

Arsharvin sighed. "When you put it like that, no."

"Then work with me here. Find some way to neutralize her."

Arsharvin raised an eyebrow. "Neutralize?"

Bondarev started. "Not that way. I mean, plant drugs in her apartment, find a problem with her visa, get her deported. Whatever it takes to stop her sniffing around my weapons program."

Arsharvin sat back, tilted his head and looked up at the ceiling. "Your whole Nebraska ploy ... it is too tenuous. I can't use any of that as evidence if Lapikov demands to see it, but I may still be able to retrieve the situation. Leave it with me."

"Do not leave it long," Bondarev warned. "I have met this woman twice, and she is tenacious. Every day she spends as a Kremlin insider is a day closer to her blowing the lid off my Groza program."

It would not have improved the mood of Yevgeny Bondarev to know that if he was to walk down three flights of stairs, into the west wing basement of the Titov central administration building where its computer center was housed, there he would have found Roberta D'Antonia deep in conversation with his Chief Scientist.

"Thank you for seeing me again at short notice, Chief Scientist Grahkovsky." She was standing just inside the doorway. There was nowhere to sit in the small office beside the chair Grahkovsky was already occupying.

"You are welcome," Grahkovsky said. She was sitting at a computer terminal, and as D'Antonia had been escorted in by a Titov security officer, she had been running her fingers over a braille printout. It might as well have been Chinese. D'Antonia could only see the small dots and bumps and had no idea if she was reading computer code, a journal publication or a letter from her mother. But then, she did wonder if Grahkovsky had even had a mother. "I assume this is about the Maine event?"

"Yes, it is. Thank you again for the warning you provided. But I was surprised when the window you provided of 36 hours came and went with no news of a meteorite strike, and even more surprised when it finally happened yesterday, off the coast of Maine, and not..."

"Not Nebraska?" Grahkovsky smiled as though at some internal joke. "Trust me; you were no more surprised than we were. But I told you, our algorithms for estimating the entry and impact point of asteroids from this field are crude and imprecise."

"I guess I am hoping, or my Minister is hoping, that in future, any predictions will become a little more ... reliable?" *Or let me put this another way*, D'Antonia thought to herself. *Less likely to be fabricated.*

Grahkovsky put her papers down on the desk and straightened them, aligning them with the edge of the desk. D'Antonia had to wonder whether she was completely blind, or whether perhaps she could see a little something, like shapes, or shadows.

"The Maine incident gave us incredibly valuable data," Grahkovsky said. "Data with which to refine our calculations, to aid our 'predictions,' as you call them. The more of these events that occur, and there will be more, I assure you, the more reliable our calculations become."

"Was the Maine event a new, unexpected event, or was it the Nebraska event, just later than projected and ... off the expected course?"

"It was the same event," Grahkovsky said after a slight pause. "Just later, and with a different entry and impact point than we had calculated. If it had been a new event, I would have advised you, as promised."

She did not sound sincere. But still, it was valuable intel. It made her earlier urgent report seem less of a fizzer if she had been right about the impending strike, just wrong in relation to where and when. And with a plausible explanation of why.

"If that impact point had been Boston, and we had been able to predict it, would we have alerted US authorities?" D'Antonia asked.

"There you go again, Ms. D'Antonia," Grahkovsky chided. "Asking me political questions. That is probably a question you should direct to your Minister or one of his colleagues."

"Yes, I'm sorry."

Grahkovsky picked up her papers again. "Now, if there is nothing else. I must get back to my work."

"Certainly," D'Antonia said. "Look. This is ... I was wondering if perhaps you'd like to join me for cocktails one night. I promise I won't ask you about your work; it would be entirely social." She took a step closer to the door, not crowding the woman. "It's just I know so few interesting people in Moscow."

Grahkovsky smiled. "Ah. And I am an *interesting* person?"

D'Antonia laughed. "Well, yes. Anyway, think about it. You have my office cell number. I promise it won't be boring."

As she closed the door behind her and nodded to the waiting security officer to show her out, D'Antonia felt a little sheepish. Was that dumb? She was about the same age as Grahkovsky, maybe a little younger. Two girls out in Moscow for cocktails, that wasn't so weird, was it? One a honey-blonde Italian, the other looking like a character from an apocalyptic video game...

OK, maybe it was dumb.

A short while later, Grahkovsky called up to Bondarev.

"Your Italian girlfriend was here earlier, General," Grahkovsky said. "Is there anything in her file about her being a lesbian?"

"What? The Minister's advisor? What are you talking about?"

"Nothing. She came by unannounced, asked me about the Maine incident, and then asked me out for cocktails."

"What? Wait." She heard Bondarev put his hand over his cell phone and call out to someone. "Get Arsharvin back here! He is still in the Center somewhere." He lifted his hand off the telephone again. "That woman is starting to annoy me. I would like you to accept that invitation."

"I am not having sex with a woman, General, even for my motherland."

"No one is asking you to," Bondarev said, a little flustered. "And I doubt that is what she meant. Italian women only ever go out in pairs or flocks, never alone. Don't you know that?"

"I had a sheltered upbringing, General. Can I assume you will at least pay for my drinks?"

"What? Yes, whatever. Please come up to my office. I need you to speak with someone about this."

"The GRU?"

"How do you know?"

"I heard you mention Colonel Arsharvin. Am I to be arrested?"

"No, but please come up and speak with the GRU, Chief Scientist. They will want to know about this interaction."

"This is quite inconvenient. When should I…"

"Now, Chief Scientist Grahkovsky."

Bunny O'Hare was also feeling greatly inconvenienced. Not only had they been forced to get up at zero dark thirty for the conference call with the RAF Skylon team in Scotland, but she had expected that one unwanted side benefit of having no operational X-37 to fly might mean she could get a little well-earned time off-base. Play a little pool. Drink a little beer. Shoot a little shit. Sleep. A lot.

They had set up two telepresence rooms on each side of the Atlantic. In one, Rodriguez had gathered 'Kansas' Severin, 'Zeezee' Halloran, O'Hare and herself. On the other side were Squadron Leader 'Paddington' Bear, his intelligence officer and Halloran's opposite number, a warrant officer called Stan (not his first name) Aston, and finally the RAF pilot with the rather impressive name, Flight Lieutenant Anaximenes 'Meany' Papastopoulos.

The US team was already online and waiting as the RAF team filed into the room. O'Hare watched with a tired disinterest until Meany came into the frame. Whirred into the frame, to be exact. She recognized him from the personnel file mugshots they had been sent when the telecon had been set up. O'Hare watched, her jaw a little unhinged, as the man in the exoskeleton found a place at the teleconference table and locked his powered frame into a balanced seated position as naturally as any of the others who were pulling out chairs.

Rodriguez and Severin had started making polite conversation, but O'Hare leaned forward and thumbed a mike. "Whoa. That's one fancy rig you got there, mate."

Meany grinned. "Thank you, Captain. I'd be happy to trade war stories one day."

"You're on, Flight Lieutenant," O'Hare said. "It'll be my shout."

"I guess that's our introductions over with," Rodriguez interrupted. "Ladies and gentlemen, we seem to all be here. Squadron Leader, if you'd like to begin?"

"Yes, Colonel. As you know, we've been authorized for a second joint-forces operation. Everyone here has participated in our Learning After Action, and, it is safe to say, there were many learnings, especially about the capabilities of these beasties."

There was no disagreement on either side of the line.

"As you would also be aware, Russia has responded to our intervention by moving not one, but two new Groza units into orbit over the continental USA. We note one of these orbits also has a potential strike footprint taking in Scotland, Eastern England, mainland Europe, Turkey, and the Middle East." He looked up, as though he could see through the ceiling. "An orbit which takes it more or less right over the top of Lossiemouth, which we do not regard to be a coincidence. So His Majesty's Government has authorized me to advise that all available resources, including our Skylon, are at your disposal."

The meeting had started more formally than Rodriguez was accustomed to, but she acknowledged his opening speech. "Thank you, Colonel, I think continued cooperation on this is in all our interests. Now, while I am told we have briefed NATO leaders on what we have seen, none are inclined to lend us the same level of assistance because, I'm afraid, the Russian asteroid field cover story is gaining more traction by the day, and also because they do not regard a 'collision in space' satisfies the requirements of Article 5 of the NATO treaty compelling them to come to our aid."

"I wonder how NATO defines 'collision,'" Zeezee wondered out loud. "Like, if a bullet hits the head of the General Secretary of NATO, is that just a collision?"

"Strike that comment from the record, please," Rodriguez said into the air. "The reason for this session is that we need to take down that Groza system, all remaining 15 units, without starting World War Three, and the math is against us. We can't keep trading one of our spacecraft for one of theirs, and the Groza is much more heavily armed than we first suspected. The missile which struck our X-37 has been identified as a modified Indian *Shakti* kill vehicle. Impossible to evade and damn near impossible to out-run. We have proven the Groza is vulnerable to missiles, but only during an attack from multiple vectors which overwhelmed its close-in weapons system."

Severin chimed in. "And if you are thinking of an attack by ground-based weapons, we refer you back to clause 1; we do not want to start World War Three. The Saudis and Iranians are already swinging at each other, and Russia is happily tossing grenades into the fire. We start swatting Russian satellites out of the sky with something as obvious as anti-sat missiles, World War Three is what we will get."

Meany raised a hand. "Colonel, are we brainstorming here, or do you have a proposal for us to consider? We can keep lobbing missiles at those Grozas, but we'd be creating debris fields so extensive no one would be able to put satellites into those orbits for another ten years."

Rodriguez and Severin exchanged a look. Which caught O'Hare by surprise, because she hadn't been forewarned of anything. She shot a glance at Zeezee, who sat, as usual, po-faced at the end of the table and gave nothing away. What? She was the only one not in the loop on whatever this was?

"We have had an approach, from ... an unexpected quarter," Rodriguez said.

"Would you care to expand on that, Commander?" Bear asked.

"Yes. It seems Abqaiq was not the only ground target to have been hit by a Groza strike in recent weeks. There was one other," she said.

Tomas Arsharvin was not a man to wait for permission before doing what was needed. If Yevgeny Bondarev said he wanted to be rid of a foreign intelligence agent who was threatening his operation, then rid of her he would be.

He commanded his own *Otriad*, or battalion, of GRU personnel, so finding warm bodies for an operation was not an issue. He had one *Spetsotdelin* or section which specialized in the rendition of high-value targets, aka kidnapping. It had conducted several espionage support operations in Russia, the former Soviet Republics, and even in Europe. Within 24 hours, he had the skeleton of a plan. Within 48, he was on the telephone to Bondarev again.

"You send me the paperwork, Major-General, and I can deal with your Italian problem by the end of this week."

"Not sooner?" Bondarev asked, only half joking.

"General, this isn't as simple as dropping rocks on people's heads from space. I have a team in the field, setting up the operation already. They will need two days. And I need to brief the individual I am going to use as bait..."

"Bait?"

If they pulled it off, Arsharvin's plan was a win-win: Bondarev would be rid of the foreign spy and the GRU would gain something too. But he needed Bondarev's help. "Yes, I will require the assistance of your Chief Scientist. She seems to have made a connection with the Italian. Don't worry; I have a team prepped to support her."

"You want the assistance of my most valuable staff member in a counter-espionage operation? Are you going to fill me in on the details of this operation?"

"Do you wish to know such details?" Arsharvin asked, surprised.

"I suppose not," Bondarev said. "But I do want my Chief Scientist back in one piece when it is done."

Arsharvin infused his voice with false innocence. "Is she currently in one piece?"

"China?" Bear asked. "China has offered to help us degrade Russia's Groza network? Why? How?"

"Pentagon assumes China got hit," Zeezee said. "Apparently, there was a seismic event near the Tarim Basin oil and gas fields a few days ago. It was logged as a small quake, but after China approached us, the seismic profile was compared to what we saw at Abqaiq, and it's a match."

"As to your second question, how can they help? They haven't told us," Rodriguez admitted. "But the approach came at the highest level; Chinese Ministry of Defense to State Department, Pentagon and now down to us for evaluation."

"Sorry, ma'am, but how can we evaluate whether they can help us if they won't tell us how they plan to do it?" Meany asked.

Rodriguez turned to her intelligence officer. "Halloran? Tell people what we know."

"Yes, ma'am. According to DIA, there is what we suspect and what we know. What we know is that China has recently deployed two anti-satellite systems, the first being the air or ship-launched JC-19 anti-satellite missile and kill vehicle combination. It was first tested in the late 2010s and is now deployed across the PLA Army Airforce and Navy. Not so interesting, for the same reason our own anti-sat missiles aren't really an option. The second is the *BX-1 Parasite* microsatellite system. This one is a little more interesting. We estimate China has about 100 of these 90 lb. microsats in orbit…"

"These are the things that physically attach themselves to passing satellites and then blow them up?" Meany asked.

"They've evolved," Zeezee said. "China learned that leaving debris in orbit is probably not a great idea, and also, not very stealth. So the latest *BX-1 build 3* clamps onto its target and uses microwave energy to fry its insides and disturb its orbit. All the enemy sees is that its bird has gone dead … the attack is virtually undetectable until you get a recon satellite or spacecraft up close and see the parasite."

"That could be a very real option," Paddington noted. "And a very fast one, depending on how quickly China could get these *Parasites* to match orbit with the Groza units."

"The third capability is unconfirmed," Zeezee continued. "We believe China has been experimenting with directed energy weapons on its *Tiangong* space station."

"Laser?" O'Hare asked.

"DIA analysts think they are testing various defensive close-in weapons systems for the station, both laser and microwave. Whether they can or are intended for use as offensive weapons is

263

debatable – the *Tiangong* is huge, it isn't exactly the sort of thing China can send all over the globe hunting enemy satellites."

"Thanks, Halloran," Rodriguez said. "It seems to us China has the capability, with either anti-sat missiles or this *Parasite* system, to help take down Groza. What they apparently lack is precise intel on which of the many Russian mil-sats in orbit *are* Grozas. And they lack up-to-date data on its offensive and defensive capabilities. They have asked us to share our intel so they can correlate it with theirs and coordinate a comprehensive strike."

Squadron Leader Bear coughed. "We need to be sure China is not talking about firing dozens of ground or air-launched missiles into space. For the same reasons we don't want to, we can't have them doing so, are we agreed?"

"Absolutely, Squadron Leader," Rodriguez agreed. "The *Parasite* option would be ideal. It leaves the Russian birds in orbit, we avoid huge debris fields or splashdowns like we saw off Maine, and it's highly unlikely Russia could ever prove why its satellites went dead."

"*If* Parasite really exists, no offense to DIA, and *if* it even works against these monsters," O'Hare said. "With respect, we had a hard time trying to burn through their skin with a high energy laser, so they definitely have heat shielding. What's to say they aren't shielded from microwave energy as well?"

"Good point," Meany agreed. "If they were shielded against the EMP burst from a tactical nuke, which would be smart, that would also protect them from microwave radiation, wouldn't it?"

"I'm not sure there is much of anything that could protect you from a limpet mine that attached itself to you and started pumping out high-intensity microwave energy," Halloran said. "My question if China uses *Parasite* mini-sats is how we would even know the Chinese attack was working? How do we see the Groza is dead if it is still orbiting?"

"Comms," Severin said. "The things must be in communication with a ground station. We can map their comms signatures; we'll see if they stop transmitting."

"Takes time, though," O'Hare said. "And it's not foolproof. Russia sees what's happening, it puts its Grozas into 'radio silence' mode, we think they're dead, and they just wake them up again later?"

Rodriguez turned to Zeezee. "Let me sum up. One: tell your Pentagon contact we need some commitments from China before we share our targeting data. The first is that they plan to use a covert space-to-space weapons system for their attack. No ground or air-to-space missiles. They won't want to confirm to us that *Parasite* exists, but if they agree, we can be pretty sure that is what they are using. Two: we want a test run. We give them solid intel on one Groza, they knock it out, and we check that it is dead. Only then will we share all our data and they can scale up their offensive. Any other thoughts before we close?"

O'Hare raised a hand. "This softly-softly approach, ma'am, if I was China? I might just say 'thanks but screw you, guys; we'll go with what we know and start taking out Grozas anyway.' Anti-sat missiles, micro-sats, whatever it takes."

"That might be what you'd do, Captain," Rodriguez observed. "But China came to us, remember. It seems they want to work together on this threat, and knowing the Chinese, they'll want to keep it low key."

Low key was exactly how Major Fan Bo of the People's Liberation Army (PLA) Xichang 27th Test and Training Base had been ordered to conduct its operation against the Russian Groza system. The PLA Strategic Support Force Network Systems Department had very quickly identified the attack on Korla as an orbital bombardment rather than a natural event. And given the large amount of open-source data being shared by Saudi and American sources claiming Russia was behind that attack, it reviewed its own data on the Groza system and reached the same conclusion as the US and UK.

Groza was an existential threat to Chinese aspirations in space, as well as to geopolitical stability, if Russia continued to use it to further its national economic goals.

Operational responsibility for responding to the Russian attack fell to Bo and his unit. Bo was commander of the Chinese *Mao Bei* program, otherwise known to western intelligence as *Parasite*. *Parasite* was indeed real. And it was capable beyond anything the western powers had imagined. Yes, the PLA had launched more than 50 *Mao Bei BX-1.3* mini-sats in the last five years. That had been impossible to hide. But it had also launched more than twenty *BX-1.4* satellites. Slightly larger than the 1.3, the *BX-1.4* weighed nearly fifty kilos, could operate at altitudes up to 1,500 miles above the earth, and importantly, it could swarm. Developed in order to be able to overwhelm defensive systems and disable large targets such as enemy space stations or industrial space construction platforms, up to four *BX-1.4s* could be linked and pilot themselves to match orbit with a target object. They would then distribute themselves around the object with equal spacing or, if ground controllers recognized the object, would attach themselves to pre-identified weak points. Once in place, the swarm would begin radiating, enabling a *BX-1.4* swarm to simultaneously target widely distributed propulsion or life support systems, communications, or weapons systems.

Bo was extremely proud of the sophistication of his weapons system. No other space-going nation could come close to matching it, and it was extremely effective. Close-in weapons systems such as lasers or ballistic weapons would find it hard to even lock onto the tiny satellites, and would almost certainly be defeated by a swarm. Once one or more *Mao Bei* had attached themselves to their target, that target was dead.

Or so he had thought. He had spent the morning reviewing a graphical reconstruction of the recent US and UK Groza engagement based on ground optical, signals intelligence, and radar observations. The reconstruction enabled him to see a 3D recreation of the battle sphere, with all combatants represented, and he could page forward and backward along the timeline of the engagement. Underneath the graphical screen, several smaller screens showed data about the engagement, from the velocity and relative distances of the combatants to the weapons used and estimate of damage inflicted.

The fight had been crude, even ugly. He shook his head, watching as the avatar for the US X-37 intercepted the Russian kill vehicle, and both were wiped from the board. At the end of the engagement, only the British Skylon remained operational, and it had all but depleted its missile store.

Why? He could clearly see the launch of the Russian *Shakti*, so the engagement confirmed what the PLA intelligence services had reported – Russia had mounted offensive weapons on its Grozas. But what else? Missile countermeasures, lasers, ballistic defenses … these could not be seen from the ground. Bo needed more data. He had every confidence in his *Mao Bei* mini-sats, even against these Russian behemoths, but he did not want to send them in unprepared.

And then there was the matter of how *many* Grozas Russia possessed. China had positively identified at least eight now, including the two believed responsible for the Korla attack. They were still orbiting, but whether they were capable of further attacks was impossible to know. They must possess powerful imaging and targeting capabilities, so it would make sense for Russia to leave them in orbit and use them for reconnaissance, even if their payloads were expended. But were there more than eight units? Even with AI assistants combing through databases of near-earth objects, they were still turning up more candidates.

It grated against every nerve in his patriotic body, but he needed whatever intel the Americans and British already possessed. Which meant they needed to work together. It was still only a year since a minor conflict over a US base on Okinawa had nearly cost the PLA Navy its flagship carrier, the *Liaoning*. The aircraft carrier was still docked in Shanghai, incapable of operations, repairs expected to take at least another year.

And now they were going to the US asking for help. But not begging. Bo knew, watching the US/UK engagement with the Groza, that China had the superior solution to counter the Russian threat. The US must know that too. He told himself the US needed China more than China needed the US.

And they were about to prove it.

Bo had been given permission to deploy his *Mao Bei* mini-sats to disable the two Russian satellites orbiting over China which had been judged to have been responsible for the Korla strike. China would not be waiting for the US to make up its mind whether to 'play ball' or not before addressing the existential threat over its own territory.

Two days later, Bondarev's 'Italian problem' had decided she would go straight from work at the Energy Ministry and not change, meeting Grahkovsky in her work clothes – a simple black pants suit and cashmere ankle-length fur-lined coat, with matching fur hat. The fur was mink, a product still allowed and in fashion in Russia. There were enough things on D'Antonia's mind on any given day; animal rights were not one of them. She had thought about changing into something more suited to a night tripping from cocktail bar to cocktail bar, but then she had no desire to spend the night warding off drunk, self-important Russian men or their bodyguards, and besides, she doubted Grahkovsky would dress up. The woman would probably turn up in her lab coat. But just to be sure, she sent her a text. "Will be going straight from work to Bar Noori, no time to change, see you there!"

She had a simple plan for tonight. Cultivation, nothing more. She had no illusions that Grahkovsky would get drunk and spill her guts about the Groza program. She had no special chemicals to slip into her drinks to loosen her tongue. When Grahkovsky had called to say she was taking her up on her invitation, she had said, "And you must promise, only girl talk, no work talk." So there would be no work talk tonight. Her goal for the evening was to put Grahkovsky in a cab at the end of the night thinking she was great company and agreeing they should do it again sometime.

With a potential source as valuable as Titov's enigmatic Chief Scientist, she was going to play a long game.

When she got to Noori at 9 p.m., it was only half full. The place didn't start jumping until 10 or 11, so they would have at least an hour to settle in, chat, have a few laughs, and put a couple of drinks away. Maybe two hours here and she'd suggest another place, more chill, where they could talk more easily.

As she walked in and checked her coat, she surveyed the bar and saw Grahkovsky across the room, already seated in a booth, with a bottle of champagne in an ice bucket beside her. Wow. Across the somewhat smoky room, in the sultry lights of the nightclub, the bald-headed woman looked strikingly beautiful. She wasn't wearing a lab coat; she was wearing a black short-sleeved, high-necked top, pearl necklace and earrings, knee-length pearl-colored skirt and black stilettos. D'Antonia smiled as she watched a man approach the booth, and then veer away at the last minute, no doubt as he got a closeup look at the crisscrossed scars on her face and bare arms. As D'Antonia approached, she noticed Grahkovsky had even swapped out her utilitarian wooden cane for a bronze one, topped with a silver handle in the shape of an eagle's head.

"Hello there!" D'Antonia called out before sliding into the booth. There was a spare glass waiting for her, and she clinked it against the neck of the champagne bottle. "You started without me."

"Yes, I'm a little nervous," the woman admitted. "Help yourself to a glass."

"Not your usual kind of place, Chief Scientist?" D'Antonia guessed, pouring herself some champagne and topping up Grahkovsky's glass.

"Something like that," the woman said. "And please, call me Anastasia."

D'Antonia held up her glass. "Let us drink it like friends, the Italian way." She wanted to get the party started. She reached for Grahkovsky's hand and saw for the first time that the pattern of tiny white scars spread over the woman's hands and forearms too. Grahkovsky's hand was cool and she half expected the woman to decline, but she didn't pull away. "See, we link arms, and both drink together – the whole glass," D'Antonia laughed, winding their arms around each other. She brought her head up next to Grahkovsky's, and they drank, cheek to cheek. "Salute!" D'Antonia said, wiping her mouth and putting down her glass. She sat back in the booth again. "Anastasia ... that's a lovely name. Much nicer than Roberta. How did your parents decide on Anastasia?" she asked.

Grahkovsky had turned her face toward the sound of D'Antonia's voice and had a curious half-smile on her lips. She didn't answer immediately, but it *was* noisy in the club, and Roberta was about to repeat herself when Grahkovsky answered, "Oh, I don't think we need to worry with the social chit chat yet, Roberta."

She lifted her cane and pointed discreetly toward a nearby table. "Do you see a group of men over there? Three, in dark suits? Take a sip of champagne while you are looking around, so they don't see you looking."

Roberta lifted her glass to her face and sipped. She saw the group Grahkovsky was talking about. They were young, fit and rich by the look of it. There was vodka in an ice bucket by their table. Two were talking, but one was looking straight at her. She made sure not to make eye contact and put her glass down, turning back to Grahkovsky. "Wow, you don't waste any time, ragazza. You would like me to invite them over or something?"

Grahkovsky picked up her champagne and sipped, then put it down again slowly. "No. I've already met them. They are GRU. They're here to arrest you."

D'Antonia's world tilted. No night out on the town, then. She looked quickly for exits.

Grahkovsky placed the tip of her cane across D'Antonia's feet. "Don't panic. They will only arrest you if you try to flee. They have men on every door." She lifted the cane away. "And I am told they know about your safe house and your second car, so if you tried to use those, you would end up in their clutches anyway."

"Sorry," D'Antonia said, stalling for time, thinking a mile a minute. "I don't understand. GRU? Intelligence service? But I have been vetted by the FSB, the Federal Security Service. This is some kind of misunderstanding."

"Apparently not," Grahkovsky said. "They are quite serious. They put poison in our champagne."

D'Antonia felt her skin chill and looked down at her half empty glass, then at Grahkovsky's, which was also half empty.

The woman had apparently anticipated her reaction. "It is quite slow-acting, but also quite deadly, I am told," the scientist said. "I was already given an antidote, but I do wonder if I will feel any effects. I am told the men over there have an antidote for you too. But it depends on your reaction to this conversation."

"This is crazy," D'Antonia insisted, keeping up a pretense of innocence. "Is this some kind of joke?"

"No. You will look directly at the men at the table now, please."

D'Antonia did so and saw that all three were looking straight at them. One lifted his jacket aside to show a handgun and lowered it again.

"I admit nothing because I have nothing to admit," D'Antonia said. "But I accept you are serious. What do you want?"

"I want nothing," Grahkovsky said lightly. She even took another sip of champagne. "You can't even taste it. I thought you would be able to taste it."

"Please, don't play games," D'Antonia said.

"I didn't realize I was, sorry," the woman said. "I want nothing, but they, the GRU, want you to work for them. They will create a natural-looking opportunity for you to meet with them, to tell them truthfully who you work for, what secrets you have stolen in your time in the service of Minister Lapikov and, if you agree to cooperate with them, I am told you can continue on exactly as you are. Go home to your flat tonight to sleep, go to work tomorrow with Minister Lapikov, keep serving whoever your foreign master is."

"If they think I am some kind of spy, that sounds highly unlikely," D'Antonia said.

"I agree," Grahkovsky said. "I told them you would doubt the truth of such an offer. And between you and me, I suspect there is much more to it than that. The whole 'cooperation' part, for example. They didn't share that with me, but I suspect that 'cooperating' with the GRU..." she tipped her glass at D'Antonia, "... might save your life, but cost you your soul." She drained her champagne and leaned her head back, frowning. "No, nothing. I am a little disappointed. Though it is excellent champagne and I do feel a little light-headed."

D'Antonia was considering her options. Her training told her to run. If there were men at the exits, speed and extreme violence might get her through. She didn't have a gun, but she had a long blade in the leather of her calf-high boots. They may be onto her safe house and reserve vehicle, or that could be a bluff. They clearly didn't know much about her, if they didn't brief Grahkovsky to at least make a guess at what service she worked for. She had money and a passport at left-luggage at Moscow Central Station. *Run.*

But then what? Die gasping in the back of a taxi as the panic and adrenaline of flight flushed the poison through her system?

Option 2: see what they had to offer. She might end up dead anyway, but when all roads lead to the grave, you might as well choose the longer one.

"You're wondering what you should do," Grahkovsky guessed. "It's fascinating to imagine what is going through your head right now. Would you care to share it with me? I might be able to advise you."

D'Antonia decided the woman was just a messenger. The worm on a GRU hook, and she had taken it. But they could have just picked her up at her apartment, beaten and drugged her. This rather more subtle approach suggested they were doing exactly what Grahkovsky intimated they were doing, trying to recruit her and turn her.

"All I am thinking right now," D'Antonia told her, "is that I do not want to die. And first and foremost, I will do what is necessary to avoid that."

"Oh," Grahkovsky said, sounding disappointed. "How banal. Well, then. We can order another drink – I doubt you want more champagne – and then we can call it a night. You could use the opportunity to flee tonight, but I suspect they will be watching you closely, and I am told no foreign service would be able to help you avoid the effects of the poison anyway, so you would surely die. Sometime in the next 24 hours, the GRU will create a natural opportunity to meet with you, something that will not seem suspicious to your foreign employers or to Lapikov, and you can speak with them. If that conversation goes well, you will get your antidote and live. If not, then I suspect I will never see you again." She raised a hand to attract a server and waited. "But honestly, I do

272

hope you will stay for another drink. We can indulge in a little of that girl talk you mentioned. It might surprise you, but I do not get invited out very often."

Maqsud Khan had left his own meeting with Chief Scientist Grahkovsky troubled and confused, as always.

Troubled by the simulation of a strike on an American mainland target. Of course, he understood that a strike on a target like Kennedy-Canaveral would have dramatic economic consequences for US space capabilities, but it would only make sense as part of a wider offensive, an all-out war against the US – in which case, nukes would be the weapon of choice, not Groza.

Yes, he was a corporal, but he was a thinking soldier, not a mindless digger of trenches. The only thing he could think of was that perhaps there was actually a shred of humanity beneath the ravaged visage of Anastasia Grahkovsky. Perhaps because both Kennedy and Cape Canaveral space stations were mixed military-civilian facilities, she really did want to find a way to reduce civilian casualties, if it was ever targeted?

He didn't raise this question with Grahkovsky because he preferred to minimize his interactions with the woman. She troubled him. Or rather, how he felt in her presence troubled him. There was no other way to describe it; he was simultaneously repelled by and attracted to her. Her moral ambivalence was repugnant. The way she treated him – as though he was an interesting insect in a glass bottle – infuriated him. But at the same time, she seemed to understand him like no other woman he had met. She saw through his actions to the man behind them, and she had been frighteningly accurate in her insights. Then there was … her. The raw physicality of her; if you saw beyond the scars, or between them, she was quite beautiful. He found her milky eyes strangely compelling, and the way she didn't really look at you, but looked through you. Her voice, when she had whispered in his ear…

He shook his head, cleared his mind, and focused on the task in front of him. To begin with, she had him running a straight targeting simulation, working with the AI she said would one day

273

make him redundant. Which would be just fine with Maqsud. He had not worked with AIs in his role inside the ICBM silos – they still relied on technologies from the previous century. In the Groza control room in Baikonur, he had a squad of human specialists working under him. But here on Titov, for these simulations, Grahkovsky used a natural language neural network that responded to commands just like one of the specialists in his team in Baikonur. But faster.

"Bring up Florida, USA, full-screen view," he said into his headset. "Center on the Kennedy Space Center."

On his main screen, the famous launch site sprang into focus. Across the bottom of the screen, a constant stream of data was running, changing every time he touched his mouse and moved his targeting crosshairs, showing latitudes and longitudes, distances from orbit, time from launch to impact, estimated margins of error for the impact epicenter based on upper atmospheric and local weather, and more.

"Center on Cape Canaveral Space Force Station, please," he said and the map adjusted. With his mouse, he drew a two-mile by two-mile box. A Groza strike did not hit as a perfect circle or square. Depending on where the launch vehicle was, it struck the earth at an angle and 'splashed,' so the damage footprint was more like a fan or oval, with more missiles concentrated near the point of impact and fewer further out.

The Kennedy-Canaveral target was an interesting one. It was not one site, but two. Two administration centers, museums and libraries, two industrial sites, with multiple launch complexes spread over an area that was about fifteen miles from top to bottom and about ten miles wide. Not an issue if you plastered it with a brace of nuclear missiles, but a real challenge if your weapon of choice was Groza.

As a target, it had already been programmed of course. Reviewing the current targeting data, Maqsud had seen that a single Groza had been allocated to cover both sites. And five main targets had been identified, none of which were predominantly civilian. Those at Kennedy were the NASA Vehicle Assembly Building and Launch Complexes 39A and 39B, from which NASA and Space Force launched the Space Launch System rocket, and SpaceX launched its Falcon Heavy. On Cape Canaveral Station, two sites were targeted, the mixed-use 'Industrial Area' containing the bases and headquarters for a dozen military units and civilian corporations and Launch Complex 40, the main Space Force heavy-lift launch complex.

Each of the targets fell neatly within the two-mile by two-mile footprint of a Groza strike. A full twenty-warhead strike had been allocated to the target, but as Maqsud quickly saw, the targeting had not been optimized for effect. Four warheads or 256 missiles had been allocated to each of the five targets, which was simple enough, but showed a lack of thoughtful planning.

Reviewing data on the buildings and infrastructure under each footprint, he determined that just two warheads or 128 missiles each should be allocated to the launch complexes themselves. While they looked on paper like the most important targets, they comprised either solid concrete infrastructure or easily destroyed but easily replaced light infrastructure like towers, fuel tanks and pipelines. A 128-missile strike on a launch complex would certainly knock it out, but a heavier strike would probably do no greater damage, nor result in a longer rebuild time.

Where the two sites were most vulnerable was in their 'beating hearts,' the two military/industrial headquarters which housed research facilities, assembly buildings, engineering works, computer servers and the personnel who served in them both in uniform and in suits and skirts. Flattening these buildings would set research and production back for months, perhaps years. Killing the people inside them, though, would literally decimate generations of vital US space expertise. To these two building complexes he *should* allocate sixteen warheads, or 1,024 missiles, to ensure maximum structural and human carnage.

The thought made him sick to the stomach.

How many people lay under the footprints he had just painted? Five thousand? Ten? Twenty?

He had the tools to be able to answer that question. His model had been populated with publicly available data, supplemented with military intelligence estimates of the number of military personnel, staff and visitors that were present at both sites on an average day.

He placed his mouse cursor carefully and then spoke into the air. "Two-mile by two-mile eight-warhead strike. Cape Canaveral Space Force Station Industrial Area. Casualty estimate in thousands, please."

The estimated casualties from a 32-ton payload delivered at these points would be four thousand three hundred injured seriously, six hundred twenty-five dead, the computer voice intoned.

Grahkovsky had challenged him to try to minimize the loss of human life. But the human capital was the real target at Kennedy-Canaveral, not the launch gantries, fuel tanks or even the rockets sitting there being readied for launch.

He compressed the strike zones to an unachievable one mile by one mile, spread them more carefully to cover the most valuable engineering, industrial and research facilities. The system wasn't designed for such a small footprint and reported large margins of error. But doing this avoided some of the corporate headquarters, more likely to be filled with marketers and accountants than engineers and scientists. It would save lives perhaps, but it would be a slightly less effective strike, less likely to set the US space program back.

"Recalculate casualty estimate, in thousands please," he said.

The estimated casualties from a 32-ton payload delivered at these points would be three thousand eight hundred injured seriously, five hundred seventy-five dead, the voice replied.

Despite the compromise, his tweaking had little effect on the death rate. He cursed and pushed himself away from his console.

You evil witch! he yelled in his mind. *You knew it would be like this. You knew you were setting me an impossible challenge.*

He pulled himself back to his console. He would not let her beat him. There was a way to spread the strike to ensure maximum damage *and* minimum casualties. He would find it, just to spite her.

Positioning the pieces

Sokolniki Park, Meshchansky District, Moscow

D'Antonia had not slept after leaving Grahkovsky at the nightclub. But she had not run either. What were the chances AISE would be able to find an antidote for whatever the GRU had poisoned her with, before it killed her? She did not like the odds.

Instead, she had remembered her grandfather's words, the time she had bent the front wheel on her tricycle.

"If you break the trunk of your orange tree, graft it to a lemon," he'd told her — a local dialect equivalent of 'if life gives you lemons...' And he had taken her tricycle, returning it two weeks later having used the two small rear wheels to make her a scooter. She'd ridden that scooter everywhere that summer.

The day after she'd been poisoned, she was called to an urgent meeting with a Mozprom executive that Lapikov told her its CEO had insisted on. He was in a cabinet meeting and asked her to deal with it and only bother him if the matter was urgent. Whether it was her imagination, stress, or the drug, she was starting to feel nauseous as she arrived at the building. The 'executive,' as she expected, was a GRU officer. A plain-faced man, in his mid-thirties, completely unremarkable and not particularly bright. He had a list of questions with him and, she assumed, a recording device. He warned her unless she cooperated, she would be arrested, interrogated, and she would not have access to the antidote for the poison Grahkovsky had given her. He told her without the antidote she would die within 48 hours, and it would not be a quick or painless death.

She had already decided to play along. To do what was necessary to preserve her freedom, for as long as she could. He asked who she was working for and she told him. She dumped her whole CV on him. He asked what information she had been tasked to obtain, and she told him that too. He asked her to name all of the AISE officers or agents she had knowledge of, and she told him truthfully she could not. He was not happy, but she had no information to offer the GRU about AISE agents or officers in Russia or elsewhere because, after all, she was an asset herself, not an intelligence officer, and she had not met face to face with her handler for several years. She did not know his name, and she did not even know if the disembodied digital individual she dealt with was even the same man who had recruited her so many years ago. Payment from AISE appeared in her parents' bank account each month so that the additional income could not be traced to her. Her parents thought it was her, sending them money from overseas. She did not tell him how small the payment was.

He asked her how she communicated with AISE, and she showed him her telephone. He handed it to a second officer, who cloned it on the spot. On it was an app, a multiplayer game, in which the participants could chat with each other. The conversations were not saved in the phone, she said, but perhaps they still existed on the app developer's server? She helpfully suggested the GRU could hack the developer and perhaps recover her conversations. She showed the officer her 'friends' list and pointed out which 'friend' was her AISE contact. It was true she played the game, and chatted with other players. But the rest was a plausible fabrication created by AISE exactly for this purpose.

When he was done with the list of questions from his initial debriefing, he confirmed what Grahkovsky had implied; the GRU expected her to work for them as a double agent. She would continue supplying intel to AISE, feeding them intelligence, both real and false. But she would have to give the GRU whatever intelligence she could about AISE methods, codes, technologies and such and share with them the tasking they gave her. They would provide her with tasking of their own. They also wanted her to provide them with intelligence on Lapikov – both his political and personal dealings – which she found to be a request typical of the Russian psyche. The one thing better than information about a foreign power was getting dirt on each other.

She agreed to it all, trying to appear frightened, helpless, hopeless. It was not a difficult act. She repeatedly requested to be given the antidote and was repeatedly refused.

The GRU officer asked what had motivated her to work for AISE and she told him it was the money. She had demanded the GRU match her AISE payments and named an exorbitant monthly sum. He had laughed. He told her that if she did not cooperate, it was not her bank balance, not her own life or liberty she would need to worry about, but that of her family in Italy. Had she not seen what happened to Russian exiles abroad? Poisoned, irradiated, gassed? He showed her a picture of her father, taken the day before. Buying groceries.

If we wanted to hurt you, he would be dead already, the man said. And your mother next.

Please, no. I will cooperate, she told him. Her plea was real enough.

When he was finished, he had her sign what he said was a 'full confession,' in Russian, then handed her a small bottle of fluid that could easily have been more poison for all she knew, but she drank it down greedily. She was screwed anyway.

But in D'Antonia's mind, there was cooperation, and there was *cooperation*. The first thing she did when she got home was throw up. A stomach full of accumulated adrenaline, bad coffee and raw fear. The next thing she did was compose a coded message to AISE on her networked refrigerator. She'd told the GRU a lot about how AISE worked, but she'd kept that communication channel to herself. Her message to her handler was short and simple:

I have been arrested; my life threatened. I agreed to work with the GRU as a double agent in return for my release. I do not repeat NOT request extraction. I understand you may choose to disavow me, but I propose to remain in place to provide AISE with intelligence on GRU methods and tasking. Respond, please.

The message would have read like a shopping list to anyone else and was as concise as she could make it. She made herself a cup of coffee and sat staring into space. She would have loved a Hollywood-style extraction; perhaps some sort of quadrotor drone landing on her roof, whisking her away to a boat in the Baltic Sea. She no longer had the poison in her blood, so while her career as an AISE spy might be over, she would be alive and free.

And in fear of what the GRU would do to her parents, for the rest of their remaining days.

It was not like AISE had such resources in any case. She knew they would doubt whether she was even the sender of the message. If she had been arrested, they would assume she had been broken and the message sent by the GRU. But they might respond.

The reply that came back would determine her next move. 'Error 404' would mean her message had been received, and she had been disavowed by AISE. No response at all, she would take that the same way. 'Order confirmed' would mean her message had been received and they wanted her to continue as a double agent, or wanted her to stay in place until they could extract her. A nerve-wracking half-hour passed. If she was disavowed, she had nothing to offer the GRU. She might string them along for a while with old intel, but the lack of currency in tasking from AISE would soon make them suspicious. They would give her a task that could only be fulfilled if she was still in contact with AISE and when she couldn't deliver on it, she would no longer be an asset, she would be a liability.

If she was extracted by AISE, what future would she have? She might be safe, temporarily, but her career would be over, and so would her usefulness to AISE. And then there was the continuing threat to her family.

Her coffee went cold.

Another hour went by with no response. *Va bene.* She would not be extracted, but it did not mean she would stay and play the GRU game either.

She walked around, checking in cupboards and bookcases to see if there was anything here she could not just walk out and leave behind. Her laptop and telephone contained nothing compromising; she would leave them both. The GRU had probably already searched her apartment while she was meeting with them, but it felt important to reassure herself. She satisfied herself that the apartment was clean. She had screwed up everything else, but not that. Then she drew the blinds and put spare clothes, makeup, toiletries and jewelry in a small backpack.

So this was how it ended. Not with a bang, or even a whimper, but in silence.

So be it. The GRU would be watching. It was evening. There was no way to leave now without risking detection. She would have to wait for the 'witching hour.' Four fifteen. The worst period on the worst watch in any surveillance duty. There would be movement sensors set up to record any movement of the building's front or back doors, but that worked two ways. It gave surveillance officers a

280

false sense of security. It made it permissible to sneak a few moments of sleep because an alarm would wake you if anyone came out the door. She wouldn't be using the front or back doors, but she didn't want attentive eyes on her building, she wanted them half shut.

She had chosen this apartment building because the roof adjoined the neighboring building and she had a key to that building's roof access door. She would go up, over to the next building, in and down. Then she would come out, hit the alley out the side of that building, a hundred yards from her own, where she had a perfectly silent *Vespa* electric scooter parked, and evaporate.

She went around the apartment turning out lights, and pulled out her hairband, shaking out her hair, heading for the bathroom one last time. She should be feeling broken, rudderless, but surprised herself as she realized she...

The refrigerator chimed, the loud ping interrupting her thoughts.

She walked up to it, keyed up, almost unable to focus on the small LCD screen.

Error 404. Disavowed.

It was clarity, at least. AISE did not trust her enough to leave her in place, nor value her highly enough to try to rescue her. She doubted now that they had even passed on her report about the possible strike on Nebraska to CIA. At the time, she'd been almost relieved. Now, she felt betrayed. Ignored. Abandoned.

She didn't feel sad, or scared. What she felt was a rising anger. If her own service did not value her intelligence, she would send it directly to those who might. She had not revealed everything to her GRU captors. Though it was true she did not know the names of any of AISE's own officers or those of their allied services, shortly after arriving in Moscow she had been tasked to provide the local CIA station with the names and biographical details of every member of Lapikov's office and her assessment of his political alliances within the Kremlin – who did he regard as his friends, and who as his enemies. To facilitate this, she had been given the download code for a modified dating app and the profile of a man on the app to whom she could deliver the data. She had pulled all the information together and forwarded it to him as a message, which the app encrypted. She had never met him, and knew that 'he' was probably just a postbox. But she still had the app, and it still showed the man's profile as 'active.'

If AISE would not listen to her, perhaps the CIA would. She spent the next sixty minutes documenting everything she knew about Groza, about Bondarev and Grahkovsky, about Russia's cover story for the system, and Lapikov's conviction that Russia was planning to use it again in support of Iran in the Gulf conflict. She left out the detail that she had been poisoned and arrested, but added a note to explain that she was forwarding the intel directly to CIA because she had reason to believe AISE was not doing so. It was a long shot, she recognized that, but she had already proven to them she was a reliable source by providing them with valuable intel on the inner workings of Lapikov's office and his place in the politics of the Kremlin. After checking her message a couple of times and adding some small details, she hit 'send' and then deleted the app from her phone.

It was a small salve on her wounded self-esteem to think that everything she had done since arriving in Moscow might not have been in vain. That *someone* might receive her report and take her seriously.

But she was still angry, and she turned her thoughts to the GRU. Threaten her *family*? That was not something you did to a girl from Sicily. She had money, contacts, resources and a Sicilian temperament.

Her next move was simple enough. After that, not so much.

Major Fan Bo's *Mao Bei* attack on the two Grozas whose orbit took them over China daily was nearly flawless. His men performed acceptably, and he commended them accordingly. But there was room for improvement.

He had not used his *BX-1.4* swarms. Those he wanted to keep up his sleeve. With the first Groza he decided that, given what he had seen of the Russian satellite's capabilities, he should assume it had layered defensive systems: the *Shakti* for engaging larger threats at great range and close-in weapons for dealing with lesser threats. He told his people to assume the Russian machine would be capable of infrared and radar countermeasures, laser, ballistic or kinetic self-defense weapons.

The small size of the *BX-1.3* would be its one advantage, at least in this first engagement. The attack would be timed to take place simultaneously on both Grozas at once. One as it entered orbit over China, the other as it departed Chinese territory. The *Mao Bei* satellites would be positioned non-threateningly, far enough away to pose no collision danger to the Grozas. They were set to mimic the frequencies of a 5G comms satellite, but Bo doubted they would be detected at all, amongst all the clutter and radio energy the Grozas flew through daily.

As the Groza drew near, the *Mao Bei* would power up. As the target drew parallel it would accelerate to match orbit and close the gap to the Groza. If it survived the approach, when it closed to within twenty feet of the Groza it would complete the attachment maneuver, using powerful magnets to clamp itself to the Groza's main dome. China recognized this strategy would have a limited 'shelf life' as enemy satellites could be fitted with degaussing fields to shake off a magnetic limpet. So the next-gen *BX-1.4* included a small harpoon which could be fired at a passing satellite to attach itself, and then reel itself in to sit tight against the body of the target.

Once in position, the *Mao Bei* triggered a high-powered pulsed microwave energy release lasting up to ten minutes. And fried the silicon brain of whatever it was riding on.

But the attack was only 'nearly flawless.' The first *Mao Bei* completed its approach apparently undetected and triggered itself. Bo could not be 100 percent sure, but it had reported performing exactly as expected, and that Groza had gone off the air immediately and irreversibly.

The second *Mao Bei* also completed a successful approach, but its powerful magnetic field was triggered too close to the Groza's tungsten-filled warheads. Being ferromagnetic, the huge tungsten warheads had proven an almost irresistible target to the small brain of the micro-sat guidance system. It had clamped itself onto one of the warheads out on the cylinder and triggered itself. They had definitely knocked out its comms system – it had stopped broadcasting – but Bo's engineers seriously doubted that this Groza would have been fully disabled. If Russia found a way to restore comms, or repaired it in orbit, it might still be a threat.

Bo castigated the officer in charge of the second attack. But he also held himself to account. The code on a *Mao Bei* mini-sat already in orbit could not be rewritten 'on the fly.' There would be a risk in any Groza attack that the same would happen. He could increase the likelihood of a successful attack by allocating extra units to an attack, but this tactic brought with it a larger chance of detection. A swarm attack would almost certainly be detected, either during the engagement or in analysis after the attack, but it offered the best chance of assured target destruction.

Still, he had learned the *Mao Bei* could approach and engage without triggering the Groza's defenses. He had achieved one certain, and one possible kill. And the operation had cost him only two 90 lb. mini-satellites.

It was a far superior result to that achieved by the Main Enemy, USA. Bo knew his country had also started a massive cyberwarfare campaign against Russia in retaliation for the Korla attack. It would take a few days for the impact to become evident, but Bo had been told 61398 Cyberwarfare Unit had been ordered to fatally compromise the computer systems of Russia's top 100 industrial and resource conglomerates. If they weren't making panicked phone calls to the Russian President already, within days or hours the oligarchs who owned the crippled companies would be.

The People's Republic was not one to run crying to the United Nations or the world press when it came under attack. Nor did it silently stand and lick its wounds. On the wall of his office, Bo had a vintage poster, printed at the time of the Cultural Revolution. Under the images of peasant soldiers and factory workers it said: 'In battle, there are only two types of attack: direct and indirect. However, out of these two, in various combinations, it is possible to create endless options.' Russia was about to learn that in the art of indirect attack, China was a grand master.

So it was with no surprise he received the news that the Pentagon had accepted the Chinese offer of assistance. He had been given the name of the US Commander with whom he was to coordinate operations.

Colonel Alicia Rodriguez.

The first thing he had done was to call for her file from PLA Central Security and he was flipping through it now.

Woman

Mid-40s

Latino

Former US Navy. Pilot. Catapult officer.

Assistant Air Boss on the Gerald R Ford-class supercarrier, the USS GW Bush.

Three years' service unaccounted for after that, before she reappeared as commanding officer of the Amphibious Landing Ship USS Bougainville. Interesting.

Then appointed Commander Space Force's 615th Combat Operations Squadron.

On the surface, impressive. But she had already lost one spacecraft in an ill-conceived, poorly executed attack on a Groza.

He enlarged the photo of the woman on his tablet and held it up for closer inspection. *Hello Colonel Rodriguez. Are you worthy to go to war with a real Space Force?*

Yevgeny Bondarev was relying on a very risky game of bluff to protect the Grozas overflying the US East Coast.

He had persuaded General Popovkin to intercede with his Navy counterpart to reposition the Cuban-based *Lider* destroyer. It was now patrolling a grid fifteen miles directly offshore from Kennedy-Cape Canaveral, in the company of a Russian *Sovremenny*-class air warfare destroyer and one Cuban Navy *Rio Damuji*-class frigate. The US had howled in protest at the flotilla operating so close to its spaceports, but Russia had responded that it was operating in international waters, conducting lawful military exercises with its Cuban ally.

The message Bondarev had hoped to send was this – if you launch another X-37, you will do so at risk. The *Lider* was armed with the satellite-killing *Nudol* missile. The US would know it was more than capable of destroying a heavy-lift launch rocket in its boost phase. But more importantly, it was also armed with a 200-kilowatt *Peresvet* high energy laser, both to attack enemy aircraft and to protect the *Lider* from hypersonic missile attacks. Named after Alexander Peresvet, a medieval Russian warrior monk, the *Peresvet* system was Bondarev's 'ace in the hole.' From the position the *Lider* was patrolling, the laser could easily engage an American rocket and either explode it outright or destabilize it enough to cause the launch to fail. And most importantly, it would do so invisibly and thus deniably.

The Americans would know this too.

Bondarev hoped the unmistakable threat would be enough to cause a pause in X-37 launches and the US attacks on his Groza system. Personally, he believed it was time for Defense Ministers and Generals to stop waging economic warfare from space. But he was just a simple soldier, and therefore took the precautions a simple soldier should take.

Including regarding his personnel.

"Captain Kozytsin, I am starting to wonder if you are worthy of the great responsibility Russia has entrusted you with," Bondarev was saying. He had risen for a 4 a.m. flight from Moscow to Baikonur to take Kozytsin's report in person. He wanted to see the man to reassure himself he still had the backbone for the task ahead. And to hear what ideas his people had been able to generate since he had reported last night that not one, but two Groza units over China had gone dark. He needed answers before he was inevitably required to provide them to General Popovkin.

"You have had all night and a nice breakfast over which to come up with an explanation for what happened. I want to know what, and just as importantly, I want to know who," Bondarev said. "I want to hear your best guess, and then I want to speak to your squad leaders myself."

Ground observation showed they were still in orbit, for now. But they were neither responding to commands nor sending data to Baikonur. It seemed, for all intents and purposes, they had simultaneously malfunctioned. While in orbit over China. Around 3,250 miles apart.

Bondarev did not believe for a second that was a coincidence.

"Yes, General," the man said, but he kept eye contact and did not sound defensive. "We have reviewed all available data up to the point we lost contact with the satellites. We have no indication of an object – either active or inactive – likely to have caused a collision. We detected no nearby objects at all at the time we lost comms. I have ordered our Cyberwarfare Unit to look for any comms radiation in the vicinity of the Grozas before we lost contact, but that will take time – it is not something we were actively monitoring." He saw Bondarev's face. "But it will be, in future."

They were standing in Kozytsin's modest office in Baikonur, two floors underground where even the rumble of a rocket lifting off out on a launch pad five miles away would be barely discernible. The office comprised a wall screen, a bare desk with a single lamp, and an inlaid tablet screen. Two chairs, neither of which were in use. A coffee pot and two cups, also not likely to be used. The only sounds were of Bondarev's displeasure and Kozytsin's discomfort.

"Go on."

"Yes sir," Kozytsin said, his Adam's apple working hard. "The attacks occurred over Chinese territory. We have ruled out laser or anti-satellite missiles. Our working hypothesis is that the Groza units were disabled by experimental particle beam weapons, fielded by the Chinese PLA." He motioned to the screen. "If I may?"

"Please," Bondarev nodded.

Kozytsin had prepared a single slide, showing a blurred aerial photograph of a ship-mounted weapons system and a column of data alongside it. "A Chinese *Renhai* Type 55 stealth destroyer, fitted with a prototype neutral hydrogen particle beam weapon. GRU has not seen it tested against satellites, but it has the advantage of enhanced focus when fired through the atmosphere. GRU believes it could have the range to allow it to disrupt low earth orbit satellites."

"Hmmm," Bondarev considered the idea. "Tell me, Captain. Does a Chinese *Renhai* stealth destroyer have wheels?"

Kozytsin reddened. "Comrade General?"

"Because one of those Grozas was intercepted as it crossed overhead from Kyrgyzstan into China. To my knowledge, the nearest ocean would be, what, a thousand miles to the south?"

The caustic remark hit home, and Kozytsin straightened. "You asked for our hypothesis, Comrade General. A Chinese attack by a particle beam weapon, ship or vehicle mounted – that is our hypothesis."

Bondarev stood looking at the photograph of the Chinese ship and made several snap decisions. "I suspect part of your hypothesis was right. The attacker was most likely Chinese. It seems we now have a three-front undeclared war on our hands." He turned to face the officer. "But that will no longer be your concern. You are relieved of your command, Captain. I am told your second in command, Lieutenant Ilya Solenko, has now returned from sick leave. Please advise him I will be taking personal control of Groza Operations for the duration of the current conflict; he will now be reporting directly to me. And ask him to call all personnel together immediately so that I can address them. You are to remain in barracks until you are reassigned. Is that clear?"

The Captain saluted, unmistakable enmity in his eyes. "Yes, Comrade Major-General."

As he left, Bondarev's thoughts were already racing ahead to what he would tell Popovkin. Firstly, that he had relieved the officer responsible for failing to defend the Grozas and was assuming command himself. Secondly, that they were now under attack by three nations – the US, UK, and China. Whether they were working in concert or alone, it was impossible to say and, at the end of the day, irrelevant. He had warned Popovkin that there would be repercussions from the use of Groza, which the Colonel-General had acknowledged, but like the soldiers below him, he was simply following the directives of his own commanders, the President and Minister of Defense.

Well, they had sown the field, now they must harvest it.

Geopolitics were not his worry. Bondarev's job was to protect his Groza units and preserve Russia's newly won superiority in space. He had now lost three of sixteen units to enemy action, and four were depleted. With nine units still operational, Groza was still a formidable platform, and he planned to keep it that way.

He was betting nearly everything on the threat of that *Lider* keeping the US spacecraft grounded. If he could take the US threat off the board, the UK would be reluctant to act alone, freeing him to deal with the new threat, China. He had expected China would react, and angrily, when it discovered the Russians were culpable for the Korla strike, he had just not expected that reaction to come so soon. But a range of diplomatic, economic and, if necessary, military options were available to persuade the Chinese to back off. Not least their newfound reliance on Russian and Iranian oil.

Bondarev was not normally a betting man, and he didn't like how few options he had right now. As it had been during the Cold War, Russia now found itself standing very much alone against powerful enemies as it tried to assert itself on the world stage. But at least during that conflict, they hadn't also been dealing with a potent enemy like China at the same time.

Rodriguez was also girding herself to deal with China. After multiple high-level contacts between the Pentagon, China's Ministry of Defense, and the two country's space forces, she was now face to face with the officer who was her opposite in the coming operation.

She'd decided to keep the meeting low key, one to one. Friendly ice breaker style introductions were out of the question since they would both be using simultaneous translation bots, and the speak/pause rhythm of tcons that went via translator bots didn't make for socializing. To add to the awkwardness, she'd never spoken with a Chinese military officer before and exchanges between the two space forces had been limited since a recent 'misunderstanding' in which US forces had shot down a Chinese fighter aircraft over Okinawa. But she was painfully aware that China was now in many ways a step ahead of the USA in the space race. Since the decommissioning of the International Space Station, China's Tiangong was the only manned space station in orbit. NASA was planning for another moon landing at around the same time as China was planning to put a manned spacecraft in orbit around Mars.

The man coming into focus on the screen in front of her was young – late thirties she guessed – and dressed in a sharply tailored green PLA army jacket adorned with a golden cord or aiguillette, tan shirt, black tie and a peaked hat with a bright red band. She was suddenly very happy she'd changed out of her combat utility uniform into her dress blues just before the call.

When they'd both logged into the translator bot, the man spoke. "Colonel, I am Major Fan Bo of the People's Liberation Army Xichang 27 Test Base. I have been ordered to cooperate with you in this upcoming operation."

The Chinese officer didn't exactly sound happy about it, but it could of course just be the translation. Rodriguez decided to give him the benefit of the doubt. "Uh, yes Major, and I have been ordered to provide you with any assistance you may require, assuming it is within my power to help of course."

The man frowned. "I need no assistance from US Space Force. I have already received all the data your government is willing to share. My specialists have examined the record of your recent engagement with the Russian system, and identified all the flaws in your attack. Unless you have new information, there is nothing I require."

Was he deliberately trying to provoke her? If so, he was succeeding. If not, he was also succeeding.

"It is a little hard to know how best to help you, Major, unless we know a little more about your attack vector." She decided to throw a shot across his bows. "For example, we assume you are using your Parasite system to conduct these attacks. Would it be valuable if we provided a distraction, for example by lasering the Russian satellite while you engage, to increase the chances your Parasite mini-sats can get through?"

Bo reached forward and muted the call, speaking to someone off-camera. So, they weren't alone after all. She hadn't really expected they would be, but the pretense of a private call might have been nice. He turned back to the camera and unmuted. "Your assumption around our attack vector is uninformed. We have multiple possibilities and will use the system with the greatest likelihood of success under the operational conditions."

She leaned forward on both her forearms. "Major, I have been advised by my superiors that it has been agreed China will not use ground or sea launched anti-satellite missiles for this operation. Both to reduce the risk it will be observed, and to reduce the possibility of targeting errors that might impact US space assets."

Bo opened his mouth to speak, and then apparently reconsidered. He gave her a thin smile. "As agreed, we will not be using anti-satellite missiles."

Rodriguez tried to change the mood. "Major, I just want to say, I was saddened to hear about the Russian attack on your citizens in Korla. I understand there was significant loss of life. You have my personal condolences and my commitment that I and my people will do whatever we can to prevent future Russian kinetic bombardment attacks be they on China, the US, or elsewhere."

Bo looked quickly off to the side at whoever was standing there, but didn't consult before responding this time. "Thank you Colonel. I cannot confirm anything about an attack on China but your sentiment is appreciated."

Rodriguez nodded. "If there is nothing you need from me, then I will sign off. We are working to move new assets into place, and I will be in contact when we have a launch date and time. Good luck Major." She wasn't sure of the protocol, but she gave him a salute.

He appeared taken aback and returned her salute stiffly. "Thank you Colonel. Goodbye." The screen went dark.

Well Alicia, Rodriguez thought. *That was one small step for Space Command, one giant backward leap for bilateral space relations.*

She had other problems to deal with, since O'Hare had kamikazed her one orbiting X-37. Right now, she had one operational and one reserve X-37 grounded at the Cape and was haggling with Air Force, NASA, United Launch Alliance, SpaceX and a half dozen other commands and bureaucracies for a priority shot on a heavy-lift rocket that could get one of her machines into orbit *stat.* It was the first real test of what she had thought were protocols Space Command had already agreed with the dozens of parties involved in lifting big payloads into space, and she was getting nowhere, even with Severin and Zeezee storming the bureaucratic ramparts.

Apparently, without a formal declaration of war she could wave in people's faces, she was regarded as just another customer trying to jump the queue.

It didn't matter to Amir Alakeel whether his country had formally declared itself at war or not. He was preparing to die anyway. He had just volunteered for a mission from which, his CO had explained, they expected many would not return.

The Natanz nuclear enrichment facility was in Esfahan province in the heart of Iran, 500 miles as the crow flew from Alakeel's base at Dhahran. But Alakeel's squadron would not be flying as the crow flies. They would be making a dogleg north via Kuwait, crossing into Iran south of Basra in Iraq, avoiding the heavily patrolled skies of the Iranian west coast. This part of their route had been cleared with Kuwait through US intervention and was the least dangerous part of the mission. Once they entered Iran, they would hug the terrain, avoiding known air defense zones around the cities of Ahvaz and Esfahan. Flying low exposed them to the risk of being visually identified and would burn more fuel. But they would be overflying Iran between 0200 and 0300 at night, and that risk was deemed better than the risk to their stealth profile if they popped up to an altitude where they would be more vulnerable to radar detection.

The Natanz facility, which had been identified in the early 2000s as Iran's primary nuclear enrichment facility, had been an obvious target for nearly thirty years and Saudi intelligence indicated Iran had gone to extreme lengths to protect it. The six-square-mile facility was buried 72 feet underground, surrounded by walls and ceilings of 15-foot-thick reinforced concrete. Alakeel had been part of many exercises wargaming an attack on Natanz, including one very realistic exercise conducted during his training in Nevada.

Although not state of the art, the air defense system at Natanz was the best Iran had in its arsenal – a Russian-made S-300 system with a hardened central command post connected to four independent radar arrays dotted around the site at 12-mile intervals and 12 Buk M3 self-propelled launch vehicles each able to independently track and launch against four targets simultaneously, and reload within 15 minutes. It was similar to systems fielded by Syria during that country's war with Turkey, and it had proven deadly against non-stealth aircraft, but had yet to claim a stealth aircraft kill in any conflict.

He lost one of his men five minutes into Iranian airspace, north of Bandar Mahshahr. The Saudi aircraft were not flying within visual range of each other – each had its own stealth-optimized route to the target. There was no warning, no arc of a missile launch, no cry for help; one moment his icon was there in the flight ahead of Alakeel, and then next, he was gone. There was no emergency rescue beacon triggered by the pilot, either. An enemy patrol? Comms failure? There was no way to know.

They had flown on.

The biggest threat to their mission was that they might bump into a lucky Russian air patrol. Signals analysis had shown Russia had based the Su-57s it sent to Iran at the Iranian Air Force Base in Esfahan. It was probably not a coincidence. Russia was happy to lend a little air muscle to Iran, but it had made sure its precious stealth fighters could take off and land under Iran's heaviest air defense cover. While they had no indication – again from electronic signals intelligence provided both from their own observations and by the USA – that Russia had set up standing combat air patrols over Esfahan, the Russian Su-57s were constantly taking off from Esfahan to patrol the Iranian west coast and the Gulf, and just as frequently landing again.

The chances they would be spotted by such a patrol were low, but in just a few minutes were about to become very, very real.

Saudi and US hackers had tried more than once to disrupt operations at Natanz with cyberattacks, but Iran had learned its lesson after Natanz was successfully targeted by Israeli hackers in 2010, and no viable attack vector could be found. Two Saudi human agents had died in 2023, trying to physically infiltrate the site to plant malicious code.

But if Alakeel's aircraft could penetrate to the heart of Iran – and if the 2,000 lb. rocket-boosted High Velocity Penetrating Weapons (HVPW) provided to Saudi Arabia by the US Air Force for this mission could break through the earthen and concrete ramparts protecting the 7,000 centrifuges below – then they might set Iran's nuclear program back years. Iran seemed hell-bent on putting nukes on its ballistic missiles, but without a steady supply of enriched uranium, it would be limited to the few weapons it had on hand, not many of which could be made compatible with ballistic missile warheads.

The HVPW had never been used in combat. It had been designed specifically for the smaller payload bay of the F-35, used the same air to ground targeting system, and was intended to strike with the hitting power of a 5,000 lb. GBU-28, which could deliver 630 lbs. of high explosive through 150 feet of packed earth or 20 feet of reinforced concrete.

That was the theory. Amir Alakeel was about to test the reality for the first time in history.

Nine of ten aircraft had made it this far. Right now, they were one hundred and fifty miles out of Natanz, flying at six hundred miles an hour, winding northeast through a low range of hills between Farsan and Chelgerd. They were not flying in a tight formation. Each machine's pilot and AI were working constantly to maximize their stealth profile, and so they were flying in train, each machine a variable distance ahead of the next, with about fifteen minutes separating the first machine to the last – which was flown by Alakeel.

They were observing total radio silence on this flight, not wanting to give away their presence to any electronic warfare unit that might be sniffing the airwaves over Iran. But each of his men knew exactly what part they were expected to play. And even though they had not used it since leaving Saudi territory, his men had chosen their own call sign for this mission: *Janbiya*. It was the name for a very iconic curved dagger from the Najran region of southwest Saudi Arabia. It was worn for ceremonies but was only ever taken out of its sheath at times of extreme conflict. The allegory was considered very appropriate for the times.

His role and that of the three aircraft at the head of the line of aircraft was air defense suppression. He had two HARM antiradar missiles in his weapons bay, leaving room for only two Sidewinder air to air missiles. In five minutes, the first of the aircraft ahead of him would turn gently northeast, skirting the mountain range that protected Natanz from the west. The other eight aircraft behind it would follow the same track. Then they would bank right, flying around the farthest reaches of the mountain range and swing south, attacking Natanz from the flat plains of its northern approaches. The first three aircraft in his squadron would also concentrate their anti-radar weapons on identified air defense targets, while the next six were each carrying two of the bunker-busting HVPW bombs, programmed to strike different points in the complex. They could be released at a range of ten miles, but with the S-300 able to swat them from the sky at ranges out to 50 miles (if it got a lock), they would have to get well within the Iranian kill zone to fire them.

Alakeel's target was an S-300 air defense array known to be sited on the mountain range, with a 360-degree overwatch on the airspace surrounding Natanz. Three other arrays dotted around the plains below supplemented its coverage and had also been marked for destruction, along with the Buk mobile anti-air missile launchers linked to them. His attack was timed to take place exactly as his other three air suppression aircraft had rounded the other side of the mountain range and were releasing their HARM missiles, so that when the Iranian air defenses went down, they went down in a single wave.

The four 'wild weasel' anti-air-defense aircraft, Alakeel included, would then use their passive sensors to search for air targets and provide cover for the six ground attack aircraft that would blow through after them.

He had picked up the signal from the S-300 acquisition unit on the hills overlooking the western approaches to Natanz about twenty minutes earlier, and it had grown stronger by the minute, without showing any sign of picking up his approach. It operated at multiple frequencies – from VHF, UHF to L and S bands – in an attempt to pick up even low-observability aircraft like the F-35. But it had to do more than just detect. It had to track, and then hand off a target to the Buk vehicles parked on the hillsides around it which then *also* had to track and lock up his aircraft to get a firing solution.

The F-35 was made for attacks like this.

He saw his HARM launch waypoint approaching in the helmet-mounted display projected on his visor. If he had not been bound by radio silence, he would have announced he was beginning his attack, and wished his men good luck and Godspeed. As it was, he locked up the signals from the S-300 array, confirmed its position, and fed the data to one of the HARM missiles as he armed them.

As he crossed the waypoint at 50 miles out from the mountains shielding Natanz, he fired.

His weapons bay doors flicked open, the big missile dropped out, and then they closed again. The flare of the missile's flaming tail blinded him momentarily as it raced ahead of him at 1,420 miles an hour, well over the speed of sound. But he was already searching for his next target. As soon as his HARM missile struck home he expected other shorter-range air defense radars to wake up and start searching the skies. He wanted a Buk, but he'd settle for one of the mobile ZSU-57 tracked anti-air guns that also dotted the complex.

His Lightning rose and fell, following the terrain below. He eased the nose up slightly, taking his machine from 1,000 feet up to 2,000, but keeping his nose pointed directly at the S-300 signal to minimize his radar profile as he watched the track of his missile on his tac screen.

Come on ... come on...

Before it reached its target, he saw another icon appear on the screen from behind one of the aircraft rounding the mountain ranges to the north. *Air to air missiles?*

Three of his aircraft had made their ingress and would have fired their HARM missiles like him, but his fourth, one of the HVPW attack aircraft, had just been fired at. He saw it desperately break off and turn toward the source of the attack as the missiles closed on it and...

It was down. He had lost another man before the attack had even begun.

Gritting his teeth, he pulled his machine into a hard bank to port and pointed it at the bearing for the missile launch, popping up to 5,000 feet and focusing his infrared and electro-optical sensors on the sky ahead of him. He barely registered the signal as his HARM missile struck home, and the S-300 signal from the hills over Natanz went dead.

Somewhere ahead of him was a Russian stealth fighter. Had to be. And it was hunting his men.

Three more HARM missiles struck home, and he saw the radar signatures of two more S-300 units go down, even as a half dozen others sprang to life as the air defenders around Natanz realized they were under attack and woke their units to life, desperately searching the skies around them. Looking over his shoulder, he saw lines of tracer fire sweeping the sky, firing blind. More HARM launches, fewer air defense radars up now. The rest of his squadron would be powering in to deliver their bunker buster bombs now...

Another air-air missile launch ahead of him. Another of his men broke away, trying to avoid it. He could stay on passive sensors no longer. He quickly powered on his phased array radar and scanned the sky ahead of him. It would alert the Russian fighter to his presence immediately, and give the pilot a vector to Alakeel's aircraft, but that was what he wanted. Anything to pull that damn Russian away from Natanz.

Tone! His radar had gotten a hit on an aircraft low to his northeast. Then lost it again. Su-57 for sure. Nothing else could attack so invisibly, and disappear from his radar so easily. He firewalled his throttle, taking his machine beyond 900 miles an hour and banking left, guessing where the contact was headed.

Over his right shoulder, he saw the ripple of massive bomb blasts light the sky as the 2,000 lb. bombs of his ground attack element struck home. Saw the radar signatures of two more Buk units go down. *For you, Zedan* ... he thought to himself. Now his men were free to do some hunting of their own, to pull away from Natanz and look for the aircraft attacking them.

His radar warning receiver screamed at him. *Missile launch.* Before he could react, or in fact because he was too slow, the F-35's combat AI wrenched his machine into a rolling bank and pointed it at the ground, firing chaff and flares as it dropped. He grabbed the stick back in time to see the missile that had been fired at him flash behind him and detonate in one of the chaff clouds.

Where was the dog?

Tone. He got another lock. It was close. Too damn close. A dark shape flashed past his wing and tried to swing in behind him. For the first time in this war, Alakeel had eyes on his enemy, and it was just a shadow in the visor of his helmet. Black against black.

The F-35 wasn't made for knife fighting. It was no slouch, but it wasn't as nimble as the Su-57 behind him. His trainers at Nellis in Nevada had analyzed engagements with the Su-57 over Turkey and Syria and shared this conclusion with their Saudi counterparts — if you let it get on your six, you *will* die.

The one thing his Lightning had going for it right now was 360-degree awareness thanks to sensors located all over the airframe. His infrared sensors had locked onto the Russian and even though his head was pressed back against his seat and his vision compressed by the force of maneuvering he could 'see' the enemy fighter behind him, a bobbing, weaving glowing icon in his helmet display, trying to get a guns solution on him. But he had trained in exactly this situation in Nevada. Trained and trained and trained again, against the insanely maneuverable American F-47 drones, which could turn with g-forces no human pilot could match.

Ninja Star, that was his only option. That was what the Nellis instructors called it. It was completely counter-intuitive, which is why it sometimes worked. But he needed altitude and bullied his machine in a yawing, spiraling roll up to ten thousand feet, pulling the Su-57 up in his wake, keeping it in his rear left quarter where it couldn't get a guns solution. Going vertical…

Now! He pulled his machine over onto its back before his airspeed bled away to nothing, dragging the machine into a grindingly slow loop at the same time as he kicked in hard right rudder. The Lightning went into a flat spin, shoving him hard against the left-hand cockpit wall, his helmet slamming into the cockpit glass. He saw the Russian fighter try to follow him up, jink in surprise as he stalled and fell away and then peel off, trying to extend away to get a new solution on him. But his nose was coming back around as his machine fell toward the ground like a 30,000 lb. leaf in an uncontrolled flat spin that would have been fatal to any other machine. As his nose swung giddily around, his AI lined up on the Russian fighter, got an infrared lock and sent one of his Sidewinders after it. *Fox One, dog.*

The missile closed on the Russian in less than a second and the explosion lit up the night sky in a cloud of flame and metal.

Breathing heavily, Alakeel countered the spin and his fighter gained forward momentum again, creeping up over 200 miles an hour to 300, 400 … If there had been another Su-57 on his six out there he could have been a sitting duck. But he got control of his aircraft again and pointed it back toward Natanz. His tac display told him all of his men were now bugging out, heading for the egress point that would take them back to Kuwait as planned.

But not *all* of his men.

As he pointed his nose at the ground and plotted his own course west, he saw the blinking icon of a rescue beacon on his helmet visor, flashing the downed Saudi pilot's location to satellites above. The man had ejected about five miles northeast of Natanz.

Three down, and they still had to fly four hundred miles through hostile skies to get home; with every Iranian air defense unit on the ground and Russian fighter pilot in the sky looking for them.

Alakeel looked at the location for the emergency beacon and knew there would be no chance of rescue. The pilot was four hundred miles inside enemy territory and he had just helped inflict significant hurt on the Iranian nuclear program. He might very soon wish he had died with his machine.

Rodriguez was late for school. The school bell was ringing, she could hear it, but she wasn't even dressed. Oh my God, it wasn't morning, it was afternoon! She was standing in the hall outside class and five hundred kids were about to come piling out of their classrooms and see her standing there naked!

Wait, no. She rubbed her eyes, realizing she was waking from a dream. But there *was* a bell ringing. Levering herself up on one elbow she fumbled for her cell phone and squinted at the clock. 0300? And the caller. Seriously?

She could hear music and voices in the background. "O'Hare, there better be a nuke inbound or there is going to be one, *outbound.*"

"No ma'am but I have an idea that can't wait," the voice at the other end shouted.

"Where are you?" Rodriguez grumbled. "If I'm not mistaken that's '*I Will Survive*' playing in the background."

"Hank's Bar ma'am and I'm on mocktails, so it isn't a booze inspired idea for a girls' only tour of the Caribbean though I do think you, me and Zeezee should totally do that," O'Hare said. "No, ma'am, I was thinking how you said we need a different attack vector, one Russia can't counter."

"I did?" Rodriguez asked blearily. "When did I say that?"

"Right after I drove our only orbiting X-37C into a Russian kill vehicle ma'am," O'Hare said. "Though you might have used more colorful language."

"Now I remember," Rodriguez frowned. She rubbed her eyes again. "What is your idea O'Hare?"

"Well, I was looking over your inventory ma'am," O'Hare said. "It is going to take you weeks to get a launch slot for *Avenger* and get it into orbit..."

"If I'm lucky," Rodriguez told her. "It seems nothing short of a Presidential Executive Order will get anyone to step out of the launch queue for us."

"Sure ma'am, I believe you," O'Hare said. "But I noticed you have an X-37B, last gen, in a hangar in Vandenburg..."

Rodriguez lay her head back down on her pillow and sighed. "I've inspected it personally O'Hare. It can be launched, but it can't be recovered. Besides which, it is an *unarmed* X-37B. It gets near a Groza, they will just shoot it out of orbit with their cannon or a damn Shakti, so we're just out one more X-37."

"What if it wasn't unarmed?" O'Hare asked. "What if ... *hey, mate, I'm still drinking that!*"

"What?"

"Bartender tried to take my Mockhito, ma'am, sorry," O'Hare said. "What if I told you DARPA has a project running with Air Force to arm its X-37Bs?"

"I haven't heard about that," Rodriguez said.

"Well, you aren't out drinking Mockhitos with the right people, ma'am. I am. And my DARPA buddies tell me Air Force has a weapon that can slot right into the payload bay of your old X-37B, plus an Atlas nose cone already prepped to take it. The 37B is smaller. It doesn't need a heavy-lift rocket, you can send it up on an Atlas V or Falcon 9."

Rodriguez levered herself back up onto one elbow, suddenly wide awake. "That could solve one problem. But I don't happen to have a free Atlas V rocket lying around the Cape ready to boost that old crate into space..."

"No, but Space Force *Vandenberg* does ma'am. I checked; they've got an Atlas V satellite launch scheduled for a few days from now.

That's a call Brigadier Parsons should be able to make on his own authority. So if he can commandeer that Atlas V for you, I may just have a new attack vector. In case China doesn't come through."

"OK, O'Hare," Rodriguez said, pulling herself up into a sitting position. "I'm listening."

After a few minutes of listening to O'Hare yell into her ear to the accompanying thump of *Bohemian Rhapsody*, Rodriguez realized her next call was going to be to a gator-hating engineer called Ross Hardy at Vandenberg. And assuming he didn't laugh outright, the one after that would be to Brigadier General Parsons.

For the first time in days, Rodriguez felt her frustration replaced by something new. Hope.

Amir Alakeel needed reason to hope.

He'd lost one man crossing the border into Iran. Two more over Esfahan itself. He had known the Iranian air defense units and Russian aircraft patrolling Iran's western borders would be on high alert and expected he might lose one pilot more getting his remaining seven aircraft out of Iranian airspace. Each pilot was flying fast and low, relying on their stealth profiles to get them past the enemy hunting them. The other six aircraft were all ahead of him, making for the Iraq-Iran border.

But somewhere before Bandar Mahshahr, fifty miles from Iraq, he lost three aircraft. He could see no enemy aircraft on his screen. No indication enemy radar had locked onto any of his pilot's aircraft. So the hunters could only be Russian stealth fighters.

His men were still radio silent, and they died silently. But one by one, Alakeel saw their encrypted ID signals disappear from his tactical situation screen.

Three did make it through.

Alakeel was the last.

But he was no longer looking to escape. He had one remaining Sidewinder missile, and before he left Iran, he intended to take at least one Russian fighter with him.

He was not blinded by rage. Turning away from the fighters he knew must have been waiting for him over Bandar Mahshahr, he pointed his F-35 southeast, hammering low and fast along the low coastal hills of Iran's northern coast. With complete certainty, into the teeth of another Russian patrol, but hopefully one that was not expecting him.

He kept his phased array radar switched off, relying only on passive infrared and electro-optical sensors to scan the skies around him.

And then he saw it. Not literally. It came up on his threat warning receiver as a big blob of radar energy that his onboard AI took several moments to analyze and identify.

Russian *Beriev* A-100 Airborne Warning and Control (AWACS) aircraft! Now he knew how his men had died. The A-100 was equipped with a *Vega Premier* Active Phased Array Radar, specifically designed to detect stealth aircraft as far as 370 miles away. Though it had probably not got a solid lock on any of his squadron's aircraft, it had apparently picked up enough returns to plot their egress route and vector Russian fighters to intercept them.

It would not be alone. There would be at least two Su-57 fighters escorting it, possibly more. And it was circling 100 miles further inland, over the city of Shiraz.

He hesitated, checking his fuel state. To attack it would be suicide. Even if he did manage to close on it without it picking him up, even if he did get through the fighter escort, he would barely have enough fuel left to make it back to the Gulf and Saudi airspace.

But it was the flying equivalent of the frigate *Sahand*. Iran did not possess any airborne warning aircraft – their last flying AWACS aircraft had been destroyed in an accident in 2009 and never replaced. So this aircraft, like the others patrolling the Iranian coast, was on loan from Russia, and no doubt crewed by a Russian aircrew.

Alakeel made a simple calculation. He had lost six aircraft. Six men. He had destroyed one Su-57 over Esfahan. The crew of an A-100 was, by memory, at least fifteen.

Even if he traded his own life for the Beriev, Russia would still stand to lose double the number of men in this one engagement than he had lost, and what was probably the most expensive asset it had moved into the theater.

With that thought, any hesitation he felt was lost. He looked at his terrain guidance screen. He was approaching the Heleh Protected Area wetlands, which were 20,000 acres of uninhabited wetland extending from the coast 50 miles inland. From there he could pick up Highway 86, a four-lane highway that wound through low hills and ranges east of Shiraz, and then it was 40 miles to the provincial city and the Beriev circling over it. It was still semi-dark, but there would be traffic on the highway. If he stayed low ... *really low* ... any returns the Beriev picked up might be confused with ground traffic.

At 600 miles an hour, it was nine or ten minutes' flying time.

It was insanity.

And that was why it might work.

He flung his fighter onto its port wing and dropped toward the dark water that was the Heleh wetlands, leveling out 200 feet above the ground. He flinched several times as flocks of birds, startled by the subsonic approach of his aircraft, lifted into the air around him, but they didn't rise high enough, and quickly fell away behind him. He let the terrain-following autopilot keep altitude for him as he concentrated on hitting the northeastern exit from the wetlands and picking up Highway 86. He nearly missed it in the gray early-dawn light, but pulled his machine into a screaming right-hand bank that sent him into the valley the highway cut through. It felt like he was so low he could clip the aerials off the cars and trucks that flashed past underneath him, but his focus was on ensuring he didn't fly his machine into a hillside as the highway snaked left and right toward Shiraz, the electronic signature of the Beriev growing stronger by the minute. It apparently felt invulnerable on its perch high above him.

Twice he felt the ghostly fingers of enemy radar play across the skin of his aircraft. So lightly that they could not possibly have picked up a return, but enough to make him realize the Beriev wasn't the only enemy up there. But they hadn't seen him. He'd made it.

And there was no time for relief, because he was on the last five-mile, slowly curving easterly section of the highway, and up ahead, he saw the lights of Shiraz. Above it, the Beriev was a ghostly green blob of radar energy. He had no lock on it, yet, but from the strength of the signal estimated it was anywhere from 20 to 30,000 feet above him.

As the green blob moved toward and then directly above his aircraft, he firewalled his throttle and put the F-35 into a screaming supersonic Mach 1.2, 900 mile an hour vertical climb. Twenty seconds. That was how long it would take him to reach 30,000 feet. That was how long he had to lock up the 150-foot-long, 180-ton Beriev. That was how long the Beriev and its escort had to see him and shoot him down. It was an eternity, and it went by in slow motion.

He armed his one Sidewinder missile and set it to 'fire on lock' mode.

He engaged his APG-81 phased array radar's air-air mode and set the software to scan the sky directly overhead for the profile of a Beriev A-100.

He ignored the sudden radar warning screaming in his ears and the alerts flashing in his helmet-mounted display.

He kept his Lightning pointed at the sky, at the green phosphorescent blob on his helmet display that could only be the Beriev, until the blob turned to an icon, and the icon flashed red and his last Sidewinder dropped from his weapons bay and speared into space ahead of him!

Without waiting to see if it hit home, he hauled his machine over onto its back and pointed it southwest to the line in the sky that was Saudi airspace.

Missile warning! The Beriev's escort had a lock on him. How could they not? His weapons bay doors were still closing and his tail streaming fire as he pulled away from Shiraz at Mach 1.3 ... 1.4 ... 1.5.

Come on, you beautiful girl, Alakeel urged his Lightning. It pumped flares into his wake, trying to decoy the missiles behind it, and he saw the coast of Iran flash by underneath him. The Russian air to air missiles would be traveling at Mach 2.5, so it wasn't a question of whether they would haul him in, but when.

Mach 1.6.

In his situational display, he saw the icon for his Sidewinder missile wink out, but the Beriev was still flying.

Or ... was it? The icon for the Russian AWACS began rotating – left, right, left – like it did when an aircraft was ... spiraling to the ground.

Kill!

He was over the Gulf now, seconds from the Saudi coast.

An explosion behind him. His machine shook. Then another, closer.

He was shoved back in his seat as his machine was jolted forward as though by the slap of an angry God, and then began tumbling nose over non-existent tail through the sky. Groaning against the violence and speed of his descent as his machine disintegrated around him, he reached for the handle between his legs and heaved.

At ten thousand feet above the ground and one thousand two hundred and twenty seven miles an hour, his canopy blew away and the rocket booster under his seat ignited, flinging him into the sky with a force that rendered him instantly unconscious.

"The joint operation with China is on," Rodriguez told O'Hare the following day. "I got launch priority on that Atlas at Vandenberg, and CIA just passed on intel from a deep cover source that Russia is planning to use its orbital bombardment system again."

"Use it on who?" Bunny asked. She was sharing a beer with Rodriguez in the Colonel's off-base apartment at Cocoa Beach near the Cape. It was something they hadn't done often enough, if you asked O'Hare, but she appreciated her friend was also weighed down with some pretty heavy responsibilities, so she just grabbed the opportunities when they arose. Plus, she'd lied about the mockhitos and sorely needed a 'hair of the dog'.

"Probably targets in the Middle East, the report says, but we don't plan to wait to find out. Together with China we are going to take the Groza system down, starting with the bird orbiting over East Coast USA. We hit it earlier, as it flies over Greenland this time, so that if anything goes wrong, it splashes down in the Labrador Sea or Greenland landmass."

"We hit it, or China does?" O'Hare asked.

"Chinese PLA Strategic Support Force will conduct its attack before the Groza hits the Greenland ice shelf. They have not chosen to inform us exactly what form this attack will take but they did share with us that they recently conducted two successful interceptions of the Groza units in orbit over China."

"They what?"

"NORAD has been monitoring comms from those units. They stopped simultaneously yesterday. However China did it, they knocked those Grozas off the air and the assumption is if they can't send, they can't receive. They're non-mission-capable." She tipped the neck of her beer at O'Hare. "Anyway, enjoy your drink, it might be your last for a while."

"You know this is not something to celebrate, right?" O'Hare said. "If the PLA can take down something like those Grozas that easily, then nothing we currently have in space is safe, including our X-37s, the RAF's Skylon … nothing."

"That thought had occurred to me," Rodriguez said. "And I suspect they are using this opportunity as a not so subtle way to show us what they are capable of."

"Parasite?" O'Hare asked.

"Could be, or could be another attack vector we haven't considered," Rodriguez said.

"When do we go up?" O'Hare asked.

"The Chinese say they'll have their assets in place inside a day."

O'Hare nearly coughed beer out her nose. "One day!?"

Rodriguez handed her a paper towel. "And there's something else. Ivan has parked a damned *Lider* missile cruiser off the coast of Florida. It fields *Nudol* missiles and a high energy laser, either of which could swat a heavy-lift vehicle launched from the Cape or Kennedy out of the sky the minute it clears the launch pad."

"They wouldn't bloody dare," O'Hare said.

"Space Command begs to differ. All heavy-lift launches out of Kennedy-Canaveral are now on hold. Anyway that was the last detail Brigadier General Parsons needed to get that Atlas launch allocated to us, so this is where you tell me I didn't use up every last favor I was owed on one of your drunken brainwaves."

"With respect, my idea for a puppy-kitten hybrid is both genetically possible and commercially attractive, but relax, this idea is solid."

"How solid?" Rodriguez asked. "You mentioned a laser. What kind of firepower can DARPA squeeze into the payload bay of an unmanned spacecraft the size of a Humvee?"

"How about *exactly* the kind of weapon the Army has just mounted on its Humvees?" Bunny said with a grin. "What would you say to a G-BAD 30-kilowatt laser?"

Rodriguez hesitated. The small Ground-Based Air Defense Directed Energy On-the-Move (G-BAD) laser that the Army had just begun mounting on vehicles like the Humvee and Stryker was a defensive weapon. It was powerful enough to hit and destroy air to ground missiles, subsonic cruise missiles and drones, but several orders of magnitude less powerful than the 250-kilowatt high energy laser that could be carried by the X-37C. And *that* had already proven ineffective against the Groza. Unless…

"You want to fly escort for the Skylon," Rodriguez guessed. "China's attack fails, we have the Skylon as a backup. Russia launches a *Shakti* against the Skylon again, you protect it with your G-BAD armed X-37B?"

Bunny winked at her. "Long-range strike capability protected by an anti-missile laser weapon. Great plan, Ally, wish I'd thought of it." She finished her beer and walked to the icebox for another two. "When is the Atlas launch slot?"

"My people in Vandenberg say they can have that X-37B prepped within another …." She looked at her watch. "…eleven hours. Then DARPA can go to work. The launch slot is fifteen-thirty Pacific, two days' time. That's how long DARPA has to get the G-BAD mounted in our X-37 and the X-37 inside an Atlas nose cone."

"A half day more than they told me they need," Bunny said. "But let's not tell them that. I'll call them now." She handed a beer to Rodriguez and tapped the neck of the two bottles together. "Thunderbirds Are Go, ma'am."

"Your new friend Meany will be happy to know you're riding shotgun again," Rodriguez observed.

O'Hare handed a new beer to Rodriguez. "You know what happened to him? Meany?"

"No, what?"

"Broke his back, punching out over Syria," she said. "I think he and I might even have been at Incirlik air base around the same time." She sounded uncharacteristically thoughtful. "Could just as easily have been me."

"Glad it wasn't," Rodriguez said. "He looks totally hard-core in that exoskeleton. You would look like a tattooed midget on stilts."

"Ouch. That hurt."

"I take it back. Make that an *angry* tattooed midget on stilts."

Manure, meet fan

45th Space Wing, Cape Canaveral Space Force Station, Florida

Being a data scientist in Cape Canaveral Security Center wasn't as glamorous a job as it had sounded. "Damn, I need a cup of coffee," Ambre Duchamp said, stretching. She was serious too. Her morning routine was a cup of coffee when she woke up, then one when she got through the Cape Canaveral Security Force patrol headquarters doors and settled at her workstation. Then another one by about 11. Each one a double shot skinny cappuccino. She knew it was too much, but she never used to need that much caffeine. It was boredom setting in, she knew it. The visitor vetting system she had designed was more or less running itself now, so all she found herself doing the last few weeks was running reports. The Risk Factor tags were generated automatically as soon as visitor data was entered and crossmatched, and sent immediately to the duty Patrol Supervisor. She'd set up another report that she ran once a week which checked the RF hits against the incident reports to see how accurate the system had been at tagging troublemakers. She was in the mid 80 percent range now but would like to see something closer to 90, so she was still tweaking the AI algorithms to see if she could break the 85 percent ceiling she seemed to have hit. Once she did that, she'd probably start looking for a new job. Running reports wasn't a job for a restless data scientist.

But that wasn't why she desperately needed a coffee.

"I'm bored..." came a small voice from the desk beside her. "When can we go and see the rocket?"

Ambre turned to Soshane, who she had sat down with some pens and paper and a coffee table book of photos from Kennedy through the years, and told her to 'draw something while momma got some stuff done.' "We'll head out soon with one of the Defenders," Ambre told her. "I got to get this done; then I need to organize a ride. OK?"

Her girl looked at her with pantomime impatience, but turned back to her drawing. "Ooookaaaaay."

Soshane's nagging had finally got to her. She knew there was a SpaceX Falcon heavy-lift launch vehicle being prepped for transport out to Launch Complex 40 and there would never be a better chance for Soshane to get a selfie of herself in front of a real rocket. Depending on how soon Ambre found herself another job, it may well be the little girl's only chance.

She swiveled away from Soshane and turned on the coffee machine that sat on her desk. Yeah, she was serious about her damn coffee. She didn't drink that swill they had in big urns out in the duty room. Tasted like tar mixed with paint thinner. Nah, she had her own New Guinea mild roast she bought online from that place that made the compressed coffee balls however you wanted them. Had her own little machine on her desk, brewed that coffee at a perfect 201 degrees with a quarter-inch of crema that just made you say 'mmmmmmm' every time.

While she was waiting for the machine to warm up, she turned back to her screen and ran her eye over the morning's RF reports. Fifteen so far, but it was only 9.30 a.m. OK, couple guys with felony assault, all going way back; low risk. Two domestic violence, coming in from Kennedy visitor center with their families on a tour, so they were flagged in the mid-risk range, especially since it was going to be a hot day out there; not good for fools with a short fuse. A couple foreign commercial visitors who ticked boxes because they were on a watch list. One diplomat, doing a tour with officers from 45th Wing Command, harmless enough…

But this one.

Ambre leaned forward, running her finger along the screen. Huh. The hit on him came from FBI. Tourist, booked on the 11 a.m. Space History tour of Kennedy-Canaveral. Russian, but then they got a lot of Russian tourists at Kennedy because of the whole International Space Station connection. Except … she double-clicked on the FBI source report that had triggered the tag.

OK. FBI had the guy on a watch list as a 'person of interest.' He wasn't under active investigation. Ambre leaned over and took her cup, sipped her coffee. "Mmm," she said aloud, thinking, *Let's have a little look at you, Sergei.* She pulled up his visitor record and nodded to herself. He'd checked in at the visitor center, as normal. No prior visits and nothing in the Homeland Security databases she had access to, though she could see he'd done two years at Penn U in Philly about ten years ago, without so much as a parking ticket. Probably nothing, right? And then...

She looked at her watch. The 11 a.m. tour should have reached the Cape by now. They usually took the tourists out to Launch Complex 34 at the Cape, the scene of the Apollo 1 disaster. "Hmm," she said, sitting back and looking up at the ceiling. This wasn't her job. The RF report would have gone in to the Staff Sergeant duty commander. He'd decide whether to hand it to one of his Defenders to keep tabs on Sergei The Russian, or just let it ride. Russian or not, a routine low-risk visitor like that would probably not get any special attention unless he did something to put himself on the Security Forces radar.

Ah, what the hell. She pulled up the GPS map that showed where every visitor on the site was currently located. It matched the chip in their visitor tags with facial recognition data from the CCTV cameras that festooned the center inside and outside buildings and infrastructure, and it showed not just where they were, but could paint a phosphorescent trail on the screen of where they'd been since checking in.

Where you at right now, Sergei? she asked herself, clicking on his portrait photo to show his location.

Well, she knew where he should have been. He should have been on the tour bus, heading either to, or away from, Launch Complex 34.

Except he wasn't.

Sergei The Russian, person of interest to the FBI, was two hundred yards from the SpaceX engineering complex, apparently on foot, and very close to the 45th Space Wing's new Central

Computer Complex. *The CCC is not on your official tour program, Sergei*, she thought. She ran the back trace on his movement history.

He checked in at visitor reception.

Got on the bus outside the Pass and ID office.

Got off the bus at Building AS, the new SpaceX engineering complex at the Cape. Then walked back down Industrial Road to the Computing Center.

Went *inside* the Computing Center. His tour ID shouldn't have let him get any further than the reception area, but his trace showed him in there for ten minutes. She'd have to pull the internal CCTV feed to see what he was doing, and she didn't have access to that.

The motion tracker showed he'd left the CCC, and was now walking down the Phillips Parkway, presumably back to the SpaceX complex. Which was a total no no. Visitors were required to either stay on the tour bus or be escorted to their next appointment – they were not supposed to go wandering around the station.

Ambre drained her coffee and reached over to rub Soshane on the back. "You stay here, honey. Momma has to talk to some people." She didn't run. It wasn't unusual, among thousands of daily tourists, for them to get the occasional stray or 'leave behind.'

She went out of her small office, up a corridor and into the duty room. A couple of guys were sitting there getting ready to go on shift, and she got a brief 'Hey' from one, a young Senior Airman called Russell something, before going into the small office out back where Staff Sergeant Danilo Verge was just putting down his phone after what had sounded like a call to his wife.

He looked over at her. "Hey, Ambre. You got something for me?"

"Maybe."

He rotated his chair a little left, a little right. "Must be good, to get you out of your little cave."

"Depends. A Russian spy sound good to you?"

He picked up a tablet and opened an app. "Juicy. Whodat?"

"I sent you the profile, and his current location."

Verge looked the data over. "What's he doing wandering around the Industrial Area?"

"What I asked myself."

Verge tapped his tablet, calling up more information on the guy. "OK, FBI tagged him as he flew in, but nothing serious. Probably just a stray."

"That's what I thought. But, you know, FBI don't tag *every* Russian coming in..."

Verge picked up a handset, looked up a number and dialed it. "I'll call guest services, ask them to patch me through to ... Oh, hey. Hi Raylene." He rolled his eyes. "I know, that must hurt some. Hey look, can you put me through to the, uh, the guide on the 11 a.m. Early Space Tour? Lyle, that's his name?" He wrote it down. "OK, yeah, put me through to Lyle." He put his hand over the mouthpiece. "Lyle, Lyle ... the guide who had a bolter last month, the one who managed to hide himself inside the Space Shuttle Atlantis. Wasn't that Lyle?"

Ambre shrugged. She remembered the incident, but not the tour guide responsible.

"Yeah, that was Lyle, I'm sure of ... oh, hey, is that Lyle?" Verge said, suddenly all friendly. "Yeah man, this is Officer Verge at Security. Look, are you missing a PAX? Russian guy name of ... Sergei?" He thumbed a button, put the handset on speaker mode, and laid it on the table between himself and Ambre.

"Russian guy, Russian guy..." the man on the other end of the call sounded sheepish. "Don't know if he was a Russian, officer, but there was one of the guests threw up in my bus. I put him off at the cafeteria on Hangar Road so he could clean himself up. Said I'd pick him up on my way back through..."

"Well, he aint at the cafeteria anymore, *Lyle*," Verge said. "He's roaming around outside the new Central Computer Complex on Phillips Parkway is where he is."

"Oh my," Lyle said. "Look, I'll be back at the cafeteria in twenty ... say ... thirty? Max."

Ambre pointed at the dot on the screen. "It *could* look like he's on his way back to the cafeteria, Sergeant. Maybe the guy just felt better, decided to get some air."

"Don't you worry, Lyle, he's my problem now," Verge said and hung up. "Thank you very much. Freaking pain in the ass, Lyle. Freaking FBI." Verge sighed and stood, walking to the door of his office and leaning out to see who was there. "Russ, you ready to move out?" he asked the young guy who had greeted Ambre.

Russell looked over, fastening a radio to his belt. Ambre had talked to him a few times. He'd grown up in Daytona, joined Space Force hoping to see the world, and then ended up in the Cape. But he was getting to the end of his four-year active duty tour and he'd actually managed to save most of that house deposit him and Maria were working on. There was this place opening up, Harbor Heights, fifth floor, sea views, had its own fitness center, pool, childcare place about a block away, looked pretty good. Maria had checked it out. In case that happened any time soon. Having met Maria once at a social thing, Ambre was pretty sure it would.

Russell stood. "Yes, Staff Sergeant, what's up?"

"Got a stray for you."

Ambre showed him Sergei's location on her tablet – he was still wandering away from the Computer Center – while Verge filled him in. "Tour guest, got sick, guide left him at the public cafeteria. System flagged him low-level risk, but he shouldn't be where he is so his tour pass is canceled. Get out there, pick him up, bring him back here. We'll ask him a few polite questions."

Russell looked at his watch. "He's at the cafeteria?"

Ambre looked at her tablet again. "No, he's stopped again. He's near there, taking his time. Probably getting a bunch of selfies."

"I'll send his tag to your GPS," Verge said. "Bring him in here when you get back." He turned to Ambre. "You want to sit in when we talk to him? Hear his story? Could be nothing, could be interesting."

"Me? No thanks," Ambre said. "I got Soshane with me today."

"Oh yeah, right," Verge nodded. "That's today?" He gave her a wink. "You owe me for that, you know. I don't sign off on that sort of thing for just anybody. We're talking a big bag of them homemade cookies, Ambre."

"Yeah yeah."

"A *really* big bag," Verge emphasized. "OK. Get rolling, Russ," Verge said and went back in to his office.

Ambre took Russell's arm as he reached for his vest and black beret and pulled them on. "Hey, Russ, do me a favor?"

"Sure, what?"

"Drop us out at Launch Complex 40 before you go get the stray? Soshane wants a photo with a real rocket in the background and I arranged for someone at SpaceX to let us in where they're putting a Falcon on the crawler…"

He looked at his watch, then looked toward Verge's office. "Yeah but, how about … first I pick up the stray, then I drop you at the Vehicle Assembly Building. You can get a ride from there? It's a long way to LC 40 and I'd catch all sorts of hell from Verge if I was playing limo driver for you and this guy suddenly went postal inside the cafeteria."

"That's not his profile," Ambre said. "He's a low-level…"

"Being a Russian on an FBI watch list is not a profile?" Russell asked.

"Well, since being Russian in America isn't a crime yet, no…" she said, but she didn't want to get him in trouble. "OK, yeah. If you can drop us at the VAB after you pick him up, at least we're halfway."

"There's our guy," Russell said a short time later as they pulled off the Parkway into Industrial Road. A heavy-set man wearing a white shirt, tie, and jacket over his shoulder was walking up the road from the CCC toward the SpaceX engineering complex. "Who else would be out walking around in this sun?"

316

Ambre and Soshane were seated upfront in the Security Force patrol car, Soshane squirming around like she was sitting on an ant nest. She'd taken one look at the police car as she and Ambre walked out to it and said, "Momma, can I get a photo with the policeman too? Bethany is gonna *die!*"

"You can't get a ride out to LC 40, hit me up again," Russell said. "I'll come get you once I'm done with Sergei here." As the patrol car cruised silently to a stop about ten yards behind the man, Russell reached over and tapped Soshane on the leg. "You want to hit that button down there?" he said, pointing to a toggle on the dashboard above the radio. "See where it says 'Horn'?"

Soshane leaned forward. "Yeah?"

"Just press that, once," he grinned.

She pressed it and the siren on the car let out a single two-tone blast that stopped the man up ahead of them in his tracks and made him spin around. It made Soshane jump too, so Ambre put a hand on her leg. "It's OK, hon, it's supposed to do that."

Russell climbed out of the patrol car and stood casually behind the door with one hand on the door frame and the other by his side. "Sir, would you mind coming back here, please?" he called out.

The man didn't appear nervous. With jacket still slung over his shoulder, he sauntered back to the patrol car and stood near the door. Russell stepped out and closed the door. "How you doing today, sir?"

The man had a sallow, pock-marked face, like he'd had the worst case of acne as a kid that Ambre had ever seen. His black hair was parted on one side and neatly trimmed. He looked solid, but not fat. And despite the fact he was wearing a dark suit on a hot day, he didn't appear troubled by the heat. "I'm fine, officer, is there a problem?" he said.

"Can I see your visitor badge please, sir?" Russell said, pointing at the badge clipped to the man's belt.

The guy looked down, unclipped it and handed it over. As Russell scanned it using the chip reader in his belt radio, Ambre saw the guy looking inside the car, at her and Soshane. He straightened up again. "I was feeling sick so the tour guide dropped me off here. He said he'd be back. Is there a problem?" he asked. His accent was comic-book-thick Russian mafia.

"Name please, sir?" Russell asked. Ambre knew it would be showing on Russell's chip reader, but he was asking anyway.

"Sergei. Sergei Grahkovsky." The man looked at his watch. "The guide said he would be back. In about fifteen minutes."

Russell nodded, put the badge in his shirt pocket. "Except he dropped you at the cafeteria, and this is not the cafeteria, sir. Can I ask why you are out here on foot?"

"Oh," the man said, swinging his jacket over to his other shoulder and pointing. "He said they could be gone about an hour … and I got bored waiting. I'm sorry if I broke any rules."

OK, yeah, maybe, Ambre thought. It kinda made sense. Except for the detour via Central Computing. *Toilet stop?* She was starting to feel like a bit of a fool for calling the guy to Verge's attention now.

Russell was taking it pretty calmly too, or maybe just wanted to keep the other man at ease, because he simply smiled at the guy and said, "OK, look. There's something wrong with your badge anyway, it isn't reading properly. Probably just a technical glitch. I have to get you to come back to base with me and sort it out. We'll reconnect you with your tour group once everything is in order." The badge thing was probably a lie, Ambre figured, much better than saying, "I'm taking you in for questioning."

Russell stepped back and opened the rear door of the patrol car to the passenger transport area. It was caged off and Ambre knew the doors could only be opened from the outside.

"This is very annoying," the man said, pulling his jacket on. He didn't move to get into the car.

"I apologize, sir," Russell said. "If you'd get in, please, we'll sort this out as quickly as we can."

"I'm hot, momma," Soshane said. The Florida sun was shining right in the window on her legs, so Ambre reached forward to the pocket in the door and pulled out a clipboard with some sort of logbook on it and put it on Soshane's legs to give them a bit of cover from the sun. "We'll be going in a short while, honey, and then you…" She heard a noise and looked up.

Russell was gone.

The man was leaning in the driver's side door, toward Soshane. Ambre grabbed the girl, pulled her toward her, and drew a breath to scream, but the man held something inside the car and pressed a button.

Spray?

That was all Ambre had time to think before her world went black.

As O'Hare and Albers were getting briefed on the operation of the G-BAD laser system by DARPA and making sure their command system at the Cape could 'talk' with the X-37B, the creator of the Groza weapons system they were about to go up against again was boarding an aircraft at Moscow's Sheremetyevo International Airport.

She had not advised the commander of the Titov Space Test Facility, General Yevgeny Bondarev, that she was planning to travel. Nor had she done as required and notified the Titov security office. She had not even told her mother.

The only person who knew she had left Russia, was her brother. But then, he had a need to know. He was an integral part of what was about to happen. He had checked in with her just before he left Russia himself. She had been making breakfast when her telephone started buzzing. It was a deliberately compact kitchen, so she just had to turn and take one step to reach the counter behind her where she always put it.

"So..." her brother said after the usual formalities. "I have my ticket and visa, money and passport on the table. Bag packed. Anything else I need to know before I get in the taxi?"

She smiled. "Nothing," she said. "How is momma?"

"She'll be fine, *Nastya*. She's a tough old girl," he said. "I told her I'll be back in a week. Don't worry about momma."

He always called her at breakfast, caught her eating her porridge and drinking coffee. She knew it was because that was when he was most likely to think of her. He had never forgiven himself for leaving her alone at breakfast that day when he was supposed to have gotten her up and ready for school. But he had left early to go for a run because he was trying out for the school football team.

And he also never forgave himself for not coming straight back to the apartment to check on her after the meteor struck. He'd gotten a message that his mother's hospital roof had collapsed and had left the school right away without checking to see if his sister was even there. When he'd gotten to the factory, he'd learned his mother was alright, and he should have started looking for his Nastya right away. But he hadn't, he'd stayed with his mother until she was examined by a paramedic and allowed to leave. His mother had asked after Anastasia and he'd lied. Said she was at school and she was fine. Three hours. Three hours they had waited for his mother to be released. Three hours Anastasia had lain weeping and bleeding on the floor of the kitchen, unable to see.

She didn't understand his guilt. Had he come back to the apartment straight away, he could have done nothing. She would have gotten to the hospital quicker, but it was a hospital in chaos. She probably wouldn't have been treated any quicker. The damage to her eyes was instantaneous; caused by the infrared flare of the explosion and then the blast wave. There was no miracle treatment for that. The cuts to her skin came from the flying glass. Yes, also from writhing on the glass covered floor in pain and confusion, but did it really matter whether she was scarred on just her head and arms or on her back and sides as well? It would not have changed the way the world recoiled from the sight of her.

She held him responsible for nothing. He was a ten-year-old boy at the time, but it was like his guilt grew stronger with each year that passed. It wasn't pity. He was genuinely proud of her, he'd told her that. But just why he held himself responsible for the effects of a cosmic fireball, she would never really understand. But she had known that it meant that when she needed his help now, he would not say no.

Anastasia Grahkovsky had never traveled outside Russia before. Her passport was completely new. The visa in it was the only page used. She had been careful to apply for the visa in good time, expecting many problems, but there had been none. She was not traveling economy class. It might be her only trip outside Russia, so she had shunned the cheaper options and gone with Lufthansa, thoroughly enjoying the feel of their deep leather and wood finish business class seats. While those around her had worked or slept, she sat listening alternately to the murmur of their conversation or to audio summaries of scientific papers. She had never attended any kind of international astrophysics conference, but it occurred to her she really should. There was so much to learn, so many great minds to learn from. She knew she could never share with them what she herself had done, what she had learned, but she felt a strange liberation, a freedom of spirit and soul, the minute the Airbus A400 ATTOL (Autonomous Taxi Takeoff and Landing) airliner lifted off the ground.

Eight hours forty-five minutes later, as the aircraft approached its destination and cabin personnel began to fuss with their pre-arrival duties, she pushed the call button and ordered herself a final champagne. Whether because of her blindness or other visible disabilities, the staff had been fantastically attentive and despite being busy didn't hesitate a moment before bringing her a champagne, pouring and putting it in her hand for her, even tidying up her cubicle so she didn't have to do it herself.

German efficiency. It was something one could easily get used to. She wondered if she shouldn't have been born a German, instead of a Russian. It might have suited her better. But then, if she had, she would not have been in Chelyabinsk when the meteor struck. Would not have become obsessed with the power of objects colliding with the earth. Would never have designed Groza. Would not be sitting on this aircraft, on the way to Shanghai.

At that moment, despite her blindness, scarring and crippling injuries, Anastasia Grahkovsky decided that if the world existed in a thousand dimensions, she would not have traded her life for any of a thousand other possible lives in the multiverse.

O'Hare and Albers could think of a thousand other lives that would have been more interesting to live than the lives they had lived for the last 24 hours. When not reading up on ordnance manuals, they had been running system checks and doing simulator time on the X-37B. Even though it was just a cut-down X-37C they found the handling and systems were generationally different — much less automated, much more manual, and the onboard AI was not much more than a glorified autopilot. Albers sweated under the workload. Not surprisingly, Bunny O'Hare loved it.

Before suiting up and sitting down with Albers to get ready for the engagement, O'Hare put a call through to Meany, whose compatriots were also busy getting his spacecraft into position for the active phase of the operation.

"Hey, there's someone here who'd like to talk with you," Meany told her. He was on videocon and she saw him tapping some keys on a console to patch the other party in. She figured it would be Paddington. She was wrong.

Meany was grinning. "Captain O'Hare, meet Angus. Angus, O'Hare."

I am pleased to meet you, Captain O'Hare, a voice said, a total clone of the voice and accent of the twentieth-century Scottish actor Sean Connery. *I hope we do not have such an exciting time working together on this mission as we did on the last.*

O'Hare leaned forward toward the camera and pointed a finger at Meany. "You programmed it to say that."

"Well, yes, but not totally," Meany admitted. "I got bored with him just saying yes, Flight Lieutenant, no, Flight Lieutenant, didn't I, Angus?"

The Flight Lieutenant assigned me a reading list on the Art of Conversation, which covered 4,120 books on the subject. By studying your own verbal interactions, I am able to tailor my conversation to a style adapted to your preferences.

"You just do your job and we'll get along fine, Angus," O'Hare said. "Which, by the way, aren't you supposed to be flying that Skylon right now?"

I am, ma'am, the AI said. *But unlike a human, I can walk and chew gum.*

"Cute," O'Hare said. "Angus, I need to talk with Flight Lieutenant Meany. I'll let you get back to whatever you were doing."

No worries, Captain.

"This is going to be a long mission if he is always that chipper," O'Hare sighed. "How good is your motion detection algorithm at the ranges we're going to be standing off, Flight Lieutenant?" she asked. "You're sure you'll pick up a mini-sat moving in?"

"Same optical sensor suite as we have on our photo recon satellites, Captain," Meany said. "We can track a jihadi riding a scooter through a crowded market in Islamabad from nine hundred miles up, so yes, we can pick up a 40-kilo mini-sat at ninety miles. I doubt the Groza has anywhere near the same optics, but we'll know soon enough, depending on how the Chinese take-down proceeds."

"Let's run through our response to a *Shakti* launch again," O'Hare suggested.

"Yes, ma'am. We should pick up the prelaunch ignition sequence for a possible *Shakti* kill vehicle launch on infrared. As soon as we see it, Skylon bugs out, engaging boosters to accelerate away from the threat, making minor course corrections to deplete the *Shakti*'s vectoring thruster reserves. You're riding shotgun, parallel trajectory. What range can you engage at, ma'am?"

"Five miles in atmo, so maybe double that in space?" O'Hare said. "We're not set up to pull data from the Skylon as we did last time, but we should be able to lock it up ourselves from fifty miles out. Track and fire are automated. DARPA is confident in their interception algorithm – confident of a hit – but the question is whether it will translate to a kill. No one has intercepted a *Shakti* with a laser before."

"If the G-BAD can knock down a cruise missile, it should be able to take down a *Shakti*," Meany opined.

"Well, you might be betting your Skylon on it, so I hope you're right, Flight Lieutenant."

"What else can you tell me about your new ride, ma'am?"

"Not much you wouldn't already have read elsewhere," O'Hare observed. "It's twenty-year-old tech by now. Like a baby version of the X-37C. Sixty percent smaller, no other weapons. But it's a helluva good surveillance platform. It got a refit about five years ago to protect it against ground-based ASAT weapons and was given limited countermeasures – infrared and radar – but it's not going to be able to outrun or outmaneuver that kill vehicle if it comes for us instead, so we're also betting the farm on that G-BAD laser." She winked at him. "Unless you want to sacrifice the Skylon to save me?"

"Never going to live that down, are we?" Meany sighed. "Comms protocols, ma'am? What is your call sign for this mission?"

O'Hare had not checked the spaceplane's ID nor discussed with Vandenberg whether the small spaceplane already had a call sign she could use, so she went with the first word that popped into her head. "Uh. Bertha 2."

Meany started writing it down, frowned and looked up. "I had not mistaken you for a sentimental woman, Captain O'Hare."

"I am not just sentimental, Flight Lieutenant, I am also bad tempered, with homicidal tendencies," O'Hare told him. "And don't you forget that."

"Very good, ma'am," Meany said with a straight face. "If there's nothing else, I'll see you in space."

Not many hours later, Yevgeny Bondarev was standing in the Groza command center, looking at the world map showing the position of his remaining Groza units as they circled the globe, which went from shoulder height up to the ceiling. All appeared reassuringly normal on that screen.

Underneath it were smaller data screens and tactical displays, and on these a situation was developing which was far from reassuring. His strategy of parking the *Lider* missile destroyer off the coast of Florida appeared to be working. SpaceX had announced that due to 'minor technical issues' its next Falcon Heavy launch out of Florida had been delayed. But Russian surveillance satellites had detected the launch of a US Atlas V from Vandenberg Space Force Base on the US West Coast the day before. The irony of that was not lost on Bondarev. The Atlas V first stage was powered by *Russian* RD-180 engines. GRU intelligence indicated it was carrying a US Space Force payload, but they had no intel on what the payload was.

That launch had bothered him. If his political masters were planning to escalate the conflict in the Gulf with another Groza strike, he would need every available unit for the storm that he was sure would break as soon as they did. Unfortunately, his misgivings about the Atlas launch had proven correct.

One of the screens he was looking at showed the bubble of space around Groza 4, which normally would be empty except for passing satellites. It was not. At the outer edge of the satellite's sensor range were two familiar but unwelcome objects. The RAF Skylon and a US Air Force X-37B. Bondarev now knew what the payload of that Atlas V rocket had been.

"How far out is that Skylon?" Bondarev demanded.

Lieutenant Ilya Solenko flinched. He had not much enjoyed reporting to the snide, nit-picking Kozytsin, but he enjoyed even less having to report to a full two-star General like Bondarev. He had been discharged from the base hospital even though he still had lung problems and his blood was showing dangerous levels of chemicals commonly found in heptyl, one of the older rocket fuels still used in Russian rocket engines. He coughed. "Ninety miles astern, sir," he said.

"Well within missile range. Once again, with a US X-37 in support. Why the B model? It's a recon and transport ship, isn't it?"

"Yes sir, recon, deployment of small payloads," Solenko said. "Unarmed, though there have been reports it is used to trial various weapons. It has a smaller profile, perhaps they thought it would be harder to observe."

Bondarev looked at the data running across the bottom of the tactical screen. "It launched from the US West Coast not long after we destroyed the one X-37C they had in orbit. I suspect it was just the first thing they had available," Bondarev said. "Or, it's a sacrificial pawn. What do you think, Captain?" he asked.

Solenko went blank. *What did he think? He could barely bloody breathe.* "Sir?" he asked.

Bondarev waved a hand impatiently at the wall. "The tactical situation, man. This is a virtual rerun of the engagement of a week ago, with the exception that the enemy is holding at extreme range. A difficult range from which to launch any kind of attack, but not impossible."

Solenko was a thin man (even thinner now after a month in and out of hospital) of little imagination. And not given to reading the minds of his enemies or predicting the future. Instead, he decided to give a status report. "Sir, I have told the men to prepare for an attack from either space-to-space or ground-to-space weapons," he said. "The 30mm close-in weapons system will be reserved for anti-missile defense. If the RAF Skylon launches a missile, or the X-37B makes an attack run, we will engage with the *Shakti* kill vehicle."

"Fire too soon and either of them could outrun it at those ranges," Bondarev warned. "It could be exactly what they are trying to do, neutralize our defenses. Or provoke us. We have only one shot, one missile, and they must know that by now."

"But we could launch now," Solenko said. "They may not be aware it has a launch and loiter capability."

It was an important detail Bondarev had overlooked. He mentally slapped himself. "Good point. How long can the *Shakti* keep station with that Groza, in loiter mode?" Bondarev asked.

"Indefinitely, Major-General," Solenko explained. "Or until the Groza is repositioned. It doesn't have sufficient fuel to make major changes to its orbital track, but as long as the Groza continues on the same trajectory, the *Shakti* can remain in position alongside it."

Bondarev tapped his hand on his thigh. "I don't like passively waiting for the Americans to make their move, Solenko. We must take the initiative here."

"Sir?"

"Launch the *Shakti*, put it in loiter mode," Bondarev said. "Either they will retire or they will attack, but in both scenarios we are prepared, yes?"

"Yes, Comrade General." Solenko turned to Karas. "Launch the kill vehicle!"

Ambre woke feeling groggy. Shook her head, but it wouldn't clear. Her vision was blurred, her head thumping in pain. Soshane!

She looked around her, tried to call out, but her voice wouldn't work.

She tried to sit up but then realized she already was. She was sitting on a concrete floor, legs out in front of her, hands tied behind her, back up against a pole. She looked up. Some kind of garage? Her vision was clearing, slowly. Soshane. It came out as a croak. She still couldn't speak.

Russell's patrol car was parked next to her, about five feet away. The space she was in was big, maybe about two cars deep and five wide. She saw a sign on the metal roller door that covered the entrance – *Exit LEFT to Scrub Jay Road, Exit RIGHT to Industrial Road*. Work, brain, work! OK, she was still inside Cape Canaveral Station. But what building was on the corner of Scrub Jay Road and Industrial? She'd had to learn the locations of every building when she was setting up her system, programming links to every damn CCTV feed. She had it. The old Fire Station. Unused now, it hadn't been in operation since the late 2020s when a new facility had been opened. It was on the historical buildings register.

"Soshane!" she croaked again, no louder now than when she'd first woken.

"Your girl is asleep," said a voice behind her. Russian mafia accent. She looked around herself, but a utility box blocked her view behind. "Close your mouth. Breathe through your nose. The effect of the spray wears off quicker if your mouth and throat aren't dry." She heard a noise like the legs of a chair scraping on the floor. "You'll be able to speak in a few minutes. I don't know about children; your daughter will maybe sleep longer."

She realized she was panting, closed her mouth, pulled air through her nose. She wasn't scared. She was terrified. And angry as hell. She concentrated on her breathing for a few minutes. Tried to speak. Coughed. Tried again. "I want … I want my daughter," she finally managed.

The sound of a chair scraping again, and then the man appeared in her side vision, moved around in front of her, carrying the chair, and calmly placed it down in front of her. He was holding a packet of gum and slipped a piece into his mouth. "Your daughter is sleeping," he repeated.

Ambre looked around herself again, but apart from the patrol car, the parking bay of the Old Fire Station was empty. "Soshane?" she croaked.

"She's not in the car," the man said. "There is an office out back. I put her there, on my jacket. She's tied up like you, but it is comfortable enough if she wakes."

Russell. The last Ambre remembered, he was holding the rear door open for the Russian. But if his car was here ... where ...

As though reading her mind, the man spoke. "The policeman is dead." He folded the paper from his chewing gum and dropped it into a pocket of his suit jacket. "I am sorry for this news. I hope you were not good friends."

She glared at him, then strained at the ties around her wrists, which bit into her skin cruelly.

"Not deliberate," the man said, watching her struggle without trying to stop her. "I hit him in the face with the spray and he went down, but he was still moving so I sprayed him again. I think I overdid it."

Ambre stopped struggling. "We're still inside ... Cape Canaveral," Ambre said, still struggling to speak. "You took the ... patrol car ... drove here? You passed about a hundred ... CCTV cameras. They'll have posted him missing ... they'll be searching for him. And you. You'll be on ... security feed."

He kept chewing his gum.

"If my sister was right about the computer virus she had me plant, then your CCTV feed is down," he said. "In case you are wondering what I was doing inside your computer center." He looked over at the patrol car. "This is really very annoying. I had done what she asked me to do, I was on my way to the cafeteria to meet the nice tour guide and get out of here. But you showed up."

She tried to yell for help, but her voice wasn't recovered sufficiently yet, and all that emerged was a strangled groan.

"If you make noise, I will have to gag you," he said. "That would be a shame. I would like to have someone to talk with, here at the end of the world."

An alert sounded inside the Skylon's command center and Meany pulled his VR helmet face visor down. "Target heat spike on infrared. Talk to me, Angus."

Heat signature indicates the Shakti kill vehicle is powering up, Flight Lieutenant. Skylon is already positioned for evasion. I recommend engaging one third power and preparing for full boost.

"Do it," Meany said.

Ahead one third on booster, the AI confirmed. Separation between the two spacecraft began immediately to increase.

"Skylon, Bertha 2. We're showing a heat-flare on infrared," O'Hare called. "Get ready to run. Where is that bloody Chinese attack?"

"Skylon acknowledging. We're already moving," Meany said. "Relying on you for that intercept if China doesn't join the party, Bertha 2."

"Got your back, Flight Lieutenant," O'Hare told him. The X-37B was orbiting parallel to the Skylon and five miles distant. But without the benefit of Skylon's targeting data, they wouldn't be able to get a laser lock on the Russian kill vehicle until it was close. Damn close.

Missile incoming, Angus said. *Going to full boost.*

Meany watched the icons on his screen as both allied spacecraft accelerated away from the Groza. "Talk to me, Flight Lieutenant," O'Hare called. "We still don't have a lock."

"Angus, relative velocity?" Meany asked, wanting to know how fast the Russian missile was hauling them in. *The Shakti is closing at a relative rate of 209 miles per hour,* Angus said. *In thirteen seconds it will be within range of the X-37's laser targeting system. The X-37 will have a 33-second window in which to intercept.*

"Bertha 2, Skylon. You copy that?" Meany said. "I hope you have that laser warming up."

"Skylon, Bertha 2. Lieutenant Albers tells me thirty-three seconds is twenty-three seconds more than he needs," O'Hare said.

Separation to enemy missile increasing, Angus intoned. *The enemy missile has reversed course and appears to be matching orbit with its host satellite again.*

Every damn time, Meany cursed to himself. Every damn time we think we have the thing figured out, it plays a new damn trick on us!

"Cut propulsion, plot a trajectory back to our missile launch point, Angus," Meany ordered.

Yes, Flight Lieutenant. Alert. The target Groza is maneuvering, Angus reported. *Its main booster has engaged.*

"It's what?" O'Hare asked. "What about that *Shakti?*"

The kill vehicle is maintaining station ten miles from the Groza. But the Groza has now engaged its main booster, Angus repeated. *It appears to be moving to a new orbit. It is too early to predict.*

Meany's mind raced. Had they spooked the Russians that badly? He flipped the Cape Canaveral comms channel on. "What do you think, ma'am? They've got the wind up them and are moving that bird to a new orbit that doesn't threaten the USA?"

He heard O'Hare give a dry laugh. "I have never seen Ivan back down from a fight, Flight Lieutenant. Never. Either this is part of some pre-planned exercise, or they are testing us out. But I can guarantee you they are not pulling back."

"What the..." Sergeant Karas muttered in Baikonur, watching a series of alerts flash on a warning screen at his master control console. "Lieutenant Solenko!"

Solenko ran to his position and took a moment to read the data before turning to Bondarev. "Comrade General," Solenko called out, "Groza 4. It is..."

"Under attack?" Bondarev guessed. Of course it was. Faced with a *Shakti* launch, the enemy commander would have little choice but to engage. It was a chess game he was prepared to play. He might sacrifice another Groza, but if he could take the X-37B or Skylon with him, the cost to the allied forces would start to tell. They would have to see that they would run out of spacecraft before he ran out of satellites.

"No sir," Solenko said, rechecking Karas's screen. "Groza 4 is ... carrying out an unauthorized maneuver."

"Controlled or uncontrolled?" Bondarev asked.

"Controlled," the man said. "I don't understand ... it has engaged main propulsion. It is repositioning!"

330

Karas was hammering keys, but looked up in distress, shaking his head. "Lieutenant, General. We are locked out … we have lost command authority of Groza 4."

On the fifth floor of the Mandarin Oriental Hotel Pudong, Anastasia Grahkovsky put down her tea, felt the watch on her wrist and decided it was time.

She had used quite a lot of her savings on the flight to Shanghai, and quite a lot again on this hotel room. Which had struck the clerk on reception as rather strange, considering the poor woman couldn't even enjoy the view – but then, she'd seen stranger things in a career in the hospitality industry than a blind woman booking a room with a view.

Grahkovsky walked to the TV screen and turned it on. She would have wished she could be there in person somehow, but in a way she was – in blood, at least. She found an English-language cable news channel and left it burbling in the background.

The news was only of vague interest to her. Saudi Arabia and Iran were still engaged in missile diplomacy. After its failed strike on Riyadh, Iran had launched a cruise missile strike on the Saudis' showcase industrial and technology hub, Jubail City, which a breathless cable TV host was explaining generated no less than seven percent of Saudi Arabia's GDP and which was now all but shut down. The Saudis had responded with a stealth attack on Iran's largest nuclear fuel enrichment plant at Natanz.

It struck Grahkovsky as entirely infantile that the two Middle East countries were firing missiles at each other, when both of them knew that it was Russia who had attacked Abqaiq. Yet there had been no attempt by the Saudis to exact revenge on Russia – that had been left to the Americans. But then she only had a PhD in astrophysics, not politics.

She'd called Maqsud Khan about an hour earlier to talk him through the requirements for the next phase of the project. He had no idea where she'd called him from, of course. Part of her yearned to tell him the truth, but he would find out soon enough, and she couldn't risk that he might find a way to abort the mission. She could have left the entire mission to her faithful AI in Titov, but she had been serious about her request to Maqsud – the strike algorithms were not optimized to cause maximum possible damage to the American launch facilities. She had made it very clear to him that he could adjust the attack parameters any way he wanted, but he must ensure the maximum possible long-term damage to US heavy-lift launch capabilities. From what she had seen of his work targeting Abqaiq and Korla, he would almost certainly be better at this than her still primitive AI.

She thought of Kennedy-Canaveral as a lioness would think of a nest of snakes it found hatching near her cubs. She wanted to crush it, to mangle it, to smash it out of existence.

She would soon hear whether she'd managed to do so.

In fifteen minutes and twenty-three seconds.

Groza 4 initiating maneuver, we are fifteen minutes twenty-two seconds from release point, the simulation AI said in the virtual control room at Titov.

Maqsud Khan had moved into the second phase of the simulation cycle that Chief Scientist Grahkovsky had assigned him. Now the simulation AI was assuming the roles of systems, weapons and propulsion operator for the simulation of a full strike on Kennedy-Canaveral. These roles would usually be carried out by the other squads on a Groza shift, but Khan had always known that one day, all those bodies would be replaced by AIs. It was just a matter of when, and it made sense of course that at Titov they were already simulating that future reality.

He checked his watch. He had found the solution to the challenge of targeting Kennedy-Canaveral. The problem was the margin of error introduced by launching on the target from the standard Groza 4 orbit over the US East Coast, which was not optimized for a specific strike on the space complex. But by adjusting the orbit to take the Groza directly over Florida he could dramatically increase precision. It was not something he would get permission to do in real life, as by prioritizing the strike on

332

Kennedy-Canaveral he was sub-optimizing the targeting of other potential targets. But he'd had to find a way to beat that witch Grahkovsky somehow. Now his simulated Groza was closing on Kennedy-Canaveral from a distance of ... he checked quickly ... 1,419 miles ... which it would cover in just under 12 minutes, arriving over the space complex at 1538 in the afternoon.

"Target acquired," Maqsud said into his headset. "Groza 4 on new track, orbit is stable and weapons are online. Groza system locked, coordinates entered and system is ready to fire. Fire order is full salvo. Weapons status please..."

Full salvo programmed, the AI responded. *Groza 4 armed, spinning up.*

"Systems check..." Maqsud intoned, trying for fun to imitate the gravelly bass voice of Sergeant Karas, but not really succeeding.

Hub green. Re-entry vehicles green. Tether locks green. No optical or electronic jamming detected. Systems go for release, the AI reported.

Maqsud had worked all through the night, tweaking and recalculating the strike footprint for this simulation. At first it seemed to him he had made little difference, reducing the number of projected dead by 720 and injured by one thousand three hundred. But then he told himself, every single one of those notional people could theoretically be a mother, with a child waiting at home. And one day his calculations might be used in a real attack. The thought was enough to keep him working until he was sure he could optimize it no further.

He set himself the goal of achieving the best possible combination of target destruction with the lowest possible loss of non-core civilian life. Grahkovsky had been right about Maqsud's ability to shift his moral boundaries. He'd solved the challenge the witch had set him by subdividing the human capital at the space complexes into two categories – core and non-core. Core were the engineers, ground staff, scientists and military personnel, and buildings directly related to space operations. Non-core were purely civilian or administrative buildings and personnel such as those who worked in museums, libraries and administrative functions. The GRU data he had access to was specific enough that it allowed him to assign a core/non-core category to every single building in the Kennedy-Canaveral complexes and then optimize the strike footprint accordingly.

He knew it was a little like wielding a sledgehammer and trying to be precise about hitting a nail, but he had done the best he could.

"You are clear to fire when in range," Maqsud told the AI, and lifted a pencil above a pad of paper, ready to start writing down casualty figures.

Theoretical casualty figures. From a single, *simulated* strike, of course.

Inside the mission center at the Xichang 27th Test and Training Base, Major Fan Bo watched the launch of the target Groza alter orbit with consternation. He had put his assets in place for a perfect interception of the Groza, and a masterful demonstration to the Americans of the capabilities of the *Mao Bei* weapons platform, and now ... now all that work was possibly wasted. Wasted!

He had taken the data provided by the Americans and fed it into China's own surveillance network, moving a *Yaogan* spy satellite into an orbit that would allow it to track the Groza orbiting over the East Coast of the USA. It had obtained a good lock on the Groza via its electronic signal radiation signature and Bo had ordered his team to bring a *Mao Bei* 1.4 five-satellite swarm into position ahead of and parallel with the Groza.

But *Mao Bei* was made to lie in wait for its prey, like a trapdoor spider. It did not chase it like a farmer chasing a chicken. He picked up his comms handset and made a call he knew he would not enjoy.

"Comrade Colonel, this is Major Fan from Xichang," he said. "*Mao Bei* satellites are in position, but the target is adjusting orbit. The attack window has been lost, sir." He listened, and then straightened. "Yes, Colonel."

Putting the phone down quickly, he snapped his hands behind his back and addressed the room, showing none of the emotion he was feeling. "Stand down!" He clicked his fingers toward his mission comms commander. "Get me a translator link to the American Colonel."

Ambre watched carefully as the Russian, Sergei Grahkovsky, went through the shoulder bag she'd brought with her from the office. She'd gotten beyond fear, beyond terror. She'd tried begging to see Soshane. She'd tried crying. Now, she was burning with anger. This guy was keeping her from her daughter. Soshane was somewhere in some dark office out back, drugged, oblivious. She had to get to her.

"Ambre Duchamp," Sergei said, turning her driver's license over in his hand. "Wow, you got a self-drive permit? Don't see many of those where I come from." He put her license back in her purse, closed it and put it back in her bag. "Nice name, Ambre. Is it French? You from New Orleans or something?"

Should she reply? She was in no mood for small talk with a killer. "What did you mean, the end of the world?"

"No, no, no," he said. "That's not how this works Ambre." He dropped her bag on the floor and leaned forward in his chair. "I ask you something, you answer me. And then you get to ask something, and I answer. Conversation, chit and chat, okay?"

Oh, God. He was crazy. But if she kept him talking, maybe someone would come. The whole station should be in lockdown by now. How long had passed since they left to pick this guy up? An hour? Two? The Cape Canaveral Station was huge, thousands of visitors, hundreds of personnel, staff of civilian operations like SpaceX, dozens of buildings, big and small ... but a Defender, patrol car and two civilians missing? Security Force must be out in strength, searching every damn building. She looked down and saw she was still wearing her staff ID badge. It was chipped. Didn't the patrol cars have GPS chips on them too? He'd sounded like some kind of hacker, the way he talked about killing the CCTV feed. Could he have disabled the GPS locator system too?

Keep the guy talking. She could do that.

"OK," she said. "Yeah, my ma was from New Orleans. Her grandma was called Ambre. It's French for Amber."

"Amber, I like that better," Grahkovsky said. "More American. Can I call you Amber?"

"You can call me what you like, Sergei," Ambre said, unable to contain herself. "Sergei? Is that Russian for jerkoff?"

Grahkovsky just smiled. "Was that your question? Or do you want me to answer the first one, about the end of the world?"

She just glared at him so he settled back in the chair. "Tell you what. I'll give you a bonus round and answer both. Sergei means 'protector,' not jerkoff. Ironic, right?" He laughed. "You have no idea how ironic. The other one, well, I don't mean the actual end of the whole world." He looked around the inside of the fire station parking bay. "Just this part of it." He looked at his watch. "In about twelve minutes to be precise."

As he spoke, a klaxon sounded outside. Not just one. Several. Ambre's head jerked up. She'd heard it before during drills. It was the alarm that sounded when there was a terrorist incident; an 'active shooter.' The klaxons kept blaring. She could imagine the scene outside, people looking up in confusion and fear. The attack at Kennedy a couple years ago fresh in their minds. Entrance and exit doors across the station would be automatically closing as the station went into lockdown. No one in, no one out. First responders including Verge's Defenders, hitting their vehicles, rushing to the scene of … whatever it was.

"Hear that? You don't have six minutes, Sergei," Ambre spat. "That's because of you. You've probably got about two minutes before a special operations team busts through that door and shoots you dead. Stick your head outside, why don't you? The street is probably full of cops, and they'll all be looking for you."

"Good. Now we're *talking*," Grahkovsky said. He stood and walked behind her again and returned carrying a tablet. He sat down again, turned it on, and tapped the screen. "You mean this street?" He turned the screen around to face her so she could see a view down Scrub Jay Road. He tapped again, flipping the view to the Industrial Road crossroads and showed her. "While you were asleep I put my own cameras up outside, so we could watch the show." Ambre's eyes fixed on the view out the side of the building. Scrub Jay, no doubt about it. As she watched, two civilians ran past on foot, and then a fire truck sped through the intersection, followed by a Security Force patrol car. They didn't stop.

"Don't worry about the 'active shooter,' there isn't one," Grahkovsky said, turning the tablet back toward himself and tapping the screen again to shut the tablet off. "Right now there are about 15,000 personnel and 5,000 visitors across Kennedy Space Center and Cape Canaveral Station locked inside their offices and labs and workshops. Waiting for someone to decide what the hell is going on and get them out or call it a false alarm and let them get back to work. Twenty thousand contractors and visitors, looking out windows, wondering what the hell is happening." He grinned. "She said it would work, and it is. I wish I had a camera inside your Security Force HQ. They must be going, how do you say, ape shit? Alarms screaming and no way to find out why or even turn them off once they realize it's a false alarm." He tapped his fingers on the tablet in his lap, and smiled. "So I'm pretty sure that looking for you, me and a missing cop is the least of their worries right now."

"*You* did this?" she asked, aghast. "Why?"

"Nuh uh," he said, wagging a finger at her. "It's my turn to ask. Let's change the subject to something more personal." He settled back on the chair, hands behind his head. "You know, I never went to Disneyland? I was going to go there tomorrow, but now I never will. What's top of your bucket list, Amber?"

Ambre didn't feel like playing his game. Her head fell back against the pole behind her and she stared up at the ceiling as the klaxons kept wailing. If he was telling the truth, no one was coming. He was right – the standard procedure during a critical incident with an active shooter was for military personnel to hit their emergency stations and for civilians to remain in their buildings, under lockdown. The Security Force would be trying to identify the source of the alarm, scouring the base to work out if it was real or false, and they'd be taking it seriously with a Defender already missing.

No one was coming for her.

When she didn't answer, he crossed a leg and continued conversationally, "No, I didn't do this," he chuckled. "My sister did: my very clever, very resourceful sister. She has been planning this a long time. She persuaded a Cyberwarfare coder to make the code I used to trip the terrorist alarms. And she made *this* herself, at home, in her kitchen." He held up the pump spray bottle Ambre had briefly glimpsed in his hand before she was knocked out. The label said, 'Hand Sanitizer.' "I tried it on a stray cat. It's good stuff. Anything she does, my sister, she does well."

Ambre looked at him blankly. What should she say? Did he expect sympathy? "Please, my daughter..."

He put the spray bottle down by his feet but didn't move from his chair. "Family is important, no? I would do anything for my sister. I nearly killed her, you know." His face contorted. "If I had stayed home like I was supposed to, got her up earlier for breakfast, she wouldn't have been sitting at the window. If I had come home earlier from school, *found* her earlier, they might have been able to save her eyesight."

Ambre had no idea what he was rambling about.

"All my life, every time I look at her, I see what I did," he said. "Now, she has asked me this special favor. It is my absolution, yes? You know that word?"

"I don't know what you mean. I don't understand," Ambre said, speaking softly and slowly. "I just want to see my baby."

He looked at his watch again, and cocked an ear as though listening to the blare of the klaxons outside. "You will know what I mean. In about ... five ... minutes."

"What the hell is that noise?!" O'Hare said, ripping her VR headset from her head.

Albers did the same. Outside, all hell was breaking loose. They heard klaxons sounding, raised voices, feet running.

Severin came bursting through the door. "Active shooter!" he called. O'Hare rose. "No, you two stay put until we know what it is. We've got armed security on the doors..." He pulled out his cell phone. "I need to get..." Then he stared at it, fumbled with the screen and cursed. "Network is jammed, dammit..."

O'Hare was pulling her VR headset back on and indicated to Albers to do the same. "This is NOT a coincidence," she muttered, pulling her virtual instruments back up. "Lieutenant Albers, we still online to Skylon?"

"Yes, ma'am. We are moving back to our previous holding position."

"Noted." O'Hare keyed the channel to her CO. "Colonel, Bertha 2. We are showing the target is maneuvering to a new orbit. We

338

need an estimate from NORAD as soon as they have a track they can predict…"

Rodriguez's voice came over the speakers in the control center. "Bertha 2, I was just about to page you. NORAD has already done the analysis. The target is now headed directly for *this* facility. We are expecting a strike. I've just been on the line with the Chinese commander. They are now out of position to intercept. If the Skylon cannot engage, you must do so. Patching intercept coordinates through now, initiate immediate full burn."

"Ma'am, the active shooter alert…"

"Let the Defenders worry about that. It's too late to evacuate the base anyway, the thing will be in range in a matter of minutes."

Data flowed across a tactical screen and Albers quickly did the math as O'Hare watched the distance between them and the target increase.

He put his hand over his headset mike. "It's going to be close. And to reach the Groza, we will have to deal with that *Shakti*…"

O'Hare punched in the intercept coordinates and firewalled her throttle with a grimace. "Don't give me problems, Lieutenant, give me solutions."

"No Chinese attack," Meany frowned, looking at the data showing the Groza was on the move and was still radiating signals energy. He opened a channel to Paddington in the Lossiemouth situation room. "Colonel Rodriguez, are you seeing this? That Groza appears to be maneuvering to a new orbit, and I see no Chinese…"

"Skylon, Bertha 2, sending you new targeting data." O'Hare broke in before Paddington could answer. "That Groza is moving in on Kennedy-Canaveral. We may also have a terrorist attack underway. All hell is breaking loose here, Flight Lieutenant, let me know if you can make the intercept."

Before he could react, an alert sounded in his helmet. *Missile alert. Missile alert, initiating evasion protocols.*

His VR view out of the virtual cockpit of the Skylon canted radically as Angus automatically spun the Skylon 180 degrees and pointed it away from the Groza again.

"Angus!" Meany yelled. "What's happening?"

The Shakti kill vehicle is again on an intercept trajectory for this spacecraft, Angus said.

Meany thought fast. He furiously plugged the data O'Hare had just sent him into his nav system and plotted an intercept. It would be close. "Angus, ignore the Russian attack. New target. Maneuver to intercept." Meany hit his local comms channel again. "Colonel Paddington, do you concur?"

Bear's voice in his ears said simply, "I concur, pilot."

"Angus, execute."

The VR cockpit view canted wildly again as the Skylon slewed onto a new heading at full boost.

Angus' voice was preternaturally calm. *Course correction initiated. I estimate we will reach optimal missile range two minutes before the target reaches the Florida coast. But to do so, we will need to deplete main booster fuel reserves to below bingo fuel state. I also estimate a 92 percent likelihood that the Shakti kill vehicle will be able to intercept us before we reach optimal missile range.*

Chaos lived in the spaces between Angus' words. In space, a missile theoretically had unlimited range. But it needed fuel to maneuver and every small course correction had a cost. That cost was as relevant for the *Shakti* arrowing in at them as for his chances of knocking the Groza out. He needed to get his Skylon within optimal range so that if the Groza changed course again, his missiles would have fuel enough to correct their trajectory. He needed to hope that O'Hare could intercept the *Shakti* before it hit the Skylon. And in making the intercept, he would burn his own fuel reserves, below the 'bingo' limit required for him to safely deorbit the Skylon.

"Forget your fuel state, Flight Lieutenant," Squadron Leader Bear's voice said in his helmet. "Continue the intercept."

In the Old Fire Station on Cape Canaveral Station, things were beyond chaos.

"Where were we?" Grahkovsky was asking. "Oh yes. Your bucket list. If you only had a short time left to live, how would you want to spend it?"

"I need a drink. Water," Ambre said, trying to buy some time to think. To avoid playing his stupid game. "My mouth is too dry."

He looked at her suspiciously, but then relented, standing and moving behind her. She heard him rummaging in a bag or something and he returned with a half empty bottle of water and held it just out of her reach. Her throat was like sandpaper. "Come now, Amber. It's a simple question. You answer mine, I'll answer yours."

"All right, dammit!"

He held the bottle to her lips and she gulped the water desperately. When she'd emptied it he threw it into a corner and sat down again.

"Your turn," he said patiently.

"My bucket list? If I only had a short time, I'd want to spend it with my daughter," Ambre told him. He'd said the world was going to end? It certainly sounded like it. The Old Fire Station was right at the edge of the Industrial Area of the station. Outside she heard someone far off, yelling directions, heard the klaxons still ringing. In the distance, a police or fire engine siren. "Can I please see her?"

He shook his head slowly. "So selfish, Amber. I am here too, you know? Should I be alone at the end of things? I hadn't planned to be. I planned to be in my hire car driving back to Orlando by now. But no, you and your friend the trooper had to ruin that. So instead I am here, and you want to run off and leave me alone. Is that fair?"

Ambre tried to keep her voice steady. "You said she's sleeping. Bring her in here. I can hold her and we can talk. I promise, just bring her in here."

"Agh!" he yelled and stood. He ran a hand through his black hair and unbuttoned his collar. "This is so damn pointless. Don't you get it?" He looked at his watch and pointed outside. "Listen to that! In a few minutes, you're going to be dead. I'm going to be dead. She's going to be dead." He paced around the chair. "At least she's sleeping. She'll sleep through it. Do you want to wake her up just so she can watch us die? So you can hear her scream? What kind of parent are you?"

Ambre fixed him with an unwavering stare. "Please. I don't want to wake her. I just want to hold her." *I want to know she's alive.* "And then we can talk."

"This is..." He stopped pacing and waved a finger at her. "Seriously." Then he stalked off out of sight behind her.

Ambre stopped breathing. He could be fetching a knife to cut her throat with and be done with her. Or his spray bottle, to knock her out again. He could be leaving them, escaping out a back door to try to make it out of the station in the confusion. In fact, why was he not? If ever there was a time to try to sneak out, it was now. He wouldn't be able to walk out any of the guarded entries or exits, they'd be locked down, but he could break through the nearest perimeter fence, try to walk out...

Her mind was racing and she jumped as he reappeared, holding a small bundle in his arms which he placed carefully at her feet, watching in case she tried to kick him. Soshane! Instinctively she reached forward with her arms to grab her, but they were still tied behind her and the rope or plastic or whatever was around her wrists dug cruelly into her flesh. She bit off a gasp, and using her feet, scooped the little girl closer to her, making a kind of nest with her crossed legs. The girl didn't stir, and in a panic, Ambre leaned forward, trying to hear her breathe.

"I told you, she's sleeping off the spray," Grahkovsky said, watching her with a look of disdain. "My sister told me one spray in the face will knock out a grown adult for up to a half hour, so a small child like her, she'll be out much longer."

She didn't trust him an inch, but now she could hear Soshane breathing, see the rise and fall of her chest, see the pulse at her neck. She pulled her legs in tighter and pulled the little girl as far up onto her lap as she could.

"OK, well, I guess you answered my question," Grahkovsky said, sitting down in the chair again, leaning forward with his elbows on his knees and his face in his hands as he watched them. "In your own way. A deal is a deal. Ask me your next question." He looked at his watch for about the fifth time. "But make it a good one, it will probably be your last."

She wasn't listening. Soshane was alive. Maybe Russell was too. Maybe despite the chaos of the base-wide emergency alarm, someone was still looking for them. Maybe not Special Operations, but Verge and his Defenders at least. Russell was one of theirs – would they just stop trying to find him in the middle of an emergency alert? Not likely. Any minute now, they'd come busting through a door, or a wall...

He reached out with one of his legs and kicked her foot hard, jerking Soshane's head in her lap. She looked up sharply. "I can just as easily take her away again," he said. "If that's what you want?"

She pulled her legs tighter. "No! No, I ... I was thinking. Uh, I want to know, what's about to happen?"

He smiled a beatific smile. "At last. A good question. She couldn't tell me everything. State secrets, you know." He looked up at the ceiling like he was wondering where to start. Or perhaps, like he was looking through it, at something else? "She asked me to plant a virus. Some code that would trigger a terrorist lockdown, keep everyone inside. I just had to go into the building where the local servers were housed and find a power point and plug in my phone..." He reached into his pocket, held out a standard consumer foldable and charger that looked like the kind of phone a million people carried. "Smart, huh? The code went from the phone and through the building's power supply and into the servers to trigger the evacuation alarms."

She frowned, asking despite herself, "But why..."

"Exactly!" he said, slapping a knee. "Exactly what I asked. Why go to all this trouble for a false alarm? Your security people find out it's a false alarm, after a while they work out how to shut it down and everyone goes back to what they were doing, right?" He sat back again, putting the phone in his jacket pocket. "Except, they don't." He crossed his arms. "They don't, I don't, you don't," he said. He nodded at Soshane. "She doesn't." He cocked an ear to the emergency klaxon and spun a finger around in the air. "My sister wanted everyone to stay put. She didn't say why, but it isn't hard to guess."

Ambre paled at the calmness in his voice, his matter of fact tone. Whatever was coming, he'd resigned himself to it.

He took one last glance at his watch. "She told me, after I planted the code, before the alarms went off, that I should get out. She said I needed to get at least five miles away."

"Some kind of bomb?" Ambre asked at last.

"More than that," he said simply. "My sister works on the Space Program. She never said what, but I know her, and I can guess." He looked up at the ceiling. "The sky is about to rain meteors."

Albers was right, dammit, O'Hare could see, with a sinking feeling in her gut, their intercept trajectory was going to take the Skylon right into the path of the *Shakti*, which was rocketing toward it once again.

"Laser up?" she asked.

"G-BAD online. Infrared sensors online. Two minutes to a lock, ma'am," Albers said.

"Will we get there in time to save Skylon?"

Albers checked a readout in his helmet-mounted display. "That's a maybe."

She cursed. She was dealing with enough maybes already. Maybe the Groza wasn't making an attack run. Maybe it would glitch. Maybe...

"This is insane!" Severin said, saying out loud what they were all thinking. "Russia goes off reservation, starts bombarding the Saudis and Chinese from space. We attack their satellites, so they *nuke* the Cape?"

"No, something is wrong," O'Hare said, shaking her head, steering the X-37B manually toward the *Shakti* intercept point painted on the visor of her VR rig. "I've been up against them before. This is not the way they work. Everything they do is like a move in a chess game. Feint, bluff, attack, counter-attack. This is something different. This is like a child losing checkers then getting up and knocking the pieces to the floor."

Their X-37B was screaming down the East Coast of the USA at about 18,000 miles an hour, tail streaming fire, and it might still not

344

be enough. Albers pointed to the panoramic monitor at a small white dot against space. "There it is," he said. "The *Shakti*."

Shakti kill vehicle one minute from impact, Angus said. *Suggest a minor course correction toward Bertha 2 to improve their probability of an intercept.*

"Approved," Meany said. "Intercept status on the Groza? Weapons status?" he asked as he checked his fuel state and winced. The problem of how to deorbit the Skylon would be a problem for tomorrow.

We will be in missile range of the Groza satellite in one minute twenty. Missile launcher deployed and powered up, systems nominal, ready to shoot. But I do not have an optimal firing solution. We will need to fire at maximum viable missile range, but outside targeting sensor range.

"Fire blind? How soon before the seeker heads on the missiles get a lock?"

They may not. If the target maneuvers again, they may not get within seeker sensor range.

"Captain O'Hare?" Meany spoke on the interservice channel. He had patched O'Hare into his comms so that they could listen in on each other in real time. "You want me to take the shot?"

Meany heard a hurried conversation between O'Hare and Albers in the background, then O'Hare came on the line. "We are seconds from locking up that *Shakti* on infrared. As soon as you get a viable solution, you shoot, Meany," O'Hare told him.

"Yes, ma'am. Spool the launcher up, Angus, fire the second you hit max viable range. Full salvo."

Yes, Flight Lieutenant, fire six missiles at range max. Fire on AI authority?

It was a question that had struck terror into the heart of AI ethicists for decades. Paddington had delegated weapons authority to Meany. Meany was about to delegate it to Angus. But it was a situation in which milliseconds could matter.

He didn't hesitate. "Angus has weapons authority."

Hub rotating. All systems nominal. Release set to auto … firing in five, four, three…

Maqsud was stirring sugar into a cup of lukewarm black tea, barely interested in the audio of the AI counting down to the simulated attack. He just wanted to skip forward to the results so that he could get the full cycle of trials done and get back on a plane to Baikonur before Grahkovsky came back from … wherever she had gone. She had made him suffer through a meal with her, which was torture not because she was poor company, but because she was not. She was incredibly well read, had more than a passing understanding of and respect for Islam, shared his taste in American jazz. He had been fascinated watching her moving around her apartment in the light of nothing more than a few candles, making and serving dinner, pouring wine for herself and mineral water for him, and never dropping a fork, never spilling a drop. He shuddered at the memory of how she had made him feel, how he felt even now. Fascinated by her, drawn to her, and repelled by her complete and utter amorality.

Warhead one released, the AI said. *Warhead two spinning up. Would you like real-time imaging of the strike zone?*

What? "Say again," he commanded.

Would you like real-time imaging of the strike zone? the AI asked.

Real-time imaging of a simulated strike? What kind of simulation was this?

"Yes, bring it up," he said, leaning forward to peer at his monitor as the AI opened a window that showed an angled zoomed view of what was unmistakably the Kennedy-Canaveral launch complex. For a simulation, it was…

He saw cars moving down streets on a sunlit afternoon. Saw boats plying the Banana River and sea off Cape Canaveral. Saw people walking between buildings … no, they were running.

His blood chilled.

Warhead two released, the AI said. *Three spinning up.*

"Abort!" Maqsud yelled. "Abort the attack."

Abort command sequence disabled, by authority of Chief Scientist Grahkovsky, the AI replied.

"Override! Abort!" he yelled, his voice on the edge of hysteria.

Abort command sequence disabled, by authority of Chief Scientist Grahkovsky, the AI repeated.

He grabbed his beard and tore at it in mortal pain.

No! Allah why? Please, no!

"Russian space to ground weapon launch," Meany said over comms, his voice half-choking. "Radar is showing a warhead launch…"

"G-BAD firing, pulse mode," Albers said. "Hit!" He turned his face to O'Hare. "No effect!"

"Override safety tolerances," O'Hare said, thinking furiously. "Go full beam!" One warhead launching from the Groza? It carried twenty.

"Two Russian warheads launched," Meany said, the pain in his voice palpable. "It's approaching the Cape Canaveral coastline, making its bombing run. Impact from the *Shakti* in … ten seconds."

O'Hare didn't know 'Lucky' Severin was a religious man, but heard him mutter behind her, "God help us."

She shot a quick look at her instruments. Bertha 2 and the Skylon were nudging 20,780 miles an hour.

"Laser hit!" Albers cried. "*Shakti* deviating. Explosive decompression."

They heard Angus' voice over the comms. *Ten seconds to Skylon missile release. Nine … eight…*

Inside the Morrell Command Center, all three Space Force officers lifted their eyes from the instruments in front of them and looked up at the ceiling.

There was no point running. You couldn't outrun a meteorite.

Soshane was still sleeping. Ambre wanted to wake her, to talk to her, to tell her she loved her. But wake her to this? The end of the world? As insane as he was, Grahkovsky was right about one thing. If what he was saying was true, it was better Soshane was asleep. He was sitting watching her, and then stood up and took a step toward them, and Ambre reflexively pulled her legs tighter, holding Soshane as close to her as she could.

Just try and take her, you SOB, she was thinking. *I'll rip my arms out of my sockets to get off this floor and then beat you to death with them.*

Her fears were realized as he reached into the back pocket of his suit pants and pulled out a knife, opening it with a flick of his wrist. She kept one leg wrapped around Soshane and raised the other, ready to kick him if he came anywhere near them.

"Relax!" he said, holding up a hand. "I'm going around behind you, and I'm going to cut your hands free, alright?"

"The hell you are," she said, crabbing around as he moved, but she could only move so far before her left arm strained like it was going to break.

"OK, look," he said, closing the knife again. "I'll drop the knife by your hands, you can cut yourself free." He showed her the knife and held it out at arm's length, holding it in two fingers, and reached over her shoulder to drop it so she heard it clatter on the floor. Her fingers scrabbled for it as he took a step back and sat on the chair again. "You have about two minutes to live, Amber. Don't waste them."

She didn't intend to. Picking the knife up with the tips of her fingers she pulled it into the palm of her right hand and opened it with the left. She kept her eyes on him as she flipped it, so the blade was pointing upward, and began sawing at the ties between her wrists. He sat watching her with a frighteningly detached curiosity.

She felt the ties break and drop, but she didn't move straight away. She knew her legs would be cramped, her arms too. She flexed her wrists behind her back, planning her move. But he must have seen something in her eyes, because he stood and lifted the chair, taking a step back and holding it out in front of himself like she was a lioness and he was a tamer. "Easy, momma. Just pick up that girl and hug her, alright? That's all you have time for. Seriously."

348

She glanced quickly over to the patrol car parked about five feet away. Clenched the knife tightly.

Yeah, you can do this, she told herself. She tensed and released the muscles in her leg, testing. They screamed in protest. She couldn't. She couldn't do it. Damn it all.

She took a big breath, pulled her arms from behind her back, shoulder sockets screaming in protest at having been locked in place so long. She leaned down and wrapped her arms around Soshane and lifted her up, cradling the little girl to her bosom like she was a baby again. She wrapped the jacket around her and held her as tight as she could.

And then she dived.

Grahkovsky jumped back, eyes wide, watching from behind his raised chair as Ambre dived forward like a legless swimmer rolling off the starting blocks in a swimming race and rolled across the floor of the garage, pulling her useless numb legs along behind her as she rolled with Soshane clutched to her chest as fast as she could and slammed into the side of the patrol car below the driver's door. Shoving Soshane wrapped in the jacket as far as she could underneath the patrol car, she crabbed under it herself, scraping the skin off the knuckles of her right hand, the hand holding the knife.

Grahkovsky looked like he was going to shout something, but she didn't wait to hear it. She spun around with her legs away from him, arms and head facing him, Soshane between her legs behind her, knife out in front of her. "You stay there, you psycho! You get close to us I swear I'll…"

She didn't get any further.

The world outside exploded. Something detonated right outside the garage and one of the steel door panels blew in, cutting Grahkovsky clean in two as it careened across the garage floor. Ambre just had time to throw her forearms over her head before a massive sonic boom burst her eardrums and brought the roof of the garage down on top of her.

On the balcony of her hotel in Shanghai, Grahkovsky was shivering. But it wasn't cold. It was excitement. Palpable. Almost sexual.

She couldn't see what was happening in the skies over Florida right now, but she could imagine, with a clarity and precision that the people huddled in their buildings across Kennedy and Canaveral, even those looking up into the sky in wonder, would not possess.

From the angle the missiles were launched at, they would appear like classic asteroids, streaking through the sky trailing huge white contrails. Growing larger as they closed at incredible speeds. Just one asteroid at first, but that was just an illusion; error of parallax. As they dropped toward the earth, they would split into segments, then split again, like a firework bursting, causing the single huge contrail to dissolve into hundreds. The eye would barely have time to register this, though, before the superheated tungsten missiles were slamming into metal, glass, concrete and flesh below.

Now. It would be happening now! She tightened her hands on the railing of the balcony, wishing she could hear it. The crash and rumble of the strike, followed quickly by the sonic booms caused by the missiles splitting the air at Mach 10.

She tilted her ear to the sound of the TV in the room behind her, waiting for the first news reports to start coming in, heart in her mouth.

Missiles running, Angus said. *Five seconds to impact.*

Meany watched in horror as another warhead launched from the Groza. Number four.

Two hundred and fifty-six missiles, hurtling toward the ground. Toward Bunny O'Hare.

Target is firing close-in weapons, Angus reported. *Missile down. Missile down. Impact* ... There was a moment's pause. *Target destroyed, debris field continuing over the Atlantic.*

Meany breathed a sigh of relief, but felt no elation. The virtual cockpit forward view from his Skylon showed the Florida panhandle below, and above it, a network of contrails still arrowing toward the earth.

The heart in Yevgeny Bondarev's chest had stopped beating.

He was watching the attack on Cape Canaveral play out on the huge wall screen inside the Baikonur Groza Control Center with the same feeling of horror that had gripped Maqsud Khan, and many of the same thoughts.

Impossible! But it was happening.

Grahkovsky. It had to be. No terrorist organization had the capability; no foreign State actor would dare. He had called her as soon as the incident had started to unfold, only to be told by her staff that she had not been seen for two days. Her sudden unexplained absence made chilling sense now.

As one of very few people in the world with a clear line of sight to the unfolding calamity that he knew was about to take the world to the brink of war, perhaps beyond, Bondarev could draw a blood-red thread from event to event and it led to only one conclusion.

The attacks on Abqaiq and Korla by his desperate political masters.

The retaliation against his satellite network by the US and UK, causing losses on both sides. China's intervention, perhaps more than once.

And now the bombardment of Cape Canaveral. If anyone was left alive in a few months to investigate it, he knew they would be asking themselves why. Why had she chosen that target, of all targets? Bondarev had a good idea, but it was one he hoped one day to put to her himself, as she sat on death row.

"Pan that image out," Bondarev said. His people had patched through the feed from a Russian surveillance satellite that was in geosynchronous orbit over Kennedy-Canaveral. Its job was usually to monitor signals and provide imagery of US space launches. Today it was showing an entirely different scene. He watched as the first missiles struck Cape Canaveral Space Station, setting buildings alight in multiple places, thick angry smoke boiling into the air immediately, indicating fuel storage facilities had been hit. He could see cars and emergency vehicles moving, hundreds of people running away from the strike zone. And some who were not.

The Kennedy Space Center did not appear to have been hit yet, though he knew that Grahkovsky would not have left it alone of her own accord.

Bondarev raised his voice. "Put all remaining Groza units into stealth mode. No radio communication up or down. Combat AI self-defense protocols only." He pulled Solenko aside. "Once you have shut the Groza network down, prepare your men here to expect a GRU lockdown. Tell them they will be interrogated. They should just tell their interrogators what they have seen and heard. They have done nothing but their duty," Bondarev said, gathering his things, not waiting for the full outcome of the strike on Kennedy-Canaveral to play out. "I will call General Popovkin and get guidance. But it is a call from which I do not expect to return, Solenko. These events happened on *my* watch, literally."

Inside the Morrell Operations Center, the personnel of Space Force dived under desks, tumbled down stairs or crouched against walls as the ceilings shook, windows shattered, and the world outside thundered with sonic booms.

Inside the windowless X-37 control center, O'Hare, Albers, and Severin were all hunkered down, arms over their heads as ceiling tiles dropped to the floor around them.

The bombardment lasted half a minute, but felt like an hour.

When it subsided, they looked at each other with expressions ranging from grim fury (O'Hare) to surprise at still being alive (Albers).

The sudden silence didn't last long. As they listened, there was a secondary explosion as a fuel tank somewhere cooked off, and new sirens added their noise to the 'critical incident' alarms that were still wailing. Fire!

"I've never been under a meteor strike before," Albers was saying. "But I don't think we were right under that one."

O'Hare was thinking exactly the same. The Morrell Operations Center was at the southern end of the Cape Canaveral Complex, four and a half miles from the Industrial Area up by Industrial Road. If she'd been laying a hurt on the Cape, she would have targeted both, but she most definitely would have prioritized the Industrial Area above all else.

O'Hare turned to Severin. "Major, I can set Bertha-2 to AI control or even hand it off to Vandenberg. I know they have a crew in a trailer over there who've been sweating my every move. Skylon can look after itself now." There was another huge explosion in the distance; another tile fell from the ceiling, and the screens in their consoles flickered again as the building shook for a second time. She shrugged. "If, you know, you think maybe it's a good idea we get out of here?"

Severin raised his eyebrows. "You want to run for cover, O'Hare? That's not like you."

"Hell no, sir!" she said. "But I suspect we'd be able to do more good out there on the ground than following a pile of space junk through the sky in here."

Maqsud sat in horror and misery, staring at the small screen on his console. He realized now what Grahkovsky had tricked him into doing, but too late. Too late.

Or, perhaps not? Something had happened to disrupt the strike. Whether it was his abort order or something else he could not see — only five warheads, or 320 missiles, had dropped before he lost communications with the Groza. *Only* 320? That had been nearly the full payload allocated to Cape Canaveral. The rest had been allocated to Kennedy, which did not appear to have been struck at all.

The rain of projectiles had struck Cape Canaveral Station in a three-mile by four-mile fan-shaped strike that took in the Industrial Area and nine launch complexes including LC 40 and LC 37, the two heavy-lift launch pads. Maqsud's compromise had been to deprioritize lower-value targets like the Space Force headquarters at Morrell Operations Center, and purely civilian structures like the Space and Missile Museum. But he'd had to accept the horrible casualty count that had gone along with targeting the Industrial Area because, as Grahkovsky had known when she assigned him the duty, the whole point of the strike was to cause massive loss of life.

But it had been a simulation. Just a simulation! A very clever, very convincing simulation.

Even as he screamed it inside his mind, he knew in the depths of his soul it wasn't true. As he watched, horrified, Cape Canaveral burned. Maqsud turned off the screen.

The AI was telling him something, but the words were lost to him. They flowed around him like the accusing air and flickering, mocking light. He was in the basement. Outside, he needed to be outside.

He walked to the door, found a stairwell and went up. He saw an exit to the ground floor but ignored it. Up. He kept going up, five floors. The stairs took him to the roof of the Titov Main Test and Space Systems computing wing. He emerged onto a tarred black roof, lined with pipes, satellite dishes and thick black electrical wires. Trees, he could see trees. He needed to see trees. He walked to that side of the building and looked at the forest, marching off into the east, deep into Mother Russia.

No boiling clouds of smoke there. No contrails. No fire.

Not yet.

Without a pause, he put his hands on the small safety railing that ran around the top of the five-story building, and vaulted over.

Ambre Duchamp was suffocating. There was no air. She couldn't breathe. Something was pushing down on her head, holding it to the ground. She tried again to draw a breath and couldn't. She began to panic, pushing up against whatever was over her head, trying to get her arms under herself, but there was no room.

Stop, Ambre! A voice yelled at her. *Think.* Her voice. *Breathe.*

She tried again, managed a small gasp. Not enough, but something. Another one. There was air. Not much. Filthy, dusty air. She coughed, and lost what little air she'd got into her lungs. Easy, girl. Pulling her head into the crook of her arm, she took in another sip of air, then another. That's it, one more.

She held the air in her lungs and pulled her face out of her elbow, trying to see something. See anything. But the world she'd woken in was dusk dark, and choked with dust. She lay her head on the ground and felt with her fingers above her head. Metal. Slippery. Greasy? Where the hell…

Under the patrol car. She was under the patrol car. The last thing she remembered was watching the garage door slice through Grahkovsky and then the loudest explosion she'd heard in her life … *listen, Ambre.* She strained her hearing, could hear nothing except a metallic buzzing in her ears. No clues there.

Soshane. She frantically scrabbled her legs, feeling something between them, something soft. Just the jacket? Or the girl, still there? She couldn't turn to look, had to feel with her thighs, her calves. Be still, Ambre, feel her. She clamped her thighs together around the lump between them, and lay as still as she could. Was that movement? The slow rise and fall of a child's chest, breathing? A cough. That was definitely a cough. She couldn't hear it, but she could feel it. Soshane was alive. But hurt? She couldn't see!

She took another sip of dusty air and coughed, then took another. Got to get out. Think. It's like a coding problem. There's a logic, a sequence, think it through. There was a bomb or something. Maybe more than one. Not nuclear or you'd be dead. You're in the garage. Under the patrol car. The roof fell down, probably crushed the car, pushed it down, so you're pinned. You're alive, you can't hear, but your arms work, your legs work, your head isn't crushed, you can cough without screaming so your ribs aren't broken. You could stay here, save your energy, and wait to be rescued. Help will come.

Except no one knows you are here.

Except maybe Soshane is hurt.

Soshane wasn't awake or she'd be panicking too. She could be lying back there between Ambre's legs unconscious, bleeding to death.

You have to get out.

She couldn't see a yard in front of her face, but sensed something there and held her arms out in front of her as far as they would reach. Her fingertips brushed metal. She tried shoving herself forward, using her toes to push, but even with her head on the side, something was pressing down in her shoulders and she couldn't move an inch forward.

Sideways?

No dice. The underside of the patrol car had her pinned.

Backwards.

She lifted her butt and found she had a couple of inches there before it hit the chassis. OK. She lifted her hands and grabbed the metal of the chassis each side of her head. And shoved.

She slid backwards a few inches. Her feet still not hitting anything. Yes. She pushed again. A few inches more. Adjusted her grip, grabbing the chassis further back. Shove. She slid backwards, taking Soshane with her, gripped between her thighs.

One more shove.

Her feet hit something. She felt it with her toes, tried pushing it, but it wouldn't budge. Realized she'd lost her shoes. What? How? It didn't matter. She shoved hard and tried to use the chassis to push it with her feet but no dice, whatever it was, it was going nowhere. Her head was where her butt had been so she found she had a couple of inches above her head now and she craned around to look, but all she saw was gray sunlight and dust or smoke-filled air. It was like the sight of it suddenly made her body realize how foul the air was and she was racked with a fit of coughing, which only stirred up more dust. She buried her mouth in the crook of her arm again and pulled in a painful breath.

Get it together, woman.

She felt with her feet. There was space left and right of the obstruction. *OK, you can get out from under the patrol car, Ambre. Solve that problem first. Then solve the next one. Get out so you can check Soshane.*

356

She splayed her legs. She was no ballerina, but she spread them out on the floor until her ligaments screamed, and she pushed back. Feet against the obstruction, twisted her hips, legs splayed. Push. Lifted her backside. Her butt was out from under the patrol car now, which meant Soshane was out. OK, twist. Twist and … there was no space to twist and roll out. She tried to picture the scene from above. There was something about two feet away from the side of the patrol car, stopping her moving out. But she could move her legs left and right. The chassis was stopping her twisting around and sliding out. It was like one of those stupid puzzles someone gave you when they ran out of ideas in a games shop. She lay there and looked down at herself in her mind's eye.

You're lying on your stomach. Bend your legs at the knees, feet in the air. Push back until your knees hit the obstruction. And then what? *Just do it.*

She lifted her feet in the air, bent them as far as she could toward her butt, and pushed again, sliding back until her knees hit the wall or beam or whatever it was, Soshane wedged up against it. Please don't wake, baby, not now.

Yes. Her shoulders were out, just her head under the car. With a desperate shove she pushed sideways and wrenched herself out from under the patrol car, Soshane sliding along the ground beside her. Feeling gingerly above her head, she tried to sit up and grab at Soshane at the same time, but slammed her head into a sharp edge above her with such force she nearly blacked out.

Dammit, don't you pass out. Don't you cry, bitch!

She felt like she was going to throw up, and she had blood running down her face now, but she scrabbled for the bundle between her legs and felt an arm, a shoulder, then Soshane's hair, and pulled her by one armpit and an arm, cradling the girl's head into her neck.

She was warm. She was alive.

Quickly but carefully, Ambre felt the girl's body from head to feet. Nothing wet. No bleeding. Nothing broken she could feel or see, not that she could see more than a foot in front of herself.

They'd made it.

And now what?

Ambre looked around her, trying to make sense of what she saw. The patrol car was down on its wheel hubs. Tires at the front and back were flat. Roof flattened so that the windows had exploded, but it hadn't been completely crushed. They might have made it if they'd been inside the vehicle when the roof came down, if they'd ducked quickly enough. But then what? They'd have been trapped in there like sardines in a can.

Like this situation is better? It looked like the side wall of the garage had been pushed in against the car and toppled so that it lay across the car forming the small triangular gap in which she had emerged. Bricks and rubble and metal meant there was no way out, either at the front or back of the car. She ducked down and looked under the car again. It was hard to see, but it seemed like the whole car had been buried except for the small tent shaped space she and Soshane had crawled out into. *You can see. You can breathe. Light and air are coming from somewhere, Ambre.* There wasn't space to even pull herself up into a crouch, but she lifted her butt and raised herself up on one arm and managed to get her eyes above the level of the car window and look back to where the light seemed to come from. There was rubble and steel there, but also a small gap about the size of a baseball in the fallen masonry – and blessed, dusty light.

Soshane stirred. Not awake, but waking.

You got to get out, Ambre. She can't wake in here. Last she probably remembers is that lunatic leaning into the car, and now she wakes up here, in this post-apocalyptic shit? Not happening.

She looked back at the baseball-sized hole again. Definitely daylight. Then raised herself up and looked inside the patrol car through the shattered glass of the passenger side window, not really sure why, maybe just for inspiration. For ideas.

Her handbag. The glove compartment had exploded, the contents strewn across the seat and floor. A flashlight. A taser. Handcuffs.

She got an idea.

358

Executing it wasn't easy. She had to lie on her back again with her head jammed into the base of the fallen wall, and then walk her legs up the side of the car until they reached the crushed window and slipped inside. Now she was almost hanging by her legs down the side of the car with her shoulders on the ground and her head at an awkward angle. Now, turn. She half rolled, half spun, scraping her abdomen across the busted cubes of broken glass still sitting in the passenger window frame, biting her lip so she didn't scream. Pushed herself up as far as she could with her arms, trembling with the effort, sure she would collapse, until one of her knees fell off the seat inside the patrol car and the momentum pulled her across the window frame and up.

She was inside the car.

Another five minutes of contortions she never knew she was capable of and she was sitting hunched over in the passenger seat, breathing like she'd just run a marathon and trying not to cough a lung up.

The next part was no easier. Reaching out of the car and down, she had to manhandle Soshane up, losing her a couple of times before she managed to get a sort of cradle rigged around her using the jacket she'd dragged out with her and pulling her up into the car with her. As carefully as she could, Ambre transferred her to the driver's seat, the roof pushed so far down on that side of the car that there was no question of Ambre being able to fit there. It was nearly down as far as the steering wheel, but the wheel was still free.

This is totally going to work. Or not. She looked around the car again. Water. There was a half bottle of water in the driver's door. She knew she had a muesli bar in her handbag, maybe even two. Always carried a snack in case Soshane got hungry. OK, she had food and water. They could stay here for hours, maybe a day. And use the car siren to signal for help. It was a plan.

She decided to test it, reached forward for the button that Russell had asked Soshane to press. Taking a small breath and preparing herself even through her deafness for the loud sound of the siren in the claustrophobic space of the collapsed parking bay, she held it down.

Nothing.

Of course. The car had been turned off by Grahkovsky. It needed to be woken up.

She reached past Soshane and felt for the car starter button.

It was a keyless model that started if the keys were somewhere inside the car. Russell had them in his pocket when he got out and confronted the Russian, she was sure of that. But Russell was dead. Where had Grahkovsky put him? He'd gassed him, grabbed him ... oh shit. Ambre turned slowly and looked into the caged-off rear compartment of the patrol car. The unmoving body of the dead Defender was curled onto the back seat with his back to her. Oh hell. Russell.

That decided it. Soshane wakes up and she's back in the patrol car at the end of the world with Russell dead in the back? She'd have nightmares the rest of her days.

Ambre reached around the steering column and held down the patrol car's starter button until the lights on the dashboard lit up. She kept her finger on the button.

Welcome to drive settings. Please choose drive mode. Do you want manual drive, or autopilot? An annoyingly calm, sexy voice filled the car.

There was no way she could set the car to auto-drive and expect to get anywhere while it was buried in rubble. It would simply refuse to move. Ambre tried to speak, and broke out in a fit of coughing. She took a mouthful of water.

Please repeat. Do you want manual drive, or autopilot?

"Manual," Ambre croaked.

Manual drive selected.

"Safety settings," she said next. "Disable collision avoidance. Disable air bags."

Warning, disabling collision avoidance and air bags may void your auto insurance. Do you wish to proceed?

"Yes."

360

Passengers detected in two seats. Please put on your seatbelts. A small dinging bell sounded inside the car.

"Seriously?" she muttered. She reached across and fastened the driver's belt around Soshane and then pulled her own belt on. Luckily it didn't jam.

Head craned awkwardly to look behind her, she maneuvered her left leg into the driver's pedal compartment and lightly put a foot on the accelerator pedal. She patted her sleeping girl on her thigh. "OK, baby, this is it. Let's hope momma isn't crazy." She put one hand on the gear shift and moved it to reverse, and then jammed her foot down on the pedal.

The 200-kilowatt, 260 horsepower electric engine in the patrol car whined in protest as the car shoved against the fallen steel and rubble and sheet metal behind it. Ambre pushed her foot toward the floor, determined to either burn out or break through. The all-wheel drive spun the shredded tires and added their acrid smoke to the choking dust inside the collapsed garage. Ambre could hear the protesting engine and screaming tires even through the ringing of her near deaf ears and gritted her teeth.

Oh please, God, she said to herself, reaching out to The Man for the first time in the whole ordeal. *I've been saving this until I really needed it. And I need it now!*

A heavy section of roof slammed down into the hood of the car in front of the shattered windscreen, causing her to jump and jam her foot down even harder.

The car shuddered and shook and then juddered a foot backward. Like ketchup out of a glass bottle, it seemed like it was going nowhere, and then suddenly, it was accelerating. It hit something lying on the ground behind it, humped over it with a clattering, grinding sound, broke through a wall of debris, and then slammed into a still burning 10,000-gallon oil tank that had somehow flown through the air and landed on its side in the middle of the road outside the Old Fire Station. Crawling out the car window, heaving Soshane out with her, she fell to her knees and crawled away from the burning fuel tank.

She was *out.*

She stopped, and looked slowly around herself.

Oh. My. God. No.

Anastasia Grahkovsky listened for one minute more to the frantic voice of the news reporter, the background wail of sirens, the beat of helicopter rotors, the blaring horns of the traffic across the water.

He had cheated her. She had ordered Khan to conduct a full payload strike on Kennedy-Canaveral, but what she had just heard reported could have been no more than five or six warheads. Cape Canaveral was burning, and the reporters were saying alarms had been triggered just before the meteor strike, but Kennedy was unscathed.

So either Khan had not executed her orders to the letter, or … yes, it was just possible the Americans had intercepted her Groza. An anti-satellite missile? Another X-37 sacrificed? Or perhaps the British had interfered again. She would know soon enough.

Alarms triggered. Sergei had done his job, then. He'd kept the personnel inside their vulnerable office buildings and labs and workshops. There had been no evacuation of the target buildings. She had been worried NORAD or Space Force would detect the repositioning of her Groza unit and try to evacuate the Kennedy-Canaveral complex, so she had paid one of Titov's cyber security staff to give her a virus that would trigger a critical incident alert at the Space Force facility. He had been able to use an 'off the shelf' product developed by Russian cyber warfare services earlier in the decade, when the Cape had been an Air Force station, because its alert system had not been updated when it was transferred to Space Force. But he could not help her penetrate the base's cyber defenses, so the only way she could insert the virus was to have it done by a physical agent.

Poor, beautiful, loyal Sergei. Had he survived, she wondered? She hoped not. The TV footage cut to a helicopter or drone view of flame and boiling smoke. A fire boat on the Banana River, hosing a burning building ashore. Then a shot of a launch complex, fuel and gas pipelines spouting fire, a launch gantry lying bent and broken on the concrete launch pad.

She could only imagine the scenes at Titov, or within the walls of the Kremlin.

She knew they would *all* come after her now. Probably the GRU first, and if she evaded them, then the Americans, or the British. Damn them all.

But she had succeeded, at least partly. She had protected her babies.

Her mother country could not be trusted as sole steward of the weapon she had created. She had seen that already when it had been used against a petty, small-minded target like Abqaiq. Then Korla? Russia could not be trusted to protect and defend it either, when such crude and unsophisticated attacks as those launched by the British and Americans could so easily succeed. She had tried to buy her progeny some time, but she had only been partially successful. No matter, she had bigger plans.

If it was to reach its true potential, Groza needed to serve more than one master. So she'd arranged for a hire car to be delivered to the hotel that evening and she would take it tonight to meet with the foreign agents with whom she had made anonymous contact before leaving Moscow.

From the 3rd department of the Strategic Support Force of the People's Liberation Army of China.

Fan Bo had been poring over the data from his aborted *Mao Bei* swarm attack on the Groza when word had started coming over international news services of a 'meteorite' strike on Cape Canaveral. At first he had thought it must be a hoax, but the vision shot from viewing platforms that were usually used to record rocket launches showed toppled gantries and smoking ruins, shocked civilians stumbling along a causeway covered in white chalky dust, and bodies being pulled out of the Banana River ... this could not be faked.

Now he understood why the Groza had suddenly deviated from its predicted orbit. He had been worried that it may have detected his ambush and repositioned to avoid it, but it was more likely it had simply been retasked for this strike.

Twenty years of service in the PLA had taught Bo not to second guess the actions of his leaders, either in the armed forces or in politics. But he had also learned it was unwise to appear unprepared when his military masters called him to action. He would order his unit to prepare attack plans for all of the Groza units flagged to China by US Space Force.

Watching the smoke boil over Cape Canaveral, he had little doubt he was about to become very, very busy.

Since leaving their control center Bunny O'Hare had been very, very busy. She and the others had run from the Morrell Operations Center to the base Security Office, to find the duty commander, an officer called Verge, standing at a makeshift desk outside the damaged building, yelling into a radio and directing his Defenders to where they were needed. They didn't have to offer their help twice. He'd sent O'Hare out with a two-way radio to round up civilians and take them out to the evacuation point set up on the Industrial Road causeway. Or call for medical help if they couldn't walk out.

She'd led two groups of civilians out by the time she'd worked her way up toward the sewage treatment plant and found the woman and child crouched in the middle of the road by a smoldering fuel tank and smashed patrol car.

"Hey there, are you alright?" O'Hare asked her as she approached. The woman was crouched in the middle of the road, a little girl clutched to her chest, the girl's head buried in her shoulder. Around them, the Cape Canaveral Industrial Area was burning.

Thick, choking smoke rolled across the road. The woman turned toward O'Hare's voice.

"Hi mate," O'Hare repeated. "Are you okay?"

"Yes," the woman managed. But she was looking at O'Hare with unfocused eyes and a flat expression on her face. Shock. She was in shock. O'Hare had seen it often enough to guess that much. She reached out a hand and stroked the little girl's hair, looking in her sleeping face. "This your daughter? She hurt?"

"Yes," the woman said. "No. I don't know."

"What's your name?" O'Hare asked gently.

The woman frowned. "Ambre."

"Surname, ma'am?"

"Uhm … Duchamp?"

"And the girl?"

"Soshane Duchamp."

O'Hare reached for her two-way radio and lifted it to her mouth. "Base? Captain O'Hare," she said. "I'm up by the Old Fire Station on Scrub Jay. I have two civilians, one adult, possibly concussed, another unconscious, a little girl. Names Ambre and Soshane Duchamp. I need a paramedic." She put the unit to her ear, listening. "No, the girl is breathing normally, no obvious injuries. OK, yeah, I think I can get them there. O'Hare out." She reached out and put a hand on Ambre's shoulder. "Ma'am, are you able to walk, do you think?" she asked.

Ambre didn't answer. She pointed at the smashed patrol car. "Russell," she said.

O'Hare looked where she was pointing. "The patrol car?"

"He's in there."

"There's someone in the patrol car?" O'Hare asked.

Ambre just nodded, and held Soshane tighter.

O'Hare got up and jogged over to the patrol car. Its roof was flattened at the back but there was enough space at the front for her to stick her head in and look inside. Uh oh. There was someone curled up on the back seat. In a Defender's uniform. And he wasn't moving.

Looking around herself she saw a piece of iron fence railing that had been blasted onto the road and jammed it into a gap between the car body and the car door frame. After putting her weight on it a few times, it suddenly flew open. She reached in and put her hand on the man's arm.

He was already cold. Whatever had killed him, it had happened a fair while earlier.

This was ten separate degrees of messed up.

About a block away, there was a massive explosion as another fuel tank went up. Bunny ducked reflexively, but Ambre didn't even react. She was just crouched on the road, rocking her daughter back and forth.

Trying not to look at him, O'Hare felt the Defender's body for an ID or badge or something and came up with a tag and a small leather wallet. She put them in one of the pockets of her flight suit and jogged back to Ambre.

"OK, ma'am, let's get you up," she said, helping Ambre to her feet. "You okay with your daughter there, or you want me to carry her?"

Ambre pulled away from O'Hare. "No. I've got her."

"Good, that's good," O'Hare said and pointed back down the road through the smoke. "We're going back down there. It's a little crazy right now with all the smoke, but you just stick with me. There's an aid station set up out on the causeway. They can have a look at your daughter and you. Alright?"

Ambre bit her lip, but she nodded. Then as O'Hare was about to start walking she grabbed her arm. "What about Russell?" she asked. "We need to bring him too."

O'Hare took her by the shoulders. "Don't worry. We'll get you and Soshane out first, and I'll come back for Russell, I promise."

O'Hare had a million questions she wanted to ask the woman with the sleeping child she'd found by the smashed patrol car and the dead Defender, but they'd have to wait for a better day.

Take-down

Presidential Telepresence Center, White House, Washington, DC

A day later, Chinese Premier Chen Minhao and US President Stuart Fenner sat face to virtual face. The off-the-books videoconference had been requested by Fenner, who was about to take some very important decisions, and while he didn't need or expect China to support them, he needed to know that the Chinese Premier would not publicly oppose them.

As Commander in Chief, Fenner had been sorely tested since coming to office in 2028, and many had doubted his military credentials having served only as a platoon leader for the 3rd US Infantry Regiment, guarding Arlington National Cemetery in Northern Virginia. But he had demonstrated a cool temperament in the Turkey-Syria conflict, cutting loose the Emirates as allies when they refused to allow him to base US aircraft there. He had shown resolve when facing off against Russia in a dispute over the Bering Strait in which Russia tried to occupy the US island of Savoonga, and prescience in pulling US troops out of Asia and the Middle East and repositioning them in Europe to face an anarchic Russia. That decision had emboldened China to support Japan to try to push the US out of its last Okinawa base, but Fenner had kept his nerve, and the US alliance with Japan had in fact been strengthened following that dispute.

It was safe to say the recent conflict over Okinawa had done nothing for US-China relations, and both parties to the videoconference still described each other as 'the main enemy.' So it had surprised Fenner when Chinese defense ministry officials had approached the Pentagon to support a joint US-Chinese operation to degrade the new Russian Groza satellite network. Surprised him until his own head of national intelligence had informed him that China itself had been the victim of a Groza strike.

The enemy of mine enemy is my friend … it was a principle as old as time and Fenner planned to make use of it now. In fact, they were already benefiting; since the attack on Florida, the Chinese had covertly disabled at least four more Grozas according to US Space Command.

Fenner gave a tight smile at the video camera as the Chinese Premier came on line. "Premier Minhao, thank you for agreeing to meet on such short notice," he said, a bot translating his words simultaneously as he spoke. He had asked for the meeting to take place without any other officials or advisors present and had instructed his Chief of Staff no recording should be made and no notes should be taken. He had met Minhao twice on the sidelines of Asia Pacific Economic forum meetings, and once during a much-publicized meeting following the ceremony to celebrate the declaration of the United Republic of Korea.

"Mister President, my sincere condolences for the victims of the attack in Florida. If there is anything we can do, either now or to assist with your efforts later to rebuild, I trust you will let me know personally," Minhao said. He had only recently taken the helm of the world's most populous nation after the former Premier Xi Ping had stepped aside following a controversial third term, relinquishing the premiership to his chosen successor, Minhao, but staying on as head of the Chinese Communist Party where he could wield power behind the scenes. Fenner also had his people working a backchannel to communicate the same thing to Xi Ping as he was about to discuss with Minhao.

"Thank you, Premier; obviously that is what I want to discuss today," Fenner said. "Premier, I think we must face the reality that in Russia, we are now dealing with a State that has gone well and truly rogue. The proxy war on Turkey, the military action to take control of the Bering Strait, the coup that followed it, and now these attacks on Saudi Arabia, China and the USA..." He looked down at a report on a tablet which had just been sent through to him. "For which the latest death toll is approaching six hundred, with several hundred more injured."

The Korla attack was still not public, but Fenner noted that the Chinese Premier did not attempt to deny it. "Our losses were of a similar magnitude, Mr. President. I have seen you have publicly laid the blame for this attack clearly at the feet of Russia. And I agree, since the transition from Vladimir Putin, Russian behavior outside its borders has seemed less … orderly." The Chinese Premier was choosing his words very carefully.

"Your actions against the Russian Groza system are proving very effective, Premier. Can we presume you will continue to prosecute your attacks on the Russian satellite system?"

Minhao muted and appeared to confer with someone off-camera and then looked back at Fenner. "I can assure you, the data you provided is being acted upon, Mr. President."

"I am pleased to hear that. But our situation since the attack on the Cape requires not only that we act, but that I am *seen* to be acting."

Minhao leaned in to the camera. "Mister President, I am aware some members of your Congress are calling for nuclear retaliation against Russia. We have also seen that Russia denies any and all responsibility for the act and maintains that it was an unfortunate natural event. For obvious reasons, we do not believe them, but we would caution in the strongest terms against resort to the use of nuclear arms."

Fenner noted Minhao's carefully emphasized use of the word 'we,' and took it to mean that he was also speaking for Xi Ping in this matter. It was good to know.

"Premier, as you know, we have called an emergency session of the United Nations Security Council for later today. At that session, we will be laying out the compelling evidence we have assembled, which proves Russia has placed a kinetic bombardment weapons system in space and that it was behind the attacks on both Abqaiq and Cape Canaveral."

"I see."

"Premier, would you be comfortable with us disclosing that Korla was similarly attacked?" Fenner asked, getting down to business.

Minhao did not hesitate or confer with his aides this time. "That would not be ... desirable ... at this time, Mr. President. We have no plan for public confirmation of the event you refer to."

"Very well. Can I ask you, if we call for punitive international economic sanctions against Russia in the Security Council, will you support us? I should point out the leaders of the UK and France have indicated their support already."

Now Minhao hesitated before replying. "We would consider supporting such a resolution," he said.

"Thank you, Premier," Fenner said, knowing he could not expect a more definitive answer in the circumstances. "And finally, if the USA takes military action against Russia, limited to eliminating its ability to carry out offensive operations in and from space, can I have your commitment that you will neither condemn these actions publicly nor will you oppose them militarily?"

Minhao's face was impassive, but his next words were delivered with passion. "We would be concerned, Mr. President, that any military conflict between the USA and Russia had the potential to escalate undesirably," Minhao said. "Publicly, we would counsel both sides to find a peaceful resolution to the current situation." He leaned forward. "Privately, as you know, we are willing to continue our cooperation in regard to the already agreed joint operations, and would not attempt to interfere in a *proportionate* non-nuclear response to the attack in Florida, limited to the domain of space and, naturally, not prejudicial to Chinese interests in any way."

Fenner read the written translation of Minhao's words on the screen in front of him to be sure he had heard correctly. There were a lot of very deliberate clauses in the Chinese Premier's words – 'already agreed,' 'proportionate,' 'non-nuclear,' 'limited to space' – but they were all conditions he could live with considering the state of relations between China and the USA. "I think your position is clear, Premier. I hope you will support our Security Council resolution later today and please, let us keep this line open in coming weeks. You may call me at any time on any issue, not just this one."

"Thank you, Mr. President, the offer is mutual," Minhao said. "Goodbye."

Fenner watched the screen go black and sighed. He needed a minute to think before walking back out of the telepresence room into the maelstrom of activity that was the White House. He did not realistically expect China to support their resolution in the Security Council, but if they would at least abstain, the US would proceed with sanctions. And none of the conditions suggested by the Chinese Premier would prevent him from taking the actions currently proposed by his Defense Secretary and National Security Advisor.

He took a sip of cold coffee from the mug in front of him and stood. He had an address to the nation to review. One that could set them on a course to all-out war with Russia.

As he turned, the door to the telepresence room opened and his Chief of Staff, Dave Moore, stepped in, closing it behind him. "Mr. President, I suggest you sit down again. The Russian President, Avramenko, is waiting to talk with you."

Fenner flushed. "Unless he plans to take full responsibility for the attack on the Cape yesterday, he and I have nothing to say to each other."

Moore was a former US Air Force Major-General and not given to political doubletalk. "Our information is that he will admit privately to you that Russia has put a kinetic weapons system in space, but that he will claim the attack on the Cape was an act of cyberterrorism, and not officially sanctioned by his government or its military."

"Cyberterrorism? Someone hijacked their satellite?"

"That's their story, sir."

Fenner put his coffee mug back on the table with care. A very deliberate act since what he felt like doing was throwing it against the wall. "Firstly, Dave, it's nice of him to admit privately what we already know to be true. Secondly, I neither believe, nor care, whether the attack on the Cape was sanctioned or unsanctioned.

That claim, even if true, would change nothing." Fenner nodded at the door. "You can tell President Avramenko to go…"

"How about I just tell him you're not inclined to take his call, Mr. President," Moore interrupted.

The Groza attack on the Cape two days earlier had been brutally effective and, Rodriguez had to admit, had exposed how vulnerable US Space Force's infrastructure was to asymmetrical enemy action, due to its reliance on US continental launch facilities side by side in Florida. If Kennedy had been hit as hard as the Cape, the US would have lost most of its East Coast heavy-lift launch capacity for a considerable period of time, leaving it only with the limited facilities available at Vandenberg. Not to mention the additional thousands of personnel years and expertise it would have lost too.

Her staff had, of course, wargamed a similar threat (assuming a terrorist incident, though) and had a solution of sorts. Right now, the X-37C that was being prepped for loading aboard a SpaceX Falcon Heavy out of Florida (and that luckily had not been moved to the Cape yet) was on its way to Vandenberg where Rodriguez had been assigned a priority Delta IV Heavy launch slot.

The RAF's Skylon had been left critically low on fuel after its race to catch the Groza over Florida, with no chance of making it back to Lossiemouth. Despite looking at an option for refueling in space – an operation not previously attempted – RAF engineers instead chose the least bad option, deorbiting the Skylon and landing it successfully on the three-mile-long runway at Hamad International Airport in Qatar. A company of Royal Marines was there to meet it, just in case any nearby Sheikh got it in their head it might make a nice addition to their fleet of executive jets.

That said, Rodriguez had been impressed by what she had seen of the Skylon in action, she had to admit. Which was why she had written a memo to 45th Wing's Brigadier General Parsons requesting urgent consideration of a proposal to purchase a Skylon Spacecraft military variant from the UK, for testing purposes. There were precedents for the US purchasing UK military equipment, the best known being the UK-made Harrier jump jets used by the US Marine Corps for decades. But she knew it would be an uphill fight.

That was a battle for another day.

Today, the war in space was about to go from cold to hot, and she was deeply chagrined that her 615th Combat Operations Squadron was to have no part in it.

Well, almost no part.

In addition to the Royal Marines there had been another reception committee waiting for the Skylon in Qatar. They were from the US Defense Advanced Research Projects Agency and in their Lockheed C5 Galaxy they carried all the fuel and equipment needed to get the Skylon airborne again.

Plus a very special, and very secret, cargo for its payload bay.

"Captain, your role in this mission is as weapons officer, is that clear?" 'Paddington' Bear was explaining, slowly and carefully, to a rather indifferent Bunny O'Hare.

"It was explained to me more as a multirole kind of thing, Colonel," O'Hare argued. "Which is why I was advising Flight Lieutenant Meany here to…"

Payload deployed, systems check complete, ready to hand over control, Angus intoned, interrupting the heated debate inside the Skylon's virtual cockpit. Bear wasn't present in person – the only two officers in the cabin were Meany and O'Hare – but he had joined via intercom when the altercation between the Space Force and RAF officers had become rather … vigorous.

"We are two hundred miles laterally and fifty miles vertically from the threat you are describing, Captain," Meany said, with patently false patience. "Also, we are in geostationary orbit, therefore unlikely to accidentally fly into a cloud of space debris of any sort, until we move from this position."

"OK, it's your spacecraft," O'Hare said ominously. "But as soon as I drop the boom, all hell is going to break loose up there and you might wish you had a little more room to maneuver, is all I'm saying." She was not in a great mood, having spent seven of the last 24 hours on a cramped and uncomfortable flight from Orlando to Lossiemouth in Scotland, and having slept only two of those.

The 'boom,' as O'Hare called it, was a Kinetic Energy Projectile (KEP) and it did not exist. At least, not on any public list of DARPA balance sheets. It was the offspring of a project that had been running in the early 2020s, in which DARPA had trial-fired a 'tungsten-rich' core inside a carbon-epoxy aeroshell to ensure it could withstand the Mach 5 plus velocities that it would need to sustain if fired either by a rail gun or dropped from orbit. It had proven that it could.

The program had been revived by DARPA five years earlier when the US got its first inkling that Russia was serious about deploying a kinetic bombardment weapon in space. Unlike the Russian 'area effect' weapon, Groza, DARPA had been directed to develop a precision-guided weapon, which it had done by fitting the KEP with the guidance system from a Trident D5 sub-launched ballistic missile re-entry vehicle. As the US had no orbital platform big enough from which to launch the KEP, it had only been test-fired from Virgin Galactic's White Knight 2 carrier aircraft, from an altitude of 71,000 feet. That test had, however, been successful, with the guidance system functioning flawlessly.

O'Hare's demeanor could be put down to two things. The first was that while she was one hundred percent certain the DARPA warhead would hit the ground somewhere (gravity would see to that), she was not at all certain the guidance system would survive the shock of atmospheric re-entry, even if it did use the same well-proven technology as an ICBM re-entry vehicle. So she wasn't one hundred percent sure it would hit its target.

The second thing impacting her mood was the knowledge that her strike was to be the signal for both a Presidential address and a major ground to space anti-satellite operation launched by multiple US Air Force and Navy units across the globe. As she sat and bickered with Meany, no fewer than six US Aegis guided missile cruisers on patrol in the Pacific, Atlantic, and Indian Oceans were preparing to fire SM-3 Block III anti-ballistic missiles at identified Groza satellites. In coordination with China, another six Grozas had been targeted for destruction by the Chinese *Parasite* anti-satellite system, though of course they still would not reveal details of the *Parasite* system. O'Hare knew from the intel she had seen that the Chinese could have been left to take out all eight orbiting Groza satellites, but a US assault on Russia's satellite network by sea-launched anti-satellite missiles of a scale almost unimaginable to O'Hare was about to begin, and the US President clearly wanted it to be seen and heeded by all.

"Thank you, Angus," O'Hare said, dropping her beef. She checked the instrument readouts on the KEP. "Shell integrity confirmed, propulsion system online, target locked and inertial navigation system online..." She hit a key combination on her keyboard. "Launch in T minus three minutes and ... counting."

She looked over at Meany, crouched in his exoskeleton in front of the Skylon control systems, hand on stick and throttle. "You've got this, Flight Lieutenant," she said, by way of apology. "Anyone who can outfly a *Shakti* kill vehicle and take down two Grozas in orbit can handle whatever happens next, no worries."

"Thanks, ma'am," the RAF pilot said. "Permission to assume you're being sincere?"

"Granted," O'Hare said. "Angus, give me an external view on the KEP, will you, and get ready to count us down?" Even though it wasn't necessary, she wanted to watch the launch of the US weapon, especially as it may be the first and only time the weapon was ever deployed.

View from Skylon to KEP re-entry vehicle onscreen, Captain, Angus said, bringing it up on the main panoramic visual display in front of both her and Meany.

It was not a very impressive sight, O'Hare reflected as she looked at the weapon. The 20 cubic feet of tungsten encased in an ablation-shielded ceramic tile sheath weighed only 24,000 lbs., and in the wide-angle camera view the deltoid-shaped missile looked impossibly small against the vast expanse of the earth below.

Did she spare a thought for the men and women who lay under the crosshairs of the target she had just designated? Yeah, she did. But they had seen what had happened in Abqaiq, and Korla, and Florida; they had put on the uniform of the Russian armed forces that morning, and they had known what that could mean.

O'Hare looked at Meany one last time, got his nod, and checked her targeting data. "Angus, you are go for launch."

Launch in five, four, three, two … KEP away, Angus said.

The warhead had been lifted out of the Skylon's payload bay and pushed out into orbit by the same robot arm Meany used to 'drag and bag' errant satellites. It was as low-tech a delivery system as any that had been discussed, but the operations window hadn't allowed for anything more sophisticated. And in the end, it wasn't needed.

Without any fanfare, the vectoring thrusters on the re-entry vehicle fired, putting it on a trajectory that would end with it slamming into its ground target in about fifteen minutes from now, with the power of a tactical nuclear penetrating bomb.

That target? Russia's principal spaceport, Baikonur Cosmodrome in Kazakhstan.

Yevgeny Bondarev had already decided that Baikonur Cosmodrome was likely to be the last duty post he would ever see. As he had expected, his call to General Popovkin had been followed a short time later by the arrival of two armed GRU officers, who escorted him back to his quarters. There he had remained under arrest for nearly 18 hours, incommunicado. He had no idea what was happening in the world outside his accommodations, but he could imagine. Both within and outside Russia, the world would be losing its mind. And it was his fault. He could blame no one else.

It had been his recommendation, some years before, for Groza to be deployed.

The Groza strikes on Abqaiq and Korla? Under his command. He could have refused to carry out the attacks, and challenged the sanity of such orders. But he had not.

The appointment of the brilliant but ultimately unstable Chief Scientist Grahkovsky? Him again.

The loss of no fewer than four Groza satellites to enemy action? Under his leadership.

The final signature on the orders transferring Maqsud Khan and approving Grahkovsky to conduct a series of 'simulations' of attacks on US launch infrastructure? His.

The security of the control system which Grahkovsky had subverted to allow her AI to take control of the errant Groza? His responsibility.

When he had been told to shower, shave and don his dress uniform, he had assumed he would be carted away to face a military tribunal. Instead, he had been bundled into a car in handcuffs, and then into an aircraft, and flown east. He was not told his destination and had no window out of which to orient himself, but as he was walked from the aircraft onto the tarmac, he recognized the facility. Baikonur Cosmodrome.

"Where am I being taken?" he asked the GRU Lieutenant in charge of his escort.

"To meet with Colonel-General Popovkin," the man replied, giving Bondarev some information for the first time in more than 24 hours. "But we have been told your aircraft will be returning to Moscow in four hours, with you on it, Major-General."

"Alive, or dead?" Bondarev wondered out loud. The GRU Lieutenant didn't respond.

After winding through two long corridors, they walked into what Bondarev quickly recognized as a situation room, on full alert. Had full-scale war already erupted? Row upon row of technicians, enlisted men and women, intelligence and other officers, were hunkered over terminals or talking in low, urgent tones. Wall screens on all sides were showing friendly and enemy dispositions, on the ground, in the air, on the sea, and in space. There was too much information for him to take in before he was pushed roughly along the back wall to a side office, in which General Popovkin and his staff were gathered around a table.

Popovkin looked up as he came in. "Ah, the man of the hour," he said with not a little irony. "Sit him down." His escort led him to a chair along one wall, where he was left for several minutes in cuffs, trying to catch up with the conversation. They were apparently preparing for a US retaliatory strike of some sort, but what kind, he couldn't tell.

"Why do you think you are here, Bondarev?" Popovkin asked, at last, the four other officers in the room staring at him with blank faces.

"I do not know, Comrade General," Bondarev replied honestly.

"I sent for you because, despite your recent lapses in judgment, you remain the officer on my staff with the best understanding of American strategic intent and capabilities," he said. "I sent for you because I wanted you here where my people could pick your brain about what the Americans might be planning in response to your attack on Cape Canaveral, without the risk of using video links vulnerable to interception or cyberattack."

Your attack on Cape Canaveral. Bondarev noted his careful use of the words.

"But events seem to have overtaken us since you boarded your flight. Look up, Bondarev," Popovkin said, "and tell me what you see."

It was a facile question, but Bondarev indulged him. "I see a ceiling in need of painting, Comrade General."

Popovkin managed a crocodile smile. "Very droll. Shall I tell you what I see? I see an RAF Skylon spacecraft parked in a geostationary orbit about one hundred and twenty miles up, directly over this Cosmodrome. I am also informed that US anti-satellite-missile-capable naval and air assets have been moved to alert status. We presume their undersea assets off our coastline have also been placed on alert. And finally, that US news networks are reporting that the US President is expected to make an announcement to his nation in about..." he looked at his watch, "... ten minutes." For a man staring over an abyss, Popovkin sounded unnaturally calm. But Bondarev could see a bead of sweat on his temple. It was all an act, a performance for his staff sitting around the table. Popovkin continued. "Aerospace intelligence believes this is all a prelude to a nuclear strike in retaliation for the attack on Cape Canaveral. President Avramenko, the Prime Minister and his cabinet have been moved to safety. And now that you are so conveniently here, please, share with me *your* thoughts."

Bondarev had nothing to lose, he realized that. So he said exactly what he was thinking. "I think they are right. I think the US President is going to announce that he has authorized a nuclear strike on a Russian target. The US public will want to see a proportional response to the attack on Florida, and a tactical nuclear strike on a Russian military facility would meet that criterion. A surface vessel or submarine-launched hypersonic cruise missile strike would be the most likely attack vector." He shrugged. "The likely target? Somewhere remote. Say Kaliningrad, Petropavlovsk-Kamchatskiy ... or here."

"How boring," Popovkin said, rising from his chair. "I had hoped you would add to the sum of wisdom in this room, but you have not." The others rose with him, but Bondarev stayed seated. He doubted there was a seat for him in whatever bunker they were headed for.

"I do have one observation you may not have considered," Bondarev said quickly, before they could leave. "If the US President is going on air in less than ten minutes, then the missiles are already flying." Popovkin paused at the door and Bondarev continued. "A US Waverider hypersonic missile fired from the Black Sea off Turkey would take sixteen minutes to reach Baikonur, so it is probably already on the way. I suggest you *run*, General."

Popovkin glared at him, then looked at the GRU guards who had brought him in. "Put him in a cell here. There is no need to transport him back to Moscow. He can be tried tomorrow and..."

He got no further. Bondarev had been wrong about the US using a nuclear weapon. But about the rest, he had been right.

Without any warning, the roof and walls of the command center collapsed on top of them.

"Bullseye, Captain," Meany said, watching the feed of their strike on his VR helmet view. The vision had shown a massive detonation deep in the heart of the building complex identified through signals and human intelligence as the nerve center of the Baikonur complex. "NORAD, Skylon. Confirming a successful strike on Baikonur."

"Skylon, NORAD. Strike acknowledged. Buckle up, Skylon," the NORAD controller said.

Withdrawing manipulator arm. Closing payload bay doors, Angus announced.

"Received, NORAD. Skylon moving out to 200 miles, we'll conduct a bomb damage assessment once the dust clears," Meany said. He pushed up his VR helmet. "That was some serious hurt, ma'am."

Hurt? O'Hare had seen plenty of hurt in her time, but probably none more than she'd seen in the eyes of that mother, cradling her unconscious daughter among the flames of the Cape a few days ago.

"The hurt has just started, Flight Lieutenant," O'Hare said sadly. "Angus, can you bring up the feed from the White House broadcast?"

Yes, Captain, do you want BBC, Fox or CNN?

O'Hare looked at Meany, who shrugged. "BBC, I guess," she said.

Anthemic music and then President Fenner's voice filled the virtual cockpit before his image flickered onto their panoramic display screen.

"... fellow Americans, and close allies. In the life of a nation, we're called upon to define who we are and what we believe. Sometimes these choices are not easy. But today as President, I ask for your support in a decision I've made to stand up for what's right and condemn what's wrong, all in the cause of peace.

"At my direction, elements of our Navy, Air Force and Space Force have moved into position to address a new threat that I had hoped we would never have to face in my term as President, but which the events of the last few days have shown to be a reality. No one commits America's Armed Forces to a dangerous mission lightly, but after perhaps unparalleled international consultation, it became necessary to take this action. Let me tell you why.

"Several weeks ago, without provocation or warning, the Armed Forces of Russia attacked Saudi Arabia with a new type of weapon, called an Orbital Bombardment Platform. The target of that attack was the Saudi oil processing installation at Abqaiq, which was destroyed with the loss of hundreds of lives. Two days ago, the same weapon was used in the attack on Cape Canaveral, which so far has cost upward of 700 lives, with many more seriously injured. Russia claims these incidents were not its doing, that they were the acts of an unmerciful God. However, proof for our assertions was laid out in the United Nations Security Council earlier today. There was no justification whatsoever for this outrageous and brutal act of aggression.

"The militarization of space in this way is unacceptable. The use of space for anything other than peaceful purposes is unacceptable. No one, friend or foe, should doubt our desire for peace; and no one should underestimate our determination to confront aggression.

"Today, the United Nations Security Council approved, for the first time in ninety years, mandatory sanctions under chapter VII of the United Nations Charter against one of its member States, Russia. These sanctions, now enshrined in international law, will deny Russia the fruits of its aggression by sharply limiting its ability to either import or export anything of value, especially oil or gas.

"But we must recognize that Russia may not stop using the weapons it has based in space to advance its ambitions. Russia has created a frightening weapon which contravenes multiple international conventions and shown a reckless willingness to use it. To assume it will not do so again would be unwise and unrealistic.

"And therefore, the US and its coalition allies are, as I speak, taking action to remove the threat of Russian aggression literally hanging over our heads, once and for all.

"We have no quarrel with the people of Russia, nor any designs on Russian territory. We will not threaten other elements of the Russian Army, Navy or Air Force. We will not attack defensive Russian missile warning satellites. But whatever offensive military assets Russia currently has in space will be brought down. The bases from which Russia has launched them will be rendered inoperable. What military assets Russia may try to place into space in the foreseeable future will be destroyed.

"To President Avramenko of Russia, I say this – by your actions, you have forfeited the right to a future in space. You have no place in the stars among peace-loving nations. Russia's time as a space-faring nation is *over*.

"Standing up for our principle is an American tradition. As it has so many times before, it may take time and tremendous effort, but most of all, it will take unity of purpose. As I've witnessed throughout my life in both war and peace, America has never wavered when her purpose is driven by principle. And on this August day, at home and abroad, I know she will do no less.

"Thank you, and God bless the United States of America." The vision cut to a panel of journalists ready to dissect the address.

"Cut the TV feed, Angus," O'Hare said. "Bring up the Skylon's infrared camera, zoom it out to show all of Russia. Windows also for the USA and UK coastal areas for known Russian ballistic missile submarine patrol routes. Notify us of any heat blooms indicative of ICBM launches."

Yes, Captain.

O'Hare turned to Meany. "You realize we could be about to watch the end of the world from 200 miles up in space?"

"Yes, Captain, but unfortunately, we aren't up there," he said grimly. "We're down here."

The *Arleigh Burke* Flight III-class missile destroyer USS *George M Neal* was sailing in the company of two older Flight II destroyers in the Western Pacific south of Guam. Onboard was a cable news network camera crew that had been choppered aboard that morning after agreeing to sign a secrecy agreement embargoing them from broadcasting anything until after President Fenner's speech.

They had their camera trained on the forward deck of the cruiser as a hatch flew open, and a heartbeat later, there was an enormous flash of light and smoke as an *SM-3* Block III anti-satellite missile punched into the air and curved away, leaving a thick white contrail of smoke behind it. Seconds later, another launched. And then another!

In all, the *George M* sent six missiles away, racing toward three targets — two Russian Groza satellites and a low earth orbit signals intelligence satellite known as Olymp-M. All three satellites had been allocated to China for secondary destruction if the US attacks were not successful, but Chinese intervention was not needed — four of the six US missiles struck their targets.

Across the globe, six other Aegis cruisers carried out similar strikes against Russian satellites, and they were broadcast across TV networks around the world in near real time.

The debris fields created by the US strikes were large and potentially dangerous to other orbiting objects, so the US limited its *SM-3* strikes to objects in low earth orbit so that the debris created would decay and fall back to earth relatively quickly, burning up on re-entry. The targeted but very public show of force was deemed to have been absolutely necessary.

China, in fact, managed the bulk of the anti-satellite offensive with its *Parasite* system, disabling in the space of the next two hours all remaining Groza units and nearly forty percent of Russia's GLONASS geosynchronous orbit military communications network. It left the network still capable of communication over the Russian mainland, but communications over Western Europe, Asia and the Middle East were severely disrupted.

Despite the entreaties of at least one general on the Joint Chiefs of Staff, no Russian early warning satellite or GPS satellite was attacked. To have done so would have been a direct attack on Russia's nuclear defense capabilities and was certain to have triggered a nuclear response. Despite the attack on the Cape, no Russian population center was targeted, though vision of the strike on Baikonur was released to the media and widely publicized, without the US detailing exactly how it had been delivered.

Luckily for Russian cosmonauts, none were in space at the time of the US attack, or their manned spacecraft would also have been targeted for destruction.

At the time O'Hare and Meany were launching their orbital strike, in Dvina Bay off the Russian port of Arkhangelsk on the Arctic White Sea, a US submersible Sea Hunter drone rose from the depths and fired two conventionally armed hypersonic Waverider missiles. Diving immediately for the terrain below them, they hugged the contours of the Northern Dvina River as they raced inland at 3,300 miles per hour, reaching their target 167 miles inland in just over three minutes.

They hit the main launch complex at Plesetsk Cosmodrome with 2,000 lbs. of BLU-97 Combined Effect Bomblets, which floated down on small parachutes before detonating in a devastating ripple across the Russian space facility, shredding metal, setting fire to fuel tanks, and flaying the flesh from anyone unlucky enough to have been caught out in the open when they hit.

Within two hours of the President's speech, Russia had been reduced from two Cosmodromes to none. From military dominance of the domain of space to bare existence. And its Groza orbital bombardment platform had been silenced, permanently.

What remained unclear, as O'Hare had pointed out, was how Russia would respond.

Russian Energy Minister Denis Lapikov had a very clear idea of how Minister of Defense Kelnikov felt Russia should respond. He could hear him yelling at President Avramenko up in the front of the Presidential Sukhoi Superjet 100, Russia's equivalent of Air Force One. They were circling over the Barents Sea northeast of Finland after core cabinet ministers like Lapikov had been bundled into helicopters and rushed to Moscow's Sheremetyevo Airport for a quick departure a few hours earlier.

Let Kelnikov yell. Lapikov knew the Russian President responded poorly to bullying, but Kelnikov knew no other way. He was not a man for sophisticated arguments. Fat, balding and vindictive, he had wormed his way into the Defense portfolio from the position of Foreign Minister after the coup of two years ago had left him as one of the only ministers still standing. He was proving right now that he was a bad choice, Avramenko had to see that. Or he would, very shortly.

Lapikov stood, nodded to his aide and gathered his papers. He had been on the satellite telephone all morning – a frustrating experience since, in addition to its declared activities, US Cyber Command was conducting an undeclared war against Russian economic institutions such as Treasury, Agriculture and Fishing, Mining, Economic Development, Industry and, not least, his Energy Ministry. Telephone networks, internal websites, email servers were all being attacked. But significantly, no Defense or police infrastructure, as would be expected if the US intention was one of total war.

Reaching the front of the aircraft and the President's offices, he waited with the Prime Minister and the Ministers of Finance, Internal Affairs and Foreign Affairs. All were silent, listening to the debate within as they waited to be called in for the cabinet meeting that might well decide the future of mankind. There were no heads of the military services aboard the Presidential aircraft, they were represented by their Defense Minister and their Commander in Chief, the President, but could be conferenced in as needed. Finally, the door was flung open and Kelnikov stood there, flushed and sweating. "Come in," he said gruffly, as though the meeting was his to convene.

Lapikov looked immediately at the Russian President, seated at the cabinet table, and saw a deep frown clouding his face. Whether it was concern at what Kelnikov had told him, or anger at Kelnikov himself, Lapikov couldn't tell.

"Sit, sit," Avramenko said, waving at the seats around the small round table. It was a cramped, close environment that lent itself to up close and personal discussion, but thankfully the President did not smoke, so at least the air was clear. The President sat back and looked briefly at Kelnikov. "Tell them what you just told me."

Kelnikov dabbed his brow with a kerchief. "They have hit Baikonur and Plesetsk. Both are out of commission. Plesetsk with conventionally armed cruise missiles. Baikonur may have been a tactical nuclear strike..."

The Interior Minister interrupted him. "There is no evidence of radiation, comrade. It was more likely a conventional weapon, a bunker-busting bomb."

Kelnikov did not appreciate the interruption. "Delivered how?" he asked loudly. "By magic carpet to the center of Russia?"

"Continue, Kelnikov," Avramenko said. "Please listen, Comrade Ministers, there will be time to speak when you have the full picture."

Kelnikov continued. "US and allied forces launched a massive anti-satellite offensive as promised. Mostly sea to space missiles, but using other, unknown attack vectors, perhaps land or space-based directed energy weapons ... anyway, we have lost communication with *all* Groza units, and nearly *half* of our GLONASS communications network."

"Is that all?" Lapikov asked.

"All?" Kelnikov bellowed. "No, that is not 'all.' As you have no doubt experienced, our commercial, industrial and communications infrastructure has been under massive pressure from cyberattack for the last 72 hours..."

"Civilian infrastructure," Lapikov pointed out. "They are going after civilian assets, not military. Economic infrastructure, not defense or security. And since the cyber-attacks started before the incident over Cape Canaveral, we cannot assume that the Americans are behind them. China is a likely source, thanks to your misguided attack on their oilfields!"

The Interior Minister, Gregor Dzubya, a former Federal Security Service major turned politician, lent his voice to Kelnikov. "It matters not whether the attacks are commercial or military. All attacks which weaken the State must be regarded equally. The Cold War was lost because of economic, not military weakness."

"We must respond in kind!" Kelnikov said, trying to build momentum. "They are trying to deny us the use of space as a domain. We can do the same. I have attack submarines off the East and West Coasts of the USA and within range of French Guiana that can deal with the remaining US and EU launch facilities. I have *Nudol* armed missile destroyers in the North Sea and Atlantic that can target their satellite networks."

"Are you seriously suggesting a cruise missile attack on the US Space Force base at Vandenberg?" the Prime Minister, Kirill Shabaev, asked, speaking up for the first time. "Have you forgotten it was *we* who attacked Cape Canaveral?"

"*After* the US and UK began a campaign of unprovoked aggression against our Groza satellite system," Kelnikov said, turning to the President. "We had not fired a single shot against the US other than in self-defense. The misguided attack on Cape Canaveral by General Bondarev's mad scientist was unfortunate, but we must react to the US attack immediately, or lose the high ground of space once and for all. Do you want to see US nuclear missiles hovering over Moscow, waiting to drop? If we give up the domain of space, what is next? The seas? The skies?"

Avramenko was going to speak, but Lapikov saw his chance and took it. He stood and held up the papers he had been carrying. "I do not hold Bondarev alone accountable for the attack on the USA, Comrade President." He placed the first few sheets of paper in front of Avramenko. "*Your* signature, Kelnikov, on the order to deploy Groza, appointing Bondarev as commander. *Your* decision not to have the same sort of controls on Groza as we have on our nuclear arsenal... and this, *your* signature on the order to bombard the Chinese oilfields."

"Stop your petty theatrics," Kelnikov said.

Lapikov continued, putting a further piece of paper down in front of Avramenko. "Your signature on the order authorizing the repositioning of two Groza satellites over the USA, one of which was used in the attack on Cape Canaveral."

"On Popovkin and Bondarev's advice!" Kelnikov said.

But Lapikov was not finished. He waved a final piece of paper in the air. "And this. A record of *your personal bank transactions* in advance of the attacks on Abqaiq and Korla. Your purchase of shares and futures in resource companies in Russia and abroad; foreign exchange, gold and platinum bullion trading!" Lapikov threw the page down in front of Avramenko. "He has been growing rich off the back of his Groza attacks. How many shares have you purchased in advance of the attacks you are suggesting now, Kelnikov?"

Lapikov was not so naïve as to expect an accusation of corruption would cause even a ripple around the table. There was not a man there who had not profited handsomely from his position of power in one way or another. But Kelnikov had played the Groza strikes close to his chest, kept other cabinet ministers out of the loop. He may have profited, but none of the others in the room, save perhaps the President, had been let in on the opportunity. A quick glance around the table and Lapikov saw he now had most of the room with him. And he had given the President the leverage he needed to shut the bellowing Kelnikov down if he wanted to.

"Enough!" Avramenko said. "Sit down, Lapikov. This is not a time for petty squabbles but ... I do have to consider this disturbing information."

"You bloody hypocrite!" Kelnikov spat at Avramenko. "Tell me you didn't profit from the forewarning I gave you about those Groza strikes."

A shocked silence followed. Lapikov looked down at the floor and smiled to himself. *Ah, Comrade Kelnikov. You are tap-dancing in a minefield now.*

Avramenko took a moment to let the silence in the room settle. "The Comrade Minister is clearly overcome with the stress of the moment," he said, his voice dangerously flat. "He will remove himself from this meeting, and from his duties." The President nodded to the Interior Minister. "Dzubya, you will isolate Minister Kelnikov pending investigation for corrupt dealing. Prime Minister Shabaev, you will assume interim responsibility for Defense. Please organize for the General Staff to conference in immediately. I will not authorize a nuclear or conventional military response to the US action, but Dzubya, I want to urgently see a plan for full scale cyber warfare targeting US and Chinese economic interests globally."

He looked down at some notes in front of him as the room waited. There must be more, Lapikov thought. There was.

"I want to increase our support to Iran," Avramenko said. "They have requested upgraded S-400 anti-air defense systems to help them avoid a repeat of attacks like the one on their nuclear enrichment facility at Natanz. They have requested aerospace engineering assistance in improving the survivability of their ballistic missiles and enabling them to mount … new ordnance types. See that they get it." He paused to see if any protests were being raised, but heard none. It was all his ministers could do to keep up, let alone think ahead. "And I want more boots on the ground in Iran and Egypt. At least one Okhotnik unmanned fighter squadron in each country and an armored Spetsnaz brigade deployed with our amphibious landing ship the Azov." He pushed his notes away. "Move a second Landing Ship with a detachment of Mi-24K *Kuryer* gunships to Bandar Abbas. We will scale back our current level of intervention in the Persian Gulf until the increased troop and materiel levels are in place, but when they are, I expect to see a plan for continued pressure on Saudi oil exports out of the Gulf."

The Prime Minister, Shabaev, nodded. "Yes, Comrade Supreme Commander." Kelnikov could do no more than fume.

Avramenko turned to Denis Lapikov. "Lapikov, you are also relieved of your duties as Minister of Energy."

Lapikov gasped. Kelnikov's face went from one of outrage to a broad vindictive smirk. But it quickly disappeared as Avramenko continued. "I am appointing you Presidential Secretary for the National Emergency. You will coordinate closely with Prime Minister Shabaev and his ministers, and with our Joint Chiefs. You will manage all press and social media communications about the current situation in cooperation with my office. You will reassure our nation, and our allies, that Russia, and importantly our economy, is untroubled by the current dispute with the USA. But your priority is the restoration or relocation of our space launch capabilities at Plesetsk and Baikonur. We cannot be left without the ability to put satellites in space." Avramenko looked around the table. "You are all busy men – if there is nothing else, this meeting is adjourned. Thank you for your service, Comrade Kelnikov. You may remain, Lapikov."

Kelnikov scowled as he left the room, and shrugged off Dzubya as the man took his arm. Lapikov was still getting to terms with the idea of his new and unexpected portfolio. As the door closed behind the others, he realized the surprise must be showing in his face when Avramenko clasped him by the forearm. "Chin up, Denis. You will get all the resources you need. I will place my Executive Office at your disposal, and my Chief of Staff will set you up and smooth the way with Shabaev. Plus, I will take Space Command out of the Aerospace Forces and make it a separate command, under your authority for the duration of the Emergency."

"Thank you, Comrade President."

"I know you want Defense," Avramenko said, "and I had strongly considered it, even before that idiot Kelnikov started yelling at people. But I need someone to focus on rebuilding our space launch capability and that will not be an easy task. I suggest immediately opening a channel to a non-aligned space-faring nation such as India..."

"Finance will be the biggest challenge, Comrade President," Lapikov pointed out. "With UN sanctions..."

Avramenko smiled. "Do not worry too much. I received an interesting telephone call last night. From a contact close to the Chinese Premier, no less. He called the Korla attack 'unwise' but also said he felt the American attacks on our satellite systems were 'regrettable.' He did not seem to feel bound by UN sanctions China did not vote to support, and offered to continue to respect our current commercial arrangements on oil and gas, on the condition that we provide the necessary turbine parts and expertise to repair the Tarim Basin compressor station. We may not be as inconvenienced by these sanctions as the US would have the world believe."

"That will certainly help," Lapikov agreed.

"Now, back to you. I will persuade Shabaev not to fill the Defense Ministry immediately. But give it six months, get the reconstruction underway, and you can have Defense." He held out his hand. "Your priority now is rebuilding our capabilities in space. Deal?"

Lapikov shook. "Deal, Comrade President."

Lapikov walked out and signaled to his aide to wait a moment longer before he started to give him a download. He walked past him and into an executive bathroom. Threw water on his face and took a deep breath. A job like the one the President had just given him, he could really have used the services of a formidable woman like Roberta D'Antonia. A networker. A fixer. Damn her, her indiscretion had resulted in an uncomfortable discussion with a GRU Colonel and had nearly cost him his own Ministry, but he had survived that little hiccup and he was still here, still in the game.

She had done him one last small favor, though. It had come in the post with an unsigned note, but he recognized her handwriting.

Dear Minister,

Sorry I had to leave without saying farewell but I am sure you understand. I hope you also understand that I am concerned for the welfare of my family now, so that is my priority. I attach some information you may find interesting and hope in some small way that it makes up for any inconvenience I may have caused.

He liked that she had not specifically asked him for a favor in return. And he had no idea how she had obtained Kelnikov's private financial records, but yes, she had more than made up for the inconvenience she had caused him.

Captain Amir Alakeel was at a meeting of a different sort. Only one of the two participants was alive.

He was standing by the grave of the young pilot, Hatem Zedan. Though Zedan was but one of the pilots Alakeel had lost in recent weeks, he was the one for whom Alakeel felt most personally responsible. But he was not sad, for the Koran said, "Those who are slain in the cause of God, He will not allow their works to perish." He was a little sad for the family of the man he had lost over Natanz. He had been paraded in front of Iranian media together with wreckage from his stealth fighter, and Alakeel had heard there were talks underway to swap him for an Iranian pilot shot down off the northern Saudi coast near Khafji. The man returning home would not be the same man who had left it, and the fact he would return home a hero would be little comfort to him and his family in the long dark nights ahead.

The strike on Natanz had not been a significant military victory: bomb damage assessments showed eight of the twelve rocket-boosted bunker busters had penetrated the roof of the complex, but only one third of it was regarded as destroyed. Its impact on Iran's military ambitions was more political than material. Saudi aircraft had penetrated to the heart of Iran and struck at its most heavily guarded facility. Yes, a number of Saudi aircraft had been shot down, but by Russian fighters, not Iranian air defenses. And Russia had lost aircraft too – its vaunted Mig-41s and Su-57s had proven vulnerable to Saudi 5th-generation fighters and it had lost the Beriev to Alakeel's impetuous attack. Their much boasted-about arsenal of ballistic missiles had proven incapable of penetrating Riyadh's Peace

Shield, causing many to question the treasury-crippling value of their efforts to arm them with nuclear warheads. And Iran's Navy had lost a prized frigate.

Though its imams still railed about Saudi perfidy inside their mosques, the Iranian provocations had been paused. Russia too was avoiding directly engaging Saudi forces, though it was moving more assets into the theater – naval, air and ground – so it would surely be just a matter of time before hostilities resumed.

From his jacket pocket, Alakeel pulled a feather. He had visited a friend of his father, who was an *alsuqur* – a falconer. The man had given Alakeel a tail feather from his most prized bird – a *Shaheen*, which he claimed was the fastest falcon in the entire country, with the medals to prove it. The feather was long, with gray and brown bands and a white tuft at the tip. Alakeel held it up to the sky a moment to admire it.

As he did so, he saw a flight of three F-35 Lightnings pass overhead. Zedan had been an introvert, a thinker. He'd apparently thought about his own death and told his family that if it should happen, he would like to be buried near an airfield, with his face to the sky so that he might spend eternity gazing up at it in wonder as he had once done as a child.

Alakeel placed the feather on his grave, and covered it in loose soil.

All war ends in defeat, he reflected as he walked away. *Only peace can be won.*

Epilogue

45th Space Wing, Cape Canaveral Space Force Station, Florida, July 2034

Bunny O'Hare had tried to avoid the scene of her crime, but it had been calling to her every waking moment of the day and night. Meany Papastopoulos had finally talked her into it, saying it was something he needed to do as well.

Like a trauma victim reliving every moment of an assault, O'Hare couldn't stop replaying in her head every single minute of their mission over North America, from the time they had been advised that there was a Groza satellite headed for the Cape, to the moment she and Meany brought it down.

She was reliving it again as she stood beside Meany, looking through a fence at the rubble-filled wasteland that had been the Cape Canaveral Industrial Area. The fence was filled with flowers and cards and photographs of the missing and the dead.

"We could have prevented this," O'Hare said, leaning her forehead against the fence. "We were the only ones on the planet who could, and we didn't."

"Yeah, too bloody right," Meany said. "We killed all these people." He was getting more than an occasional sideways glance from other people at the fence. Exoskeletons like his were not a common sight yet and there was nothing subtle about its constant whirring every time he shifted his weight or took a sideways step.

O'Hare shot him a look. "You don't mean it. I do."

"I'm not being funny. I mean it. You should have anticipated they'd send that Groza at the Cape. Instead of hitting it over Canada, you could have set us up between that Groza and Florida and we could have easily intercepted it."

"You're right," O'Hare said miserably.

"Bloody right I'm right. And I wasted precious seconds powering in the opposite direction when that Shakti launched on us. Running away, when I should have been running toward it." He gripped the wire of the construction barrier with white knuckles. "I killed these people too. You weren't the only one up there."

O'Hare closed her eyes and laid her head against Meany's shoulder, then sensed someone standing beside her.

"Hey you," a voice said.

She turned, to see the woman and child she had rescued. The child was holding a small bunch of flowers it looked like she'd picked herself from a grass verge somewhere.

"Oh hey ... uh ..."

"Ambre," the woman said. She reached out a hand and clasped Bunny's hands in hers. "You know I tried to find out your name, to thank you. But they wouldn't tell me. I went through the base personnel list, could probably get busted for that, but there were so many female officers in Space Force could have been you, I gave up." She let go of Bunny's hands. "She got me and Soshane out," Ambre said to Meany. "You know, that day?"

"You got yourself out," Bunny said gently. "Is how I remember it. I was just the one who found you."

Ambre smiled and squatted down next to her daughter. "Go ahead sweets, put down your flowers."

"There's more than yesterday even," the girl said, pointing. "And more pictures."

"Every flower is a thought honey," Ambre said. "And every thought counts. Right? Miss..." she turned to Bunny.

"O'Hare," Bunny said. "People call me Bunny."

"People call her a lot of things," Meany said, face neutral. They watched as Soshane put her flowers into a gap in the wire mesh security fence. She retreated behind her mother's legs to stare at Meany.

"I come here most days after work. Thought maybe I'd see you here one day, but I wasn't really sure I'd recognize you. I was kind of out of it when you found me," Ambre said. "But I noticed your friend here, and then I saw you."

"Nick," Meany said, reaching out his hand. "RAF Space Command. Pleased to meet you ma'am."

"Are you half robot?" Soshane asked him, sticking her head out.

"Soshane!"

Meany laughed. Crouching wasn't easily accomplished in his exoskeleton, but he could go down on one knee, so he did. He knocked his knuckles on his articulated shin. "I suppose you could say that young lady."

Soshane reached out and touched it. "How come you wear it?"

"Soshane, don't be rude," Ambre chided.

"That's fine," Meany told her. He was still down on one knee and twisted a little so she could see the spinal support column behind him. "I need it because I broke my back jumping out of a fighter plane and before you ask why I jumped out of the fighter plane, it was on fire and before you ask why it was on fire, that was because a Russian man in *his* fighter plane got angry I was shooting at him and so he shot at me and what is the lesson there, miss?"

"That Russians are bad people," Soshane said. "That's what they say on TV."

"Well no, they aren't," Meany said, straightening up again. "They've got bad leaders right now, that's all. What I meant to say was be careful who you get mad at because they might get mad right back at you." He looked at Ambre and shrugged. "Sorry, I'm rubbish with kids."

"You're doing fine," Ambre said. "She's just a busybody." She gave her daughter a little shove. "Go see if you can find any new pictures Soshane." The girl gave her a dirty look, but started wandering down the fence line, looking at the photos and drawings that people had pinned on the wire. Ambre looked directly at Bunny again. "I almost didn't recognize you in … civvies," she said. She sounded like she was referring to Bunny's jeans and t-shirt, but she was looking at her tattoos and facial jewelry.

"No, well, I'm not actually with Space Force," Bunny said. "I was just a contractor. So I haven't really been around much since … you know." She punched Meany's arm. "But the Tin Man was in town for a couple of days so we thought we might come out here and pay our respects, sort of thing."

Ambre looked at Bunny and then at Meany and crossed her arms. "You both look like you could use a decent home-cooked meal." Before they could reply, she nodded in the direction of Soshane. "We always eat early so she can do her homework and get to bed so you'll still have plenty of time to head into Port Canaveral and find a bar. Least I can do to say thank you."

Bunny didn't even hesitate. "A home cooked meal would be awesome, Ambre."

"It's a third-floor apartment, but we have an elevator," she said to Meany.

"Why, are you afraid I'll beat you up the stairs?" he asked.

"Oh, he's a wiseass," Ambre said to Bunny. "I like him."

Roberta D'Antonia hadn't had a home-cooked meal for months.

She'd been sitting in an anonymous apartment in Stockholm, Sweden, eating pot noodles when news of the Groza strike on the Cape had broken.

And she'd heard the US President's address sitting in a bar in Stockholm's Gamla Stan district. Knowing that for all his measured, angry words, there was very little America could do if Russia wanted to put another Groza-style system into orbit. It would contract third-party nations, it would claim to be putting commercial satellites into space, and the next generation of Groza satellites would be better defended, stealthier, more deadly.

Which was why she had used her first two weeks of freedom pulling in favors and putting together a dossier on Lapikov's nemesis, Defense Minister Kelnikov. Lapikov was many things, but not a mass-murdering swine. If anyone had to be behind the trigger of Russia's weapons of mass destruction, she wanted it to be him.

After sending the package of documents about Kelnikov to Denis Lapikov, she turned her attention to securing the safety of her own family. From her contacts in AISE, she had learned that the Russian GRU had put a price on the head of Chief Scientist Anastasia Grahkovsky. They wanted her dead. Not dead or alive, just dead. There was a contract on offer.

D'Antonia picked it up. She didn't want the money that was attached, she had another reward in mind, one that involved the GRU leaving her family the hell alone if she took care of Grahkovsky for them. They agreed to her terms.

She learned that the scientist had flown from Moscow to Shanghai. A tip from a colleague in Shanghai had led D'Antonia to the Haidian District of Beijing, where it was rumored a blind, scarred and bald foreigner had been seen entering and leaving the Chinese National Space Administration headquarters in a government vehicle.

D'Antonia doubted that Grahkovsky worked in the building, but bet on the likelihood she would need to go there occasionally to brief Chinese officials. She paid for a street vendor to keep an eye on the entrance to the CNSA underground garage, and after a couple of weeks, she struck gold. She had Grahkovsky's car followed back to a gated CNSA research compound on the outskirts of Beijing and set up watchers again, to keep track of the Russian's movements. She returned to Sweden, and waited. Over the next three months, Grahkovsky was rarely seen leaving the compound – it must have included living quarters – but once each month, she did.

Like tonight.

It seemed that her night out with D'Antonia in Moscow had given Anastasia Grahkovsky a taste for champagne cocktails, and on the last Friday night of the month, she left her compound and went to a nearby jazz club, where she booked a private booth. According to the staff at the club, she would order a couple of cocktails, take in the music, and then order a car to take her home. Occasionally one of the other patrons at the club would get up the courage to speak with her. Once, the staff had seen her leave with another guest, both of them quite drunk. She was usually in the company of one or more bodyguards, but tonight she was alone, and seemed quite content that way.

D'Antonia walked into the club, knowing that Grahkovsky was already there. She had people inside who had eyes on the woman, and she was in her normal booth, off to one side of the stage. There was no sign of protection. A whisper-thin woman was singing Amy Winehouse in a voice that was pitched far too high for D'Antonia's tastes, but she ignored the aural assault, and the stares of the locals in the club, as she moved through the tables to Grahkovsky's booth.

She slid into the booth without speaking and waited.

Grahkovsky turned her head to D'Antonia as though listening, then smiled. "Ah. I recognize that perfume. I knew someone would come. I'm almost glad it's you."

"You were not that hard to find," D'Antonia said.

"Because I am not hiding," Grahkovsky said. She turned her face back to the stage, and sipped her champagne. "I love this song. *I'm No Good.* Do you know it?"

"Yes. But I prefer the original," D'Antonia said.

Grahkovsky reached for her cane. "I suppose you want me to come with you. Whose intelligence service is waiting for us? The Russians or the Americans?"

"No one, it is just you and I," D'Antonia said truthfully.

"Ah. Of course." Grahkovsky fingered her glass. "I did think the champagne tasted slightly bitter tonight. Except, there is no antidote this time, is there?"

"I'm afraid not," D'Antonia said. The woman's calmness was unnerving.

"How long do I have?" she asked.

"About..." D'Antonia checked her watch, "... ten minutes."

"Good. We'll hear one more number, then. Will you stay with me for a few minutes more?" the woman asked.

"I can do that." The woman on the stage bowed to subdued clapping, then launched into a rather lovely version of *Summertime.*

Grahkovsky hummed along. D'Antonia watched her warily, but she showed no sign of panic, no tensing of muscles, no indication she was going to try to fight or flee. "You wanted to be found," D'Antonia decided. "That's why you're here alone."

"Yes. I don't want to sound melodramatic, signora, but Anastasia Grahkovsky, that little girl from Chelyabinsk, she died long, long ago. All that has existed since then has been an idea. That idea became Groza. Russia was not worthy of it. So now that idea, in all its terrifying potential, has been given to China." Grahkovsky drained her champagne and dabbed her lips with a napkin. "You have killed me. And if not you, it would have been someone else. But Groza lives on."

"I pity you," D'Antonia said.

Grahkovsky's hand tightened on the stem of her glass. "I am indifferent to your feelings about me."

"Yes, that is why I pity you," D'Antonia said. She rose, taking Grahkovsky's cane with her. "Goodbye."

She walked outside the club to find a fresh breeze had blown through, sweeping away the smog and the rain that had shrouded the city ever since she had arrived. Looking up, she could actually see stars.

Perhaps the idea of Groza was unkillable. But it was no longer a threat. And at least for now, the sparkle of the night sky was beautiful again.

/END

But your reading adventure doesn't have to end here. Look on Amazon for other novels in the Future War series (Kobani, Golan, Bering Strait, and Okinawa.)

Author's note

I must start with a confession. Orbital is the novel in the Future War series I have most been looking forward to writing, and the one I have been most nervous about. Predictions of any kind are fraught with uncertainty, and none more so than predictions about warfare in the domain of space.

We are on the doorstep, unfortunately, of an unprecedented militarization of space. If you doubt this, look no further than the list of nations which now have dedicated Space Force commands. And the advent of pilotless or unmanned spacecraft has made 'bloodless' conflict in space possible, another element which increases the risk of that conflict occurring.

The reason for my nervousness, though, is the great passion with which those interested in the realm of space guard their beliefs about how war in the domain of space will or will not develop. Many of the technologies in this novel are either in early prototype phase or, like the Skylon, only now attracting the investments needed for them to see the light of day. So, many of my predictions will not be realized, I fully accept that. This doesn't make them less valuable to explore. For help with the many technical elements of how these future weapon platforms might operate in space I am indebted to the online expert community of Quora and my team of beta readers. Any deviations from science fact are done for literary or plot purposes, so all blame is mine!

Will the technologies discussed in this novel be deployed by 2034? As with any novel in the Future War series, the answer to this is simple: some will, some won't. But let me explain my reasoning for including them.

The Groza Kinetic Orbital Bombardment System does not exist, yet, though all the technology to create it does. But it is a fact that Russia deployed a terrifying weapon in space during the Cold War, called the Fractional Orbital Bombardment System (FOBS) — a suborbital missile which could circle the earth and fire nuclear warheads at any target on the planet, striking it in half the time an ICBM missile would take. It was in operation between 1968 and 1982. I was a child when this weapon was operational and had no idea it was circling over my head. I doubt most people on the planet knew! FOBS was specifically banned by the 1979 SALT II treaty, but was already being discontinued by Russia for economic and practical reasons. ICBMs stored in silos were cheaper to deploy and maintain than constantly sending rockets up to circle the earth; and submarine-launched ballistic and cruise missiles could reach their targets nearly as quickly. But this novel is based on the speculation that if Russia did it once, it may do it again. With recent advances in technology like the RS-28 *Sarmat* missile and with the cost of putting large payloads into space likely to fall dramatically over the next ten years, temptation may once again meet opportunity and result in a weapon such as Groza.

The US X-37 Orbital Test Vehicle exists. The US Air Force currently operates a spacecraft known as the X-37B, a small 'space shuttle-like' pilotless space craft that holds the record for the longest time in orbit by a reusable space craft. The X-37C is currently a plan on a drawing board at Boeing, and if it sees the light of day, it will most likely be due to a future need for the US to have its own capability to lift astronauts into space (it is envisaged it will be able to carry a crew module accommodating six personnel). I believe it is reasonable to expect that with the move to modular payload bays in almost all future weapon platforms, the X-37C would also be weaponized.

The RAF Skylon Single-Stage-to-Orbit spacecraft is more than just an idea on a drawing board. The British Government partnered with the European Space Agency in 2010 to explore potential designs for the Skylon. Key to its development was a new engine, and Reaction Engines Sabre motor has been chosen, with industry partners Boeing, Rolls Royce and BAE Systems underwriting development. The consortium has announced ambitious goals for the first Skylon: a max speed in atmosphere of five times the speed of sound (3,800 mph), peak altitude of roughly 92,000 ft and, on return to the ground, a turnaround time of approximately two days, able to complete at least 200 suborbital flights per vehicle. The first test flight of this commercial 'spaceliner' concept is scheduled for 2025. This novel speculates about a later Skylon marque, Skylon-D, with similar specs but capable of achieving low earth orbit. It is reasonable to believe the RAF would explore the potential of such a platform for military space operations.

The Chinese *Mao Bei* 'Parasite' satellite defense system already exists and has been observed in action. In 2001, Chinese State media reported that China was testing a 'parasitic' micro-satellite that could latch onto another satellite and destroy it on command. In September 2008, China sent two men into space on the Shenzhou-7. During their time in orbit the astronauts released a *BX-1* micro-satellite. Within four hours of its release the micro-satellite flew within 27 miles of the International Space Station at a relative speed of 17,000 mph. A collision between the *BX-1* and the Station would have destroyed both objects and been fatal to the astronauts aboard the Station. The *BX-1* did not strike the Station, but demonstrated China's ability to develop and deploy a maneuvering micro-satellite with ASAT capabilities. It is reasonable to speculate that by 2034 this technology will have matured, and include the ability to swarm. Of all the weapons described in the novel, I regard this one to be the biggest 'game changer.' Cheap to deploy, simple to operate, difficult to detect and avoid, it gives China the power to easily and covertly destroy or disable almost any enemy spacecraft or satellite in orbit. Think about that.

The ALFA-S or Air-Launched Flexible Asset (Swarm) is currently under development by Hindustan Aeronautics Ltd and NewSpace Research and Technologies. It is expected to finish testing in 2023 and is yet another example of the underestimated advances being made by the Indian aerospace industry. India already supplies weapons to Saudi Arabia and conducts joint naval exercises. It is reasonable to speculate that an export version of the ALFA-S would find its way into the Saudi inventory.

The *Shakti* Kill Vehicle already exists. In 2019 India launched it aboard a Prithvi Defense Vehicle Mark-II and successfully intercepted a satellite in low earth orbit. India already jointly develops weapons systems together with the Russian Federation, notably the *Brah Mos* hypersonic cruise missile. It was considered reasonable therefore to speculate that it might export the *Shakti* technology to Russia.

High energy laser interceptor systems already exist. Russia tested a carbon dioxide laser system in space known as Polyus as far back as 1987. The US AN/SEQ-3 Laser Weapon System is a 30-kilowatt laser already deployed on the USS *Ponce* as a close-in defense weapon against airborne threats. The US Army is in active development phase for several platforms including the 50-kilowatt Multi-Mission High Energy Laser (MM-HEL), which will be mounted on infantry fighting vehicles or HUMVEEs. It is also progressing its Indirect Fires Protection Capability-High Energy Laser (IFPC-HEL), a 250 to 300-kilowatt weapon to engage drones and aircraft, with a target service entry date of 2024. In 2018 China revealed its LW-30 30-kilowatt vehicle or ship-mounted laser defense weapon system. This novel assumes that the challenges of how to power such a weapon in space will be overcome in the next 14 years. It is therefore reasonable to speculate that this technology will be mature in Army and Navy use by 2034, and ready for trial in space, where a recoilless directed energy weapon would be ideal.

Space to space autocannon defense weapons have already been deployed in space. The Russian Salyut 3 military space station was armed with a Rikhter-R 23mm autocannon in the 1980s, based on the weapon in use in Russian fighter aircraft at the time. With the advances in sensors, targeting software and thrust vectoring that have taken place in the intervening decades, it is reasonable to expect that mounting autocannon weapons on spacecraft, especially for defense against incoming projectiles/missiles, would be both achievable and desirable.

Meany's exoskeleton exists in various prototype forms. US Special Operations Command had a project (TALON) which developed a prototype combat version which has not been deployed. At the 2015 Special Operations Forces Industry Conference, Revision Military displayed a prototype Kinetic Operations Suit. Launched a year prior, the suit features a powered, lower-body exoskeleton to transfer the weight down to the waist belt and supports it with motorized actuators on each leg. The exoskeleton supports a body armor system capable of stopping rifle rounds that surrounds 60 percent of the operator, compared to 18 percent with current armor vests. To relieve weight, the leg actuators pick up each leg and move it as the person moves, and take the weight of the helmet, armor, and vest down through a rigid, articulated spine, transferring weight from weak areas of the neck and lower back. A small power pack powers the suit, and a cooling vest pumps water through three yards of tubing under the suit to maintain core temperature; the power pack has a cooling fan that can be heard in close proximity, but it is thought that won't matter after breaching a door. The Kinetic Operations Suit has undergone live-fire testing and combat scenarios and successfully performed the same tasks as currently outfitted operators in similar amounts of time. Similar systems are in development for civilian use to help people with spinal injuries to walk again. I think it is fair to expect that within 15 years, while they may not be widely available, they will be in use.

On the topic of a possible Saudi-Russian armed conflict, I have been thinking about the potential of this for some years, since pricing disputes surfaced several years ago between Russia and the OPEC Plus group including Saudi Arabia. It was quite chilling when, even as I was writing the final chapters of Orbital, a new cold war started between Russia and Saudi Arabia over production quotas which saw the price of oil fall 25-30 percent globally. This price war, together with the COVID-19 pandemic, saw the price of a barrel of crude oil in May 2020 futures contracts fall below zero. The prospect of a heavily armed nation such as Russia, whose economy is dependent on energy exports (60 percent of exports, 30 percent of GDP), facing economic ruin due to catastrophically low oil prices is quite frankly frightening. Under Vladimir Putin Russia has shown itself to be a tough negotiator, but also, some would say, a rational player – though there are few signs it is truly working to reduce its current dependence on energy exports. Chinese energy demand may replace declining demand from Europe, but like the US before it, China is trying to reduce its reliance on imported energy. This novel speculates on what might come after the reign of Putin, if a collapse of energy prices in 2033–34 really pushes Russia to the brink.

Finally, a note on US Space Force, which was established as an independent branch of the US Armed Forces in December 2019. It is currently organized under the US Department of Air Force and the Chief of Operations for Space Force, a former Air Force Brigadier General, is also the Commander of US Space Command. Where US Space Force will eventually be anchored, and where its headquarters will be based, were still unknown at the time of writing. But it is reasonable to speculate that current Air Force space operations units will transition to becoming dedicated Space Force units, and that space-centric facilities such as Cape Canaveral and Vandenberg will eventually be transferred from Air Force to

Space Force. A hundred other constellations are also possible, but I went with this one!

You are welcome to debate any of the assumptions and predictions made in Orbital. Just drop in to my Facebook page at https://www.facebook.com/hardcorethrillers/

PAGASA: Preview

Read on for a preview of the next novel in the Future War series -
PAGASA: This is the Future of War.

A little fish
Subi Reef, South China Sea, December 9, 2034

It was the most heavily fortified Chinese installation in the South China Sea. But Bobong Huerta knew it also had the best damn crab fishing anywhere for fifty miles.

His only crewman, Gonzales Maat, hadn't liked the idea of going anywhere near it. He had a scar from a tuna hook that ran down the right side of his face and it turned white when he was angry. It was white now. "Why we got to sail 20 miles to Subi? They never going to let you in man, the way our government been yelling about things lately. Chinese are not going let anyone even near Subi."

"I been fishing Subi fifty years," Bobong told him. "Best damn crabbing anywhere at the base of that reef and people too scared to go anywhere near it. Rich pickings, man."

"You been drinking your breakfast again, haven't you? It's like you *want* them to take your boat. How are we supposed to get home? Swim?" Gonzales pointed at their radio. "Probably been hailing you the last half hour."

"Radio don't work," Bobong grunted.

"I know that. They don't know that."

Watching the big white Chinese Coast Guard motoring toward them from the mouth of Subi Reef's harbor, Bobong wasn't so sure; maybe Gonzales was right. It was pushing toward them at about ten knots, a half mile off but already dwarfing their little blue and white fishing boat. Gonzales recognized it, or at least the type. China used them to chase away any boat they didn't like. If they were in a good mood, they just yelled at you with bullhorns, or blasted you with high-pressure water hoses. If they were in a bad mood, they'd drive straight at you, try to capsize you with their bow wave. It made Bobong want to spit. Coast Guard? They were six hundred miles from the Chinese coast!

Bobong looked past the white ship to the reef, maybe a mile off. It had just been a coral atoll when he was a kid. His father would take him there and they'd fish the lagoon inside for jacks, largehead hairtail. Drop crab pots on the reefs around it, and every one came up filled with crab. It was an hour or more out of Pagasa Island, where they lived, but it had always delivered. Then the Chinese came. Started by chasing off the Philippine and Vietnamese fishermen, and then about twenty years ago they started building. First just pouring concrete over the reef so it wasn't submerged at high tide. Built a small dock. Then a big one. A runway for helicopters and jet fighters. Then they put in missile emplacements, barracks and warehouses and workshops. A lighthouse. Dredged the middle of the atoll and turned it into a deep-water port so they could anchor the big Coast Guard cutters like the one headed right for Bobong and Gonzales.

It wasn't a reef anymore; it was a Navy base. He wasn't dumb. He knew that. But Bobong had been stewing on it for years and he finally couldn't stand it anymore. These waters belonged to everybody. His family had been fishing here for a generation before the Chinese came. He had as much right to sail here as anyone. And he was sick of sailing past it knowing there was good fishing right here.

"He's coming straight for us. Gonna impound your boat," Gonzales said again. "Damn drunk old fool."

Standing up in his wheelhouse, Bobong spun the wheel clockwise, turning starboard to let the Coast Guard cutter know he'd seen it and was moving out the way. It corrected course too, kept coming straight at them.

"Maybe they will, maybe they won't," Bobong told Gonzales. "Was a time when you'd approach like this, the Chinese either waved you off, or waved you in. Sometimes they were friendly, let us drop some nets and pots. They didn't bother us; we didn't bother them."

"That was *ten years ago*, Bobong," Gonzales told him. He nodded at the cutter, a few hundred yards off now. There was a guy standing on the bow, filming them with a camera. Another one beside him with a rifle. Gonzales pointed at them. "You think they feeling friendly today?"

He'd barely finished speaking when they heard the engine note of the Chinese cutter change. Its bow lifted out of the water, the bow wave rising higher as it suddenly accelerated.

Straight toward them!

"Get us out their damn way, Bobong!" Gonzales yelled.

Bobong already had the wheel hard starboard, turning his little boat the best he could, but all he was doing was putting it beam-on to the incoming cutter. He pushed the engine throttle full forward. It just coughed and choked at the flood of fuel.

The bow of the Coast Guard ship was like an ax, looming over them. Bobong whirled around, grabbed Gonzales and shoved him as hard as he could toward the door out to the stern. "Get out, man, jump for it!"

He just had time to see Gonzales dive clear, when the Chinese vessel was on him. He'd yelled so loud, pushed so hard, his lungs were empty when the cutter slammed into his boat just forward of the wheelhouse. His little boat folded like paper under the weight of the 2,400-ton warship. Bobong suddenly found himself twenty feet under the water in a welter of bubbles, wood and oil, his sinking boat dragging him down with it. He tried finding a way out of the wheelhouse – a broken window, the door, anything – but water was still pouring in, smashing him back against the wheel.

Sixty-year-old Bobong Huerta drowned scared and angry, screaming for his papa with empty lungs.

Learning moments
Hong Kong Harbor, January 7, 2035

Karen O'Hare had never been aboard a superyacht. In fact, now she thought of it, she'd never been aboard a yacht of any kind. She'd sailed on a destroyer – not her own choice – and piloted an unmanned submarine while sitting comfortably ashore, but that was the closest she'd ever wanted to come to actually being a sailor.

She was perfectly at ease pushing a stealth fighter through the sky at Mach 2.5 with a Russian K-77 missile on her tail, but put her on a deck at sea with nothing but the ocean deep and sharks and box jellyfish and stingrays and giant octopuses around her … no thank you. Sure, it might have something to do with the fact Karen 'Bunny' O'Hare didn't have gills or webbed feet and couldn't swim to save her own life, but she didn't have feathers either and she wasn't afraid of flying.

"So how big is that thing?" Bunny asked the water limousine driver who had picked her up at 9 p.m. from a wharf near the ferry terminal and driven her to Repulse Bay on the other side of Hong Kong Island.

The ship that lay dead ahead of them had five decks that Bunny could see above the water, and probably two or three below. At the rear was a dock for a smaller boat that anyone else would probably call a luxury yacht in itself. Even sitting still, the behemoth looked fast.

"The *Sea Sirene?*" the limo driver replied, almost dismissively. "She is 62 meters long and 12 across the beam. Draft three and a half meters. Tonnage, about 1,280."

"Is it as sexy on the inside as it is on the outside?"

The man shrugged. "I've never been aboard it."

"Well, give me your cell number, I'll send you pictures of me at the swim-up bar with a daiquiri."

"I doubt that," he said with a smile. "I'm not taking you to the *Sirene*. Mr. Sorensen's new yacht is behind it."

By 'behind it' Bunny took him to mean 'smaller than'. Because as they approached the *Sea Sirene*, Bunny couldn't see any other ship.

As they swung around the bow of the superyacht, she got her first glimpse of the ship hiding behind it. It had only four decks above the water, which explained why it wasn't visible, but what it lacked in height it made up for in length. The area in front of the low, curved superstructure was at least two hundred feet long, and it had a newly arrived tiltrotor chopper parked on it, the blades still turning.

"The White Star *Warrior*," the man said, putting on his best tour guide voice. "A 120-meter aluminum and titanium trimaran hull, rotating master stateroom, indoor and outdoor dining for up to 30 guests, indoor cinema, gym and spa, jacuzzi, and a 25-meter lap pool."

"What, no roulette table?"

He ignored her. "The entire ship is designed for a zero-carbon footprint. The 70,000-kilowatt engines…"

"Kilowatts, that's like…"

"94,000 horsepower."

"Right."

"The engines are powered by hydrogen fuel distilled from seawater and can drive her at up to 20 knots…"

"I fly jets," Bunny told him. "So, 20 knots is kinda … not fast."

"Cruising."

"Ah."

"And 30 knots when aquaplaning."

Bunny turned her face away. "Still not fast," she said to herself, refusing to be impressed. But if an alien ship landed on earth and floated on the water, she was pretty sure the White Star *Warrior* is what it would look like.

Bunny was more interested in the tiltrotor. For a start, it had wings. Secondly, it had two turboprop engines turning rotors at the end of the wings. And lastly, it had two turbofan *jet* engines tucked in under V-shaped tail fins. But it disappeared from view as the limo driver swung his boat around to the back of the ship where there was a water-level fantail landing dock and two sailors – a man and a woman – in cream t-shirts, pants and spotless cream shoes to help her out.

There was also a woman in a red silk lounge suit with a cream blouse, leaning up against a bulkhead by a door and watching O'Hare negotiate the transfer with amusement. She was somewhere in her early 40s, tall, lithe, with long raven-black hair. Not exactly beautiful. Handsome was the word you'd probably use if describing how people look was your thing. Bunny preferred to judge people by how they handled themselves, by their range of creative swear words, and the variety and location of their tattoos and/or piercings.

"Ok, I got it," Bunny said, waving away one of the sailors. The tall woman kept her hands in her pockets and detached herself from the wall with a shrug of her shoulders, stepping down to greet O'Hare.

"Ms. O'Hare, I am Sylvie Leclerc. Would you like to come with me?" French accent. Of course she had a French accent.

She led the way, taking the steps up to the flight deck two at a time despite the three-inch heels she was wearing. They passed one deck level on the way up but didn't stop.

Damn show off. Bunny had already decided she didn't like her. Yet.

As they emerged into the cooler night air, Bunny's nostrils flared. She could still smell that heady alcohol-to-jet fuel smell coming off the aircraft crouched on the deck, see the shimmer of the heat over those turbofan engines. The thing was matt black, with the White Star Lines logo in plain white on the doors. It wasn't a copter, wasn't a plane. It reminded her a little of a Bell-Boeing Osprey special ops aircraft, but those jet engines at the rear ... not an Osprey.

"You like?" Leclerc asked, pausing as they reached it.

"Can I touch?"

"Be my guest."

Bunny walked closer and ran her hand over the angular wheel housing and got her first surprise. It felt like rubber but buried in the skin were small irregularities.

"Stealth coating?"

Leclerc smiled and nodded, folding her arms and watching O'Hare with interest. "Oui."

She walked around the rear of the aircraft, Leclerc following. "Twin General Electric TF40 turbofan jet engines."

"Correct."

A sliding door to the interior was open and Bunny peered inside. It wasn't fitted out like an executive ride. The compartment inside was very spartan, with everything that might move either strapped down, locked in or stowed in netting-covered racks. "Modular payload bay," Bunny guessed. "This one is a personnel module. There are other modules?"

"There are," Leclerc confirmed.

Bunny walked around to the front of the machine. She was too short to hop up and see inside the cockpit and the door was locked (she tried it), but on the nose of the aircraft she spotted two round ports. They were barely visible to the eye, marked only by a circular break in the smooth metal of the aircraft's skin. She looked under the nose of the aircraft, at bulges in front of the forward wheels.

"These are gun ports," Bunny decided.

"They could simply be concealed landing lights."

"Yeah, they could. But they're not."

"Mr. Sorensen is waiting."

The French woman led them off the deck, past the lap pool and into a poolside salon with tiered birchwood benches around the jacuzzi, which thankfully was both empty and switched off. Bunny imagined the effect the designer was going for was 'Finnish sauna'. A trolley with iced water stood at the end of the pool and one of the sailors who had met her down at the waterline and followed them up poured Bunny a glass and set it down on a bench, which Bunny took as an invitation to sit.

"I'll be back," Leclerc said, disappearing deeper into the ship.

Leclerc found the elderly owner of White Star Lines standing in his oak-paneled office, flipping through mail on a tablet PC. She'd only been working for him for six months and still wasn't at ease in his presence. He'd never once engaged in small talk, even on a recent 10-hour direct flight from Hong Kong to Moscow in his executive jet. He'd sat across a coffee table from her and not said a single word except to reply politely if she asked him a question.

Karl Sorensen was 78 years old. He was the 25th richest man in the world and his White Star Lines was one of the leading mercantile shipping and port management companies on the planet. What made it a very sustainable company was that since the early 2000s it had been the cargo carrier of choice for the US military. Whenever the US went to war, it was White Star Lines that transported the Seabees, the dozers, tanks, trucks, and materials to make it happen. Containers bearing the White Star Lines starburst logo were almost as ubiquitous as the Stars and Stripes wherever the US was constructing its bases.

He looked over at her as she walked in. "She is here?"

"Yes."

"Let's make this quick. I don't like Australians. Noisy." He flipped the leather cover of the paper-thin tablet shut in his idiosyncratic way. It never left his side; in fact, it rarely left his hand.

Leclerc suppressed a smile and followed him aft, finding O'Hare standing on the deck with one foot up on a bench, looking back on the chopper on the flight deck.

Well, she was focused, Leclerc gave her that. About shoulder high to me, cropped, dyed platinum hair, pierced nose, eyebrow, lip and no doubt ... elsewhere. Tattoos on both arms where the black t-shirt stopped, also on her neck and ankle; the ankle tattoo just visible above combat boots. She had a pleasant face, but apparently an abrasive personality, which Sylvie had been warned she might need to 'manage' if the next few minutes were to go well.

Sylvie Leclerc was used to managing people. She'd managed billionaires, foreign intelligence officials and government ministers. So, she was sure she would be able to...

"Hey, you. Do you have anything other than water?" Bunny asked Sorensen as he approached her.

He frowned. "Yes. Of course. You wish for..." He snapped his fingers at the young sailor standing discreetly against a wall.

"Ginger ale, lots of ice," Bunny told the sailor. "Because what I really wish for..." she looked back at the chopper, "is to fly that thing."

Leclerc inserted herself between the smiling Bunny O'Hare and the billionaire with the embarrassed expression on his face. "Ms. O'Hare, this is Mr. Sorensen, the owner of White Star Lines."

Sorensen held out his hand tentatively, and O'Hare shook it. Leclerc breathed a sigh of relief. Alright, so she had some basic social skills, that was a plus.

"It looks like an Osprey, but it's not," Bunny continued. "What it really looks like is an A10 Warthog and an Osprey had sex and that is their ugly love child. You must have some kind of heavy-duty helo deck if you can land that thing on it."

Sorensen still looked confused, but Leclerc was glad to see he didn't dismiss O'Hare out of hand. "Sit, please," he said, as O'Hare took her drink from the sailor. "I have some questions."

"So do I," Bunny told him.

"I am sure. But this is my ship, I am the one looking for a pilot, so I get to ask my questions first."

"That's fair."

Leclerc took a glass of water and sat on a bench at a discreet distance. Far enough away so as not to intrude, close enough for another intervention if it was needed.

Sorensen opened his tablet cover and tapped the screen. "Why were you discharged from the Royal Australian Air Force without privileges?"

"Assaulting an officer."

"Insulting?"

"No, ass-aulting. With a flight helmet. To the jaw." She pointed at her face.

"What does it mean, a discharge without privileges?"

"No severance pay, no pension."

"I see." He flipped through some tablet screens. "Then Defense Advanced Research Projects Agency, DARPA, field-testing unmanned weapons systems in combat theatres: Syria, Alaska, Okinawa, Florida."

"Yes. Totally classified. And none of those jobs after Syria were supposed to be in combat theatres, by the way. The wars started after I got there."

"Yes. Do you love war, Ms. O'Hare?"

Leclerc saw O'Hare flinch. "I hate war. But it seems war loves me. And look, I love flying fast jets, I love testing new systems and making them work so that only the bad guys feel the pain when they are used, and they don't turn on their owners or innocent bystanders like some kind of robotic Armageddon death machines."

"Robotic, Armageddon…"

"Death machines, yeah. If it was up to the politicians and generals of most armies, including your customers, most wars would be fought in cyberspace, or space space, and if a war was

416

forced out into the open, the skies and seas would be full of machines fighting each other with no soldiers, pilots or sailors getting killed, which sounds just dandy except it never works that way and the people who end up dying are old women, mothers with kids and young guys from Detroit who just signed up because they needed a job to pay their father's medical bills. But people like you don't need to worry about that because you can just get in your chopper with your ginger ale on ice and..."

Intervention time. "Mr. Sorensen and I would like to know, what is it you believe in, Ms. O'Hare?" Leclerc asked.

Bunny didn't hesitate, she didn't hum and haw. "I believe I am the best damn pilot of anything that can swim, crawl or fly. That's what I believe. And if I can put that to use in a way that lets me go to bed with my conscience and wake up in the morning still good friends, it's a good day."

"You are a mercenary," Sorensen said.

"My arse," Bunny replied.

"Sorry?" Sorensen frowned.

"She means no, Mr. Sorensen," Leclerc explained.

"I mean no. I was a combat pilot. Now I'm a test pilot. I am a computer coder, proficient in about six digital languages. *And*, on Okinawa, I learned Ikebana." Leclerc thought she caught O'Hare winking at her.

"That is some form of the martial arts, I assume," Sorensen said, nodding. "I learned karate, in Copenhagen in my youth."

"Well, it's a form of art, but not so martial," Bunny explained. "Japanese flower arranging. I rock it." She pointed at a spray of orchids on a table and fake-shuddered. "That, for example, is just vulgar."

Sorensen stood, flipping his tablet cover shut. "I do not believe in assertions of competence, Ms. O'Hare," he said. "I believe in demonstrations." He turned and walked off.

Bunny watched him go, then turned to Leclerc. "So, I take it I didn't get the job?"

Leclerc stood, motioned to the sailor who had been tending to them, and he disappeared out a side door. "That will depend," she said.

The sailor reappeared with a man who was clearly a pilot. He was carrying an extra flight suit and helmet.

Leclerc explained. "You will have one hour with the pilot to familiarize yourself with the machine out there on the flight deck. And then you will be given a mission to execute…"

Bunny's eyes narrowed. "What mission?"

Leclerc took the flight suit and handed it to Bunny. "Oh, I think you'll enjoy it. We need a pilot who can get into, and out of, 'difficult' environments. So, you will take off from this ship, fly Mr. Sorensen's aircraft directly over the People's Liberation Army Guangzhou East Air Base at no more than 10,000 feet, and then return here."

"That's it?"

"That's it."

"No drug running, no picking up shady guys with wraparound sunglasses, no taking video of secret Chinese army weapons…"

"No. But I will be honest. The Chinese government does not allow civilian aircraft to overfly its bases. Guangzhou East is protected with Qianwei-2 vehicle-mounted infrared homing missiles and radar-guided 57mm anti-air cannons."

"OK."

"Plus, a Russian-made S-400 anti-air radar and missile system."

"Right. Not OK."

"No. But if you make it back here alive, we will check your flight data, and if you did indeed overfly Guangzhou East and make it back, you will get the contract."

Bunny sat, thinking about it. "You coming on this flight too?"

"No. Definitely not. Nor is Mr. Sorensen's pilot."

"I'll be alone."

"Yes."

"I could just steal Mr. Sorensen's nice stealth chopper and disappear."

"I doubt that. I mean, you could probably steal it, but you couldn't disappear. There is nowhere on the planet Mr. Sorensen couldn't find you."

"I was just joking. And I would do this, why?"

Leclerc sat again, close to O'Hare, lowering her voice.

"Because I have studied your background, examined your methods, and I know you can. I was the one who got Mr. Sorensen to agree to this little test, because I know you will ace it. And if you do, a new world will open to you that will quite simply blow your mind."

"I have a heavily-armored mind," Bunny told her. "It is not easily blown."

Leclerc leaned even closer. "Mr. Sorensen has been buying up military prototypes from all over the world for the last five years. Near-production systems that competed for weapons contracts and narrowly lost or were ... how do you say ... discontinued because of politics, or budget cuts."

"Systems ... like that tiltrotor out there?"

"Oui. Aircraft, naval vessels, weapon systems, land, sea and underwater drones, Chinese, Israeli, American, Russian, Indian ... and the technical crews to sustain them. You may even have worked on one or two..."

"Why? I thought he was a shipping magnate, not an arms dealer."

"Not to sell. To deploy, for the protection of his fleet. It is an uncertain world – Mr. Sorensen's very expensive ships and their cargoes sail dangerous waters."

Bunny O'Hare had a feeling that the big brown eyes, olive skin and sotto voce French accent of Sylvie Leclerc probably worked on 99.9 percent of people, male or female. Not to mention her perfume, which if Bunny were a perfume person, she would totally ask for the name of.

But Bunny was more a deodorant person than a perfume person, and sultry sotto voce voices were just annoyingly hard to hear, especially on the deck of a yacht out in the middle of Hong Kong's Repulse Bay. There were a million reasons why she should just ask to be driven back to the ferry terminal and only one reason why not.

It was sitting fifty yards away, still ticking as it cooled down in the heat, and it was calling to her: *come on, are you pilot enough?*

"I'll do it," she told Leclerc. "What happens if I get killed?"

"Then you won't get the contract."

"OK. Can't fault that logic."

The vertical takeoff aircraft crouched on the deck of the superyacht like a cougar waiting to leap into the air. Bunny had seen enough to recognize it now.

"This is a V-290 Vapor, right?" she asked Sorensen's pilot as she pulled on a flight suit.

He nodded. "A prototype. This one supplemented the two turboshaft tiltrotor engines driving the props with two GE turbofans for added speed. The props are only used for takeoff or landing. Once we go lateral, propulsion comes from the turbofans."

"More speed, but less range?"

"Not enough range for the US Army or Navy, apparently, because they didn't go with this version. But fine for operations off a ship deck. Mr. Sorensen has a private jet for longer trips." He had a Swedish accent. Former air force, she'd guess, the way he carried himself. He'd told her his name was Rolf.

Bunny pulled on the helmet he was holding out and adjusted it to fit, throwing the cable hanging off it over her shoulder as she walked toward the cockpit of the Vapor. As they walked around the dolphin-shaped nose, she patted it. "Mr. Sorensen's private jet fitted with Gatling cannons too?"

"You don't need to worry about those," he smiled. "You are going on a sightseeing trip. So, we only need to familiarize you with flight and navigation systems, not weapons."

"Righto."

The Vapor's instruments and nav systems were pretty standard, so most of her hour of instruction was spent doing takeoff and landing go-arounds so that she could get used to the transition between vertical and lateral flight. The flight computer handled most of the transition automatically, her helmet visor was constantly feeding her with handling and instrument cues, and the Vapor handled much more like an aircraft than a helicopter, so Bunny picked it up reasonably quickly.

After their final landing, the pilot looked at his watch. "Time's up. I think you're good to go."

"Alright. Keep my ginger ale cold, will you?"

He had been about to climb out and paused. "I would not have accepted this dumb challenge. It is a one-way trip and when China shoots you down and examines the wreck, it could cause problems for Mr. Sorensen's business."

Bunny bristled. "Well, I guess that's why you are a glorified taxi driver and I am an ace combat pilot, Rolf."

He let the barb slide right past him without reacting. "The nav system will automatically log your position. We've filed a flight plan to Guangzhou civilian airport for you as cover. It's in the nav system. You don't need to fly right over the top of the air force base, just get within its physical perimeter and bug out."

"Any other special conditions or rules?"

"No. Good luck," he said, without feeling.

As she lifted off the deck and transitioned to horizontal flight, she reviewed the flight plan they'd filed and immediately decided to junk it. She didn't trust the wizened old shipping magnate or his svelte French sidekick for a moment, and wouldn't be at all surprised if they'd already tipped off the Chinese authorities to be on alert for an aerial incursion, just to make things interesting for her.

Pushing her sidestick forward, she took the Vapor down to wavetop height and started skimming across the harbor just over the masts of the sailboats and freighters that festooned the water. As the big turbofan jet engines kicked in, the broad-bladed propellers that helped her take off vertically folded back like the ears of a running rabbit, to reduce drag. She headed west, around Lantau Island, and swung out into the more open waters of the South China Sea. The ingress route they had plotted for her would have taken her straight up the Zhujiang River, which led directly from Hong Kong to the port and city of Guangzhou. Fifty miles out, fifty back, at the Vapor's cruising speed of 300 knots, it gave her a total flight time of twenty to thirty minutes.

Not including any time spent dodging Chinese ground-to-air missiles.

This Vapor had a top speed of about 600 knots, but Bunny wasn't interested in its top speed. She was interested in its stall speed. How slow could she go and still retain lateral flight control?

Circling an area of clear ocean, she gently pulled back the throttle. At around 100 knots, the flight computer started automatically engaging the turboshaft-driven rotors at the Vapor's wingtips to provide supplementary vertical lift, and it didn't like it when she canceled them.

Stall warning, engage tiltrotors. Stall warning, engage tiltrotors.

With landing flaps extended, the Vapor's handling started getting dangerously sloppy at 75 knots or about 85 miles an hour. She decided 90 would be manageable as long as she didn't try anything radical.

Pulling up the nav map, she replotted the waypoints for ingress to the People's Liberation Army Guangzhou East air base. It was basically a transport hub, not a fighter base, though a quick Google search told her there were also attack helicopters based there. She could probably outrun them but had no desire to even try.

The waypoints she laid in avoided the Zhujiang River entirely. It was too obvious. Instead, she would hit the Chinese mainland south of Guangzhou and fly up the S105 Nanshagang Toll Road at treetop height like she was some rich kid in a Ferrari burning up the expressway at a hundred miles an hour and not worried about speeding fines.

Infuriatingly slow for an aircraft, sure, but slow enough that a ground radar, if it could see her at all, might mistake her for a fast-moving ground vehicle.

She squinted at the map, talking out loud to herself. "So, ride the S105 all the way to Guangzhou city limits, turn right onto the S81, then take the S4 which ... bloody beautiful." The final branch of the highway network was an expressway that actually went *across* the long runway at the PLA air base. She could fly right down the expressway, a hundred feet off the ground, and power right across the Chinese air base from south to north before doing a loop around a botanical garden and getting back over the expressway for the trip home.

Too easy, O'Hare.

Well, except for the fact she couldn't use the Vapor's otherwise capable radar, because it would give her position away. So she was limited to using the passive radar warning receiver, which could tell her if she was being tracked by Chinese air defense radar, or aircraft, or if someone fired a radar-guided missile at her, but forget evading a heat-seeking missile, because though she did have flares she could try to decoy it with, she would be going too slowly to evade anything. She would be putting a lot of faith in the Vapor's stealth characteristics.

Still, it was her plan, and she went with it.

Expecting to be hailed by Chinese air traffic control at any moment, she pointed the Vapor's nose at the huge container terminal on Longzue Island and sailed over the massive cranes with just feet to spare before picking up the expressway. It was a river of headlights, and traffic was flowing but didn't seem to be doing much more than about sixty.

Dammit, even crawling through the sky near stall speed she was thirty miles an hour faster than anything down there.

"Well, we're going to find out how good Chinese air defense radar is, Bunny my girl," she told herself aloud. "Whoa!"

A pedestrian crossover appeared right ahead of her and she just managed to get her nose up in time to lift the Vapor over it, stall warnings screaming in her helmet again, the faces of some very surprised late evening commuters burned into her retinas as she flashed past them and dropped the Vapor down above the traffic again. She wondered if the trailer truck drivers just below could see her matt black silhouette against the night sky as more than just a black on black shadow. She hoped not, because if they could, she would probably be leaving quite a few heart attacks in her wake.

She flipped one of the Vapor's view panels to show the radar warning receiver plot. Strong signal coming from Guangzhou Baiyun International Airport north of the city, as you'd expect, and an even stronger one from the military airfield to the east. But no lock on her aircraft, and no hail on the air traffic control frequency. Yet.

"S4 exit coming up. Damn you are good, O'Hare," she said, giving herself a little mental pat on the back as she swung the Vapor onto the turnoff that would take her along the expressway that crossed the air base runway.

On the lookout for the dangerous pedestrian crossovers she saw an object up ahead of her, right in her path. A sign of some sort? She squinted.

Oh, shit.

Sitting over the highway, right in her path, was a Harbin Z-9 attack chopper. It was the most common of China's copies of the deadly French Dauphin and it was hovering with its two 23mm cannon pods pointed straight at Bunny.

Not only had someone tipped the Chinese off that she was coming, they had also predicted exactly how she would attack the problem of getting herself into and out of the Chinese base. That damn French, it had to have been her. *I have studied your background, examined your methods...*

Was she that predictable? *Well, predict this.*

The need for stealth now irrelevant, O'Hare hit the toggle to retract her wing flaps, pushed the Vapor's throttle fully forward, and her machine leaped forward, pushing her back in her seat.

Straight at the Chinese attack chopper.

She was playing aerial chicken at a closing speed of 460 miles an hour, betting the Chinese pilot would get out of the way. It wouldn't open fire. Send her crashing down onto a busy highway below? Not a chance.

As if to prove her wrong, a stream of tracer fire started spitting from the cannon pods of the Z-9 and with a twitch of her stick Bunny rolled right, the 23mm shells flowing past her like a stream of laser light.

"Well that's just *reckless*, that is," Bunny muttered aloud. She rolled level again, blowing past the Z-9 as it spun on its vertical axis, trying to follow her with its cannon still spitting fire, but it couldn't rotate fast enough. Did it carry heat-seeking missiles? She was dead if it did ... her two turbofan engines pouring flame as she pulled away.

Guns, she needed bloody guns. She flicked the radar warning screen away and pulled up a systems menu. Of course, the guns weren't called guns. There was no 'weps' menu either. That would be too damn easy. Auxiliary systems? She punched the icon and saw menus for the sound system, emergency lighting … ah, right. Countermeasures. Arm? *Hell yes*. Twin 20mm guns up. Chaff and flares up.

Her helmet view changed to show a targeting reticle that followed her head as it turned until it reached the limits of the gun's gimbals. But it also showed her something else. An ammunition counter. It showed 'RNDS: 0'. They hadn't loaded her guns. Of course they hadn't.

Craning her head around and looking over her shoulder, she put the Vapor into a skidding bank so that she could get a look behind her and saw the Chinese chopper falling behind. If it had missiles, she'd have been dead already, but she was out of reach of its cannons now.

Maybe this was going to work after all.

From the corner of her eye she saw a flash of light and reacted instantly, hauling the Vapor around in a stomach-wrenching turn as she pumped out a stream of flares. Heat-seeking ground-to-air missile, had to be! Sure enough, an arrow of fire lanced overhead and disappeared into the night.

Down, she had to get lower!

The expressway over the runway was raised on concrete pillars and she dropped the Vapor down below the level of the expressway, so that as she pulled her machine around, she was looking back at the Chinese airfield through the expressway supports.

She saw an aircraft taxiing out for takeoff. There was another, already speeding down the runway.

"Oh, come on! That ain't fair!" she yelled, thumping the canopy beside her head with a gloved fist.

The air base Google entry had mentioned transport aircraft and choppers. It hadn't said anything about damn fighter aircraft. But that's what she was looking at. She only got a glimpse, but if she was guessing, she'd guess they were J-10 Vigorous Dragons. Light.

Fast. Big guns. And they carried half a dozen missiles. They looked like small Eurofighter Typhoons.

They would reel her in and swat her from the sky within minutes of getting airborne.

"Screw this." She looked desperately around her. To her right was the cityscape of Guangzhou city. She could hide in among the skyscrapers maybe? For how long? And they'd be sure to send those damn Harbin helicopter gunships in after her. She was crossing over the river now and out of an instinctive desire to stay as low as humanly possible, she started following it southeast, away from the city, her jet wash kicking up twin furrows of water behind her.

Minutes, she probably had *minutes* before those fighters lit up their search radars and locked her up, stealth coating or not.

Ahead of her on the water was a huge freighter. She'd become a bit of an expert on merchant shipping after a few months spent watching shipping ply the lanes between Alaska and Russia, and she recognized this one immediately as a crewless autonomous container ship. It had a radio mast and radar dome where the wheelhouse superstructure would have been and could navigate itself between ports, only needing a human pilot – usually sitting in a control room hundreds of miles away – as it was entering or leaving harbor.

Bunny grinned as she recognized the large star on the flat stern and the name; White Star *Magellan*. Well, wasn't that ironic?

Chopping her throttle and dropping her flaps, she circled around and lined up on the long deck, tightly packed with containers. This time she let the automatic landing system deploy the wingtip tiltrotors as she positioned herself right over the middle of the dark foredeck between two cranes, matched speed with the ship, and ever so gently dropped the Vapor down onto the containers on the deck of the *Magellan*.

On the observation deck of the White Star *Warrior*, Sylvie Leclerc glanced at her watch for about the 100th time and paced over to the starboard railing, looking out over the water toward the north.

"Will you please stop stalking around like that?" Sorensen asked her. He was sitting on a leather couch, looking through a contract. "Or at least take off those heels. She is dead. It should have taken her thirty minutes, and she's been gone two hours. You should be spending your time finding a new candidate."

Leclerc spread her hands on the railing, still staring into the night sky. "A shame. I really thought she…"

Really thought she … what? That she could pull off an impossible mission with all the odds stacked against her? No, of course not. But Sorensen had insisted on the unorthodox test.

So, the brash Australian had failed. At best, she was now languishing in a Chinese military prison or hospital. At worst, she was dead, and the test had cost Sorensen his expensive toy.

As she looked across the water, she saw a massive container ship gliding through the bay about five hundred yards away. It was dark except for the pilot lights on its bow and stern, and a few LED lights on its large onboard cargo cranes. A light on the bow showed it was one of Sorensen's ships. Nothing special in that, the chances of any particular container ship being one of his were about forty percent.

A sound reached across the water to her. Engines. Aircraft engines, spooling up. The sound seemed to be coming from near the container ship. Definitely an aircraft … she could hear the *whap whap whap* of rotor blades. But where? A small darker-than-night shadow detached itself from the blackness of the ship's deck and rose into the air.

"*Le diable!*" she exclaimed. "I don't believe it."

Sorensen looked up. "What?"

Leclerc pointed. Within a minute, Sorensen's Vapor was hovering over the deck of the White Star *Warrior*, with O'Hare flipping them both a sardonic salute from the cockpit as it settled onto its landing gear.

Sorensen stood, not waiting for Bunny to climb out. "I still think you are making a mistake," he said, and walked into the cabin.

Leclerc waited by the railing as Bunny approached, pulling her helmet off as she walked and running a hand over her close-cropped hair to wipe off the sweat. Leclerc could see the faint outline of a tattoo under the stubble.

"I have a complaint," O'Hare said as she approached Leclerc.

"I'm sure you have many."

"Well, true, but one *big* one. It was impossible to connect my cell phone to the sound system in that thing," Bunny said. "I had to listen to Rolf's bloody Celine Dion playlist all the way back here."

Muara Container Terminal, Brunei, January 7

"You have a complaint?" the Chinese businessman standing opposite Abdul Ibrahim asked in a tone that implied he had no interest in hearing it.

"Yes, Mr. Lim, I do. You promised me five rib boats. I do not see any."

They had just opened Lim's containers after Ibrahim had arranged for them to be delivered to a quiet corner of the terminal. His men were still going over the inventory and checking everything off, but Ibrahim didn't need an inventory to see that what he was looking at were *not* the inflatable rubber raiding craft known as rib boats.

Lim patted the hard-shell hull of one of the boats. "These are ex-US Navy Mark V special operations craft. There are three here, assembled, and two more, crated. You can assemble them yourself, or just use them for parts."

"I asked for rib boats," Ibrahim said, not ready to let go of his gripe yet. "Fast, light. Not these things."

"And rib boats I have delivered. Each of these 'motherships' can carry sixteen men, or ten men *and* a rib boat across its stern, which I have included in the shipment. They are powered by twin 12-cylinder diesel engines driving water jet propulsors that give them a top speed of 50 knots."

"We're not entering them in a race," Ibrahim scowled. "Where we're going, nothing moves faster than 30 knots anyway."

"But a little extra speed is useful to have up your sleeve, no?" Lim insisted. He was a large, round man, and it was hot inside the container. He dabbed his forehead with a stained rag. He rested a hand on a crate near the stern of the boat. "Not to mention these."

"They do not look like AK rifles," Ibrahim commented, bending down and reading the stenciled labels on the side. "We agreed AKs, and ammunition. *'Mark 19 40mm'* ... what is this?"

"Grenades, for the forward-mounted grenade launcher." He gestured further up the container. "*Those* crates hold a 7.62mm Gatling gun; you mount that behind the wheelhouse. Or a .50 cal machine gun, you have the choice, I included ammunition for both, and you have a set for each boat."

"We can't board a vessel with a mounted .50 caliber machine gun."

"No, your men will find your rifles are in one of the other containers." Lim ran his rag over his neck. "Not AKs. M16s. Do you have any other complaints?"

"I guess not. How did you get a hold of US surplus equipment?"

Lim started walking outside, toward the cooler air. "Not your concern." He pulled an envelope from his pocket and handed it to Ibrahim. "Here is the data on the target. Photographs, plans of the ship's construction. It will be leaving Singapore on the 9th at 0600 hours. That will put it off the coast of Brunei at about 0900 on the 10th. How do you plan to approach it?"

"Not your concern." Ibrahim repeated Lim's own words back at him. He looked over the information Lim had provided. "It has an escort."

"Yes, as we discussed. The White Star *Andromeda*. It controls the navigation of the *Orion* and has the usual defensive systems to defeat piracy, so you may need to incapacitate it to approach the *Orion* safely."

"What is the *Orion*'s cargo?"

"I have no idea."

Ibrahim blinked at him. "Why the hell would I hijack a ship if I don't even know what the cargo is worth?"

"Oh, you seem to have misunderstood my instructions," Lim said. "I said I wanted it 'intercepted'. Perhaps I should be clearer."

He dabbed his face again and put the rag in a trouser pocket. "You will find a case of magnetic limpet mines in one of the containers. I want the White Star *Orion* and all its cargo *destroyed*. Put it on the bottom of the South China Sea."

Ibrahim considered this. "So, it's an insurance job."

"Sure. If you like. An insurance job."

"Alright, be mysterious, Mr. Lim. What about the crew?"

"As you know, the *Orion* is semi-autonomous. There will be the usual security party aboard, maybe a couple of engineers for any repairs needed while it's underway. That's all."

"I mean, what do you want us to do with the crew?"

"Do what you like, they are no concern of mine. Take them hostage, ransom them if you want to. Send them to the bottom with their ship if you don't." Lim looked at his watch. "Are we done here?"

"No. When we agreed our price, I assumed I would be able to offload the cargo and sell it. If I'm *sinking* this ship, I'm making a lot less than I thought. I have men to pay. That escort ship will be armed. Some of my people could be injured or killed and that means I have to pay their families compensation. I will need more."

Lim appeared unconcerned. "How much more?"

"Double," Ibrahim blurted, getting ready to haggle. "Half up front, half on completion."

"Very well. Anything else?"

Damn. He should have asked for more. Clearly, he was underselling his services. It was too late now. "Uh, no. I guess not."

Hong Kong Harbor, January 7

There's an old joke about a guy who dies in a car accident and finds himself in limbo. Saint Peter tells him he's lived a good life, but he's no saint, so it could go either way. Saint Pete has decided to let him choose for himself whether he goes to heaven or hell. An angel gives him the tour of heaven, showing him the soft clouds, harp-playing angels and manicured lawns full of nuns and priests playing croquet. Then he goes down to hell and is shown around by the Devil. He sees the casino, the bordello, the bars and restaurants, horse racing and dance parties full of people doing drugs, and it's a no-brainer. He chooses hell.

"Great!" the Devil says. "Go back to limbo, have a good night's sleep, come back here in the morning."

He does, and the next morning takes the elevator down to hell. As he emerges, the doors slam shut behind him and he finds himself in a torture chamber full of screaming people. The Devil is standing there, waiting to greet him with a glowing-hot branding iron. "Welcome to hell," he says.

"Wait, what happened to the casino, the bordello ... the dance parties?!" the guy asks desperately.

The Devil steps forward. "Oh, that was yesterday, when we were recruiting you. Today you're staff."

The difference between the Devil and Sylvie Leclerc, as far as Bunny O'Hare could see, was that she put O'Hare through hell during the 'interview' and was now showing her heaven.

"I told you I would blow your mind," Leclerc was telling her. She was holding out a flight helmet for O'Hare to put on. It was large, with a wraparound visor, but with none of the usual cables ... just connections for an oxygen mask.

"Don't consider it blown yet," O'Hare told her. "I used to fly F-35 Panther fighters. I've used Gen IV helmet-mounted display systems before."

"This," Leclerc said, handing it to O'Hare, "is not Gen IV. It is not even Gen V. It is Gen Z, and to call it a helmet is an insult. To obtain it, Mr. Sorensen had to buy the company that designed it."

"Yeah, yeah," O'Hare said, but the moment she pulled it on, she lost the ability to speak.

She was no longer sitting in a lounge chair on the deck of the White Star *Warrior*, she was back in the cockpit of the Vapor. In front of her were the multifunction display panels, on her right, the flight stick, on her left, the throttle. Looking down, she could not only see the aircraft's rudder pedals, she could see her own feet! She experimented by pushing her right foot down, and the image of the right foot in her visor pushed the rudder pedal down. "*Whoa.* Get out of town." She held her hands out in front of her and saw two gloved hands that flexed their fingers in synch with her flexing the fingers on her own hand. "How does it *do* that?"

"Millimeter radar, reading the environment," Leclerc told her. "It will be more precise once it is configured specifically for you."

Bunny tried to grab the flight stick and move it, but her 'virtual hands' passed right through it, as though she were a ghost.

"If you are trying to manipulate the controls, you will need VR gloves," Leclerc said, guessing what Bunny was trying to do. "The system can read your foot movement easily enough, but for the precision needed for flight controls, you need pressure simulation gloves which send signals to the unit accurate to a fraction of an inch and enable you to feel like you are touching the controls yourself."

"OK, nice toy," O'Hare said, looking around her. As she turned her head, she could see out of the Vapor's cockpit windows and, turning her head over her shoulder, the view continued as though she had a 360-degree panoramic window behind her. "Kind of like the distributed aperture camera system on an F-35 Panther."

"More than that," Leclerc told her. "Much more. Please sit back, watch and listen. The Vapor out on the deck is currently keyed to recognize my voice commands."

Bunny leaned back expectantly.

"Vapor, start all engines please," Leclerc said.

Inside the helmet, a deep male voice began speaking. *Ensuring all personnel are at minimum safe distance. Starting turboshaft and turbofan engines. Engines to idle. Park brakes, on. Do you wish to power up navigation and avionics?*

"Yes, initiate navigation system."

Initiating. Engine startup complete. Navigation system, online. Avionics, nominal. Vapor is ready for takeoff.

"No freaking way," Bunny said. "You're flying it remotely via the mike in this helmet?" Looking out the virtual windows, she could see the tiltrotor propellers on the tips of the aircraft's wings spinning up. Over the sound being piped into the helmet, she could hear the physical sound of the rotors beginning to thump from the aircraft out on the deck, feel the blast from the props on her own body through the open entrance to the top deck lounge.

"Oui. Vapor, engage trail protocol five."

Engaging trail protocol five. All systems nominal for launch. Confirm launch."

"Launch confirmed."

A hundred points of data began flowing across the virtual screens on the instrument panels 'in front of' Bunny, showing nearby aircraft, shipping, relative altitudes and speeds, instrument readouts and system states. The noise from the deck outside rose to a crescendo. With a jerk, the view in Bunny's helmet began moving as the Vapor lifted off the deck and rose to a position 500 feet above and a hundred feet behind the White Star *Warrior* and hovered there.

Bunny couldn't stand the suspense; she ripped the helmet off her head and looked out of the top deck lounge to where the Vapor was standing. *Had been* standing. It was gone. Standing to look out a side window, Bunny could see the aircraft hovering patiently behind the ship, its blinking nav lights just about the only thing visible against the skyline.

Bunny stared at the helmet in wonder. "OK. Mind, blown."

Leclerc smiled. "That's a station-keeping protocol. It orders the aircraft to trail its host ship at a safe distance and adjustable altitude, to extend the range of the ship's sensors, and so that it is ready for … other commands." She took the helmet back and spoke in the same neutral tone. "Vapor, return to base and shut down."

Without her head inside the helmet, Bunny couldn't hear the aircraft's verbal response, but she saw it easily enough. The thud of rotors grew louder as the aircraft circled around to the front of the ship and, after a somewhat painstakingly slow approach, dropped onto the helipad and cut its engines.

Leclerc put the helmet on the sofa between them. "You are familiar with the concept of data fusion, yes?"

"From my time in air force and space force, sure," O'Hare told her. "Helps pilots with situational awareness, threat identification. Don't tell me that helmet can also access US military data sources?"

Leclerc shook her head. "Not without permission," she answered, somewhat obliquely. "White Star Lines has its own security and intelligence Risk Group that has access to the most advanced civilian satellite and open source intelligence databases. The helmet gives you 24/7 real-time access to that intel with a simple verbal request. Also, you can pull up the radar and communications feed from any of several hundred White Star Lines ships globally, so that you can see what their radars are seeing and communicate with their comms officers, again, in real time. Most White Star ships are fitted with all-aspect radar systems that enable them to monitor both surface *and* airborne contacts. For safety reasons, of course."

"Of course. You had better stop now, or you are going to need to put plastic covers on these seats," Bunny told her with a dead-pan expression. "So, if *you* can fly that aircraft with a voice command, what does Mr. Sorensen need a pilot like me for?"

"Mr. Sorensen does not," Leclerc told her. Reaching out to a table beside her, she lifted a tablet PC up, turned it on and handed it to O'Hare. "I do. Please read this carefully. If you agree to the terms, just apply your thumbprint to the end of the document."

Bunny took the tablet from her. The first part of the document was a standard employment contract, like she'd signed a dozen times, both in the air force and outside it. She looked at the salary, sign-on, and sign-off bonus and saw nothing she didn't like, until she scrolled to the final page.

SECRECY AND INDEMNITY

The undersigned agrees that they will not disclose any information obtained in the course of their employment to any person or agency outside of White Star Lines, unless authorized in writing by a senior executive of White Star Lines (Executive Vice President or above). This agreement does not prevent the undersigned from cooperating fully with an officer of the law of a recognized police or security force engaged in official duties, or an officer of a recognized military service. Failure to respect this agreement will result in forfeiture of all salary and bonuses owed and civil action for damages related to theft of intellectual property.

The undersigned further agrees to indemnify White Star Lines against any legal proceedings for property damage, injury or death caused by or occurring to the undersigned during the execution of their duties.

The indemnity agreement Bunny could live with, even though it sounded rather extreme, but the secrecy agreement had her attention. "Uh, this," Bunny said, showing Leclerc the screen. "I had to sign something like this when I worked with DARPA on top-secret military projects. Why all the secrecy if I'm just going to be flying for a civilian shipping company?"

"Well, that is, how you say, a 'Catch 22', Ms. O'Hare," Leclerc shrugged. "I can't tell you that until you sign your contract, including the secrecy agreement."

Ah, what the hell, I'm already in at the deep end. Bunny scrolled to the bottom of the document where a green square said, "Apply thumb here." The tablet beeped and the document flashed, then disappeared from the screen. Bunny handed the tablet back to the French woman.

"Merci. You are now a member of White Star Risk Group, Ms. O'Hare," Leclerc said. "It is a pleasure to have you on my team."

Bunny narrowed her eyes, looking at the woman in the red silk lounge suit and high heels dubiously. "Uh-huh. You work for this Risk Group?"

"Non. I run it. Before joining White Star Lines I was a section head in the DGSE, the Direction Générale de la…"

"French CIA, yeah, I know it."

"I was head of the department of Irregular Warfare, Naval Intelligence. And before that, I served in the French Navy. But that is old news." Leclerc held out her hand. "Welcome to *Operation Fencepost*, Bunny O'Hare."

Pagasa Island, Spratly Islands Archipelago, January 7

In the Filipino Tagalog language, 12-year-old Eugenio Maat's home was called *Pulo-ng Pag-asa*: Island of Hope.

Eugenio didn't see a whole lot of hope in the faces of the people around him. Mayor Reyes had called everyone in for a meeting in the school hall, and the Philippine Marine Lieutenant was there sitting up front next to him. He had introduced himself as Captain Heraldo Bezerra, but Eugenio and his friend Diwa called the guy 'Cat Hair' because his spiky black hair stuck out from under his baseball-style cap like a cat that had exploded. He was rarely seen without his cap on, even inside. He was standing beside Mayor Reyes, who had sweat rolling down his chubby cheeks.

It was stuffy in the school hall because it had been empty all day and so the air conditioning hadn't been turned on. So stuffy only half the people on the island, maybe fifty, were inside the hall. The rest were sitting on chairs outside where a loudspeaker had been set up.

"You know that hair?" Eugenio whispered to his friend Diwa. "You think it's actually a wig and the hat is sewn on? Maybe he takes the hat off, and he's completely bald." Diwa giggled, covering her mouth so the troops at the front of the hall couldn't see her laughing.

His Ma bent down and pinched his arm. "Be quiet, you." Eugenio's Ma was a big lady, and she wasn't happy. The mayor and the Lieutenant were still getting their microphone set up, but she wasn't in a mood to wait. She stood, and suddenly everyone in the hall stopped talking.

"Mayor! Hey, Conrado."

The man looked over and winced.

"Conrado, what are you doing to get my Gonzales back?"

Eugenio sat up, waiting for the answer. His Dad, Gonzales, and Bobong Huerta had not come back from their last fishing trip. His father had made one call to tell them Mr. Huerta was dead, but that he himself was OK and being held in jail on Subi Reef by the Chinese, and then the call had been cut off.

Reyes fidgeted uncomfortably. "Now, Maja, you know it's complicated. I've been on the phone with Puerto Princesa, they got to go to Manila..."

Eugenio's Ma scoffed and turned her face to the naval officer, who was fixing a microphone to a stand and trying to make out he wasn't involved. Not yet anyway. Eugenio's Ma involved him.

436

"You, Lieutenant. The Navy is supposed to protect our fishing boats. But Bobong Huerta is dead and my husband is a prisoner, what kind of protection is that?"

"Yeah, Navy," someone up the back of the hall said in support. "What you going to do?"

The Philippine Seabee Lieutenant, Heraldo, straightened and tapped the microphone, then switched it on and tapped it again. He leaned in to put his mouth closer to it. "Ma'am, we don't know what happened on Subi Reef, but we have a situation here now…"

"You're damn right we have a situation," Eugenio's Ma said quickly. "The situation is my husband, Gonzales, is a Chinese prisoner and you are doing sweet nothing about it."

People behind Eugenio started calling out. Most were agreeing with his Ma. Others were yelling other stuff they were unhappy with. Mayor Reyes was waving his hands like he wanted people to calm down, but that just made them yell more. The Lieutenant stepped back from the microphone and put his hands behind his back.

It was all too strange to Eugenio. His father a Chinese prisoner? His father was probably the one guy on Pagasa who was most China-friendly. Gonzales Maat had once saved a Chinese fishing crew when its boat was in trouble and towed them back to Mischief Reef. The Chinese military there gave him a thankyou letter in Chinese, which he framed and put on his living room wall. Gonzales would get in arguments with other fishermen when they complained about Chinese fleets overfishing the sea around Pagasa. He'd say there was no way to beat them, so maybe it was time to join them. "Those Chinese fleets, Eugenio," his father told him, "that's the future of fishing." His opinions didn't make him popular, even Eugenio could see that. Eugenio never actually heard him say Pagasa should be a part of China, but he never said it shouldn't either.

When people calmed down a little, the Lieutenant stepped back up to the microphone. The Filipino Seabees had come to the island about six months ago. There had always been a small squad of Marines on the island, like about twenty, but in the middle of last year the Seabees had arrived. They'd come to fix the air strip and the harbor, but to Eugenio it looked like they mostly just lay around in the shade unless the Lieutenant was shouting at them.

"I understand you're all upset, but it's not just a matter of asking China to give Gonzales Maat back. He's been charged by the Chinese with terrorism."

"That's a lie and you know it. You got a boat in the harbor," Eugenio's Ma said. "You go over there, and you get him. Or what is the Navy good for?"

Not much of a boat, Eugenio was thinking. It held about four sailors and had one little machine gun on it. He couldn't see the Chinese being too worried about it.

"Ma'am, that boat wouldn't make it a hundred yards out of the harbor. China has two Coast Guard frigates anchored offshore. You've all seen them, some of you have tangled with them. You can't even get your fishing boats out of the harbor – they aren't going to let our patrol boat out, and they've warned they'll shoot down any aircraft flying in."

"We don't fish, we starve!" Someone up back called out. "We don't get supplies from Puerto Princesa, we starve. And that includes you, Navy man."

At least we have water now, Eugenio was thinking. One of the good things the Seabees had done was fix the pipes to the underground tanks that caught the monsoon rains, and hook up some new solar cells and batteries so that they had power to the water plant that made fresh water out of sea water in the dry season.

Speaking of rain, Eugenio thought he heard thunder off to the south, high up. He looked out a window, but the sky was clear. Not a cloud. *OK, that was weird.*

The US Navy MQ-25 Stingray had started life as a refueling drone which the US Navy could launch off carriers to extend the strike range of their short-legged F-35C Panthers and F/A-18 Hornets. But the failure of Navy's unmanned combat drone program to deliver a carrier-launched long-range reconnaissance platform had seen the Stingray fitted with a reconnaissance module to enable it to perform that role as well. Carrying 15,000 lbs. of fuel, it had a range of nearly 18,000 nautical miles and could stay aloft for more than 40 hours.

The Stingray currently approaching Pagasa Island had launched from the carrier *USS Doris Miller* 700 miles west of the US naval base at Guam and had completed its 1,300-mile journey to Pagasa in just under three hours. The next ten minutes would decide if it would survive to complete the journey back to its mothership.

It had been tasked to secure optical/infrared imagery of every inch of the 70-acre island and the nearby Chinese base at Subi Reef. On approach to the island, it had engaged its radar detection suite, to assure itself there were no missile-targeting radars in the Operations Area capable of locking and tracking it. It was not a stealth design, so any halfway decent ground or air-based radar would be able to see it, and that meant a missile or aircraft could be sent to kill it. It had detected low-powered surface radar, probably from China Coast Guard vessels, but nothing else, and was in any case flying too high for them to intercept it.

It was a clear evening, with good visibility from 40,000 feet to the surface, and as it neared the small rocky outcrops, it began streaming vision and data back to the *Doris Miller*. From that moment, it was doomed.

On Subi Reef, 20 miles away, the Commander of Subi's Red Banner 9 anti-air missile battery had been patiently waiting, like a spider waiting for a fly, for the US aircraft to enter the airspace near his military facility. He had kept his radar array in passive mode, tracking the aircraft only by the radio signals it had been transmitting to the satellite controlling it – because he had known for some time by the pattern of the transmissions exactly what it was: a US MQ-25 Stingray. Chinese signals intelligence ships trailing US carrier groups had long ago developed the algorithms needed to identify US surveillance drones based on the pattern of their radio communication with the satellites to which they sent data and from which they received their commands.

The Red Banner unit had conflicting orders. China had declared a state of emergency in the region due to the contrived 'terrorist attack' on its naval base at Subi Reef by Bobong Huerta and Gonzales Maat, and any Philippine aircraft entering its self-declared air defense perimeter – which now included Pagasa Island – was to be shot down. So as not to inflame international tensions further, the order did not apply to other foreign aircraft, but if the aircraft was an unmanned surveillance drone, like the one he was tracking, he could track it and ask for permission to engage. As the US Stingray started streaming data via satellite back to the *Doris Miller*, the signal was detected by the Red Banner array, its position was confirmed and a missile oriented on the bearing of the signal. Bringing his phased-array radar online, the Red Banner commander sent a brief pulse of energy down the bearing of the Stingray's radio signal, got a solid return, locked the US drone up and called his superiors.

Who called theirs.

When the order to engage was finally relayed, the drone was almost directly overhead. The Red Banner commander acknowledged the order and fired his missile, all inside a second.

The unit's HQ-9C missile was never going to miss. At *four times the speed of sound* the Chinese missile covered the distance to the Stingray inside fifteen seconds, homed on the drone using its own radar, and erased it from existence.

While the Chinese anti-air missile crew was celebrating, so was the naval intelligence analyst aboard the *USS Doris Miller*. They'd lost a Stingray to a Chinese missile attack, sure. It was a loss they would have to learn from. But they had taken beautiful high-resolution images of every square inch of both Subi Reef and Pagasa Island, not to mention the seas around them and the ships upon those seas.

The analyst got started on the task of making sense of them.

Liberty Crossing Intelligence Campus, Virginia, January 7

Carmine Lewis was trying to make sense of the situation on the screen in front of her.

As Director of National Intelligence (DNI), she had a hundred intelligence analysts and their support AIs to 'context' the intel she was looking at, but she'd asked for it raw so that she could try to make sense of it herself before she called the President.

There was no doubt, though. Carmine was looking at the most profound cyber-attack on US interests since … well, since the last one. But this one was *sophisticated*. And it had an angle that perturbed her greatly as she sat staring out the window of her apartment at the slow-flowing Little Patuxent River outside.

Since the US had adopted a public policy of 'retaliation in kind' for State-led cyber-attacks on its institutions or infrastructure, most of the big players in cyber warfare – China, Russia, North Korea, Israel and Iran – were more cautious in the 2030s than they had been during the gold rush years of cyber warfare in the 2020s. China and Russia had learned that they could try to hide their activities behind criminal hacker collectives and disavow knowledge or involvement, but it made no difference to the nature or strength of the US retaliation. An attack traced to China or Russia would result in an even more damaging counterattack in kind. You tried to penetrate the network of one of our defense contractors and steal designs for our next generation frigate? Fine. How about we shut down your stock exchange for a few hours?

Mutually assured destruction was a language the superpowers understood, and the US had started applying it to cyberspace in the late 2020s with good effect. While it didn't *stop* cyber warfare, it made the activity as high risk as all other forms of espionage, causing State actors to think hard before they committed an attack because the benefits had to far outweigh the risks.

Which made this latest attack all the more worrying.

China's People's Liberation Army (PLA) had six cyber warfare hubs, and Strategic Support Force Base 32 Guangzhou was a well-known, well-studied and, luckily for Carmine, well-penetrated adversary. Base 32 had its focus on supporting PLA operations against Taiwan and in the South China Sea.

The CIA had managed to recruit sufficient human sources within the ranks of Base 32 that the US National Security Agency (NSA) had its work delivered to it on a plate. No sooner was a cyber offensive planned than CIA agents within Guangzhou had leaked intelligence on the attack, and if the Advanced Persistent Threat teams of Base 32 found a new attack vector, NSA or CYBERCOM were usually forewarned and forearmed. Any attacks that got through in the last couple of years were those that were allowed to 'succeed' so as not to raise suspicions among the commanders of Base 32.

It seems we got complacent, Carmine mused.

An Advanced Persistent Threat Team traced to Base 32 had been scooping up communications between the US State Department and the Philippines government, in an operation that had not once come up on Carmine Lewis's radar. Communications between the US Embassy and other US government agencies were heavily protected and regularly audited for vulnerabilities. But those of allies such as the Philippines were less so, so Base 32 had focused its energy on exploiting the fact that China ComTech had won a huge telecoms contract serving both the Philippines Departments of Foreign Affairs and Defense.

Exactly as the US had warned the Philippines in advance of their signing the deal.

According to the intel Carmine was reviewing, China had been intercepting the US Embassy's unencrypted mail and phone calls to their Philippines counterparts for close to two years. Top secret data exchanged between intelligence agencies hadn't been compromised, but the hundreds of daily emails and phone calls between Embassy staff and Philippine government officials had been.

Carmine had reviewed the intel personally to make sure it was solid. She'd looked up reports on similar attacks against other allies. She'd cross-referenced with human source reports from within Base 32 trying to understand how this had slipped under CIA and NSA's radar. She'd done a keyword search of the minutes of National Security Council briefing documents to pull out anything related to the Philippines, Taiwan or the South China Sea over the last two years, to give her an idea of just what topics Embassy staffers in Manila might have been asked to feed in to.

And only then, after a shot of coffee to sharpen her mind, had she made the video call to President Fenner.

"Please hold for the President," the White House operator said, forcing Lewis to sit through a mixtape of jazz standards chosen to be so inoffensive they made her teeth grind.

"Hey Carmine, what's up?" a voice broke in over the muzak. It was his Chief of Staff, Chuck Abdor, not Fenner. His two-term veteran right hand was often delegated to take his calls, and Carmine was used to incoming calls being vetted by Abdor first. She and Fenner were ... close. Brother–sister close. If she'd wanted to, she could reach him directly on his cell, and he'd have picked up straight away. Everyone in the West Wing knew that, but she always observed protocol if she was calling the President in her role as DNI.

Carmine didn't sugarcoat what she had to say. "Chuck, I think our Embassy in Manila has given our entire game plan on the Spratly Islands to China."

Abdor remained calm, as usual. "By entire game plan, you mean..."

"Timetable, diplomatic strategy, command structure, force strength and composition..."

"But the Embassy staff are not across all the detail. Only the broad strokes."

"Except State has been sloppy. The Embassy has been asked very specific questions to help feed into briefings for Cabinet meetings and Secretary of State interactions with our *Fencepost* allies. Any competent AI can take those questions and the answers they got to reverse engineer the detail."

"Dammit. You're sure? Of course you are, or you wouldn't be calling."

"We're sure. I checked the raw intel myself. We recently learned China has been siphoning up Embassy comms with the Philippine government for the best part of two years. We ran the Embassy email and voice traffic through an AI, looking for everything related to the Spratly Archipelago, and then analyzed it to see what actionable intel China could have milked from it..."

"Phase one of *Fencepost* has already been initiated," Abdor said, sounding less calm now. "The White Star convoy will sail from Singapore in two days."

"I know. And I'm sorry, Chuck, but according to our analysis, China knows what we are planning."

"The President is in a meeting with the Secretary of Commerce. I'm going to pull him out, and we should probably dial in the

Secretary of Defense. State too, since they'll end up carrying the can for this. Can you hold?"

"Of course."

Carmine had been playing the Washington game long enough to know her information would not be welcomed, either by Defense Secretary Phil Kahn, who would now need to gather his staff to reconsider every single element of what was opaquely known as *Operation Fencepost*, or by Secretary of State Victoria Porter, who Carmine knew would devote the coming days, weeks or even months to trying to prove Carmine wrong and avoid taking any blame for the leak of intelligence on her watch.

That thought had Carmine reaching for the coffee pot again, wishing it was a bottle of bourbon instead. Victoria Porter was a DC politics cage fighter, but Carmine had done her due diligence. She'd faced her down before, which didn't make it something she ever enjoyed, but she was ready for her.

Bring your best game, Madam Secretary.

An eternity of jazz standards flowed by until finally the music was broken again, and three screens opened up on the laptop in front of her. In the feed from the Oval Office she saw Abdor and Fenner. The rest of her screen showed Kahn, in a dark suit, white shirt, and red tie with a US flag background, and underneath him, Porter, in a white blouse and blue blazer, glasses down over her nose as she continued working on some papers while the meeting got started. Nothing Porter did in view of the President was an accident; this particular pose was intended to signal that whatever Lewis had to tell them, it couldn't possibly be as important as what Porter was currently doing. She only deigned to look up once Abdor started speaking.

"Thank you for joining Mr. President, Cabinet colleagues ... Carmine, why don't you tell these good people what you told me?"

Carmine laid it out, in more detail this time. She only got as far as the Chinese telco hack before Porter started in.

"Why wasn't NSA able to protect against this?" she asked. "We've known about this vulnerability since China ComTech won that contract."

444

"Yes, Madam Secretary, and I understand NSA Cyber Security repeatedly warned State Department Manila staff about sharing sensitive information in the clear with our Philippine allies..."

Secretary of Defense Phil Kahn – a bullish but competent former four-star General – was used to Porter's tendency to target the person and not the ball, and he interrupted impatiently. "We can play the blame game later, Victoria; right now I'd like to hear what we think China knows about *Operation Fencepost.*"

Lewis laid it out in plain English. "Mr. Secretary, they know we have decided to help the Philippine government fortify its outpost on Pagasa Island in the Spratly Archipelago."

"Exactly what do they know?" he asked.

"We are completely confident they know we are sending building materials to enable the Philippine government to rebuild its air and naval base there." Lewis paused. "We suspect, but we aren't sure, they also know the plan includes anti-air, anti-ship missile batteries and a detachment of US Marines."

Porter went on the attack again, unable to contain herself. "You 'suspect'?"

"Yes, Madam Secretary. We fed our AI everything that had been passed over the infected Philippine network infrastructure by Embassy staff, either text or voice, and had it prepare a report on likely US intervention in the Spratly Archipelago. It was basically able to reconstruct *Fencepost* Operations Orders at Strategic, Operations and Tactical level."

"But this is an AI *we* programmed, analyzing data *we* fed it. You have no guarantee, whatsoever, that China has reached the same conclusions."

"I am confident they could have."

Porter scoffed. "We can't rewrite our entire strategy for the South China Sea based on 'could have'." And to reinforce her disdain for Lewis's interruption, she pushed her glasses back up her nose and looked down at her papers again.

Lewis knew better than to wade into a game of hypotheticals with Porter and remained quiet.

"I don't like it," Kahn said. "This might explain why China has put Pagasa into lockdown now, and why there have been other ... developments."

That got Secretary Porter's attention. She took off her reading glasses. "What 'other developments', Phil?"

He looked annoyed, though Kahn really only had two settings, annoyed and about-to-be-annoyed. "Space Force is monitoring a Chinese task force nearing readiness at Dalian Naval Base and multiple-source intel indicates it is headed for Pagasa Island."

"The phrase 'task force' worries me," Abdor said, apprehensively.

Kahn consulted a tablet in front of him. "It's relatively small. A *Yushen* class helicopter landing ship with an escort of two *Luyang* class missile destroyers," he said. "But it had just come off exercises and was supposed to be going into maintenance, not cycling up again for deployment."

"Small, but potent," Lewis pointed out. "The *Yushen* is an assault ship equivalent to our *America* class. It can field two dozen helos, two thousand Marines. And the *Luyang* destroyer is their version of our *Arleigh Burke*, a multirole platform with advanced anti-air and anti-ship capabilities. Two of those would give China anti-air area denial capability over hundreds of square miles."

Abdor tried to sum up the conversation. "Whether or not our people in Manila have given away anything material, China appears to have decided to force our hand. It's a flat-out footrace to see who can put boots on Pagasa Island first."

"China already has several hundred Marines on Subi Reef," Kahn pointed out. "Sixteen miles away. They already have frigates offshore, air cover. If they put their Marines on choppers, they could fly them in tomorrow."

"The troops they have on Subi Reef are not combat troops, except for a small detachment of Commandos. There are a hundred armed Philippine Navy and Air Force personnel on Pagasa," Lewis pointed out. "Chinese troops would have to roll in hot and take the island by force. They wouldn't want the humiliation of failure, so they'll wait for the *Yushen* to get in range and do the job properly."

Fenner had risen from his chair and Carmine could see him pacing in front of his desk, as he often did when agitated. He'd been quiet until now. He had a pinched, narrow face and long nose, atop which sat small round rimless glasses of a type that had been fashionable several years ago. His bushy silver hair was swept across his forehead and he ran a hand through it now. "What is the status on our convoy?"

Kahn looked at some notes. "Two civilian ships loaded and at berth in Singapore, waiting for our frigate, *USS Congress*, to meet them and escort them into the South China Sea. *Congress* is also carrying a detachment from 1st Battalion, 10th Marines, to help site the new missile batteries."

"Why can't the damned convoy just sail now, if it's ready? The *Congress* can meet it closer to the island and escort it past those frigates before the Chinese task force gets there," Fenner said. "What am I missing?"

"The quickest route between Singapore and Pagasa is straight up the west coast of Borneo, Mr. President," Kahn told him. "Those waters are infested with heavily armed pirates and an unescorted convoy would be a juicy prize."

Abdor broke in. "If we stick to the current time schedule for *Fencepost*, when would the *Congress* and that convoy reach Pagasa?"

Kahn consulted his notes. "Three days."

"And our estimate of when the Chinese task force could be within helicopter transport range and start landing troops on Pagasa?"

"Three days."

Fenner stopped pacing. "Well, it's pretty damn obvious to me. We need to get that convoy there first. It needs to sail, at risk, right now. *USS Congress* can meet it halfway."

"Yes, Mr. President. Since we are advancing *Fencepost* Phase One, I suggest we also advance Phase Two."

"Are the assets in place?"

Kahn nodded. "The *USS Doris Miller* Strike Group is currently 1,300 miles east; the *USS Idaho* is one day out..."

Lewis hated the necessity but had already agreed to the logic. When she and others in the Cabinet Security Committee had recommended Fenner sign off on the 'military intervention' that was *Operation Fencepost*, they had foreseen it would provoke a kinetic reaction from China. Apart from the inevitable diplomatic howling, everything from missile or air strikes against Philippine and US forces in the South China Sea, to cyber and space-based warfare was possible. In the event the Chinese Navy or Naval Air Force was deployed, *Fencepost* Phase Two envisaged unmanned aircraft from the *Doris Miller* being forward deployed to the former US Clark Air Base on Luzon, 500 miles away. Their Fantom and Sentinel drone pilots would remain safely aboard the *Doris Miller* and fly anti-ship or anti-air missions remotely from a thousand miles away, as needed.

Low-level targets – small Chinese military bases on reefs and atolls within a hundred miles of Pagasa Island – had already been identified, and the conditions under which they would be attacked agreed. They included Subi Reef, just 16 miles from Pagasa, but also the air and naval bases at Mischief Reef and Fiery Cross Reef.

The *Virginia* class submarine *USS Idaho* was their weapon of last resort if China moved significant naval assets into the Spratlys – such as one of its three new carrier strike groups. *Idaho's* Long-Range Hypersonic Weapons (LRHW) were the most potent ship killers in the US Navy arsenal. Hiding deep under the waves until needed, *Idaho* was their guarantee the Chinese Navy would pay dearly if it tried to escalate, but sinking a Chinese capital ship would almost certainly provoke an all-out war with China.

Fenner nodded. "Makes sense. But I sincerely hope China backs off and we never need to use them." He clapped his hands briskly. "To work, people, I am sure you all have plenty to do."

Kinetic politics

Pagasa Island, Spratly Islands Archipelago, 1201 a.m. January 8, 2035

A half a world away on Pagasa Island, Captain Heraldo Bezerra of the Philippine Navy (PN) Seabees had more than enough to do too.

He'd just hung up from a late-night call with the Lieutenant Commander who was his CO, who had warned him Brigade Intelligence had received indications Chinese forces were planning to insert troops to take Pagasa Island, possibly inside the next 48 to 72 hours.

That news had not surprised him. Heraldo was a pessimist by nature and he knew China regularly rotated a rapid-reaction Jiaolong Commando force of 100 special operations troops through Subi Reef who could be choppered over to Pagasa within 30 minutes. Offshore, China had the two *Jiangwei* class multirole Coast Guard frigates Heraldo had warned the islanders about, which Chinese troops could use to call in indirect fire support. On Subi, Mischief and Fiery Cross reefs, China had built landing strips and naval air bases which could host up to 70 aircraft.

To defend Pagasa, he had around a hundred combat engineers, armed with rifles, a few squad automatic weapons, grenades, some shoulder-launched anti-armor missiles, but mostly ... shovels. In the harbor, he had a patrol boat with a .50 cal machine gun on it, barely even suited to the job of scaring away Chinese fishing boats. Air support? None. The Philippines Air Force consisted of a handful of light attack aircraft it used for counter-insurgency operations, none of which had the range to even reach Pagasa, let alone defend it.

But Heraldo was not so worried about the risk of Chinese troops landing on Pagasa. He wasn't even worried about the Chinese blockade of Pagasa and the risk they could eventually run out of everything except whatever fish they could catch from the shoreline.

He was much more worried about the fact he had been told a month ago that he needed to urgently complete a deep-sea pier extending out from the harbor, to allow ships with a deep draft to dock. What about the repairs to the air strip? They could wait. What about completing the repairs to the harbor itself? Also, a lower priority. The missile emplacement he had his men digging on the summit of the low hill? Yeah, keep going with that, but the pier was the priority. With only a month to get it done, the only option was to build a half-mile-long floating pier, capable of bearing a 30-ton load. They wouldn't have time to drive supports into the sea floor, and he had to allow for the 15-foot difference between high and low tide, so he'd opted for a cable-tie design, anchored to the coral and sand below with one-ton concrete blocks.

They'd started a half-mile out and built inwards, so at least his men weren't out there too long in boats where they'd probably attract the ire of those frigates. But they still had to complete the last twenty yards between the pier and the concrete dock to which it was going to be fixed. A week ago, he'd been told about the convoy that was coming their way. Suddenly the mysterious orders made sense. An auxiliary feeder ship and a US frigate would be tying up at his pier! A massive freighter would be anchored offshore as its cargo was ferried to the island.

That was why he wasn't too worried about the food situation. The convoy would be bringing everything they needed, from food, to building materials. Nor was he too worried about Chinese commandos or PLA Navy frigates. They wouldn't dare invade with a US Navy frigate tied up at *his* pier.

But now he'd been advised that rather than three days to complete the last stage of the pier, he would only have two, and they still had to lay and fix in place the last wooden beams that formed the ramp up onto the shore.

He looked at his watch. Midnight. Four hours' sleep. He'd just close his eyes for a few hours.

Eugenio and Diwa could have made their way across Pagasa blindfolded. They knew every track, rock and tree on the island and had their own names for some of them. In the south of the island was the Rancudo Airfield, its packed red dirt strip running west to east, with a few military buildings and a barracks alongside it, and the old lighthouse in the middle which doubled as a control tower. To the west, the runway had crumbled into the sea, and to the east, it was only above the waterline at low tide. In the middle was a large square the size of a football field, covered in sea grass. Eugenio had never seen anything more than a light plane land on it, or helicopters; both ends of the runway had fallen into the sea and never been repaired.

The villagers' houses were all on the eastern shore of the island, and on the opposite shore in the west was the Naval Station Emilio Liwanag, which if you asked Eugenio was a pretty grand name for a few slabs of rust-stained concrete and a rotting pier. But it was where the Philippines Marines docked when they were rotating troops onto the island, and it was where their parents said the action was now, with Chinese ships coming and going from Subi. Eugenio and Diwa hadn't been over there since the Seabees arrived, and tonight they were going to check it out. Eugenio fumed impatiently, waiting for his mom to go to bed so he could sneak out, but it was not until just before midnight she finished watching TV, checked to see he was asleep, and went in to her room. He had to give it another fifteen minutes so that she was settled, then shoved his pillow under his sheet to cover his absence and dropped out of his bedroom window to the ground below.

In the middle of the island was the tree-covered hill Eugenio and Diwa called 'Pinya' or Pineapple Hill, because the trees growing on its low slopes didn't grow straight, they stuck out at all angles, like the leaves on the top of a pineapple. The Seabees had put up big halogen lights on top of the hill and Eugenio could hear the sound of machines working up there. They were building something. North of Pinya was just scrub, with only one track, and no one ever went that way if they were going to the docks because it took longer and you had to climb the slope of Pinya on the way up, which no one wanted to do on a hot day.

And it was always a hot day on Pagasa.

Eugenio went to Diwa's house and tapped on her window, then waited in the shadow of a tree for her to join him. As she came running up, she started complaining about it being so late, but he spun on his heel and started walking fast, sticking to a track in the shadows so they weren't likely to run into a random Filipino Marine. "Come on, we'll go to the base first and get our binoculars, then you can moan all you like."

Eugenio and Diwa's 'secret base' was a concrete bunker and radio listening post, built by the Japanese in the late 1940s to monitor shipping to the north because the Japanese Navy was worried about a US invasion of the Philippines through the Spratly Archipelago. It was also marked on the maps of Japanese pilots in case their aircraft were damaged, and they had to ditch in the sea. But when a US reconnaissance force checked Pagasa Island in November 1945, they found no Japanese troops on the island and their cursory search failed to find the well-disguised bunker.

It remained deserted until 1956 when a Philippine businessman established a colony on the island, calling it 'Freedomland'. The fishermen he paid to relocate there found the bunker and stripped it of anything useful – some furniture, wiring, empty filing cabinets and a typewriter with Japanese keys – and then forgot all about it. The vegetation reclaimed it until Eugenio and Diwa, out exploring one day, saw a sea bird fly out of a hole in the hillside and decided to investigate. It was *big*, going deep under the hill. Over the next few months, they cleaned out the birds' nests and guano and made it their 'secret base', moving in an old mattress, two folding chairs, some 'borrowed' solar-powered lamps, a crate for a table and, slowly, more of their more precious possessions – like a pair of binoculars with one lens that still worked – and their most prized possession, a battery-powered radio a pilot had given them so they could listen to aircraft flying around overhead, though a lot of it was in languages they didn't understand.

"I want some peaches," Diwa said as they pulled aside the green curtain covering the entrance. She went in first, looking for the battery-powered lamp they kept on a hook on the wall, but Eugenio didn't follow her in. He'd seen something strange. Out to sea, to the north. The eyes often played tricks around nightfall; he'd learned that from being out at sea on fishing boats. Especially on nights like tonight on a new moon when all there was to see by was the light of the stars. But that's what had stopped him, because out to sea, he'd seen a string of lights. Tiny blue lights, like bulbs on a wire, bobbing up and down.

Diwa found the lamp and turned it on, and the blue lights vanished as Eugenio's pupils slammed shut. "Turn that off!" he told her.

"What?" She was holding the lamp, looking at him with a frown.

"Turn it *off!*" he said as loudly as he could, without yelling.

"Alright, wow." Diwa switched the lamp off.

There they were again. But larger now? He watched for a full ten seconds as the small blue lights grew slowly and the distance between them grew too. They spread out left and right.

Totally. Weird.

And that was all the thought he managed before the lights suddenly disappeared, turning into arrowhead shadows that streaked *right over their heads.*

They never heard the cruise missiles' sonic booms, because before they could even reach Eugenio's ears, their warheads were detonating with a thunderous roar.

Three hours earlier, the three Chinese H-20 stealth bombers had taken off from their base in China's Northern Command opposite Taiwan, and fifty miles out of Pagasa they radioed their PLA Navy contact.

"Sword, this is Scimitar, approaching release point."

As Eugenio and Diwa had been approaching their secret hideout in the forgotten Japanese bunker, the Jiaolong Commando unit waiting on underwater delivery vehicles, or UDVs, off the coast of Pagasa, radioed back.

"Scimitar, Sword, we are in position and awaiting strike."

They had not waited long. At thirty miles, the Chinese stealth bombers released six Sky Thunder cruise missiles and then banked, turning back to their base in the north.

The four dark cylinders swept over Eugenio and Diwa's heads on tails of blue fire and then fanned left and right. From the bellies of each of the cruise missiles, 260 anti-personnel bomblets were flung into the sky, scattering indiscriminately in the missiles' wake. Within seconds, the 92 acres of Pagasa Island were covered with 1,500 bombs.

Eugenio paddled backward into the bunker as the dark shadows blasted overhead, crashing into Diwa and knocking her down. Neither had time to even draw breath before a ripple of thunderous blasts rolled over their heads. Diwa screamed, holding her ears. Eugenio continued scrabbling backward, trying to reach the darkest, furthest corner from the bunker entrance that he could find.

No sooner had the first ripple of explosions died than a second rolling wave of thunder swept over the island as each of the six

Chinese missiles finished delivering its load and buried itself in targets across the island.

Eugenio put his hands over his head, and he started screaming too.

As the barrage of missiles ended, six hundred feet downhill from the bunker, 12 commandos of the Jiaolong assault team came ashore. The planners of *Operation Fencepost* would have been surprised to see that they were so few, but then they had grossly overestimated the number of Chinese combat troops based at Subi Reef. It had been a long time since China had rotated a company of the valuable troops through the base. More recently, only platoon-sized detachments had been deployed.

The rapid escalation of the conflict over the island had also taken Chinese planners by surprise.

So, when the Jiaolong Commando had been ordered to prepare a lightning strike on the Philippine island, their commander had decided his best idea was to split his small force into two waves. One force of 12 commandos to sneak ashore under the cover of a cruise missile bombardment using their fleet of underwater delivery vehicles, the other to be airlifted in as soon as the local Philippine garrison had been suppressed. A much lower chance that way of losing a chopper and its payload of elite troops to a Filipino shoulder-launched missile.

So far, the plan appeared to be working. To their east, south and west, dozens of Philippine combat engineers lay dead, shredded by the cluster bombs dropped by the Sky Thunder missiles. Dozens more lay wounded, or simply stunned by the horrific force of the attack.

But not all.

Pulling himself to his feet in the wreckage of one of the barracks buildings by the airfield, Captain Heraldo Bezerra jammed his service cap back on his head and looked about. Around him, among the bodies of the dead and the cries of the wounded, the surviving men of his detachment were dragging themselves and their comrades out from under blasted timber and shattered glass. One was sobbing, head buried in his knees, blood trickling from his ears. As he surveyed the carnage, Heraldo realized two things.

They had either been attacked from the air, or by naval artillery. It made no sense unless China planned to land ground forces. So, whatever he did next, he had to do it *fast*.

As if to hammer the thought home, from the direction of the harbor Heraldo heard shouting, then the staccato rattle of automatic rifle fire. Ignoring the cries of his wounded, he scrabbled in the wreckage of the hut, lifting aside debris, looking for his rifle. *Or any damn weapon, dammit.*

No, he told himself. *You're not thinking clearly, Heraldo.* He turned to a man two feet away from him, trying to pull the strips of cloth that had been his shirt together to cover his bloodied torso. "You!" he said, grabbing the man's arm. "Help me move this debris. We need to find the radio!"

Heraldo Bezerra had never thought of himself as a military officer. Not really. He was an engineer, commanding construction workers. But the Philippine Marines had given him weapons and trained him and his men to fight, and without even realizing it, as he reached for the radio to contact his troops at the summit of Pinya Hill, Heraldo Bezerra was about to become a combat commander.

It was 1209 hours on Pagasa Island, January 8, 2035.

And the dying had just begun.

PAGASA IS OUT NOW ON AMAZON

Other books in the Future War series

(Each novel in the Future War series is a self-contained story, with some recurring characters.)

Praise for 'Bering Strait'

"BERING STRAIT is a riveting thriller. It is 2031 and a new cold war between America and Russia is starting. Perri Tungyan is a Yup'ik fisherman, just 17 years old. He lives on Saint Lawrence Island in the Bering Strait and, as he awaits the weekly shopping drone at the Gambell airstrip, he notices several specks in the sky. These loom larger and larger, identifying as aircraft, and Perri suddenly realizes that he is the only one who knows what is happening. Russia has started to take control of the Strait. Russian ships move in to block the entrance and exit to the Strait and a no-fly zone is imposed over Western Alaska. The lives of eight people are about to be turned upside down as Armageddon approaches...

The action is intense and the plot unique. There are plenty of twists and turns to keep the reader on their toes and keep their attention while it soars along at a fast pace. The characters are developed nicely throughout the story, each having their own part to play and meshing with one another seamlessly. You soon begin to empathize with them and they are a likable bunch of people too. This story is unmissable and slightly scary because it isn't set very far in the future and, given recent world events, isn't out of the realms of possibility. Great story, highly recommended for those who want a tight, gripping tale to lose themselves in."

- Readers Favorite, 5 stars

Praise for 'Okinawa', winner of Publishers Weekly Star, and Best Political Thriller 2020 Readers' Favorite Awards

Holden's intense second Future War novel (after Bering Strait) is a riveting take on the near future of warfare and global politics, peopled by a large cast of well-written characters. In 1942, Chinese-American soldier John Chen interrogates captured Japanese pilot Tadao Kato. In 2033, Japan and China sign a landmark treaty, and

Chen and Kato's great-grandchildren, Li Chen and Takuya Kato, are both pilots ordered to participate in the first-ever Sino-Japanese joint military exercises. But the supposedly peaceful Operation Red Dove turns deadly when a secret government-funded Chinese hacking group takes control of a DARPA drone and targets American Navy assets on Okinawa. Takuya's friend Mitsuko, a political radical, may be the only person who can stave off a global war--because the death of her father has just made her Japan's first empress.

This page-turner is filled with extensive cultural, interpersonal, and tactical detail, from the unspoken meaning in a cup of tea to the military decisions that move battleships. Holden dispenses with stereotypes and crafts well-defined characters from multiple countries. Particularly memorable are the many richly characterized women, including outspoken, driven Mitsuko; brassy Australian drone pilot Karen "Bunny" O'Hare; conflicted hotshot Li Chen; brilliant hacker Frangipani; and big-hearted 103-year-old gardener Noriko Fukada. The human face they put on the conflict makes each development feel real and evoke powerful emotions.

The crisp dialogue is a pleasure to read and balances the tension with genuine laughs. ("Don't lose those," Bunny tells a sonar tech taking custody of her facial piercing jewelry. "I'm both sentimental and violent.") Readers will be on the edges of their seats as Holden ratchets up the danger to civilians as well as sailors and pilots. This military thriller, which honors servicepeople while strongly questioning the value of war, is both highly enjoyable and deeply thought-provoking.

Takeaway: Any fan of military thrillers will be riveted by this near-future novel that sets Japan, China, and the U.S. at the brink of war. Great for fans of Hiroshi Sakurazaka's All You Need Is Kill, Clive Cussler's Oregon Files."

- Publishers' Weekly BookLife 'Editor's Choice':

Praise for Kobani, winner of 2021 award for Best Political Thriller, Readers' Favorite.

Reviewed by Pikasho Deka for Readers' Favorite

Kobani by author FX Holden is a political thriller set in 2030, based on the geopolitical trends of current times. The Kurdish and Turkish forces are fighting a never-ending battle with the Syrian Armed forces backed covertly by the Russian government. American reluctance to directly join the war efforts of their Turkish allies ends when Russian state of the art stealth fighter jets named Felons bring down two 4th gen-combat drones of the American-led coalition. Told through multiple POVs including the likes of Marine Gunnery Sergeant James Jensen, an AI weapons handler, Royal Australian Air Force Flying Officer Karen 'Bunny' O' Hare, Flying Officer Meany of the Royal Air force, Lieutenant Yevgeny Bondarev, Israeli Intelligence Agent Shimi Rahane, and many more, Kobani is an action-packed war novel that keeps you hooked till the last page.

FX Holden's novel mirrors today's geopolitical trends and deftly showcases their possible repercussions a decade down the line. Kobani is a realistic depiction of a hypothetical war between world powers following their current political, strategic, and ideological stances. With compelling characters, cleverly written dialogue, and a riveting narrative that freezes your blood at times, Kobani is a blockbuster of a novel. I thoroughly enjoyed it and was particularly impressed by Holden's realistic depiction of war and global geopolitics. The plot moves at a breakneck speed, with the action sequences described cinematically in vivid detail. Overall, I found Kobani to be a smartly written political thriller. I would highly recommend it to fans of action-oriented political thrillers.

The Future War series is available on Amazon